I0630580

The Sheriff

A Donna Parker Novel

By

Dallas Dunlap

The Fifth Book of the Narvaez County Series

Other Books by

Dallas Dunlap

The Cabin: A Time Travel Adventure
The Food
Blood Spirit: Book One
Blood Spirit: Book Two

E-reader versions available for Kindle and Nook.

For excerpts and previews, see the Narvaez Now website at www.dallasdunlap.com

The Sheriff

ISBN-13: 978-0692360132

ISBN-10: 0692360131

This book is a work of fiction and any resemblance to any person living or dead (or any vampire, living or undead) described herein is purely coincidental. Narvaez County, Florida, is a fictional location. The Miasma and Koth may or may not be fictional locations.

The technology for time travel may or may not be entirely fictitious.

Dedication:

I want to thank all those who have read my books and given me feedback and encouragement.

In particular, I want to thank my friend and colleague, Jennifer, who read my work and provided invaluable suggestions and criticism early in the creative process. Without Jenn's help, the Donna Parker character wouldn't be the same.

Chapter One: The Missing White Girl

Donna Parker-McCready, the Sheriff of Narvaez County, was blonde, young, and beautiful, which she tried to downplay by wearing the non-descript Department uniform. Her long hair, restrained in a ponytail, flowed halfway to her waist. Her eyes were crystal blue, but sometimes assumed a flinty hardness. She was, looks aside, competent, educated and tough. She had killed two men in separate incidents on her way to the top, and she had led the raid that incinerated the notorious serial killer Michael Dalton, along with his mistress and fellow murderer, Anne Rutledge.

And she had been head of Major Crimes and then Acting Sheriff during the crisis of last fall and winter when a World War II era hallucinogenic chemical had been released in the county. Or, at least, that was the official version.

She was finding that being the Sheriff was not as much fun as being a lower ranking cop had been. Even heading up Major Crimes, she had been able to occasionally jump on a call if she was close to the scene. But as Sheriff, she was never close to the scene. The job was paperwork and meetings and schmoozing with local bigwigs. Sometimes she didn't feel like a cop at all. Sometimes the job was just stupid.

Like the complaint in front of her. A road deputy named Nathan "Nate" Gibbs had been accused of soliciting sex from a woman he'd stopped for speeding. *Why do I even have to read this bullshit?* She wondered. She looked at the time and then at the assignment calendar. Lu Herrera had been the shift commander when the alleged incident had occurred. She attached the complaint to an email to Herrera asking him to investigate.

The intercom buzzed. "Lieutenant Ferris to see you, Sheriff."

"Send him in," Donna said tiredly.

The door opened. "Good morning, pretty lady," Ferris said as he stepped inside.

Donna liked Ferris. He was tall, well built, clean cut, and smart. He was an African American, and his full name was Thurgood

White Ferris, although he used the nickname "Whitey." Donna and Ferris had had a few strange adventures together, of the type nobody could talk about these days.

"Close the door, Lieutenant, and have a seat," Donna said.

He did.

"Two things before we get started," Donna told him. "First, you're a lieutenant and head of Criminal Investigations. You don't need to wait for the front desk when you want to see me. Just come on back. If my door is closed, knock. Second, no more of this 'pretty lady' bullshit while we're at work. If we're at lunch or something, fine. But at work, I'm 'Sheriff,' or 'ma'am.' Okay?"

"Yes, ma'am," Ferris replied.

"So, lieutenant, what do you need?"

"Have you seen the missing persons report from Citrus?"

"Should I have?"

"It just came in. A nineteen year old from Beverly Hills. Three days ago she told her parents that she was coming down to Ruffin to see a friend and party. She hasn't been seen since."

"How boring is Citrus County that people have to come here to party?"

"That's what I was wondering."

"So, a missing persons case. What else?"

"It reminds me of a case four years ago. Construction workers found a skeleton of a young white female when they were clearing a building site out on the west side. Nobody ever found out anything about her."

"Jeez…I think I was a low ranking deputy in Pasco at that time. I never heard of that case. Have you been here that long?"

"Less time than you, ma'am."

Donna frowned. "So what makes you think they're connected?"

Whitey Ferris leaned forward. "The vampire killings and the…whatever…last fall might skew our perception. But, in a county this small, how many disappearances and unidentified corpses is normal?"

"Pretty damn few," Donna said. "I see your point."

"So, can I look into that cold case as part of this investigation?"

"Whitey, this is a paramilitary organization. I know Sheriff Kessler, Sheriff Watson, and Paul McCready, when he was in charge, ran the place like it was a fraternity or something. But there is a chain of command. Your immediate superior is Henry Klass, head of Major Crimes. I'm not officially telling you how to proceed, but here's what I'd do. Run the case by Henry and make inquiries about the old case on your own. Don't tell him you spoke to me about it. He's new to the job and I don't want to undercut him. Okay?"

"Yes, ma'am," Whitey said.

"Anything else? I'm a busy girl."

"What's the deal on that magazine interview?"

Donna laughed. "It wasn't a magazine interview at first. Rick Piers of *Narvaez Now* and Susan Muller of the *Tampa Herald* were doing a feature on the new, young, woman Sheriff. They asked me about rumors that Paul and I were nudists. I just told them the truth. Suddenly, it's syndicated."

"The church ladies won't like that," Ferris said.

"Whitey, the southern women, when they were young, thought nothing about skinny dipping in the nearest sinkhole, or having pool parties where they got drunk and took off their clothes. They gave blow jobs to their boyfriends in the front seat of the pickup in the parking lot. Then, they get a little older and they 'find the Lord' and put all that sin behind them. Even so, I happen to know that a lot of them sewed house dresses with Velcro fronts and a lot of them have orders from their husbands to get naked as soon as they get home from work.

"It's not the southern church women I'm worried about. They forgive a little sinnin' when you're young. It's those stick up the ass old Yankees that might be a problem."

Ferris shook his head. "I knew there was a reason my mother told me to stay away from white women."

"Your mother *was* a white woman."

Ferris bellowed out a laugh. "For sure. She's the one that would know."

Donna laughed with him.

"So when are you inviting me over to one of those naked parties y'all are having?"

Donna looked at him sympathetically. "Whitey, you know I'd invite you if you weren't my employee. Remember, you caught Naomi and me out by the pool that once, and you didn't see me scurrying off. But you are an employee and there are so many laws…"

"I know, pretty…Sheriff…I was just having some fun with you."

Donna looked up with a tight smile. "Anything else?"

"Nope."

"Okay, then. Good luck."

"Back at you."

After Ferris left, Donna felt a little sad. She liked men and she was very sympathetic to their needs. Indeed, if she weren't already married and if he were not her employee, she would have been happy to have sex with Ferris

She was fantasizing about that when Henry Klass came to her door.

"I've got something I thought I'd run by you," Klass said. "We just got this missing persons request from Citrus County. Lieutenant Ferris has a hunch that it might be connected to this cold case…"

Donna sat and pretended that she had never heard this before.

"What do you think, Sheriff?" Klass finally asked.

"It sounds like a long shot," Donna said. "I'd work the bars and any possible friends or acquaintances first, if I were you. If nothing turns up, have at it."

"That's what I was thinking," Klass agreed. "I'll pull the files on this old case."

"Good luck, Henry," Donna said.

ꕥ

Donna was having lunch at Molly's, a mom and pop restaurant across from the county courthouse. It was a place frequented by Sheriff's personnel and attorneys. Donna's husband, Paul McCready often ate lunch there as well because it was near the offices of his company, Conquest Security, which had all but taken over the old bank building just a block away.

"Howdy, Sheriff," McCready said as he slid into the booth across the table from her.

"Howdy, stranger," she replied easily. Donna smiled with pride. He was ruggedly handsome and expensively dressed. He was rapidly becoming one of the more influential men in the county.

"I'm glad we could get together, he said. "I haven't been home much lately. I just got back from New York and I'm headed for Seattle tomorrow."

"What did you have going in New York?"

"It was a McLaury thing. I plopped a hundred grand on some deal they're buying into."

Donna raised an eyebrow. "That's a lot of money? Will it pay off?"

"McLaury tells me it will, and he knows."

Donna didn't want to think about the implications of that. "What's doing in Seattle?"

"A presentation for a big contract. I've got to be there to talk to the company board after my people do the presentation. If we make the sale, that's two to three mil in profit."

"Damn!" she said.

"So, how's with you, babe?"

"Oh, the County Commission wants my office to take the jail back over. The facility is falling apart and the private company doesn't want to renew. They want a proposal but, jeez, with all the crap I've already got and now, the jail?"

"I'll do it," McCready said.

"What?" Donna wasn't sure she'd heard him right.

"Conquest Security will take over the jail. This other stuff is all for show. We've already got the proposal written. We'll use McLaury contractors, McLaury concrete, McLaury financing. We can underbid anybody. We get the jail, contract for five years, and turn it over to you if you're still Sheriff. You'll have a new facility. Conquest might make a little money. McLaury enterprises make a ton of money."

"So you get the short end of the stick?"

"I'm heavily invested in McLaury's businesses."

"So, how am I going to write a proposal?"

"Get the county administrator to do one for you. Or, hit the county up for money for a consultant. Do the best proposal you can. We'll beat it."

"That doesn't sound ethical somehow."

McCready laughed. "Babe, we're living in a country where torturers go free and you're talking ethical?"

She frowned for a moment. "Home tonight?"

"Bet on it, babe."

"I've got to tell you, Mister Husband, my ass is getting soft from not enough spanking."

He laughed. "I'll fix that for you."

"And I've got a few places that need to be filled in, too."

"I've got just the tool for that, as well."

She laughed. "It looks like I'm talking to the right guy. What are you having?"

"Split a pizza?"

She thought. "That's a lot of calories."

He laughed. "You know me, babe. I'll make sure you work them off."

Chapter Two: The Vampire Danielle

The Sheriff of Narvaez County, Donna Parker-McCready, stood at her tile kitchen counter and looked into the blackness beyond the wide window. There were no blinds. Privacy was not a concern here. Her house was an enormous structure perched on tall stilts facing the Gulf of Mexico on its west, and on its east a tall gray wall that kept out intruders and blocked voyeurs. In the day, the kitchen window overlooked a carefully landscaped quasi-forest of mown grass and saplings in planters and, two hundred feet distant, the parking lot, done in river gravel with plastic edging retaining the stone. But her husband, Paul McCready had decided to light the parking lot with motion sensor lamps, so that at night it was as dark as one could still be in the light-polluted twenty-first century. Even with the kitchen illuminated only by the light in the oven hood, the window over the sink was a glossy blackness.

Donna was sipping wine, a cheap Chablis.

She was naked, as she always was at home, except for those occasions when they had guests who were not privy to her lifestyle. She could see her reflection in the window, and stared at it critically. She was, by all accounts, stunningly beautiful with an athletic body honed by a regular exercise program, enhanced sometimes when her husband ordered her to do pushups or to swim some laps. Her breasts were large, incongruous on such a body. Her eyes were crystal blue and she had naturally blonde hair that fell below her shoulders, as her husband wanted. She had creamy skin and a deep all over tan.

She wasn't sure about her body sometimes. The attorney, Sharon Becker, and her boyfriend, Dave Leeper, would visit sometimes to relax in the nude and sip wine and hang around the enormous pool. Sharon was also a natural blonde, and curvy. Donna compared herself to Sharon and felt that maybe she, Donna, had too much muscle or was maybe too skinny. Such insecurity would be baffling to any man, who would find both women dizzyingly attractive.

Donna's life so far had been a story of amazing fortuitous success. As a young girl she had formed a vision of the man that she must have, a strong potent man who would keep a firm hold over her. Her young life had been devoted to finding such a man, and she had gone from one affair to another looking for him. She had been friendly and cute and very good at her job as a deputy, and so had been loved by the men she knew, and the women took vicarious joy in Donna's sexual adventures. Finally she had found Captain Paul McCready.

McCready was moody and distant, but he had the commanding presence Donna had been seeking. She had set her sights on him and finally, with the help of the old Sheriff, Tommy Watson, had been placed in McCready's division.

On her first date with him, he had wordlessly compelled her to take off her clothes by simply staring at her with his fierce, hungry stare. He hadn't hesitated to put her in handcuffs and give her the hottest sex she'd ever experienced. After that, in a darkened restaurant, Donna had explicitly offered to place herself and her body at his disposal.

For a long time, Paul had been amused by Donna's kinks and cravings. She had developed a set of rules under which she would, in tribute to him, remain nude when they were at home together, and would remain in ritual poses, generally on her knees, when she was in his presence.

He had tolerated that, and sometimes played with her, making her do pushups, or tying her up. But one day, he had talked with her alone and told her that he was building a wall around their property. She would not be allowed to wear clothing while on the property (except when they had guests) and she would be in chains when they were home alone.

That had been one of the happiest days of her life.

So she stood in her kitchen sipping wine, wishing that Paul were home instead of off in Seattle. She craved the chains and the rough sex, and afterward lying exhausted in bed beside him.

She heard the puppies scurrying around, and went into the laundry room. Sure enough, they had spilled their water dish. She toweled it up and refilled the dish and returned to the kitchen automatically, her train of thought unbroken.

She should have been completely happy and satisfied, and she was. But she was thirty-one years old. Next would come thirty-two.

The corroding winds of age were swirling around her. Soon there would be wrinkles, and gray hair. Her knees would give out, and her slave concubine lifestyle would go away. She tried not to think about it. *I think too much. Enjoy the now.*

The buzzer sounded. Someone was at the front gate.

There was an intercom mounted in the wall at the end of the long sink counter. She pressed the switch. "Who is it?" she asked.

"Danielle Travis," came the reply. "I'm here to see Paul McCready."

"Paul's away right now," Donna replied. "Is there anything I can help you with?"

A long silence, then: "I'm not sure. You're the Sheriff, right?"

"Yes," Donna said, amused.

"I think you might could help me, then."

Donna sighed. She looked up at the wall clock. It was 9:15, *and darker than…fill in the appropriate metaphor.*

"Okay," Donna said, "I'll buzz you in. Park in the lot and take the sidewalk on your right. It's dark as hell, but there are motion sensor lights, so the walk will light up as you go along."

Donna couldn't place the name "Danielle Travis," and was simply curious. Besides, she was home alone and could use some company. So she opened the gate and watched as the female figure came striding up the walk.

Oops! thought Donna. *If I can see her, she can see me.* Donna scurried out of the kitchen and across the living room, to the stairway door where she kept her "emergency" bathrobe. On impulse, she stalked the sixty feet or so to the big wood panel that Paul had installed to enclose a large desk and office. She opened his desk drawer, found one of his guns, a Glock 17 in its holster, and stuck it in the pocket of her robe.

So, Donna was ready for anything when the dramatic doorbell chimed.

When she recognized Danielle Travis, it was a punch in her solar plexus. She gasped in terror and her heart began racing. Danielle smiled at her wide-eyed, open jawed fear.

"Come on, Donna, it's just me. I won't hurt you."

Donna took a few deep breaths, calmed down, and motioned the vampire inside.

"What do you want here?" Donna asked, unafraid but heart still pounding.

"I'm a lawyer, you know," Danielle told her. "I had litigation in Miami, and decided to do a little driving afterward. I thought maybe Paul McCready might help me find more work in this state. I'm a member of the Florida bar, you know."

She stopped to appraise her surroundings. "Besides, since the incident with Arianne, I've been overcome with curiosity. You might almost say that I'm on a religious quest."

"Wine?" Donna offered.

"Thank you, yes."

Donna motioned her to sit, and she took a seat on the sofa.

Donna returned with a tray holding the bottle of wine and two glasses.

"The wine is dirt cheap," she apologized. "But it does the job for me."

"It will be fine," Danielle assured her. "Nobody can really taste the difference. It's all posing and snobbery."

"So, a religious quest, you were saying?"

"Before we go further, Donna, I think it's only fair to tell you that I've *charmed* you. I could see that you were terrified of me, and I know that you have moral objections to what I am and what I've done. So, I've put a little spell on you and now you find that you like me. Do you find that fair?"

Donna was still standing, wine glass in her right hand, the left arm across her chest, holding her robe closed against the weight of the gun. "I don't know that it's fair," she said, "but I can't do anything about it."

Danielle smiled. "Realistic? I'm glad. So, let's have a little talk. Just us girls."

Donna regarded her with suspicion. "About what?"

"You're nationally famous, you know," Danielle said. "That syndicated story about the naked Sheriff was reprinted in San Francisco. I'm surprised that you can admit to being a nudist in someplace as backward as rural Florida."

Donna shrugged. "There are a bunch of nudist camps right next door in Pasco County. It isn't that radical. We're just a husband and wife behind a ten foot wall, and a few close friends. Who could object? We'll see if it makes a difference in the next election."

"Was copping to it early a political move?"

"No. I was doing an interview and this reporter, Susan Muller, asked about the rumors. I confirmed them and I said, sure, I go naked for my husband. What's the problem?"

"That's brave," Danielle said. She had drained the wineglass and set it down on the coffee table. Donna leaned forward to pick it up, and her robe fell open.

"Oops," Donna said, "I didn't mean to flash you like that."

"It's quite all right," Danielle replied easily. "I got to see your tan. I wish I could get a tan."

Donna, for the first time tonight, noticed Danielle's extreme pallor. "What does happen when you're caught out in the sun?"

"Sunburn," Danielle said. "Extreme sunburn and peeling. It doesn't last long, not like a human sunburn. We heal from injuries right away. But it's painful and annoying at the time."

"How about indoor lighting?"

"It doesn't bother us."

Donna refilled Danielle's wine glass.

"You don't have to wait on me," Danielle told her. "I can pour my own wine. I didn't come here to impose."

"It's a habit," Donna said. "When Paul is home, I wait on him hand and foot. And on our guests, when we have any."

Danielle regarded her. "Really? I took you for a modern, liberated woman."

Donna giggled. "In the outside world, yes. At home, I'm Paul's slave concubine."

Danielle had a puzzled look.

"I'm turned on sexually by submissiveness," Donna explained. "From the time I was a little girl. All my life I looked for that commanding man, that warlord, who could put me to use…order me around and control me the way I wanted. I almost thought that I'd missed out, and then I found Paul."

"That's surprising. You don't seem to be that way in your public persona."

"I am, though, in private," Donna assured her. "Paul forbids me to wear clothes while I'm on the property, keeps me in chains in the evening, and doesn't allow me to sit or use furniture when we're alone. I kneel, knees spread and hands behind my back. I can't conceal anything."

"I wouldn't have thought Paul was like that."

"He wasn't, at first. I introduced all that stuff and insisted on practicing it. Last fall, something changed his mind and he jumped right on it. I'm completely his prisoner when we're home alone."

"His familiar," Danielle said.

"No, his slave concubine, his sex toy."

"Tomato, tomahto."

Donna shrugged. "Whatever. He's what I need and he keeps me busy."

Danielle took her meaning. "Sex?"

"Yes, several times a day."

Danielle smiled tolerantly. "You mean you're not exhausted?"

Donna laughed. "Oh, no. I'm a horny girl. I'm ready any time."

"Maybe he charms you, too," Danielle suggested.

"You could say that," Donna laughed, but then caught her meaning. "Oh, no! Not that way. He's not a vampire."

"He has the blood of the most powerful vampire there is," Danielle pointed out. "*Charm* is very basic. His success in business…from a police bureaucrat two years ago to millionaire CEO...well, let's just say he's got something going for him."

"The McLaurys let him buy in to all their deals, now," Donna objected.

"And they do that, why?"

Donna's certainty began to crumble. "Even if he has the power, I would know. I could fight it."

"Not really, Donna. *Charm* is subtle, and charm used for love would be powerfully addictive. If he uses *charm*, he really does own you."

"No," Donna insisted. "I don't believe that."

Suddenly, Donna noticed Danielle. The vampire was beautiful, even dressed as she was in a casual button shirt, shorts, and boat shoes. She had shapely, muscled legs and a face that seemed made of porcelain, framed in soft dark hair that reached her shoulders. Donna felt herself blush, as she realized that she found Danielle *very* attractive. She found her attention focused on Danielle's breasts, they were of the size and shape people called "perky." Donna found them tremendously alluring and was consumed by an almost overwhelming desire to take off Danielle's shirt and get her mouth on one of those perky breasts. Then, the area between Danielle's legs became mesmerizing. *To pull those shorts down her legs, and get my tongue on...oh my God!*

Danielle held out her hand and said, "Stay right there, Donna."

Donna, her womb wet and hot with lust, was near to screaming in frustration. She slipped off the tiny bathrobe and there was a dull clunk as it hit the floor. Helpless, she let her hand slip to her groin, and began to massage herself, letting the edge of her hand rub against her clitoris with furious speed.

Suddenly the lust was gone, and she was standing naked in front of Danielle, hand on her crotch. The overwhelming humiliation brought her to tears, and she dropped to her knees.

"It's just that easy," Danielle said. "There is a little sex involved in every social transaction. I just leverage it. I simply have to spread out my *charm* and let it hum in your brain, and you find me likeable. Just slightly more intense and I can have you irresistibly, lustfully, drawn to me."

Donna, indignant, bent down to pick up the bathrobe.

"Don't bother," Danielle said. "If your master wants you naked, you should stay that way. Show me around."

Donna was still red with embarrassment but she found Danielle's command irresistible. "What would you like to see?"

"Show me your chains," Danielle said. "Show me what Paul McCready makes you wear."

Donna nodded and padded to the closet, where she produced her chains from the cedar trunk. She demonstrated the waist chain with its threaded split link, and the complex wrist and ankle cuffs that needed special tools to lock and unlock. Finally she showed her the heavy steel collar.

Danielle held the collar in her hands. “This is quite nice. He had you measured and fitted for these, didn’t he?”

Donna gave a bitter laugh. “He spares no expense for his little blonde slave.”

“What else is in the box?”

“More chains. More devices.”

“Let’s look,” Danielle said. She effortlessly pulled the heavy trunk from the closet and opened it.

“Lots of lengths of chain,” Danielle noted. “Lots of those pretty round padlocks.” She moved some chain out of the way. “Spreader bars.” She rummaged some more. “Ooh, look at these!” She held up two curved steel shafts, one long and thick, and one smaller. “These look uncomfortable. Does he put them inside you often?”

“He never does,” Donna said. “But sometimes he bends me over like he’s going to. He likes to pretend scare me. He used to tell me that I was going to work in chains doing landscaping, but when spring came, he hired a landscaping company. I spent a couple of months expecting to be buck naked in chains doing hard labor.”

Danielle laughed. “What would you do if he did plug you up with these?”

“I’d put up with them as long as he wanted.”

“Wow, Donna, he really does have you under his thumb.”

“I love it, though. It’s what I’ve wanted ever since we first went out.”

“Does he beat you?”

“No. I’d like him to whip me. I bought him an expensive riding crop for Christmas. He gave me half a dozen light swats on the ass but he’s never used it on me again.”

Danielle was delighted by that. “He won’t beat you?” she said with a laugh. “The bastard!”

“In my fantasies, he beats me until my body is covered with welts and I’m screaming in pain.”

“Some fantasies are best left unfulfilled,” Danielle observed.

"I fantasize about being kept in a cage, too. Ever since I was a little girl, I've longed for it. Kept naked in chains, whipped, displayed in a cage. So far, I've got one out of three."

"I've spent time naked in a cage," Danielle said. "It's uncomfortable, boring, filthy, and terrifying. You don't want that."

"Maybe for a couple of days?" Donna persisted, chastened.

Danielle said nothing.

"What else would you like to see?"

"What's upstairs?"

"Bedrooms."

"Show me."

Donna started toward the stairs.

"What's wrong with the elevator?" Danielle asked.

"I'm not allowed to use it. The slave thing, you know."

"Of course," Danielle said, and followed her up the steps.

"Damn!" Danielle exclaimed when she saw the master bedroom, which took up the entire third floor, "You could house half a dozen San Francisco lawyers in this space."

Donna was alert. "That's where you live? San Francisco?"

"Yes," said Danielle, an edge to her voice. "I live and work in San Francisco and my real name is Travis. I'm not your enemy, Donna. I'm just curious, that's all."

"But you've charmed me, so I can't fight your orders."

"I'm not the one who keeps you in chains, Donna. I'm just keeping things pleasant between us."

"Pleasant!" Donna grumped.

Danielle smiled. Then she saw it. "Ohmigod, there it is!" She walked over to where Donna's antique chess set was displayed on a small table.

"What?" Donna asked, lagging behind.

"I am the beauty who lives to be ravaged," Danielle quoted, "the slave who owns her master," Danielle quoted.

"What are you talking about?" Donna demanded.

"I am anthropomorphic Death," Danielle continued, "and I feel like playing a game of chess."

Donna was silent, puzzled.

"A dream, of Michael's," Danielle explained. "He dreamed about you before he ever saw you, you know. You were always naked, your pubis shaved…like it really is. You told him that you were anthropomorphic death…He described your chess set. Here it is. Here I am with you, and you are naked, just like he saw. And you're living as a slave – the slave who owns her master."

"What do you think the significance is?" Donna asked. "It was a dream."

"Michael and your husband think that some objects that exist in the real world are symbols, and also exist in the Miasma."

Donna sighed. "What else in the dream was real?"

"He said that the dream took place on a huge marble expanse surrounded by a carved stone balustrade, and you were at an immense height. Ohmigod!"

"What?" Donna asked, growing impatient with this crazy vampire woman, *charm* or no charm.

"Your house, Donna. Your house is a great height…it's three stories tall and up on stilts besides. Your house…this bedroom…is that stone island in the air in the Miasma."

"Maybe," Donna allowed, not believing it.

"Let's look outside," Danielle said eagerly, pulling Donna to the big glass doors. They went out onto the deck and looked out over the black ocean. There were no lights on the water, and it was a view into an infinite darkness, lit only by the tiny pinprick stars.

Donna stood, nervously shifting her weight from one leg to the other, scratching the scars on her arm which had started itching.

"The owl on the dresser," Danielle asked. "Does that have any significance?"

Donna turned her face away from the sea and looked back into the room. "The owl is an aspect of Antala, the Mother Goddess," Donna said. "The ceramic piece is an altar. I kneel there to pray to the Goddess, my mother. I write my prayer on a slip of paper, and burn it with the incense."

"I want to understand it," Danielle said. "I want to understand it all."

ଔଡ଼

Paul McCready was amused.

His wife, totally naked, was standing in front of his chair but, instead of standing in her discussion position…arms behind her back, legs apart, the military at-ease position…she was paying no attention to her stance, and was gesturing with her hands.

"Paul McCready, did you *charm* me?"

He smiled tolerantly. "Donna, you know how charming I am."

Donna was steaming. "Goddammit! You know what I'm talking about."

"You're raising your voice, Donna. I take it you're upset?"

"You are God damn right I'm upset, Mister."

"Where did you get this idea, Donna?"

"Danielle Travis, that's where."

"Ah, yes. She told me she'd be in the area."

"You told me her name was Danielle Smith."

He sighed. "Donna, they all call themselves Smith."

"Back to the question, sir."

"The fact is, Donna, I do have some of the power to *charm* people. You knew that already. Did I charm you? Once in a while, when you were really dragging, yes, I might charm you to get you hot and bothered again."

Donna clinched her fists, shook, and screeched a strangled: "Arrgh!"

"I don't see the harm, unless you're getting friction burns inside." He was having difficulty restraining his laugh.

"You took advantage of me!"

"Really, Donna? You mean locking you up in chains and screwing you, which you agreed to, by the way, isn't taking advantage of you? But making you feel good about it is?"

She calmed down and took some breaths. "The difference, Paul, is you keeping me in chains is something I wanted you to do and have asked for you to do. But if you can charm me into feeling however you want me to feel, then I don't have a choice."

"Women!" Paul said. "For two years you've been doing everything you can think of to try to be my slave. Now you find out that you really are my slave, you get pissed."

"I really am, aren't I? Really your slave?"

"For all practical purposes, yes."

She started to cry.

"Donna, baby, do you want out of the deal?"

She started bawling at that.

"Come here, babe. If you're going to cry, sit on my lap. I'll hold you and make you feel better."

She squeezed her eyes closed and tried to bring her crying under control. Hating herself for her weakness, she sat on his lap and buried her face in his shoulder as he stroked along her back. Neither spoke for several minutes. She felt the hunger in her groin and raised her head. "Are you doing it again, Paul?"

"Swear to God, babe, no."

She stayed in his lap for a while, her face against his shirt. Abruptly he leaned forward, forcing her to her feet. "Come with me," he commanded.

He gripped her arm and walked toward the laundry room, forcing her to walk faster than was comfortable. He forced her down the back steps and out to the pool area.

"Take six laps around the pool," he ordered.

Without a second thought, she leaped in and felt the water force its way into her nose, and had the taste of chlorine in her mouth. She began to swim.

The pool was enormous, of a size standard for apartment complexes rather than private homes. She swam to the end, and as she turned to make the corner, she looked back. She could see in the distance that Paul had taken off his clothes and was standing naked watching her, his erection waving with his motion. She was amused. She swam to the next corner, turned, and swam back. She looked up at him and smiled as she swam past him. Another lap. And another and another. After the sixth, Paul motioned her to stop, bent down, got his arm around her waist and lifted her bodily from the water.

He handed her a towel. She dried off and started to wrap it around her, and then remembered her rules. She tried to dry her hair without success.

Paul spread a blanket on the decking. "Lie down with me," he said. His voice was gentle, but she took it as an order.

He lay down on the blanket, one arm behind his head. She lay beside him for a few minutes, not touching. Then, unable to bear it any longer, she rolled on her side and rested her head on her chest. "Oh, Paul," she said helplessly.

"As pissed as you were, you jumped right into the pool when I told you to," Paul noted. "And that was without any vampire trickery from me. What is it you really want, Donna?"

"I don't know," she whispered. Neither said anything else.

Her head resting on his chest, and his arm now crooked around her and his hand on her lower back, she couldn't help but notice his penis, hard and pointing up at her.

It fascinated her. It always had. Her hand wandered to his scrotum and drifted slowly along the shaft. She gave it a squeeze, and brought her hand to feel the silky skin of its head. She rubbed her hand around in the secretion and, unable to resist, began kissing his belly until she had reached the place where she could touch it with her tongue and finally take it into her mouth.

She loved this, to feel him in her mouth and to use her mouth to drive him to madness.

He did not seize her hair or hurry her, and when he gushed into her mouth he sighed and Donna felt proud that she had been the instrument of his pleasure. And she began to cry again because she loved him so much.

଩ঌ

That night they were side by side in bed, naked, covered by a sheet. Donna lay on her side, her back to him, miserable. Out of hurt pride she refused to lie against him or do anything sexual to encourage him. And he didn't try to touch her, which also made her sad.

In the early morning, he nudged her. "Get up," he said. She sat up and yawned. He got out of the bed, went into the bathroom and grabbed a towel to wrap around his waist. "Get dressed," he ordered. He found a pair of slacks and put them on, pulled on a tee shirt, and took the elevator downstairs.

Donna, in her default clothing, a buttoned shirt made of thin fabric, and shorts, went down the steps.

“Come here, Donna,” she heard him call as she emerged from the stairway. He was sitting in his big chair. She put her hands behind her back and went over to face him.

“How do you feel this morning about our discussion last night?” he asked.

“I don’t know, sir.”

“Do you want out of the deal?”

She squeezed her eyes to keep from crying again. “I don’t know, sir. The *charm* thing was a major betrayal.” *There! I’ve said it without breaking down.*

He nodded sympathetically. *God damn it! His eyes make me melt every time!*

“Here’s what we’ll do, Donna. We’ll take a break from the deal. Let’s take a week. No more kneeling or nudity, no more chains, no more ‘sir’ or ‘my lord.’ We’ll just be two people living together.”

“What happens when the week is up?”

“Then you decide whether you want to continue the deal.”

She took a deep breath and felt panic in her chest. “What if I don’t?”

He shrugged. “We’re still married. We can live like normal married people. Two more or less equal people, living together. We’ll see if it works.”

“Do you think that would work?”

“It would work for me. So the ball would be in your court.”

“Jesus, sir. I don’t know.”

“Take a week. See how you feel. You’ve been in this pressurized, fantasy derived scenario for several months now. Take a break. Be normal for a while.”

“What if I decide I want the deal?”

“Then you shall have it. The rules come back. The chains in the evening. And this time, there will be no illusions.”

His eyes again! Now she saw the eyes that had gotten her out of her clothes that first day together…fierce, predatory, commanding.

“All right, sir. A week.”

“No more ‘sir,’” he reminded her. “Now, let’s have breakfast together like a normal husband and wife.”

Chapter Three: Shelley Lowndes

The missing Citrus County girl's name was Shelley Lowndes. She was nineteen years old and had been living with her grandmother. Her mother had thrown her out because she didn't get along with the new boyfriend. *Or she got along with him too well,* Lieutenant Ferris thought. Ferris had deployed Al Cadbury and Corinne Green to work the bars in Ruffin, but he didn't have much of anything for clues. There were only a few photos of the girl to flash around and the bar patrons, by definition, were going to have unreliable memories anyway. *She'd be using a fake ID if she hit the local honkytonks. No way this is going to work.* But what else was there? How about her car?

Meanwhile, Sheriff Parker-McCready was sitting in Henry Klass's new office, *which used to be my office*, Donna thought. She was nostalgic for her time sitting in the glassed in room, peering through mini-blinds at the cops at their desks. She liked the slightly too high desk and the cushy office chair and the dark wood paneling. She had taken over the office from Paul McCready when he had left the SO for the first time. *Now, it's Henry's and it isn't the same.*

Klass had bought into Whitey Ferris's hunch that the four year old body and the missing Citrus girl were related. On its face, it wasn't that plausible, but for the past two years the department had been dealing with crimes that had magical overtones. Klass didn't know what Donna and Ferris knew about why that was true. But Ferris had convinced him to look.

So, he'd gone down to the Economic Development Department and pulled up some old township and section maps.

"There was nothing in that area four years ago," Klass told her. "Nothing."

Henry Klass was thin and a little over forty. His dark hair was thinning and he wore glasses. He wasn't the kind of guy Donna longed to have sex with, but she had told herself that she would probably do Klass, except that they were both married, because she felt so much sympathy for his harried life. Klass had seen her naked once, at the side of Old Bushnell Road when she'd had to change out of wet, mud covered clothes after crawling through a cave. She let him watch because it would have been cruel not to.

Donna refocused and examined the plat maps. "Where was the nearest road?" she asked.

"Officially, here," Klass told her, and pointed out the line on the blueprinted map.

"Was it paved back then?" she asked.

"Those roads aren't paved even now. This is Monarch Estates. The place was platted and the roads cut through back in the Seventies. But the developer went broke, or something, and it just sat there for thirty years. There's Glisson's Lake, where people used to go to catch rays and do some fishing, till the big wheel pickup people tore the beach up. Those mud boggers and the ATV fans kept the place torn up and scared away buyers for decades."

"I don't like the sound of that," Donna said. "You get that type of people, you've got too many suspects. Did anybody live there then?"

"A lot of people. People dragged small campers in and stayed there. There were a couple of cases in the Eighties where drug smuggling planes cracked up trying to land on the limerock roads. I'm sure plenty of them didn't crack up, too."

"So she may be drug related?"

"Good chance."

"If the place was so out of control," Donna asked, "how is it that people were building a house?"

"The McLaurys," Klass said. "When they wanted to merge their bank, Monarch Estates was a big non-performing asset. They needed to get rid of the riff raff and sell lots."

"How did they do that?"

"Bill Sullivan," was Klass's reply.

"The Sheriff before Kessler?"

"That's right."

"So," Donna said, "If Sullivan cleared everybody out in, what? 1999, 2000? The murder didn't take place until 2007 or 2008, so somebody was probably living in the area at the time of the murder. Can you get down to the Clerk of Courts and see who owned these lots, and who was getting homestead exemptions back then?"

Klass's face fell. "That's a lot of paperwork, Sheriff."

Donna put her hand on his shoulder. "I know it is, Henry. Bob Kessler should have done that back in the day. But he left it to us."

Klass nodded. "What are we looking for?"

"That map makes it look like the site where the body was found is, what?" She counted squares. "Maybe an eighth of a mile off that road. We need to see if anybody has aerial photos of that area dating back to that time. Unless there's a road we don't know about, this wasn't a body dump. She had to be walked back there."

She turned to go. "Sheriff," Klass said, "The reason I know about this place is I had a few beers with Barney Kobe once."

"The anthropologist?"

"He used to be Kessler's chief deputy. He probably worked this case, or knows who did. And he's an expert on county history. The other guy who could help you is Sheriff Watson. He practically ran the department under Kessler."

"Help us, you mean," Donna corrected him. "This is your baby. Your case."

"Got it," Klass said.

ঔ

Donna met her husband at his reserved table at the Fireside, the nearest thing Ruffin had to an upscale restaurant. She looked around at the cypress plank panels for a moment and then pulled up a chair. "How is it going today, Paul?" she asked.

He looked up. He was stirring a swizzle stick in his drink. "I'm doing just great. How's my sweet Donna?"

She made a face at him.

"What are you having?" he asked.

"Salad for me," she said.

"I'm thinking a steak smothered in onions," he told her.

"You eat a lot of red meat," she commented. "Have you ever noticed that?"

He shrugged. "Back in the Fifties an average, hard-working kind of guy was called a meat and potatoes man."

"What's your point?"

"Those guys are just now starting to die off. It can't be that bad for you."

"What are you drinking?" she asked.

"You're going to get on me about drinking, too?"

"I was just asking, sir."

He held up a warning finger.

"I mean, I was just asking, sweetie."

"Better," he said, smiling.

"Well, what is it?"

"Sparkling water and lemon."

"Seriously?"

He held the drink out for her to taste. It was soda water and lemon after all. "Son of a gun," she said.

The waiter came and took their order.

"I've got a proposition for you," she said when the middle aged waiter was out of range.

"Okay, let's hear it."

"How about this: You promise me that you won't use charm or glamour or whatever on me, and we go back to the deal."

He grinned. "Nope."

She raised her voice in frustration. "Why not?"

"Because, babe, way back at the very start of our relationship, you offered me the complete control of and use of your body, without any restrictions."

"Paul!" She was irritated to hear herself whining.

A young woman brought their salads. "A side salad for you, sir. A Fireside dinner salad for you, ma'am."

Donna thanked her politely and turned to face Paul. "If you're going to use mental power on me, it eliminates my choice in matters."

"It does," he agreed. "And that brings you completely under my control. You'll be like a fly in amber. I'll do whatever I want with you."

She watched his face and decided that he was teasing her. When he was seriously making demands of her, his eyes were fierce and predatory. But today he had a mocking expression.

"I don't see how I can accept that…" She'd almost said "sir."

"So, no deal?"

"I've got five more days to decide."

He grinned. "Okay. Eat your salad."

ঙ

After Paul left, Donna remained at the table and dialed Whitey Ferris. She determined that he was in Ruffin, so she asked him to meet her at the McCready table at the Fireside. She ordered a sparkling water and lemon wedge to sip while she waited.

"Had lunch?" she asked as he sat down.

"No, ma'am," he said. "I was on my way to Molly's when you called me."

"Order whatever you want, Lieutenant. I'll put it on my tab."

Ferris frowned. "You don't have to do that, ma'am."

"Don't be ridiculous. If Paul were still acting Sheriff, you wouldn't hesitate to let him buy."

Ferris looked down, embarrassed.

Donna signaled the waiter.

Donna liked hanging out with Ferris. He had a puppy dog affection for her and was, besides, big and well built. She suspected that he was well hung as well, and it ate at her that she might never find out.

"So, Whitey," she began after the waiter took their orders, "what's new on your Citrus M.P.?"

"Her name is Shelley Lowndes. She turned nineteen last October. She likes to drink and party and run around with boys…older boys of course. Some of the people whom Citrus S.O. has interviewed say she likes to smoke dope. No word about harder drugs. She had one more or less regular boyfriend, a guy named Ron Naismith. He's twenty-eight years old and apparently a little more conservative than she is. She borrowed his car and told him she was going to visit some friends in Ruffin."

"Is he a suspect?"

Ferris shrugged. "I wouldn't say so. Citrus is keeping all options open, but there are three guys who say they saw him give her the keys that afternoon. He can pretty much account for his whereabouts for the night she disappeared and the day after. Besides, the dude wants his car back."

Donna nodded. “What kind of car?”

“A very old one. A Chrysler LeBaron. 1994 model.”

“That is old. What kind of condition is it in?”

“He claimed he kept it cherry. Even so, getting parts for cars that old…”

“What kind of work does he do?”

“He does general construction.”

“So he’s unemployed?”

“Yep.” Ferris shook his head sadly.

“Are there any leads on our end?”

“Not so far.” Whitey leaned back and stretched. “I’m hoping Citrus can find out who she was coming down here to see. Meanwhile, I BOLOed the car.”

“What else are you working on?” Donna asked.

“I’ve got the crew deployed on some burglaries. If you want I can pull up….” He produced his smartphone.

“Never mind,” she said. “I can pull it up later. My concern is that we’re not even sure this girl came here. I’m all for working a case as hard as we can, as long as we’re not taking resources away from cases that we have a better chance of clearing.”

“I understand that, ma’am,” he said.

She grinned. “What? I’m not your pretty lady anymore?”

Ferris looked flustered. She touched his hand. “You can call me whatever you want when we’re at lunch. But you have to be proper when we’re in the office or on a scene.”

“Yes, ma’am…Damn, you got me confused.”

Donna was delighted. “Oh, Whitey, you’re so cute! You’re my favorite cop to flirt with.”

The server, a sturdy looking woman, a redhead in her late thirties, brought their orders. Donna had ordered breadsticks and Whitey had asked for smoked grouper with a variety of sides. “Would you like me to refill your drinks?” the server asked. Whitey held up his ice tea and the waitress headed for the drink station.

“You’ve got to help me eat these,” Donna said, pushing her plate of breadsticks toward Ferris. “I’ve already had a salad and I don’t want to get fat.”

Ferris made a show of peering at her chest.

"You could use a little filling out there, white lady."

Donna clapped her hands together and tilted sideways in laughter. One thing that she was secure about was the size of her breasts. Almost everybody commented about them, either complimenting her to her face or, sometimes, she heard expressions of marvel spoken behind her. As in: "Nice ass, and did you see those tits?"

When she recovered from her laughing spell, Donna said, "Whitey, you're not supposed to be looking at those. Haven't you found a girlfriend yet? You should be looking at her equipment."

"It's hard to find a decent woman these days," Ferris replied, assuming a hangdog expression.

"There's your problem. Don't look for a decent woman. You want a sex maniac."

Whitey laughed.

Donna spent a pleasant hour with Ferris. He was touchingly loyal to her, and hanging out with him always left her feeling cheerful and refreshed. So the report on the missing Citrus County girl was just a small part of the conversation. But hanging with Ferris brightened the rest of the day.

When she got back to her office, Lu Herrera was waiting for her. He was the Shift Commander usually from 4:00 pm to midnight, but he also covered the midnight to 8:00 shift fairly often, since that unpleasantness was rotated among the high ranking officers.

It wasn't yet 3:00 pm. "You came in early, Lu, have a seat." Donna settled herself behind her desk…Tommy Watson's old desk.

Herrera plopped a folder onto her desk and then sat down. Donna opened the folder. "Gibbs. He's the…refresh my memory, Lieutenant."

"You asked me to check out a citizen's complaint on him."

"Oh, yes. Offering to tear up speeding tickets in exchange for sex, right?"

"That's the one," Herrera told her.

"So, Lu, what did you do with it?"

"What you'd expect. I investigated and then sent a copy of the file over to Abigail Norton in Internal Affairs."

Donna rocked her chair back. "What did you find?"

“This complaint is pretty dubious. The woman who made the complaint doesn’t want to take it any further. She says that she has to live here, and she doesn’t want any trouble with the police.”

Donna frowned. “Did she give in to him?”

“Conflicting statements. She told me that she’d refused his advances and he let her go. But I had Marge, from Rape Counseling Services, take a run at her. The woman told Marge that she’d performed oral sex.”

Donna drummed her fingers on the desktop. “To get out of a two hundred dollar ticket, it might be worth it.”

Herrera looked shocked.

Donna shrugged. “To a woman with some experience, a blow job isn’t that big a deal. It’s almost a first date kind of thing. And two hundred dollars is big money when you’re working part time at eight bucks an hour. Is she married?”

“Yes. The husband is unemployed.”

“There you go, then. She doesn’t have any money to pay the ticket. She did what she had to do and she doesn’t want to tell the husband. Was force used?”

“Keep in mind, Sheriff, that the details come from Marge on the Q.T. I’m not putting this in my report.”

“Understood,” Donna said.

“She told Marge that he got in her car and made her pull off the road. She was afraid not to cooperate.”

“Okay, what did he say?”

“He says it never happened. He says the charge was probably drummed up by his former girlfriend. She’s pissed that he broke it off with her and she’s been trying to get him in trouble.”

“How about his day log and dispatch?”

“The only stops he made were for male speeders. There’s no record that he ever pulled this woman over.”

Donna sighed. “The classic he said-she said and she doesn’t want to press it. There isn’t much we can do. What’s your gut on this?”

“I looked back over his record since he got here, and over citizen complaint files since Gibbs got here three years ago. There have been two similar complaints, but the complainants were from out of state and didn't have enough detail to identify the deputy. But Gibbs would have been in the cluster of possibilities."

"So you believe the woman?"

Herrera shrugged. "I don't dismiss her story."

"Where was Gibbs before he came here?"

"Manatee," Herrera said. "And here's where it gets dicey. A former girlfriend filed a criminal stalking complaint against him and it actually went to trial. He was found not guilty, but Manatee SO shit canned him anyway. He grieved the firing and he got a settlement and was allowed to resign. There's nothing negative in his official employment record, but…"

Donna frowned. "I don't like this kind of thing, Lu. If he's really doing what that woman says he was doing, this could blow up in our faces. We'd have a high profile sexual assault case and this report…" She picked up the folder and waved it. "Proves that we knew about a sexual predator but let him keep working. Keep on it. Check out his supposed ex-girlfriend. See if she has any connection with this…" Donna noted Herrera's consternation.

"Sorry, Lu. Do you want me to hand this over to CID?"

Herrera shook his head. "No, I started it. We don't want to generate an official criminal investigation if there's nothing there. I'll do the legwork for now. If anything pops, the detectives can have it."

"Okay. Let me know if you want to boot it to somebody else."

Donna was worried. Lu Herrera wasn't a detective. She'd given this case to him as a personnel matter. But he was working it like it was for real. *Maybe it is*, she thought.

ꕥ

When Donna arrived home, she drove her car through the big steel gates, parked it in the gravel yard, then got out of the car and started unbuttoning her shirt. Then it hit her. *We're not doing the deal right now.* One of the rules that her husband had imposed on her under the deal was that she was to strip completely in the parking lot when she got home and then proceed naked to the house, two hundred feet away. It felt odd to walk up to her own house while fully clothed. She decided to use the front steps, since she was no longer restricted to the disreputable looking back stairs.

When she got inside the house, her husband was not in the living room. She found him in the kitchen, stir frying vegetables.

"Hi, babe," he said when he saw her. "I hope you're up for Chinese."

"I am, sweetie." She stepped and kissed his cheek. "What's with the nicey-nice?"

"When the deal is suspended, I'm always nice to my cute young wife."

She beamed with pride. She ran her hand down his back. "And your cute little wife is always nice to you, deal or no deal."

"Could you set the table, babe?"

She smiled at that. Under the deal, she usually ate while kneeling on the floor. Being allowed to sit at the table and eat with utensils made her feel like royalty. *I could get used to this*, she thought. But with that thought came a darker one, that she had been used to this for two years, but her need to be dominated and controlled had outweighed her need to be respected and pampered.

She considered where to put her own setting. Paul, of course, would be at the head of the table. Should she be at the opposite end, where he would have a clear view of her? Or should she sit next to him, within his reach? She decided that she wanted to be in touching range. As she put the silverware on the napkins, she had a brief fantasy. She was dining with Paul and some other people, and she was nude. The table was glass, and everyone could look down and see her thighs and her sex.

She wondered why that image was more erotic than her usual mealtimes under the deal, in which she was always naked, sometimes sitting at the table but usually kneeling in full view on the floor. *Maybe it's the other people*.

She decided that she didn't understand herself very well. She had gone to see the psychiatrist Sonia Taggart a few months ago, when Sonia was in hiding. She had told Sonia all about Paul, and the deal, and the wall. To the psychiatrist, the determining variable had been that the sex play didn't interfere with work and the rest of her life. And it had been Dr. Taggart who had pointed out that being kept in chains by her husband really meant just three or four hours a day. Even on weekends, he seldom kept her in restraint longer than that. But Donna hadn't told Dr. Taggart that she believed, seriously believed, that she, Donna, also had an existence in the dream world which was called (by those who knew of it) the Miasma. And that Paul existed there, too, as a powerful warlord.

She wondered what Sonia would say about the demi-goddess Ba-el Shanah, the slave concubine who was owned by the warlord Paul of Koth.

And I didn't tell her that I think about sex all the time. That when I meet a man, I think about what it would be like to sleep with him. That my life is a collection of sex fantasies interrupted by work once in a while.

With a start, Donna realized that a normal existence in which she played the role of a normal middle class *(Well, upper class now, I guess)* housewife would require more restraint, more role playing, than the role she played under the deal…the slave concubine who served her master's every whim and was kept on her knees, in chains.

I guess that's my natural state, she thought. *In all the worlds.* The thought didn't trouble her. She was worried, though, that the deal might fall through and that her husband might make her live like everyone else.

The food was good. Paul was an excellent cook and, since he had acquired money he had also acquired new tastes in food. He had made them stir fried vegetables, chicken chow mien poured over rice, and a plate of fresh fruit cut into squares.

"Mmmm," she breathed. "This is really good."

Paul smiled.

"How was your day?" he asked.

She had to censor her discussion, which troubled her. Paul was no longer part of the Sheriff's Department, not even as a reserve deputy. So she couldn't tell him about the deputy *What was his name? Gibbs.* who had been accused by the female motorist. Nor could she talk about the progress on the jail, as that would be a conflict of interest and probably a Sunshine Law violation. So she talked about her lunch with Whitey Ferris and the missing white girl.

"How is Whitey these days?" Paul asked.

"He's doing well."

"Does he still have a crush on you?"

Donna didn't like the direction the conversation was taking. "A little, I guess."

"Do you encourage it?"

She felt the heat in her face. "I flirt with him, Paul. But I've made it clear that I'm married and that we can't pursue anything. Does that bother you?"

He shrugged.

"Well," she said, getting bolder, "are you jealous of him?"

"Donna, you'd feel neglected if I didn't wonder about things like that. I know how you are…how sexual you are. I trust you, though. I'm just curious about your feelings."

"How can you be jealous when you're willing to show me off naked to other men?" She wasn't angry now, just curious.

He thought about that. "Not so many other men. Just Jerry Corbin and Doug Ackerman."

"Still."

He smiled. "You're the one who brought in Doug. That was you and Naomi, doing your nude sunbathing thing. As for Jerry…that was a way of validating the deal. That I could make you go naked for him, somebody you didn't know, showed who was in control."

"And Whitey?"

"If he weren't your employee, I'd be fine with inviting him over and showing you off naked to him."

"That's very strange…" She stopped herself before she addressed him as "sir."

"Not strange at all. I'm very proud of you. You're stupendously beautiful. I love to show you off."

Donna found herself beaming with pride.

"Have you thought more about the deal?" she asked him, changing the subject.

"You're the one who has to think," he said. "You're the one who offered the deal in the first place. But your offer was complete submission. It wouldn't have the same meaning to me or to you if you put in restrictions."

"Do you love me, Paul."

He looked at her, surprised. "Oh, baby, you know I do."

She sighed and patted his arm. "I know, sweetie." She thought for a moment. "I never doubted that you love me. Maybe you love me too much to be as harsh with me as I need you to be…" She looked up at his face. He had an expression of concern. "But I couldn't expose myself like I do, make myself as vulnerable, to someone who didn't love me."

He grinned. "It's a dilemma."

She smiled wistfully. "It's a temptation, you know. If I let the deal go, I know that you'd love me and pamper me, and I would have such a sweet life, such an easy pleasant life. But deep inside, I have this craving…I need chains and rough handling and restrictions and humiliation. I need to be naked and leashed and on my knees at your feet. That need is deeper and more compelling, I think, than my need for a normal life."

"And the deal?"

"I haven't decided yet. I've got four more days."

He laughed.

She stood up. "More wine?"

"Sure, since you're up, babe."

"Where are the dire wolves?" she asked, making conversation.

Paul had brought home two female German Shepherd puppies, one coal black and one the black on tan color associated with the breed. Paul had named the black one Donder and the other Blitzen. Donna thought the names funny, since they were the names of two of Santa's reindeer in the famous Christmas poem, but Paul had solemnly assured her that the names were German for Thunder and Lightning, and were perfectly appropriate for a pair of fierce guard dogs. The dogs were half grown now, and the couple had taken to calling the pups "dire wolves" after the enormous dogs possessed by the warlord of Koth in the Miasma.

"I'm sure they're out hunting great elk as we speak," Paul told her.

"If you let them run wild all the time, you won't be able to control them," Donna warned.

"If we keep them locked up in the house all the time, they'll become oversized house dogs."

"I'll go call them," Donna said. She headed for the laundry room and the back stairs.

Chapter Four: Consultations

The following day, Donna ditched work.

Her best friend, Naomi Spears, also had the day off due to the quirky rotation of hospital shifts, so Naomi took the first opportunity to visit since Paul had installed the wall. Donna, barefoot but wearing a yellow sun dress, stood by as Naomi pulled her car into the gravel lot and stepped out. Donna offered to carry her bag for her.

"I forgot, you're the beast of burden for the household," Naomi said. She handed her the backpack but retained her hold on the shoulder strap of her oversized purse.

"Yep, that's me," Donna replied cheerily.

"But you're wearing clothes. What's up?"

"Oh, Paul and I had a little fight and so our deal is off for a while."

"The walk is new," Naomi commented. "The last time I was here it was a sand trail." Indeed, from the edge of the gravel lot to the old concrete driveway in front of the house, a four foot wide walkway had been constructed of paving blocks.

"Yes, Paul had that put in so I wouldn't track sand into the house." She laughed. "He terrorized me for a week. He had the materials delivered and threatened to make me work in chains every weekend until it was done. But, of course, he already had a contractor signed up to do it."

"It looks nice," Naomi said.

They walked up the front steps. Donna was already finding Naomi's bag burdensome, so she was happy to set it down in the floor and flop onto the sofa.

"So what was the fight about?" Naomi asked. She was already wandering into the kitchen."

"Vampire powers."

This stopped Naomi's kitchen mission and brought her back into the living room. "What?"

"Paul has picked up something along with his vampire blood. Now he has the power to charm people like the vampires do. He's been charming me."

Naomi laughed. "Charming you in what way?"

"He was using vampire charm to make me want sex."

Now Naomi laughed uncontrollably. When she had exhausted herself, she sat down beside Donna. "So tell me, Donna, when have you ever not wanted sex? You think about sex all the time."

Donna was irritated. She proceeded to tell Naomi about the visit from the vampire Danielle Travis, and Donna's subsequent confrontation with the arrogant and mocking Paul McCready.

"How do you know this Danielle character is a vampire? How do you know she's not somebody Paul hired to play with your head?"

"I've met her before, Naomi."

Naomi nodded. "Tell you what, girlfriend. Let's mix up some drinks and sit by the pool and get wasted."

"I'll sit out in the sun, but I've got to limit myself to one drink. I'm the Sheriff now and I might get called to work. And if there's one thing that Paul might beat my ass over, it's drinking and driving."

"He still lets you sunbathe naked?"

"I can if I want. It's just that he doesn't require me to go naked all the time, since the deal is not in effect."

"Whew," Naomi said, "I was afraid you two really had gone Republican."

Beside the pool, lying naked on bath blankets, Donna told Naomi about the latest hangup in the deal.

"You know, Donna, getting a promise like that doesn't mean anything. There's no way you can enforce it. If he decides to just lay down some of that 'morbid glamour' all you can do is accept it."

Donna frowned.

"Of course, the club girls in the city pay good money for drugs to keep them horny. You're getting yours for free."

"You're saying I should just give in?"

"I didn't say that," Naomi told her. "I'm just saying that getting him to promise you doesn't solve your issue."

Donna stood up and walked over to the table where the ice and the drink mixes were parked. She looked out over the vast pool, liquid, blue and inviting, surrounded by white pavement and white fencing so bright that the glare made her squint. She gazed at Naomi. Naomi's deep tanned skin and coarse dark hair, her black pubic hair and the brown nipples on suntanned breasts made Donna sigh in admiration. Donna loved to look at Naomi, who seemed so sensual and perfectly proportioned. Donna loved to look at nude people in general. She liked to see thin broad shouldered men with their penises dangling and the dark pubic hair against the inevitably too pale skin where their shorts had blocked the sun. But Donna was turned on by female bodies too, bodies so perfect and elegant and always looking like they should never be covered.

She wished that Paul were here, to bend her over his knee and dig his fingers into her passages until she was moist and writhing. She laughed at herself. *I'm pretty far gone,* she thought, *when seeing Naomi makes me hot.*

She handed Naomi another drink, took a sip on her own Shirley Temple, and tapped Naomi on the breast. "I'm going to take a dip and cool off," Donna said.

ଔ

When Paul got home, it was nearly seven and the two women were still out by the pool watching the twilight overtake the sky. Both were still naked, and neither was shy about being that way around Paul. Paul took the exhausted ice bucket inside and refilled it. He came back and mixed each of them a drink. Donna was surprised to find that he had handed her a fully loaded margarita.

"It's a nice night," He said. He sat down by the tile table.

"It is," Naomi said. Both the women were sitting on beach towels, Donna feeling slightly guilty about putting her weight on her butt instead of her knees. Paul didn't seem to care though.

When it got dark, Paul suggested that they go out to the boat slip. Beside the slip was a long floating dock and they walked out to its edge, where the water splashed onto their feet. The three of them stood, Paul in the middle with his arm around each woman. Donna felt his hand squeeze her breast. She wondered idly if he was doing the same to Naomi. She found that she didn't care. She could see lights on boats far in the distance, and could see the stars in the clear moonless sky. She could feel the breeze tickling her bare skin and she felt an amazing sense of peace.

Later, in the vast wood floored living room, the naked women shared a blanket on the floor with the exhausted Donder and Blitzen. Paul told some of his adventures as CEO of a growing company. Naomi told of some harrowing cases in her cardiac intensive care job. Donna talked about the SO and some cops whom they all knew.

When conversation reached a lull, Paul found a movie to watch. But he didn't last long. "You kids have fun," he told them. "Grandpa's got to take his nap now."

Donna and Naomi watched the movie and both fell asleep.

Donna was awakened in the middle of the night by the silky feel of a quilted comforter being spread across her. She raised her head and heard Paul's voice. "It's okay," he whispered. "It's three AM. Go back to sleep."

Donna realized in horror that she was lying face to face against Naomi, their breasts touching. Donna had one arm across Naomi's back and the other between Naomi's thighs. She lay paralyzed until she heard the elevator rise. She wondered how to handle the situation, but found herself oddly comfortable on the unyielding floor, and so went back to sleep.

ঔ

Donna feels the hard cobblestones on her bare feet, so the walk is, if not painful, at least uncomfortable. Her groin and buttocks are a little sore, as her lord made hard use of her this morning and the night before. She wears a red scarf on her head, maintained in place by a metal hoop that fits her like a crown. She has another scarf tied around her waist, so that the knot is on her side and the scarf trails along the outside of her right leg. Other than that, she is naked. Upon her wrists are golden cuffs, tied so that her hands are behind her back. Around her neck is a gold torq, the symbol of her lord's ownership of her.

She is being led through the streets by another slave, this one a pretty girl less than twenty years old, whose legs are thick from walking while carrying weight, and whose shoulders are broad and strong. That girl is allowed the dignity of two squares of cloth made of rough hemp, one front and one in back, hanging from a rope around her waist.

Donna, whose name here is Ba-el Shanah, is, in the scheme of things, a high ranking slave. She is not compelled to work like the lesser women, for she wears the red silk of the harlots, or concubines. She might sweep, or tend a fire, or fetch wine or tea for her lord, but other than that she doesn't labor. Her sole purpose in life is to give pleasure to her lord and, although he has numerous other women in his cells and cages, it is Ba-el Shanah whom he loves above everyone else.

It happens that Ba-el Shanah is the daughter of the Mother Goddess, known in this realm as Antala. Paul of Koth rules Tug and Shenzi and Whist, as well as Koth, because he has won those lands in battle. But all know that his power comes from the sword given him by the Goddess, a sword forged by the Goddess herself, and tempered in her tears. And all know that the Mother Goddess favors him because he is loved by her daughter, the slave goddess Ba-el Shanah.

Ba-el Shanah has skin of honey, and soft hair the color of straw. Her lord has adorned her with shackle cuffs made of gold, and, when she is presented at table, has her covered head to foot in dresses of red silk, a fabric more valuable than gold. But today, he is having her led through the streets so that the people can look upon her nakedness. She is tugged along by the slave who holds the rope strung through the loop on Ba-el Shanah's torq, and half a dozen soldiers set the pace.

Crowds line the narrow streets of Koth. People press forward to try to touch her.

Sometimes Ba-el Shanah has pity on someone. A mother holds up her sick baby, and Ba-el Shanah kisses it. A blind man, pushes forward and is nearly clubbed by a soldier, but Ba-el Shanah bids her guards to let him touch her. The guards lead him to her and he drops his stick and falls to his knees. Ba-el Shanah lets him feel along her body, not flinching when his hands wander between her legs, or when he reaches up and squeezes her breast, as though it were an overripe fruit.

As Ba-el Shanah watches him, the white cataracts that cover his eyes begin to dissolve, and when she bids him stand, his vision is restored. The people who had gathered round to watch his sightless groping back away, awestruck.

Ba-el Shanah is the daughter of the Mother Goddess, and Ba-el Shanah's mercy is Antala's mercy. There is no moral order or theology. Ba-el Shanah is a captive demi-goddess, and her whim, or the whim of the Mother Goddess, is unbound by any covenant or obligation.

The soldiers hurry her along. The troops wear boots and helmets made of bronze reinforced with boar's tusks. They have skirts made of thick leather strips and breastplates of bronze over heavy leather doublets. They carry shields that are big enough to protect their torsos and there are moon shaped cuts on the inner edge of the shield so that they can hold up their shield and there is space for them to use their short spears. The soldiers are trained to march, and the duty of guarding these two slaves annoys them.

But Ba-el Shanah must be displayed. The reverence of the people for their warlord lies in the fact that the Goddess has armed him against his enemies, and that she has given him her daughter to be ravaged at his pleasure. So, although Paul of Koth may choose to decorate his possession with fine fabric when it suits him, he must show the world that he possesses and controls the daughter of the Goddess.

In Koth, there is sympathetic magic. The rutting of the warlord and the demi-goddess inspires the Mother to give birth to the grain and the new lambs when the winter turns to spring.

The Mother appears to Ba-el Shanah as a great owl, taller than a man. The owl is inscrutable, with orange eyes the size of saucers and snow white plumage except around the eyes, where the feathers are gray and set in such a way as to make each eye appear to be sunk in a concavity. Ba-el Shanah knows the owl, and is not terrified of its size or potential ferocity. She looks around. The soldiers are stopped, one in mid stride. The crowd and the supplicants are frozen. The buildings are stark...rough wood assemblages done with lime chink and sporting ragged awnings, or irregular stone structures two stories tall, the gaps between the stones filled with globs of crumbling mortar.

The world of Koth begins to dissolve.

Donna finds herself in a place familiar to her...a great marble floor high in the sky, bounded with elaborately carved stone balustrades. In the center is a gazebo held up by fluted stone columns that support its peaked tile roof. Although the gazebo appears small in the vastness of the marble expanse, Donna knows that inside it are many worlds. Donna stands, naked except for her red scarves and gold cuffs, her hands still bound behind her and she still the painted Kothian whore, her eyes circled with henna dye and her sex and nipples rouged.

The owl regards her.

The moon is a great yellow ovoid, so close that its craters and mountain ranges pock its surface and its round solidity seems to be pushing out of the flatness of the sky. On the dark horizon, Donna can see the black jags of hills and mountains far below her, for this stone island is high in the sky.

"Sit, my daughter," the owl says.

Donna backs up and sits, knowing beforehand that there is a bench behind her. Two girls, dressed as Kothian slaves bring out a small stone table. They wear loosely woven ponchos that barely cover their breasts and privates, and which are belted with thick rope. They set the table down and return with a heavy stone chair, made with armrests like a throne. Another girl, this one naked, brings out two rough terra cotta mugs and sets them on the table. Yet another woman, this one wearing only a rough loincloth hanging from a rope around her waist, brings a huge pitcher and fills the mugs. Donna doesn't see where the women come from, nor where they go. They are all similar in appearance...skin that is darkened by long days in the sun, nearly black hair, doe eyes, and big dark nipples on breasts that jiggle as they move.

The giant owl regards all this. When all the women have scurried away, the owl begins to change, to become shorter and thinner until it becomes a human form, a woman naked and commanding. She, too, is deeply tanned and has large brown breasts. Her pubic hair is a neat black triangle. Her eyes are dark, and when Ba-el Shanah looks into them, she knows that she is seeing into the blackness between the worlds.

The Goddess sits in the chair across from Donna.

"Your hands are still bound, my daughter. Shall I free them?"

"They're fine for now, my mother."

The Goddess smiles. "Do you love your bonds, Ba-el Shanah?"

"I do, mother. I am the possession of the Great Lord, and no other existence is possible for me, except as his bound slave."

"But as Donna, you are unhappy?"

Donna is surprised. As far as she can recall, the Goddess has never addressed her by that name. She has always come into the Miasma as the slave concubine Ba-el Shanah, a fantasy woman with whom Donna identified early in her life, and who has been continuously elaborated since Paul became her lover and finally the ruler of the fantasy world called Koth.

"I am not unhappy, my Mother. I'm conflicted."

The Goddess becomes suddenly less imposing and more of a confidante. "Tell me about it, Donna."

Donna sighs. "As Ba-el Shanah I am happy. Even though I'm a concubine and a slave, I am a demi-goddess and healer, and my lord is made greater by his ownership of me. But in the real..."

The Goddess smiles a gentle smile. "In the real, there are no gods, only ideologies with imaginary supernatural authority. Your craving for chains and subservience is viewed as a type of sickness and, if your fellows knew about it, they would view you with contempt. Is that it?"

Donna thinks for a moment. "It's more than that, my mother. I would accept being Paul's slave, and whatever bonds and restrictions he could impose on me if I knew that all this is real. I would like to be sure that I am not insane."

The Goddess's words are musical and seductive. "My daughter, when you were young, did you not pray for me to send you a man such as Paul?"

"I did, mother."

"And did you not pray that I would send you blood to replace that which was lost, and save his life?"

"I did, mother."

"Listen carefully, my child. Did I not take Paul, who was but a man in the real and but a daydream in your mind, a warlord who whipped you and kept you caged...did I not start with Paul and your

fantasy warlord, and did I not create Koth and all its history and all its future, and make Paul ruler of it?"

Donna is not so sure. "I guess so," she admits reluctantly.

The Goddess smiles at Donna's uncertainty.

"Now, Donna, is not Paul, the Paul of the real, more than an ordinary man?"

"He is to me, mother."

The Goddess slaps her hand on the table and raises her voice. "No! He is more than a man. In the Miasma I gave him the sword of Koth, with which he banished the Dark Lord Zis from Koth, and with which he drove the Blood Spirit from the real."

This is news to Donna. She makes a note to ask Paul about it.

"I am made of thought, Donna. In the Miasma, I am a powerful goddess, the Mother of Worlds, because the Miasma is thought and the worlds are thought. But the real is congealed thought, built by eons of beings thinking and imagining, so the real and all the real worlds are material. I exist in the form you see me because you think of me this way. Do you understand?"

Donna doesn't, but she nods anyway.

"I cannot move solid things, child. I can't make a storm arise, or appear before an army and drive it back as I can in the world of Koth. But I can act through thought. I can induce a tree to grow in a certain way, or a dog to bark or not bark. I can make a man angry or kind. And, Donna, I can change the mind of a heartless vampire, and make him feel pity for the man and woman who once killed him, to the point that he will share his haunted blood. This I can do and I have done. Do you understand, my daughter?"

Donna blinks, slightly afraid. She senses that the Goddess is angry.

"Donna, my daughter, you are bound to the warlord Paul, but the bonds are bonds of thought. In the real you are your own woman and you can walk away from him. There is no law there that supports what you are to Paul. It is all just thought, acting out a fantasy."

"What do you advise, my mother?"

"I do not advise you, child. You must decide. But in the Miasma, I gave Paul the sword of Koth. In the real, I gave him the blood of vampires. He has haunted blood, and he has the power of

charm, along with the physical powers he has acquired. The blood is haunted by the vetala, the Blood Spirit. But, in Paul's case, I haunt it, too. And I have made him more than a man. And I have made him a stern master for my daughter, Belshana."

"And if I walk away?"

"Then, you will slowly forget about Koth and the Mother Goddess, and you will become ordinary. The effect of the haunted blood will dwindle and Paul will become just another man. You will be happy together, or not. Eventually the Miasma will be just a dream to you."

Donna finds herself appalled by the prospect.

The Goddess stands and walks behind Donna, and begins to massage her shoulders. Donna feels the warmth and relaxation flow through her. The Goddess brings her warm hands down to Donna's breasts, and kneads them, and lightly brushes her nipples with her fingertips. Donna shudders with arousal.

"My daughter, I have told you more than you should know, and you will soon forget all that I have said. But the core of this knowledge will slumber deep within you, and, without your awareness, it will guide you in your deciding.

Donna, who is now Ba-el Shanah, is walking a little too fast for comfort, being tugged along by the slave who holds her collar rope, and the slave is being urged along by impatient soldiers.

The main street of Koth is only a few hundred yards from the waterfront, and Ba-el Shanah can hear the seagulls and smell the fishy smell of the ocean. She also smells the smell of urine and sweat from the assembled ragged crowd, and the smell of meat cooking at the food stands ahead. She thinks that she will bid the soldiers stop, and share with her a lunch of roasted goat. Her feet are a little sore, and her legs are getting heavy. But it is a fine day.

Donna awakes to the mixed smell of coffee and frying bacon. She is surprised to find herself covered by a comforter on the living room floor, with the naked woman lying beside her. She sits up and Naomi stirs.

ઉ્ઈ

Donna and Naomi sat naked at the kitchen table as Paul stood, serving them coffee and juice.

"I love coming here," Naomi said. "I end up feeling so decadent, waking up naked on the floor, with a hangover."

"Would you like some aspirin?" Donna asked.

"No, coffee usually does it."

Paul was wearing a tee shirt and jeans. "Work today?" Donna asked.

He laughed easily. "Later. What passes for work is just talking to people, and it will be ten or so before there's anybody to talk to. How about you?"

"I was thinking of going in at noon, so I'd be around until about eight," Donna said. "I like to make an appearance on the night shifts once in a while. Is that okay with you?"

"Even when the deal is on, you do your job and set your hours the way you see fit. That's basic, Donna."

"You're such a sweet husband," she said.

"I'll leave you two ladies to eat while I put on some grown up clothes," Paul announced. He left the kitchen.

When he was gone, Naomi looked up and smiled. "Things got a little personal last night, Donna. Your hands kind of wandered in your sleep."

Donna blushed. "Naomi, I am *so* sorry."

Naomi laughed. "Shit happens. I could have pushed you away."

"Maybe we shouldn't fall asleep together," Donna said.

"I'm fine with it if you are, Donna."

Donna laughed. "Maybe we should work on lezzie sex. Next time you and Doug come over, we could make out and entertain the men."

Naomi squealed in delight. "Donna, you are such a dirty girl!"

"I am," Donna said. "I devote myself to it."

Naomi smiled. "Do you want to shower together? I'll wash you if you'll wash me."

Donna was surprised by this and found herself blushing. "Now who's the dirty girl?"

Naomi giggled. "I can be as dirty as you can."

Donna stared into her eyes. "Okay, Naomi. You're on."

After Naomi had left, Donna was sitting at the breakfast table wearing one of her sun dresses, a bright yellow garment with red flowers and a pleated front. She liked it because of how she looked in it the mirror, standing in her bare feet. The dress concealed her cleavage but reached only to mid-thigh, which highlighted her tanned muscular legs. So she sat at the table reading reports on her laptop, with her legs crossed and feeling desirable.

Paul came into the kitchen, adjusting a cuff link as he walked.

She looked up, removed her reading glasses, and said to him, "I'll take the deal."

Chapter Five: Evening Shift

Donna had supper at 7:00 PM at Molly's, across from the courthouse. The restaurant was a mom and pop, with bead board wainscoting and bright yellow drywall, freshly painted. The proprietors had no pretensions about atmosphere and did not pretend to specialization. Breakfasts were salt and fat heavy concoctions of eggs, grits, bacon or sausage, sausage gravy over biscuits, and similar health foods. The rest of the day, the menu could be a "home cooked" meal of meatloaf, roast beef, or fish with vegetables and potatoes, or deli sandwiches, or pizza. Tonight, Donna was splitting a pizza with Lu Herrera, the shift commander.

"I should tell you," Herrera said between bites, "there are rumors about you and Whitey Ferris."

She gave him a squenched face frown. "There are always rumors about me, Lu. Whitey and I are friends and we spend a lot of work time together. But that's it. I go straight home to Paul."

Herrera shrugged. "Your private life is your concern. I'm just letting you know."

"I appreciate that," Donna said, untruthfully.

"On the Gibbs thing: Gibbs's theory that the girlfriend is the instigator of the complaint doesn't check out. I had to really press him to even get the name of the woman out of him. I checked her out. She's really bitter."

"So she had motive?"

"No, not bitter in a stalker sort of way. She never wants to see him again. I took Marge with me on the interview and what I got was this: At least twice he got drunk and either threatened her or struck her. She showed Marge a scar on her breast that she said came from Gibbs burning her with a cigarette. According to her, it was Gibbs who stalked her after *she* ditched him."

"More she said-he said," Donna noted. She sprinkled some Parmesan on her pizza slice.

"Could I get y'all some more drinks?" came a sweet voiced drawl from the server. The server was young, looked eighteen or so, had pleasant brown hair, glasses, and a nametag that said "Sheila."

"I'd like a refill, Sheila," Donna said pleasantly. "Ice tea. Unsweetened."

"I'll have another Coke," Herrera told her.

Conversation was suspended as the young lady refilled the drinks and used a rag to dry the plastic tablecloth.

Herrera continued as though the interruption hadn't occurred. "She's the one who left the county. She had a good job as a paralegal, but she quit without notice."

"Where is she now?"

"Pasco County, Dade City."

Donna closed her eyes. She noticed that her eyes felt tired pretty often now. She hoped that she didn't need anything more than reading glasses.

"Gibbs isn't sounding too good, is he?"

"No ma'am."

"Is it possible," she asked, "that you have something against Gibbs? Have you ever had any run-ins with him?"

"No, ma'am," Herrera said, hiding his indignation. "I don't think that I ever heard of this guy until you handed me the complaint to check out."

"I'm sorry to question you, Lu. I have to cover all my bases."

"I understand, ma'am."

Donna was moderately irritated that Herrera, and in fact, all the people she'd known for years, now addressed her as "ma'am." She had almost demanded it when she had been a lieutenant, and then a captain. But she felt like an intruder in the organization now that she was Sheriff.

"What's your recommendation on this complaint? Do you want to file it as unfounded?"

Herrera regarded her. "In my opinion, Sheriff, we should leave it open. He seemed evasive to me. I think his reference to the ex was made up bullshit designed to throw us off. Without subpoenas for phone records, or sitting down the complainant and the ex and grilling them, we can't confirm or deny a connection. He would know that. And, if he actually did what the complaint alleges, how many women has he done this to who didn't file a complaint?"

Donna thought about that. *If I were young and broke, would I suck off a cop to get out of a ticket that would cost me more than a week's pay?* With a sick feeling, she decided that she probably would. *And while I'm kinkier than most women, I don't think I'm easier. I think most girls would do the same thing, when push comes to shove.* She imagined herself, working twenty or thirty hours a week and barely able to buy food, pay the rent, buy gas to get to work. She imagined that Gibbs was what Herrera believed he was, and she felt anger boil up.

She didn't show it. "When Gibbs realizes that we're not dropping this, he'll lawyer up."

"That's the PBA's problem," Herrera said.

ꕥ

Henry Klass had foisted off the task of going over plat maps to Corinne Greene. Corinne was a mousy looking but very smart woman who had some serious attendance problems and so had ended up on the 4:00 PM-12:00 AM shift. That was the busiest time period for regular police work, but for detectives the shift was relatively quiet. Most detective work was knocking on doors and writing reports during the day. True, a lot of contacts with potential witnesses had to occur around dinner time, but that was scut work. Corinne and Richard Dykes had that duty.

"Show me what you have," Donna said.

"The area started getting built up around 2003 or 2004," Greene told her. "If we assume that the murder occurred within about a year of the discovery, there were eleven structures within about two miles of the site that seem to have been continuously occupied, meaning that somebody claimed a homestead exemption on them. To find out more, we'll have to get teams out interviewing those people."

Donna nodded. "Eleven residences that were occupied during the general time frame when the murder occurred?"

"That's right."

"Good work, detective. What else do you have?"

"The Property Assessor used aircraft back in those days to check for illegal structures and additions. Of course, they use satellites now."

Donna already knew that. "Okay…"

"Here's the 2006 aerial of the place, and the 2007, and the 2008." She used her pen to indicate a spot. "Here's where the body was discovered. You can see the foundation of the structure on the 2009 photo. Before the construction started, there was no roadway or tire tracks from the road to the burial site. The doer walked the victim in there."

I wonder how he persuaded her, Donna thought. *A gun in her ribs? Or did he lure her somehow?* "The last I heard, we didn't have a cause of death," Donna said. "Has anything changed?"

Corrine shook her head. "No. You know how it is. Insects. The sand shifts. If he'd shot her, we'd have something. If he cut her throat or strangled her, or suffocated her, there'd be no trace on the bones. We're lucky there's even an intact skeleton. The deputies that excavated her wrote that she was under five feet of dirt. If he'd just left the body out, or buried her in a shallow grave, animals would have dug up the body and scattered the pieces. We wouldn't have anything."

"Why would he bury her so deep?" Donna wondered aloud, not expecting an answer.

"Respect? Maybe he knew her. Or maybe he was naïve, and thought that he was making the body harder to find."

"Which leads to another question," Donna said. "What kind of a man can dig a pit that big in a short amount of time? And the shovel? Did he carry it with him when he took her out there?"

"There are a lot of burly men who live in this county," Corrine observed.

"Yes," Donna agreed. "And one of them killed this lady.

ଔଓ

Donna spent the rest of the shift hanging out with the troops. She got caught up on the gossip with Lori Collins, the chief dispatcher on the evening shift. She radioed a couple of road deputies whom she didn't know and met them for coffee at a local restaurant. She did some paperwork and wandered home at a quarter till 9:00.

Paul McCready was already in bed, with a lamp on, reading something on his Kindle.

Donna stripped and got into bed beside him.

"How'd it go?" Paul asked.

"Same old same old, sweetie. You know how it is."

She was lying on top of the covers, braced on her elbows. He lightly stroked her back, and she let her head drop to the sheet.

"I have a confession to make, sir."

"You don't have to call me 'sir' yet. The hiatus in the deal runs another couple of days, and then we'll have the big discussion."

"This is a 'sir' kind of confession."

She heard the amusement in his voice. "Go ahead, confess."

"Naomi and I were messing around last night."

"I kind of guessed that, Donna. I covered you up, remember?"

"We took a shower together, too. And we washed each other, if you know what I mean."

"Does this mean you're giving up men?"

She was astounded. "Oh, God no, sir." She rolled over to face him. "I was just telling you. I'm just being honest."

He took the opportunity to squeeze her breast.

"Do you plan to keep doing it?"

That threw her. She thought for a moment. "If you don't forbid it, and she wants to, maybe."

He laughed. "To tell you the truth, Donna, I always thought you two had something going anyway."

"Really?"

"Come on, Donna? The way you two were always naked together?"

"Well, this was the first time."

"Okay."

She wasn't expecting that. "You don't mind?"

"You're a sex obsessed girl, Donna. And pretty soon, if you don't change your mind in the next two days, you're going to be a prisoner again. So, no, I don't mind if you and Naomi want to get each other off. I like Naomi. I think that she's good for you. When I'm not home with you, anything you do that doesn't endanger our relationship is okay. Your body is yours, except that I'm the only man allowed to use the holes in it. Is that reasonable?"

"It is. You're awfully easygoing for a slave master."

"In some ways. In others not so much. But getting it on with another woman is okay. You don't even have to tell me about it, except that, if I ask, you have to be truthful."

"I would never lie to you, sir."

He pinched her abdomen. "Enough 'sir' for now. You'll have plenty of time for that kind of thing. What would you like to do now?"

She grinned. "You know what I'm obsessed with, sweetie."

Chapter Six: A Clue

It was the Sheriff who found the connection. Not because she was particularly smart, although she was. It was simply that she was the only person who had seen both documents: the background report on Nathan Gibbs and the plat maps of the area around the site where the unidentified corpse had been discovered back in 2008.

Gibbs had been divorced from Linda Hannity Gibbs in 2006. Five acres, a house, and a pole barn near the grave site were owned by a Gerald and Leanne Hannity. They had moved away in 2010. The Hannity site was a little less than a mile from where the body had been found.

But where were the Hannity's now?

It took Whitey Ferris more than a day to find them. It turned out that they had, for some reason, become unhappy with the Florida dream and had returned to Chagrin Falls, Ohio, an upscale suburb in the Cleveland-Akron area. Ferris had tried to reach the Hannitys by phone and found his messages going to voicemail. He contacted the Chagrin Falls P.D. who verified that the Hannity family still lived in Chagrin Falls, but that they were seldom home.

Sheriff Parker-McCready finally booked Whitey a plane ticket to Cleveland, first class and sent him on his way. So a plain clothes Thurgood Ferris, now armed only with his Narvaez County badge and ID, found himself in a rental car staking out the Hannity house in Chagrin Falls.

Twice, the local P.D. had stopped to question him and Ferris had spent some time convincing them that even though he was an African American, he was a Florida law enforcement officer and, yes, Florida is in the United States and yes, he had checked in with the local police chief. Three hours spent watching a driveway, and coincidentally inspiring unease in the neighborhood, was rewarded when the Hannity couple arrived in their white SUV.

The Hannitys were in their late sixties and modestly affluent. They had a stately Colonial house and an adequate amount of money. They had moved out of Florida because the place had become too "honkytonk," which was their way of saying filled with aimless and somewhat demented Southerners and pregnant with lunacy and prospective violence. Ferris sympathized and learned that Hannity had been an insurance company executive who had plenty of money and was planning on funding his daughter's college career when she became involved with that redneck cop from Sarasota or Manatee, wherever the hell he was from.

Bottom line, when Linda's marriage to Nathan Gibbs broke up, it hadn't healed the breach between daughter and parents. Linda had stayed with them until sometime in 2007 – They couldn't recall the date. Then one day, Linda had taken off without leaving so much as a note.

"Has something happened to her?" a worried Leanne Hannity asked.

"No," Whitey Ferris said, lying through his teeth. "We're actually doing background on Nathan and we're looking for anything hinky in his past."

"I'm sure you'll find something," Gerald Hannity said. "He was a piece of pure white trash."

The hairs were already standing up on Ferris's neck.

"Did she happen to take her car when she left?" Ferris asked.

"Why do you want to know that? Do you think something has happened to her?"

"We're trying to locate her," Ferris said. "We'd like to interview her. It's difficult to trace women. They change their names all the time…go for months between jobs. You know how it is. Sometimes the simplest thing is to follow DMV records of tag transfers."

Hannity looked relieved. "Yeah, she took her car. It was a…" He snapped his fingers. "Leanne, what do they call that little rice burner she drove?"

"A Miata," Leanne Hannity said. "A Mazda Miata. It was the new style, 2005 I think. She loved that car."

As he was poking along through Solon, headed for I-77, Ferris reviewed what he knew. *We've got Linda. What happened to her car?*

ᴓᴓ

"Next time you feel like springing for a first class ticket, how about sending me to someplace nice, like Rio or Barbados."

"Wasn't the weather nice in Cleveland?" the Sheriff asked, as she slid her feet off her desk.

"It was the first time I've ever seen snow. And it's damn near summer."

"Well, don't complain. I don't do this for everybody. It comes out of my personal account. What did you find?"

"They were the parents of Linda Hannity Gibbs, and Linda has been missing since 2007."

"Jesus!" Donna exclaimed. "This sounds bad for them. What else do we know?"

"She left home in her own car, a 2005 Mazda Miata, and they never saw her again. I'll start working DMV records before I go home."

Donna nodded. "When you get a chance tomorrow, see if you can find who her dentist was. We need to get a positive ID on the body."

"Meanwhile, that piece of shit is still out there with a badge, writing speeding tickets."

"He's still an alleged piece of shit, Whitey. We've got to nail him to it."

ଔ

When Donna came home that evening, Paul was already there. He had fixed a nice meal of pork chops and mixed vegetables. He invited her to sit.

"Still nicey nice," she noted.

"I've decided to postpone till Saturday morning. That gives us time for a discussion and you don't have to work the next day. Or do you have something going?"

"Not that I know of," she said.

"Okay, then. How do you like the food?"

"It's very good, Paul."

"Enjoy it. Hot food may be a luxury for you soon."

"Yum," she said.

They ate in silence for a while, but Paul suddenly had a question. "Donna, what did Danielle want?"

"Excuse me?"

"You said that Danielle visited you the other day and that she clued you in to the fact that I was charming you. But that couldn't be the reason she came to see you. What was?"

"She said that she was on a religious quest. She wanted to know about you and me. She said that I was your familiar, which got that discussion started. But she also was curious about our dreams, and the house, and the Mother Goddess and the land of Koth."

Paul raised an eyebrow. "Really? That's very strange. What did you tell her?"

"I answered everything she asked. She had me charmed."

"Of course," Paul remarked, as he dug into his food.

☙❧

There was progress the next day. Whitey Ferris, after getting through about a third of the list of dentists in Narvaez and adjacent counties, reached a Dr. Biscomb who had treated Linda Hannity. After some back and forth, which required Ferris to hang up and have Biscomb call the Sheriff's Department to verify that Ferris really worked there, Biscomb agreed to copy and send the dental records of Linda Hannity to the State Medical Examiner in Leesburg so that a forensic odontologist could compare them to the teeth of the skeleton discovered in Monarch Acres in 2008. Of course, then Ferris had to work the phone until he reached Assistant Medical Examiner Harry Owens, who did most of the ME work for Narvaez County. Owens located the old records which, thank God, were available by computer. So the hang-up would be the time needed for the odontologist to get around to the comparison.

In the meantime, Sheriff Parker-McCready took time from her busy schedule to write up a detailed presentation that would, when she had a little more evidence, persuade a judge to issue a warrant that would allow her to arrest Nathan Gibbs on a charge of first degree murder.

Meanwhile, the presumed innocent Gibbs still worked for her, answering calls and ticketing speeders, completely unaware of the shitstorm that had been stirred by that single citizen complaint.

Chapter Seven: The Deal

It was Saturday morning, and Paul began the day by fixing breakfast for himself and Donna. He made a nice omelet that had cheese and chunks of fresh tomatoes and scallions. There was fresh coffee and grape juice and English muffins with marmalade. Donna wore a cute dress, a sleeveless number that showed her shoulders and a little cleavage and which displayed her legs nicely. It was white with blue and red flowers and had a wide red belt. She was barefoot. She seldom wore shoes in the house.

Paul wore slacks and a polo shirt. He waited on her as she ate, and offered her more.

"I think I'm through, Paul," she said as she pushed her remaining half cup of coffee aside.

"Into the living room then, for our discussion," Paul told her.

He sat in his overstuffed chair and she stood on the area rug in front of him, her legs slightly spread and her hands behind her back.

She felt the tension in her gut.

"Before we go any further," Paul said, "I want you to go up to your desk and write a handwritten offer for me, spelling out exactly what it is that you're offering in this deal."

This surprised her. He had never asked for the deal in writing before. It had always been her deal and its terms were, to say the least, flexible.

It looked like flexibility was no longer going to be a feature of the framework which governed her relationship.

He hadn't specified, but she took the stairs.

I don't know what's wrong with me that I want this, she mused as she trudged up the narrow staircase, her wrists crossed behind her back. *But I do want it, and I always have.* Her heart was thumping with excitement and plain old fear. *I'm walking into a trap, but it's one I set for myself.* This was it. She had been preparing herself for this her whole life.

Once at her desk, she found a legal pad and considered it for a moment. She had already thought about what she wanted. Once she had consented to Paul's use of *charm*, she had essentially given up all power in the relationship. He had the means to compel her to do his will, and she had agreed to allow his unnatural compulsion.

So no more pride. No more hesitation. When I agree to this, I'm his. She thought of the Borg in Star Trek: *Resistance is futile. I'm voluntarily making myself helpless before him. I will have no option but total obedience.* The realization was a lump in her gut. For a second, she felt a stirring of rebellion, but then: *Pride is stupid. This is what I've dreamed of since I was a little girl. It's what I've always wanted.*

Now that she had to write into words what she wanted, she had to stop and think. *What is it, exactly, that I've always wanted since I was a little girl?* She had always fantasized about the dream warlord who held her captive, who had her lashed for his amusement, who kept her in a cage to be ravished at his pleasure.

Paul McCeady - Paul of Koth - had replaced her unnamed master as the object of her fantasies. When Paul spoke, she could hear the gruffness of his voice as a rumble in her chest. The Paul of the real world was not as tall and muscular as his incarnation in Koth, but he was muscular enough, and strong in other ways. When she stopped at his downtown office he was her emperor in coat and tie, but her eyes always wandered to his hands...big rough hands with thick meaty fingers made that way by a lifetime of working with *things*, hard manual work. She knew what those fingers felt like against her bare skin or inside her body. His fists were hammers that had brought down two gunmen at her wedding. The physical strength with which he so dominated her was also her protection.

She loved to have him spank her with those big hands...spank her and probe her intimate recesses. The slight pain of the blows against her ass was made more erotic by the knowledge that he was restraining himself, that he had the strength to cripple her but that he would not. Because he loved her.

His love made it safe for her to act out her most lurid fantasies of submission, to expose herself to him completely, to give herself over to sweet degradation and beg for more.

The sight of him shirtless overwhelmed her, made her wet, made her want to squeeze her cheek against his broad chest as he wrapped an arm across her back and gripped her bare breast with his rough hand.

Whenever she saw him naked and proud she could not resist the urge to drop to her knees and take his sex against her face, into her mouth, to work him into a frenzy such that he either spent himself in her mouth or pushed her to the floor and took her until she was limp rag exhausted and lying on the hard planking in a puddle of sweat.

Her nudity was her submission. His nakedness was his arrogance and his power over her.

His slightest displeasure, even a raised eyebrow, made her cringe in shame. His smile or the slightest words of praise made her warm and happy. His hand on her shoulder made her quiver with desire.

By now, she was fully attuned to the role she chosen in their relationship. To keep herself covered in the presence of her True Lord was to disrepect him. She would always stay naked and open for him. And the rules that he, and she, had made for her felt completely right. Why should she not kneel for her master? And why, once she had chosen this debasement, would she require the use of furniture? A hard floor was all that she deserved. And her hands? Why shouldn't she keep them always behind her so that her breasts and her sex were constantly revealed for her lover to inspect and fondle?

She thought fondly of the times she had lain on the hard floor, her wrists clamped behind her back, her head resting against the hardwood. *Or the blanket when I'm outside, chained to a tree.* She closed her eyes to remind herself of the blindfolds, or the times she lay abandoned in chains in eerie velvet darkness in the middle of the day. *How do I feel about all this? It's not that I'm always aroused by it* although she was always on the edge of arousal when she was restrained, either by Paul's chains or his commands. It felt so right to be so dominated, so secure in the knowledge that her master had her in his control - both to protect her and to use her.

I don't know why I love this so much. But she saw something clearly now. Paul's charm, his vampire magic, his other-worldly mastery of her was right and she had been stupid to fear it. If he was to be her perfect master, he required the power to arouse her into sexual frenzy. He required the power to make her overcome fatigue or resentment or fear so that she could serve his lust with mindless, helpless passion. The Goddess had been right to give him that power.

It wasn't that she wanted less of Paul's domination. She wanted more. She wanted more restriction, less choice. She wanted to be compressed to her essence...a lowly animal that lived only to please its careless owner.

There was a word for what she wanted to be. The word was mystic and scary, but she desired what it meant with all her heart. She began to write.

She tried to think of all the things a man might want from a woman who was giving up all control. Should she be specific, or should she use broad terms that gave him maximum latitude? She began her offer, with a heading: "From Donna Parker-McCready to Paul McCready: An Offer."

She began: "I, Donna Parker-McCready offer myself to be your slave." She stopped and looked at what she had written. *I'm actually asking him to take me as his slave.* Although they had both used the term, usually in a joking or ironic manner, there was nothing humorous in seeing it written down in black, on the yellow paper.

She shook her head to clear the fog of unease.

What would he want? Sex, obviously. She agreed in advance to perform any sex act whatever that he demanded of her, and to allow him to do whatever he wished to her. There would be no further need for permissions or to enlist her cooperation. She granted him access to each of her body orifices. He could take his pleasure there, or torment her with gags or plugs or vibrators as he chose. She agreed to wear whatever clothing he required her to wear or, as was more likely, to go naked for him.

She agreed that he could restrain her with chains or straps or rope, however he wished for whatever duration. He could confine her in whatever conditions he wished for as long as he wished. He could inflict pain or discomfort of whatever intensity for whatever length of time.

She kept thinking and kept writing. After an hour, she plodded downstairs with her three page missive and handed it to him.

He put his tablet computer aside and read her offer. He had an expression of amusement which irritated her. “Donna, do you really want to be a slave? Remember, you’re committing this to writing.”

“I’m your slave already, right?”

He frowned. “I think that ‘sex toy’ captures it better. ‘Slave concubine’ was more a figure of speech.”

“What’s the difference?”

He thought for a moment. “If you were my slave, you would be my property, to do with as I please. You would be giving up all control over your daily life, outside of work of course. You’d have to go along with anything I decide.”

She shrugged. “Sounds good to me, sir.”

He chuckled.

“You’re sure, Donna? That’s a pretty serious difference.”

“I’m very serious, sir. I would be cheating you if I offered my submission and then had a bunch of exceptions. I’ve decided to go all in. No more complaints or negotiation from me. You tell me how it’s going to be and I obey. No options and no choices.”

He raised an eyebrow. “Okay, then. I will hold you to it, though.”

“I expect you to, sir.”

He held up the paper. “I’m allowed to torture you any way I want?” he asked.

“That’s correct, sir.”

He raised an eyebrow. “Flogging? Electric shocks?”

She squirmed as she hesitated. She felt the familiar lump of fear in her groin. *Why am I hesitating? I wrote it!* Finally: “Yes, sir. If you wish.”

“And marks? You’re agreeing to any tattoo?”

“Sir, yes, sir.”

“And I can have you branded?”

Another tingle of fear. “If you wish, sir.”

He smiled. “Turn around,” he ordered.

She obeyed and felt him trace his finger along her buttocks. “A P on this butt cheek and an M on this one. I can burn my initials into your ass?”

Her voice was flat, defeated. She didn't fear tattoos. In fact, she was intrigued with the idea of having an intimate tattoo that marked her as a slave. A brand, though, would hurt. But she was resolute. "If you wish."

He laughed. "That's my brave Donna. I see that you have an elastic clause. I'm allowed to do anything that's not listed here as well, correct."

"Yes, sir. That's correct."

He looked up at her and his eyes were hard. "Donna, I want you to go back upstairs and recopy this, adding that I have the right to use charm or glamour on you however and whenever I choose to do so."

She flushed. "I think that the elastic clause covers that, sir."

"I want it spelled out," he snapped.

For some reason she almost rebelled at this. She reddened and her abdomen tensed. "Yes, sir," she finally said, and went back upstairs.

She returned sometime later with her revised version. He read it. "You're saying that you want the right to end the arrangement if you give a thirty day notice?"

"Yes, sir. I thought that was a reasonable time period."

"It's unacceptable, Donna. I want you to stipulate that once you have signed this letter, you have no rights within the deal. It can only be ended if I wish to end it."

This was like a blow to her gut. "Sir…"

"You've offered to be my slave," he said reasonably. "If you have the right to quit, you're just playing, aren't you."

She closed her eyes and tried to think. Everything had seemed so simple before. Now…

"I'd like to think about this, sir."

"You can have until, say, six o'clock."

"Thank you." She gave him a quick kiss and fled upstairs.

She was frantic and on the verge of tears, but finally decided to call Naomi.

Naomi was not sympathetic. "Donna, it must be nice to be rich and be a Sheriff and have time to play dominance games. Some of us have to work."

"Naomi, I need advice. You know Paul."

Naomi sighed. "Okay, what is it? But make it quick. I've got things to do before I have to start getting ready."

Donna outlined the issue with the notice clause.

"Jesus, Donna, it's not like he can take you to court. This is just a promise that you're making to him. If you want to do it, do it. If this freaks you out, tell him to forget the deal."

Donna sighed, thanked Naomi, and began writing the third draft of her offer.

She brought it downstairs and stood in her pose as he read it. She noticed that he was now holding the riding crop that she had bought him. The sight of the whip caused a shudder of excitement.

"This is acceptable, Donna. I see you signed it."

"Yes, my lord."

"So, take off your clothes." His voice was stern, self-assured.

She complied quickly. She had worn no underwear, so it was just a matter of pulling off her dress.

He caressed her sex with the crop.

He sighed. "Donna, I don't understand these dark needs that you have. But I know that you have them, and I will accommodate you in satisfying them. But we aren't kidding here. If you want to be my slave, that's what you will be…for real. I will meet your needs, and you are damn sure going to meet mine. Are you clear on that?"

Donna was shocked by the menace in his voice and the hardness in his eyes. She shuddered but said nothing. She felt her heart flutter. *He is the despotic master that I've always desired. I hope I'm strong enough for this.*

"Do you have any questions, Donna?"

She was shaken from her thoughts. She looked straight ahead. "Am I to be punished, sir?"

He leaned back and rubbed the tip of the riding crop along her mons. "Why do you think that I might punish you?" He sounded amused.

I am. He's really going to whip me! She stammered out her answer. "For rebelling against *charm* ? For messing up on my written offers?"

"Maybe you deserve some punishment, Donna. What would you suggest?"

Punishment! She had bought the riding crop for him to whip her, but now that being flogged was a real possibility, she was frightened. She felt her knees tremble.

"You could use the riding crop on me, sir."

He smiled. "The riding crop isn't all that big a deal. It might sting a bit but you like that sort of thing. It might be more of a punishment to blindfold you, put you in chains hand and foot, and leave you that way all weekend. Wouldn't that be better than a little flogging?"

"You could do that, too, sir," she agreed, feigning indifference.

"Maybe both?" he offered. "Maybe chain and blindfold you, flog you and leave you."

She almost grinned. She recognized his solemn teasing. "Even better, sir."

He laughed. "No, I'm not going to punish you, Donna. The deal is pretty punitive already. What I am going to do is deprive you of freedom, dignity, and privacy. That's what you've offered. Right?"

"That's correct, sir."

"Here's how it will work. I want you to be a sex toy, not a drudge. So, you won't have regular chores or assignments. But since you're going to be a slave I'll put you in chains sometimes and make you work, just for the hell of it.

"I know you fantasize about getting whipped, but I don't have any real desire to beat you. But you *did* buy me this thing," He brandished the riding crop. "so I won't rule it out. The temptation could get to be too much. Confinement? If I kept you in a cage, I'd be stuck with feeding you and cleaning up after you. That won't be happening.

"So, things will be much like they have been. When you're at home, you will go naked at all times unless we have guests who aren't in on the game. Of course, during the day you can come and go as you please. You have an important job and I expect you to attend to it. It has priority over the game.

"Otherwise, when I'm at home you will keep your hands behind your back as before. Expect to be in chains. We'll handle meals like before. You may not sit on your ass or use furniture while I'm here with you. You kneel or lie on the floor. You will maintain your favorite pose on your knees, or whatever other position I want you to hold.

"I will drill you on certain poses. I will want you to assume them instantly on command. When I'm in the mood, I'll make you dance." He grinned. "You're going to become an expert belly dancer."

"When I'm not here, you can do whatever you want. Of course, the deal is off when we have guests. But when we're alone, I expect you to be my perfect little slave concubine. That means instant obedience to commands. Understood?"

"Perfectly, sir."

"Turn around."

She was startled by his confidence, his arrogance. *He knows that he is already my master and he takes my obedience for granted.*

And she did obey. He quickly put the handcuffs on her wrists.

"Handcuffs, sir?" She was a little disappointed that he wasn't using the expensive, more restrictive cuffs and chains. That equipment had been purchased just for her, in imitation of her role in Koth. The cheap Smith and Wesson cuffs now clamped on her wrists were designed to hold common criminals. *But after all, I'm just a slave now. Nothing special.*

"We'll save the custom stuff for special occasions," he told her. They take too long to put on and take off. Police cuffs go on and come off in seconds, so you'll be wearing these a lot."

"As you wish, sir."

"Now, Donna, get on your knees and please your master."

ଓଃଛ

Paul kept Donna in chains, first the handcuffs and then the more elaborate bonds until Saturday evening. After he extricated her from her steel shackles, he took her up to bed and they lay smooching, which was Donna's term for kissing and fondling, until they were overcome with passion and made love. Donna awoke at her usual time the next morning, went down to the screen room gym, and did her exercises. She took her mandatory laps around the pool, showered, and returned to the bedroom, where Paul was still snoozing. She climbed in beside him, caressed him until he was tumescent, and used her mouth to relieve him.

He sent her downstairs while he dressed. Twenty minutes later he came down to the kitchen. He ordered Donna to fix breakfast for him, and to stand by the table as he ate, in case he needed anything. Then, when he was finished, he ordered her to kneel. He scooped cold scrambled eggs, cold grits, and cold bacon strips into a steel salad bowl and stirred the mixture until it was an undifferentiated mass. Then he gave the dish to Donna, who lacking utensils, had to eat the unappetizing glop by scooping it up with her fingers.

When she was done, Paul put Donna's waist chain, wrist and leg cuffs on her. He hobbled her ankles with a plastic coated cable and connected her wrists with a twelve inch chain. He put a straw hat on her head and helped her out to the walk which ran between the gravel parking lot and the old driveway that ran up to the house directly from the street. He left her standing while he went into the screen room and found a push broom for her.

"I want you to do the walkway first," he told her. "I don't know how long it will take you to sweep a two hundred foot walk, but we'll find out. There is more work for you to do when you're through with this."

Donna took it in stride. She had, after all, pushed for this ever since she had first met Paul. It was she who had first offered the deal, long before Paul had claimed it for himself and imposed it on her. So she was happy in the cool sunlit morning, naked and in chains, sweeping the sidewalk, her bare breasts jiggling with each move.

As Donna patiently swept the yards and yards of pavers, she watched the birds in the sky and the two half grown dogs frolicking in the grass. On her left was Paul's great wall, and for the first time Donna realized that it was an homage to the much taller wall that surrounded the household of Paul, warlord of Koth.

Paul of Earth had his walled estate now, and he had his slave concubine.

I have my warlord now, and I am his perfect possession.

Chapter Eight: The Unidentified Skeleton

The Sheriff of Narvaez County had, just an hour ago, returned from a one and a half hour lunch with Whitey Ferris at the dark, private table all the way at the back of the Fireside Restaurant, the table on permanent reservation for Paul McCready. As they sat eating a relatively expensive lunch of salmon and associated sides, Donna was having a warm fantasy that she and Whitey were lovers and that, instead of going back to work, they were going to find a room at a rundown hotel, and that he would ravage her by the dim light of an incongruous Tiffany lamp.

A major problem with the fantasy was that there was no hotel remotely like that anywhere near Ruffin. There was an old motel called by various names, the Ruffin Inn, being the latest. It consisted of a string of separate cinder block shacks, rather than rooms in a single building. And there was the Tangerine Hotel, a four storied stucco monster on the side of a hill near the town center. But she only knew of that because her father had told her about it. The Tangerine had been converted to a nursing home in the mid-Eighties.

The other problem, of course, was that she was not only the wife, but the personal property of Paul McCready.

So the lunch with Ferris had involved conversation which was trivial and which avoided the main issue. Whitey Ferris deeply longed for her, and Donna was powerfully attracted to Whitey. And for Donna, the slightest attraction had a sexual component.

So Donna, her womb afire, burned for Whitey while he told her the details of his latest attempt at finding a steady girlfriend. Donna had seen, but not met her. Her name was Shawna Wheeling and she was a bleached blonde twenty-five year old with a really nice body (and Donna noticed such things), a nice tan and a navel ring. Whitey had also let slip that the girl had a labia piercing, "…a ring stuck in her business…" but when he'd realized what he had said, he'd become embarrassed so Donna had to move the conversation on. The issue, of course, was that Shawna was white. Her parents lived in Pinellas County and Shawna was sure that they would *not* be cool with her dating a black dude.

Donna didn't see the problem. *Just don't tell them.* In Donna's view, Shawna should forget about family and all that tedious bullshit and just take advantage of Whitey's magnificent body and that big dark penis, which Donna imagined to be roughly fourteen inches long and as thick as a Red Bull can.

This led Donna to wonder if she could risk sliding her hand down inside her pants and pleasuring herself. That tempting chain of thought was interrupted when someone knocked at her door. "Come in," she said automatically, but was embarrassed to find herself blushing. Of course, that made her blush more, so when Henry Klass came into her office, his first reaction was to ask if she was all right.

Donna looked up at Klass's concerned face and had to suppress the impulse to begin giggling hysterically. "I'm fine," she said, trying to sound businesslike and sober. "What do you have, Lieutenant?"

"The teeth don't match," Klass said.

Donna blinked. "On the body, you mean?"

"The Monarch Estates cold case, yes."

"Dammit!" Donna exclaimed. "If the body isn't Linda Hannity, who the hell is it?"

Klass shrugged.

Donna was annoyed. She, like Paul, was a fan of a GUT, a Grand Unified Theory. If you had one bad guy who was guilty of one thing, he was probably guilty of something else. Solve one crime and many others would be solved along with it. She had already decided in her mind that Nathan Gibbs was a rapist, and it followed that he might be a murderer as well, particularly since his ex-wife had disappeared and his last girlfriend had fled the area. Now she didn't have the proof she needed to arrest him or even fire him. All she had was one citizen complaint that the complainant no longer wanted to press.

Donna thought for a moment. "You know what, Henry? We're not making any progress on the Shelley Lowndes case are we?"

"No, ma'am. We have no evidence whatsoever that she was ever in this county."

Donna nodded. "Tell you what. Try to find out what happened to Linda Hannity. We do have the info on her last known automobile. Can you run that down for me?"

She half smiled as Klass rolled his eyes. "Yes, ma'am. I'll see what I can do."

"I'm going to make a few phone calls, Henry. If I reach the person I want, I'll be out of the office the rest of the afternoon."

After Klass left, she spent a moment considering whether she should get some labial rings. Not the little decorative type, but something big and thick that Paul could attach a leash to. *I probably shouldn't give him any more ideas,* she thought. She turned to her computer and pulled up a list of phone numbers.

ଔ

Barney Kobe was a huge man, Donna guessed that he was six foot six and from his massive shoulders and bulging abdomen, she guessed that he weighed well over two-fifty. He had a tanned, leathery face and hands and coarse dark hair. She already knew that he was a Cherokee Indian by heritage but she would have guessed at a Native American heritage had she not known that. Donna hadn't yet had a sexual fantasy about him, although she probably would eventually. Kobe had once been Sheriff Kessler's right hand man until something strange had happened back in the early 2000s. He was now a forensic anthropologist and, more importantly, he had been a consultant for the Medical Examiner back in 2008.

She had driven nearly an hour and a half to get to Kobe's Gainesville lab.

"Sure, I remember the case," Kobe said. "Sheriff Kessler and Tommy Watson were both keen on solving it, but we didn't have much to go on. You have to remember, back in those days finding an unidentified corpse was a big deal. In the Seventies and Eighties, corpses turned up all the time because the county was all woods and a great place for body dumps. In fact, that's how the serial killer, Michael Dalton, came to your attention, as I recall. But by the 2000s, the county was pretty built up."

"Okay," Donna said. "What can you tell me?"

"Come with me," Kobe said.

He led her from his small cluttered office through a hallway. She found herself in a large room that had a "Raiders of the Lost Ark" ambiance. There were wooden filing cabinets along with four drawer steel cabinets spotted apparently randomly around the room. There were two rows of tables, and along the walls were cabinets that housed rows of drawers, each about eight inches tall with worn varnished faces and brass handles and tiny keyholes.

It took Kobe only a few moments to locate the file. He set it on a table.

The file consisted of eight by ten glossy photos of individual bones.

"This is pretty cut and dried," Kobe said. "This is a female…easily determined by the wider pubic bones, and the sub-pubic angle as reconstructed. Additionally, we have the skull. The supraorbital margin, the glabella, the mastoid process are all sized and shaped as we would expect in a woman. The fusing of the epiphyses and the growth stage of the clavicle lead me to believe that she was older than twenty-eight. The fact that the sutures in her skull are not completely fused leads me to believe that she was no older than thirty-five, and most likely younger than that.

"She was five feet six inches tall, give or take an inch. She was in good health. From the presence of two crowns in her teeth, we believe that she was at least middle class as far as income goes. She had a good diet and trace minerals in her bones have led others – I wasn't doing mineral analysis back then – others to believe that she had lived for some time in the area north of Tampa Bay.

"She had probably never given birth, based on her pelvic bones. But, given the state of disassembly of the skeleton, we aren't a hundred percent certain of that. She was of Caucasian ancestry, based on her gracile bone structure. What else can I tell you?"

"Can you get DNA?"

"We probably could, from tooth pulp or bone marrow, if we had anything to compare it to."

She nodded. "How long was she buried?"

"From the degree to which groundwater and local minerals have infused the bone, I and others believe at least one year, probably no more than two."

"Cause of death?"

"No skeletal evidence regarding COD."

Donna nodded glumly. “Thank you, Doctor Kobe. You’ve answered all the questions I had.”

Kobe laughed. “As I said last time we met, call me Barney. Tell me, Sheriff, what made you drive all the way up here? I could have sent you all this stuff by email.”

“I don’t know, Barney. It’s an old case. I guess I just wanted to get a feel for things…how things were back then. I’m going to do my best to find out who this woman was.”

“I appreciate that, Sheriff. Glad to be of help.”

Donna gathered up her things and started to the front of the building. She sighed. She hadn’t spent as much time in Gainesville as she’d spent driving here, and now she was going to make the long drive back. *I guess I learned something. Her age, anyway.* She was tired. She wondered what Paul had in store for her. She hoped that it involved lying down.

Chapter Nine: Naked Lunch

Weeks passed. Donna's work life was largely concerned with administration and with politics. She got to know the Republican leadership and the business community well, and she had mastered the art of nodding sympathetically when they said rat's ass insane things about the Constitution and about the President, who they imagined to be a Hitler figure bent on turning the US into something resembling the former Soviet Union. Her lunch hours were mainly concerned with fence mending and flak catching. Whitey Ferris was a frequent lunch companion although she also had a few meals with Dan McLaury and Tommy Watson.

Usually, she did not see Paul during the day because both of them were so busy, so she was surprised when Paul telephoned her. "I've sent out for some pizzas. Would you like to have lunch with me in about half an hour?"

Donna tipped her chair back and looked around her office. She actually had nothing scheduled from noon until two. "Certainly, sir. I'll come right over."

She arrived at Paul's headquarters to find a group of people, including Jerry Corbin, Paul's secretary, Mrs. Wannamaker, and Sharon Becker, along with several people she didn't know. Sharon looked dangerously cute in a sleek, barely work appropriate short dress. Donna felt a brief flash of jealousy. When he saw her arrive, Paul picked up a pizza box, one of a stack on somebody's desk..

"Folks," he said, "enjoy the pizza. The Sheriff and I have some business to discuss."

There was laughter.

"And this is important business, so I don't want to be disturbed for an hour or so."

More laughter.

Paul led her back to his office, which was a spacious room done in a pleasant beige, a bank of file cabinets painted to match the walls. The tops of the cabinets supported a verdant jungle of ferns and coleus and other foliage. An entire wall was windows, covered by mini-blinds. Paul's desk was enormous, *bigger than our bed,* and except for a phone, a computer monitor and a keyboard, completely bare, an expanse of dark reddish wood varnished to a mirror finish.

Paul locked the door, placed the pizza on the desk, and seated himself in his office chair. He did not invite Donna to sit.

"Take off your clothes," he ordered.

Donna blinked. She had guessed this was coming but she hadn't expected him to be so abrupt. She felt the sting of insult. But she didn't hesitate. *He's only taking what I offered. Slaves don't have dignity.* She unbuttoned her shirt, stripped off her gray NCSO tee shirt, removed her bra, and placed these in the side chair. She started to unzip her slacks, but glanced nervously at the window and stopped, suddenly doubtful.

"Go on," Paul said evenly. "If anybody can see you, they won't know who you are."

Donna nodded soberly. *Not my choice. I don't have choices.* She felt her abdomen tighten. *Shame? Fear?* She kicked off her shoes, removed her pants and panties, and finally her socks.

She stood, naked with her wrists crossed behind. She felt a surge of pride that she had obeyed so readily in this unfamiliar place.

"Come here," Paul ordered.

She knew to keep her hands behind her back. She walked over and stood in front of her seated husband, in her military at-ease position.

Paul stood, grabbed her shoulders, and manhandled her around. He clamped handcuffs on her wrists and then turned her to face him. "Kneel," he ordered.

She was in familiar territory now, her Sheriff role completely cast aside. Now she was just Paul's sex toy in one of Paul's spaces, and her True Lord was putting her through her paces.

She complied, assuming her standard posture…toes touching, knees spread wide.

He sat back down, took a slice of pizza, and held it to her mouth. He teased her, making her lean forward to bite it. When she had finished a few bites, he set the slice down and took time to fondle her breasts.

"Would you like a soft drink?" he asked. She nodded.

He stood up, went to what she had taken to be a closet, and got two cans of Sprite from a small refrigerator. He popped them open, took a swig from one can, and held the other to her mouth so she could drink. He resumed feeding her.

He stopped feeding her so that he could eat two slices himself. He ignored her as he ate. When he was through, he offered her more food and drink. She ate until she felt full, and then shook her head when he offered her more.

Paul smiled, had another slice of pizza, and as he ate, stared at her, a twinkle in his eye. She smiled, suppressing a giggle. This wouldn't work if either of them started laughing.

He affected a haughty tone. "I guess you know what comes next."

She did. She knee walked closer to his chair as he unzipped his pants. He grabbed a handful of her hair and pulled her to him. *This is why I'm here. Time to go to work.*

When he was through, she rested her head in his lap, her ear against his shrunken penis.

"Here, wash it down with this," he told her. He held up a Sprite.

Some of the soft drink dribbled from her mouth, and he watched it trickle down her chin and neck and finally onto her breasts. He liked that, and poured a little more of the cold sticky fluid onto her chest, so that it traced between her breasts and over her abdomen.

He stroked his hand through her hair.

"God, Donna, I love you," he whispered. "You make me feel so good."

She smiled happily. She would never admit that she loved sweet talk from him. She didn't want him to be nicey-nice. But once in a while, when she pleased him, she enjoyed hearing him tell her. She was his woman, a martyr to his pleasure. And, to tell the truth, what she wanted most from him were orders and commands. She required nothing but that he use her however he wanted, but when she performed well enough to tear an admission of satisfaction from him, it brightened her day.

She knelt there, glowing with happiness as he stroked her hair and face.

After a while, the time was up. “Get up,” he said brusquely. When she obeyed, he stood and roughly spun her around, nearly causing her to fall. He caught her, his hand on her waist.

He unlocked the cuffs.

“There are some new toothbrushes in the drawer of the sink. There are towels, washcloths, and soap in the cabinet. Get cleaned up in the bathroom and come back and get dressed.”

When she came back, she put her hands atop her head waiting for his inspection, but he scarcely looked up from the computer screen. “Go ahead, get dressed,” he told her.

She did. When she had reassembled herself into the chief law enforcement officer in the county, he stood up and pulled her to him. “You always get a kiss when I fuck you,” he said, and gave her a long deep kiss, his tongue ravaging her mouth.

When he stepped back, she laughed. “Not much foreplay, sir, but the after play is nice.”

He had her sit on his desk for a moment as he typed something. The intercom sounded. It was Mrs. Wannamaker. “Sir, Miss Becker has something for you to sign.”

“Send her in,” Paul said.

Sharon Becker apparently had the office key. Donna heard some scratching sounds and the door opened. Sharon grinned when she saw the handcuffs on the desk. “I know what you’ve been doing,” she teased.

Donna blushed.

Paul signed the form and quickly slid the handcuffs into the drawer. Sharon was beaming as she left.

“That was embarrassing,” Donna whispered as Sharon closed the door.

“Nothing to be embarrassed about,” Paul said. “You’re my wife, and this is my company. I don’t answer to anybody, and you only answer to me.”

cgeo

On the drive back to her headquarters, Donna wondered why the way Paul was treating her so aroused her. He had always been gentle and sweet to her unless she practically begged for him to tie her up or otherwise use her roughly. But since he had seen her other self in the Miasma, he had realized what she wanted. And he was giving it to her good and hard. She loved his new arrogance and his rough handling. She could hardly wait to get home and have him clamp her in irons, and take what he wanted from her.

She was barely settled in at her desk when Whitey Ferris knocked.

"We found her," he said.

Donna knew who he meant.

"Linda Hannity married Louis Flanagan in Santa Monica, California, in December, 2007. She died in August, 2008, in that city of a berry aneurysm. That's…"

Donna held up her hand. She knew what it was. "A stroke?"

"Yes, ma'am." Ferris was somber.

"You're sure it's the same Linda Hannity?"

"Yes, ma'am. It turns out that her fingerprints are on file. I tried to call you, but it went to voicemail."

"I was tied up," Donna said without irony. "I'm sorry to hear that. Did you put the new husband in touch with the parents?"

"No, ma'am. He's dead. He shot himself that September."

Donna shook her head. "Well, that's a freaking happy story, isn't it? Will the California authorities notify the parents?"

"I gave them their contact information."

Donna sighed. "That's good work, Whitey. It's a dead end but it's damn good police work."

"It's a maze, Sheriff," Ferris said. "You go down one blind pathway, cross it off, back out and try the next one."

"That's a good attitude. Lunch tomorrow?"

"If you want, Sheriff. You're the boss."

"Tomorrow it is. Let me know if Shawna wants you instead."

"I will, ma'am."

☙

Donna Parker brought her Jeep to a stop on the river gravel parking lot, her bumper pointed at the sign that said "Reserved for Sheriff." She got out of the Jeep and stood beside it, squinting against the bright sunlight and feeling the brisk sea breeze against her face.

Except for a few distant contrails, the sky was clear blue. She could hear the roar of the Gulf and could smell the fish smell of the water, less than two hundred feet away. She heard the squawk of nearby gulls. She felt good.

She had decided to come home early. There were no meetings with county officials, no local VIPs to suck up to and nothing much happening with the investigations she'd been monitoring. So, here she was, home in the midafternoon.

She bent down to untie her shoes. She slipped out of her oxfords, peeled off her white socks, balled them up and stuck them in her shoes. She undid her gun belt and, while she was at it, undid her other belt and let her pants fall to her ankles. She stepped out of her slacks, picked them up off the gravel, folded them, and put them on the car seat. Next, she removed her shirt, then her gray tee shirt, and she was standing on the gravel in her bra and panties. Feeling amused, she undid her bra, pulled off her panties, and stood naked beside her Jeep.

She enjoyed undressing outside like this, and today she had the luxury of taking her time. Smiling, she packed her clothing, shoes, and weapons in her pack and pulled the strap onto her shoulder.

But she thought better of it. She set the bag back on the car seat, walked around to the front of the Jeep and stood resting her butt against the grill.

She caught herself. *The rule! I'm home now.* She crossed her wrists behind her back and stood, feeling the cool sea breeze against her bare skin. She felt aroused.

After a few moments she walked back to the side of the car, grabbed her bag, and started toward the house. She enjoyed the rough gravel against her bare feet, and the abrasive feel of the long concrete walkway. After the two hundred and fifty foot journey, she arrived at the front of their home. She didn't go up the front steps, nor did she walk past them to the elevator. Instead, she opened the flimsy door to the screen room, walked under the looming stilt house, and took the rough back steps up to the laundry room. She was, after all, just a slave.

In the laundry room, she set her bag atop the dryer and walked, wrists crossed behind her back, to the kitchen.

She chopped up some lettuce, purple cabbage, tomatoes, and cucumbers to make a salad. She put it into her metal bowl, poured some Italian dressing on it, and dropped to her knees. She ate with her fingers, since her True Lord wasn't there to tell her to use utensils. But she was used to this. In fact, she now ate most of her meals like this, kneeling with her knees spread and not allowed to use forks or spoons. Or, her hands clipped behind her, she might eat using only her mouth, like an animal.

When she was finished eating, she washed the bowl and dried it. Then she put her hands behind her back, walked to the laundry room, and grabbed her bag. She carried it down the steps and back to the pool area. After pawing through the rumpled clothing to find her phone, she parked her bag in the shade under the house. Her phone clutched tightly in her hand, she walked, her wrists crossed behind her back, out into the sunlight. She was tempted to sit in one of the several lawn chairs, or to sprawl on one of the chaise lounges, but these were forbidden her. Instead, she found a beach blanket and unrolled it on a sunlit portion of the concrete deck.

She kept her hands behind her as she carefully knelt on the blanket. She had used vigorous exercise to strengthen her knees and thighs so that she could kneel or stand in a smooth motion, straight up or down, without using her hands or losing her balance.

She remained kneeling in her display position for a while, letting the wind caress between her thighs. At last, she lay prone, her legs apart and her hands at her side, palms up. *I'm becoming a very good slave*, she thought. *I can keep the discipline even when he's not here.* She felt proud. She knew that Paul did not insist that she follow the rules when he wasn't home, but he cut her too much slack. Leniency by her master was no excuse for her. She had resolved to be enslaved and it was up to her to follow the restrictions. In this world, Paul had no soldiers or other slaves to impose his will on her and make her behave.

She would have preferred compulsion, to be forced to obey. That wasn't feasible. She had to fill the gap by going beyond mere obedience. She had to internalize her status, live it even when she was by herself.

She wondered what had happened to the dogs. *Probably out playing by the other house.*

She closed her eyes and felt the wind and the baking sun on her back, and her ass, and her thighs. She was in a submissive pose, the same pose she assumed when Paul gave her the "belly down" command, or gave her a palm down hand signal. *I am so well trained,* she thought happily. Holding this pose aroused her and she was tempted to slide her hand under her hip and pleasure herself.

That used to be one of her favorite things, alone in the bath, a glass of wine beside the tub, music playing in the distance. Or alone, in her bed, with nobody else around. But since she had accepted the Deal, she had decided to deny herself that simple enjoyment. She was Paul's now, and her pleasure was his to control. If he denied her, she would just have to burn with unquenched desire. And when, as he sometimes did, he ordered her to caress herself while he watched, she would assume whatever position he indicated, and massage herself vigorously, moaning and writhing as she did so, because she was a slave, and had no dignity, and she knew that he wanted a show.

Sometimes he would make her stop before she was finished. He would clip her hands behind her and let her simmer, fondling her occasionally to keep her hot, making her writhe for agonizing hours before he deigned to take her and let her grind frantically against his hard intrusion.

Thinking about it aroused her even more, but she held her pose. Eyes closed, she drifted into the land of Koth, where she was the concubine Ba-el Shanah. This time, she didn't seek out the Mother Goddess but, instead, found herself in a cage, her hands chained above her head, the Great Lord looking down at her from his throne. Two guards unlocked the cage, took her out, and, with the butts of their spears, prodded her toward the Great Lord.

She was awakened from this dream by Donder's wet tongue licking her cheek and, less than a second later, by the shock of an explosive impact against her upper buttocks. She rolled over and started to get to her feet, but Paul's pointed finger commanded her into her kneeling display position. Her butt was hot and stinging from the blow. She saw the riding crop and realized that he'd smacked her with it.

There was a little flare of resentment, but that vanished quickly. Now, the pain was metamorphosing into a pleasurable tingling heat, stinging but erotic. She wished that he would smack her again.

He regarded her imperiously. “Slave girl, tip forward,” he ordered. She complied.

He stepped behind her and she felt the steel handcuffs lock onto her wrists. Between the blow from the riding crop and the restraints on her wrists, she was liquid with lust. He grabbed a hank of her hair and pulled her to her feet.

“I see you got home early today, Sheriff.” he said.

“I did, my lord.”

“Good,” he said. “I’m in that kind of mood. I feel like putting you through the wringer.”

She felt a shudder ripple through her belly. *I love this,* she thought. Nothing stimulated her so much as fear and she always cultivated that emotion as she tried to guess what torment Paul had in store for her. Paul would never hurt her, but she carefully walled that knowledge away. She worked herself into near panic, imagining what uncomfortable restraints Paul might place on her, or how he might spank her or, *please! please!* whip her. The leaden lump in her lower belly would start as dread but slowly turn into arousal as her fantasies became more lurid and explicit.

This is why I am what I am. When she was helpless in Paul’s hands, and aroused, it was the most intense sensation she’d ever felt. And he could keep her going for hours, ignoring her as she lay chained and wet, then fondling her, commanding her to play humiliating games, or hold uncomfortable poses. *I can melt into a puddle of pure ecstasy. All I’ve got to do is whatever he says.*

That was what made Paul different as a lover. He had that *hold* over her that made her his adoring subject, that submerged her will and stripped away her defenses so that she cried when she was sad and giggled when she was happy and writhed and moaned when she was stimulated and ready for love. He could maintain her in that state for days, a lust filled animal aching for his rough hands on her helpless body.

I really am his slave, she thought. *I'm so consumed by love for him that, even when he's not here, I will follow his rules. Obedience is written into me, and I will scribe over it again and again until I'm nothing but his instrument.*

She broke one of her own rules and raised her downcast eyes to look into his face. He had a half smile, but his eyes were hard and predatory. *He really is my True Lord. He really does own me now.* She knew that he was many times stronger than a normal human, and that if he used his vampire *charm* she could not resist his will. She could not break her gaze, though she felt lightheaded and her thighs were trembling. *I love him,* she thought desperately. *I love him more than anything in the world.*

She was desperate for him to put his hands on her. She hoped that he would make her suffer before he brought her to climax.

Chapter Ten: Contempt

It was almost 7:00 PM, and the days were getting longer, so that it was early twilight. Donna was in her kitchen kneeling beside the black shepherd, Donder, giving the dog a thorough belly rub as it lay on its back, tongue lolling out, blissful eyes staring at nothing. Donna heard the gate alarm and straightened up, leaving the disappointed dog looking around and wondering why the pleasure had stopped. Donna, wrists crossed behind her back, scurried to the window to watch her True Lord drive through the gate. She saw Paul's big black SUV roll to a stop on the gravel. She stood and watched the gates close.

She was naked, as she always was at home. Nudity was her discipline and she had imposed it on herself long before Paul had demanded it of her. Normally, she would go to the living room and pose kneeling, knees spread wide and hands behind her back, facing the door. The first thing Paul should see when he arrived home was his beautiful slave concubine, open and hiding nothing from him. She half turned to go and assume her position, but she saw Paul walk around the car and open the passenger side door. Curious, she watched as Paul took the hand of a woman and helped her from the car.

Donna couldn't recognize her. She had expected Sharon Becker but this woman had dark hair. Donna's usual pattern had been interrupted, so she didn't know whether she should go upstairs and dress. But, since Paul hadn't called to warn her, she suspected that he wanted her to greet him at the door as she was. Her next fallback was the white bathrobe she left hanging inside the stairwell.

Paul's rule for her was nudity, and even when guests dropped in she was allowed only minimum cover. So he had bought her a bathrobe that only reached to mid-thigh, and he had made her restitch it so that it would barely close around her. Only by tightly cinching the belt could she keep it from falling open, and even with it belted, she had to hold it closed with one hand to conceal her breasts. It was a clever way to embarrass her, to make her self-conscious when guests first came to the door. She smiled. *He's good at this. So attentive to details.* She put on the undersized robe and waited for Paul and his guest.

She was stunned to recognize Danielle Travis, dressed for work or a business dinner. She was wearing a nice pleated blouse, a plaid skirt, and a matching jacket. She had a black hat atop her head.

"Evening, Sheriff. You know Danielle, I believe."

Donna didn't know how to react. She nodded to Danielle, but she could not keep the look of horror from her face.

"Go on upstairs and put something on," Paul told her, his voice gentle.

Danielle countermanded him. "Really, there's no need, Paul. I know what she is to you. Remember, I've met her before."

Paul shrugged. "Whatever."

"She can lose that silly robe, too. It's designed for flashing. There's no need for it."

To Donna's shock, Paul told her, "Lose the robe, Donna."

Donna stood, transfixed, disbelieving. She felt her face redden, her knees were wobbly with fear. *Paul has brought this creature into our home!* She gasped out a breath. But she noted Paul's impatient expression and she knew what he wanted. She dutifully removed the robe, folded it over her arm, and took it back to its hook behind the stairway door. She stood for a moment inside the tiny enclosure, so terrified that she was afraid she would pee, humiliated that she would be exposed like this to this monster. She folded her hands together beneath her chin and squeezed. Her thoughts were incoherent but she knew that she had to obey. She stepped back into the living room, stark naked and rubbing her hands together nervously.

Paul snapped his fingers. "Watch those hands, Donna."

Donna felt her heart thudding. She quickly put her hands behind her back. *We're doing the game in front of a vampire!*

Paul led Danielle into the island of furniture which was set up farther into the vast living room. He seated Danielle on the sofa. "Would you like a drink?" he asked.

"I would," Danielle answered pleasantly. "Whatever you're having."

"Donna," Paul called. Donna was standing thirty feet from them, near the kitchen door. "Mix us up some martinis. We want two vodka martinis, extra dry."

She had to choke out her answer. "Right away, sir." She stepped behind the counter of their living room bar and mixed the drinks, her hands trembling, her heart racing. *I hope Paul doesn't see how scared I am.*

Paul and the vampire were sitting side by side on the sofa, and Paul was spreading some papers on the coffee table. Donna stood in front of them, in her serving position, feet apart, supporting the round tray with her right hand, resting the left at her side. They ignored her while she stood there, mouth open, eyes staring straight ahead. Finally, Danielle deigned to stand and take the drinks. She handed one to Paul and resumed staring at the paper while Donna stood, naked and unnoticed, in front of them.

"Babe," Paul said, *That's the first hint that he even remembers that I'm here.* "I don't know what you were planning for dinner, but whatever it was, toss it into the refrigerator. I want steaks tonight: nice big thick porterhouse steaks."

"As you've probably already guessed," Danielle announced sweetly, "I'd like mine very rare. I like to taste the juice."

Donna shuddered as she obediently padded into the kitchen.

She had been cooking a roast in the oven. Donna shut off the stove and went to the refrigerator to check for already thawed meat. No steaks. By now, Donna's terror had turned to exasperation. She sighed and took some frozen steaks from the freezer. She wondered if she would be allowed to eat with her husband and his guest. Finally, she decided. *Screw it. I'll get one for myself. If he doesn't want me to eat it, he can fucking tell me.*

She shook her head in annoyance. *There's no telling about that. Sometimes he lets me eat like a queen, and sometimes it's cold slop on the floor. He's so goddamn unpredictable!*

She put the steaks in the microwave, made an eyeball guess as to the weight, and set the defrost cycle accordingly. *What else?* Paul would want some kind of starch. She could nuke some whole potatoes. And he'd want a cooked vegetable and a salad. She decided to fix enough vegetables for all three of them. Danielle, not being much of a vegetable person, probably wouldn't want any. And Paul might decide, for some reason, that Donna couldn't have any. That was fine. She'd eat them cold out of her steel bowl tomorrow.

Donna had made a large salad, put some corn on the cob in a pan to boil, and had three steaks on the grill when Paul and Danielle came into the kitchen. She heard Paul mixing another round of drinks. She smiled. Paul got mischievous when he got a few drinks in him. His mischief usually involved tormenting his slave concubine, and she loved it. Paul was explaining to Danielle how he obtained whole sides of beef direct from an organic farm somewhere in north Florida.

Donna felt a hand on her ass, and she smiled. She shuddered as spidery fingers lightly walked up her back. She tensed when she realized that it was Danielle's hand. Donna dared not turn around.

It didn't take long to grill the steaks. Donna set two plates on the table, one, of course, for Paul and one for Danielle, who had stepped out for a moment. Then Donna took her station standing slightly behind Paul, arms behind her back, ready to serve him if he needed a refill of anything.

Danielle returned, but instead of sitting down to eat, she stood in front of Donna. Danielle held her gaze and, with a sharp fingernail prodded her just where her labia joined. Then, slowly, she drew her nail up Donna's abdomen, with just enough force to make a scratch. When she reached the crease of Donna's left breast, Danielle cupped the breast in her left hand and with her right thumb and forefinger, squeezed the nipple hard. Donna sucked in air in surprise. Danielle then traced her sharp fingernail around the aureole. Donna was frozen with terror. She felt the fear as a sexual urge in her groin, and she started to tremble. She could not hold back her tears.

"You really have her trained, Paul," Danielle marveled. "She's completely obedient and docile, but completely aware, as far as I can tell. Look how terrified she is, but she won't change the position you left her in."

Paul turned around and looked up. "Danielle, stop it!" he commanded. "Sit down and eat. Leave her alone."

Danielle backed up. "Remember who you're talking to, Paul McCready." Her voice was a snarl.

To Donna's amazement, Paul crossed his arms across his chest. "I appreciate your capacity for violence, Danielle. But I am the master of this house and you are my guest. I expect decent behavior."

Danielle blinked, startled. After a moment she said, "You're right, Paul. I'm sorry." She sat down next to him.

Paul motioned Donna to sit on his lap. He clasped her to him and held her as she sobbed, dripping tears onto his shirt. His gentle stroking of her hair and his hand on her bare back stimulated her to more crying, even as she was getting progressively more embarrassed by her loss of control.

Finally, she sat up. Paul took the heavy linen napkin and dabbed the tears from her face.

"Donna, honey, go upstairs and take a few minutes to compose yourself. Then put on some clothes and come join us if you feel up to it."

Donna stood. "I'm fine, sir."

He raised an eyebrow. "Donna?"

"Sir," she insisted, "it's okay. I'm fine."

"Do you feel up to eating?"

She thought. "Yes, sir."

"Then fix yourself a plate and sit down and join us. Danielle and I are having a discussion, and we might ask for some contribution from you."

Danielle cocked her head. "You really do love her, don't you?"

"More than anything," Paul said.

Donna was so overcome by that statement that tears welled in her eyes and she was afraid she'd start crying again.

"When I was here before, she said that she was your slave concubine."

"That's exactly what she is," Paul said.

"I assumed that was more or less equivalent to a familiar."

"No," Paul replied. "For whatever reason, Donna needs to be mastered. So, I give her what she wants. At home she's not allowed freedom or dignity. I make her follow strict rules and I impose rigid discipline and robotic obedience. That's how she wants to live, but it's a lot of pressure on her and the stress makes her weepy sometimes. But I treat her this way because she wants it.

"I love her," he said huskily. "She's my one true love."

Danielle frowned. "I'm sorry, Paul. I misunderstood."

Paul shrugged. "I accept your apology, but it was Donna who was crying."

Danielle looked up at Donna. "Donna, I'm sorry I terrorized you. I mistook your status."

Donna said nothing until she saw Paul's raised eyebrow. "Apology accepted, Danielle," she said, as sweetly as possible.

Donna was near ecstasy from Paul's matter of fact declaration of love. She got herself a nice steak, some veggies, and a glass of wine and sat herself down on the other end of the table from Paul. Danielle and Paul held a long conversation about the Miasma, and Arianne, and the land of Koth. Donna was allowed to speak only when spoken to, so she rather lost the thread.

ઍ

But she was singing as she cleaned up the kitchen while Paul was driving Danielle back to her motel. When Paul returned, he didn't bother to put her in chains for what remained of the evening. Instead, he sent her up to the bedroom. They went to bed early, to read and watch TV. And when Paul pulled her over to him and lifted her so that she could straddle him, she made love furiously in the on top position, until she couldn't come any more, and had to topple over and feel her legs turn to rubber.

ઍ

In her office the next morning, Donna was thinking about – what else?-sex. She decided that one night like last night, atop her inexhaustible lover, was worth a couple of dozen quickies in which Paul took her in the ass or in the mouth. *If a girl has to have an owner, he's the guy to get.*

But some things troubled her. First was the scary fact that Paul was completely comfortable having a vampire as a guest, and that he was secure enough in his position to scold one of these unpredictable killers and compel her to back down. She knew that Paul had a few vampire abilities, mainly the power of *charm,* and the physical strength that allowed him to haul Donna around as though she were weightless. But Danielle was a full vampire. What did Paul have that was stronger than that?

And what was Danielle's deal? Michael Dalton had been in a hurry to get the hell out of Dodge, once Paul had brought him Arianne from the afterworld. But that experience seemed to have aroused Danielle into something like a religious quest. Danielle had pumped Donna for knowledge about the Miasma and the associated characters, gods, and dream worlds during the first visit. Last night had been more of the same. Donna had been restricted by her position to talking only when asked a direct question, but Danielle had been getting as much information as possible from Paul. She had clearly not charmed Paul, and she hadn't bothered to charm the terrified Donna, either.

Finally, there was Paul's account of the vetala, which he now called the Blood Spirit. He claimed that the epidemic of hallucinations and dementia of last fall and winter was the result of a demon that he had ultimately vanquished, using the sword given him by the Mother Goddess. Donna was miffed that he had told Danielle about this, but had not previously let Donna in on that little secret. Donna had naively assumed that the bullshit government story about a sixty year old chemical dump had some underlying factual basis.

So an uncomfortable truth began to seep through her body and mind like a ground hugging fog. *I am completely enslaved to a man who is far more powerful than I thought, and who doesn't always tell me the truth. He befriends vampires and has talks with demons. He has gone from being a CEO of a small security company to a multimillionaire in a few months. And I am so in his power that I don't even wear clothes.*

ꕥ

She had lunch with Whitey Ferris at Molly's, across from the courthouse. It was friendly and fun enough but there was a certain glumness to it. They had made no progress on their cold case, the skeleton at the construction site. And Whitey's relationship with Shawna was at a standstill. She liked the sex well enough, but she was going to hold her commitment at that, because she couldn't face her parents with the reality of an interracial relationship. "My dad is old school. He would just freak."

“What the hell,” Whitey asked, despondently, “the President is black. There are all kinds of black professionals, black celebrities. When is this shit going to change?”

Donna didn’t have an answer but she patted his hand, and eventually settled into holding it. “I don’t know, Whitey. I don’t know.”

Chapter Eleven: Another Missing White Girl

The Narvaez County Sheriff Department never forgot about Shelley Lowndes, but there simply was no evidence that the young woman had ever been to the county. The media had lost interest after a couple of weeks, the grieving parents evaporated from public awareness and the missing white woman was truly gone, reduced to a handful of framed photos on a mantle in Beverly Hills. Then came Marilyn Rogie.

Marilyn was a pleasant young woman of twenty-three. She came from a respectable family-her father was a retired New York policeman-and she was from the Pine Hills area. In the local media, Pine Hills, heavily populated by transplants from the North, was a lot more important than Ruffin and the eastern part of the county in general, which was populated by Southerners and by older working class retirees. So the loss of Marilyn was hyped as a community tragedy. Moreover, Narvaez was simply closer to Tampa than Citrus was. Shelley Lowndes had gotten a lot of press in Ocala, but Marilyn was big news in the huge Tampa Bay area.

To Sheriff Donna Parker-McCready, what was eerie about Ms. Rogie's disappearance is that she went missing from the Ruffin bar known as the Long Branch.

In Donna's younger days, she had often put on short shorts and a tied off blouse and gone prowling for men at the Long Branch. But more ominously, so had the vampire known among the Community as Arianne, and among the humans as Anne Rutledge. An unfortunate construction worker named Gil Hunley had met his fate at Arianne's hands after being lured away from that local bar and club.

There was a clue, though. Marilyn Rogie had left her car, a new Ford Focus, in the parking lot. She had gone out with girlfriends. Her friends had seen her talking with various young men. Nobody had seen her leave.

Whitey Ferris had asked for the surveillance disks immediately, but the camera setup was the same as it had been during the Hunley investigation. There was a single inside camera. It was mounted over the door and was aimed directly at the cash register. It wasn't designed to monitor the customers. It was designed to keep employees from stealing the proceeds. The camera looked down on customers entering or leaving. You might be able to ID a woman from her hairstyle and clothing. If a man walked past the lens, and he was wearing a hat, forget it.

Donna knew all this, but she had been a cop for a long time now. She knew how frustrating missing persons cases were. So she didn't dismiss Whitey's hopes. Instead, she went into the side room where Ferris was examining the videos frame by frame, and she put her hand on his right shoulder and leaned close so that her breast touched his left arm, and stood, her cheek almost touching his. "Do you see anything, Whitey?" she asked, her voice a whisper.

She saw the bulge rise in the crotch of his pants and she felt a little guilty, but also a little thrilled.

"No, pretty lady," Ferris answered softly. "There are four or five women that could be her. I can't tell anything about the men."

"Goddamn ACLU would get rid of all these cameras." Donna straightened up, blushing, when she heard Henry Klass's voice. "But we could have found this girl by now if we had more surveillance footage."

Donna smiled. *If the bitch had been wearing a radio collar, that would have helped, too. Do you want to require those?* Instead she said, "We've got to work with what we've got, Henry."

She turned to face him.

"At least we've got the car," Klass said. "We know that she didn't just run away on her own."

"Speaking of which," Donna reminded, "has anybody checked her financials?"

"No," Klass replied, his voice laden with sarcasm, "we all just got our badges yesterday." He hissed out an exasperated sigh. "Of course we checked. She owes about six g's on a student loan, she's current on all her bills. She pays off her credit card every month, and she has four thousand in her savings account and three hundred in checking. Money wise, she's fine."

"Boyfriend?" Donna asked.

"She had a fiancé, lived with him for nine months. They broke up four months ago."

"Is he a possible?"

"He's in Afghanistan," Klass said tiredly.

"Shit!" Donna snapped.

Klass and Ferris both stared at her, shocked.

"I'm sorry, guys," Donna told them. "I know you're busting your butts on this. It's just so goddamn frustrating."

Later in the day, Donna had to face the broadcast media and do a few sound bites that would depict her as a tough determined Sheriff. She promised that her department was doing everything possible to find this woman. She managed to hide her underlying pessimism. The interviewer recalled how the gruesome Michael Dalton case had started with the discovery of a body in the State Forest in "rural Narvaez County." Donna assured her that the two cases were not in any way similar. *But they really are.*

Before she went home, Donna did something she almost never did. She stopped by the Fireside for a drink. She bought herself a margarita at the bar and started back to the McCready table when she passed former Sheriff Tommy Watson and Dan McLaury, who were sitting at a table drinking what looked like gimlets.

"Well, there's the naked Sheriff," Watson greeted her.

Donna was mildly irritated. "You haven't forgotten that yet?" She joined them at their table.

"As an old law and order guy, I was scandalized when I read that interview," Watson said. "As a man, though, I was wondering how I could wangle an invitation to those naked goings on."

Donna pinched his cheek. She was happy to see him looking healthy again. "Tell you what, Tommy. Just drop by some time. Paul won't mind showing me off, and I certainly wouldn't mind letting you look me over." She turned to McLaury. "Sorry, Dan. The invitation doesn't extend to you."

McLaury laughed.

"I'll be dropping by as soon as my heart can take it," Watson said.

She had a drink with the two men. It cheered her up a little. She sat and talked with the two until the buzz wore off, and she started home.

ଔ

When she had finished her shower, she reported to Paul, who was sitting in his living room chair. He had his Kindle in one hand and the riding crop in the other. She stood as he teased her with the crop and winced as he probed it into her cleft.

"You're a little late today," he said.

"I stopped for a drink with Tommy Watson and Dan McLaury. I waited a half hour to let the booze wear off."

He nodded. "That's okay, Donna." He stared into her face. "You look stressed. Tough day?"

"Another missing person."

"Sorry to hear that. Those are tough."

Donna was alarmed by the kind look on his face. "Sir, please don't get all nicey nice on me because I had a tough day. I'm here now and I'm yours to use and abuse."

"Okay, turn around."

She stood with her back to the chair as he went to his office and returned. He clamped standard handcuffs to her wrists.

"You're right that you need to be in chains at home," he said. "But I don't feel like doing the whole rigmarole. So these are enough. And since you can't do anything with your hands behind your back, I'll have to fix supper and feed you. Problem?"

"No, sir."

"Good. For the time being, I want you to sit here on my lap and let me fondle your naked body until I get hungry enough to get up and fix some food. Does that meet with your approval?"

"If that's what you want, I have no choice," she answered, her voice husky.

He gave her a hard slap on the ass and dragged her by the handcuff chain back to the chair. "Let's sit down and you tell me about your day," he said.

As he kissed her and squeezed her breasts, Donna was distracted by her thoughts about the missing woman. But Donna had become very skilled in her art. She gave Paul McCready not the slightest hint that she was thinking about anything other than his attentions.

Chapter Twelve: Naomi

Naomi Spears watched, amused, as Donna stripped naked in the parking lot. "This is sort of a major rule," Donna explained. "And I have to be the one who carries the luggage, too."

Naomi forced herself to walk slowly while Donna trudged up the walk naked, her feet bare against the concrete pavers of the walkway. Donna had been helping Naomi clean her vacant house east of Ruffin, and get the lawn and landscaping under control. The task had involved frequent wine breaks, so Donna's head was spinning slightly. Even so, Donna took her slave role seriously and she was weighted down by her own tote bag hanging from a shoulder strap and Naomi's suitcase in one hand and Naomi's backpack in the other. When they arrived at the house, Donna told her, "You go ahead in the front door. I'm taking the back stairs."

Donna dropped her tote bag off in the laundry room, then paced past Naomi and then Paul who was sitting on the living room sofa reading. She carried the suitcase and backpack up to the second floor then took the opportunity to go on up to the upstairs shower.

Once showered, dried, and made up, she hiked naked down the two flights of stairs, her hands dutifully held behind her back, and arrived in the living room where Naomi and Paul were talking. The TV was on but nobody was paying attention.

Donna did her little rotation to show Paul how clean she was. Paul patted her affectionately on the butt.

"I hear you told Paul about our shower the last time I was here," Naomi said, with a hurt tone in her voice.

"I'm sorry," Donna said. She dropped to her kneeling position. "I felt that I had to tell Paul about it."

"It's cool," Naomi said. "It's cool with him, cool with you and me."

"Good," Donna replied brightly.

"Would you girls like something to eat?" Paul asked.

"I could go for some food," Naomi said. "How about you, Donna?"

"Donna no longer has a choice about things like that," Paul told her.

Naomi gave Donna a strange look. "Alrighty, then."

Assuming that Paul intended to put her to work in the kitchen, Donna started to stand, but Paul put his hand on her shoulder. "I'm learning to do Chinese," he said. "Does that suit you, Naomi?"

"That would be great," Naomi replied.

"It will take about an hour. I'll be cooking chicken chow mien and rice, along with stir fried stuff."

"I guess we'll have to wait," Naomi said. Then she asked, "Can Donna put on some clothes?"

"I'm afraid that's out of the question," Paul replied. "Donna has a hard and fast nudity rule."

Naomi sighed. "I guess that's between you and her."

Donna and Naomi talked about things…their jobs, Doug Ackerman's work, hairstyles, dresses. Finally, Naomi leaned close to her. "You're really kind of a prisoner here, aren't you?"

"I am," Donna said. "It's actually more severe than a prison, since I'm in chains. But it's only a few hours a day. From about seven until we go to bed, I have zero freedom."

"No offense, Donna. But that's kind of creepy."

"It's what I've always wanted. Now I've got it. I'm cool."

Naomi shook her head.

Paul chose to let Donna eat with them, sitting at the table. Donna was glad of that. The meal was good, the conversation pleasant, and Donna felt content after a day of physical work. As the meal ended, Naomi asked, "So what do you guys usually do after supper. Is that when you put Donna in chains?"

Paul gave an embarrassed laugh. "You disapprove?"

"Not at all," Naomi said. "If anybody ever brought something on herself, it's Donna. I was just wondering."

"On a weekday she gets hooked up as soon as we're both home. On weekends, it varies. Usually I only chain her in the evening, but sometimes I make her work outside all day in chains."

Naomi laughed at the absurdity of it. "Can I see them?" she asked.

"Donna," Paul said, "go get your chains."

Donna got up from the table and retrieved her paraphernalia from the trunk. She carried the cuffs and chains back to the kitchen, where she laid them on the table.

"The waist chain goes on first," Paul said. He had Donna stand motionless as he cinched the chain and fastened it with the split link. Next the collar…" He took the heavy two piece device and locked it together on Donna's neck. "Then the wrist cuffs, and finally the ankle cuffs." When Donna was collared and cuffed, he showed Naomi how her wrists could be crossed and clipped together, and how they were locked to the waist chain. "It's a very strict restraint," Paul said. "But it doesn't hurt her. The goal is to restrict her movement so that she has no use of her arms whatever. Finally, the leash." He clipped the leash to her collar.

Donna stood expressionless, decked out in shiny steel, unable to move her arms and with her head locked in place by the collar so that she could only face straight ahead.

"Would you like to take her for a walk?" Paul offered. "I'll clean up the kitchen while you're out. Just walk her back and forth a couple of times along the wall. She can give you a guided tour as you go."

"Seriously?" Naomi asked.

"Sure, why not? I walk her in the evening all the time. She likes it. And it's a nice night."

Paul showed Naomi how to get to the back steps from the laundry room. He let the dogs out first and they scampered downstairs. Naomi followed. Donna, deprived of the use of her arms, was last in line, bent slightly forward as Naomi pulled on the leash.

They began the walk.

It was a warm night. The sky was a milky blue as a bright moon directly overhead lit up the ground fog. Neither Naomi nor Donna spoke for a while. Finally, Naomi asked, "Don't you have a problem with the fact that the dogs run free while you're on a leash?"

Donna laughed. "I don't mind. Paul is making a point about where I fit in here."

"What point is that?"

"That I'm not free, that I have no rights. I'm just his sex toy, his slave. I'm not as free as his animals."

"Do you think that's healthy?"

"It's what I want. For some reason, knowing that Paul has total power over me is incredibly erotic. The more he restrains me and humiliates me, the more aroused I get. On my knees, in chains, looking up at him, I'm just a quivering glob of sexual hunger. I want him to totally dominate me, use me up, and leave me lying gasping on the floor."

Naomi glanced over at her. "I'm sure it's intense. But you could get hurt."

Donna thought about that for a while. "Naomi, in Koth, Paul is the warlord and I am his concubine slave. I was made for that kind of world. Here, I'm kind of weird."

Naomi laughed. "I think the word might be whack."

"I've been reading up on these things," Donna said. "The criterion for judging whether someone is sick is how much distress the condition causes. But, I can still orgasm with non-sadomasochistic sex. And my sexual needs aren't interfering with my work. So by those rules, I don't need therapy."

"Maybe," Naomi responded. But you have this delusion that you're from another world. Doesn't that indicate that you might need help?"

Donna stopped, causing an uncomfortable jolt to her neck as Naomi kept going, leash in hand. Naomi turned to face her.

"You believe in vampires, Naomi. You met Michael Dalton. Do you believe that he was a vampire?"

"I'd have to say he was."

"Before I met Paul, I saw him in my fantasies, living in this Bronze Age kingdom. We found the cluster of worlds called the Miasma. We believe all this because we started investigating and everything else followed."

"Donna, has it occurred to you that Paul might be conning you? Using bullshit to convince you that you're destined to be his slave?"

"No," Donna insisted. "I have seen things, and I had a witness, that proved that there is an afterlife that we know as the Miasma. I can't get into details but…"

Naomi turned and tugged on the leash, throwing Donna slightly off balance. "Okay, slave girl, let's walk. I want to do this whole wall at least twice."

"That's a long way," Donna objected.

"You need some exercise, to clear your head of this foolishness."

As she trudged along, slightly out of breath, Donna told Naomi the story of Arianne and how Paul had brought Arianne back from the Miasma.

"And Whitey Ferris saw all this?"

"Yes," Donna insisted.

"Okay," Naomi reluctantly admitted. "Maybe you're not crazy. But who cares? I'm getting off on jerking you around. Let's go a little faster."

Naomi began powering along at a rapid pace, the way a nurse in a hospital walks toward an emergency. The hard pull of the leash bent Donna forward and, her arms pinned behind her, she had to half walk, half stumble through the grass and sand. Donna felt the heat as anger reddened her face. But she stifled the flare of emotion. *I'm a slave in chains. It's Naomi's right to make me walk as fast as she wants.*

Naomi half dragged her to the corner where the wall turned toward the Gulf. She slowed down and let Donna walk beside her, still bent forward by the leash which Naomi now held with her left hand, while she rested her right on the small of Donna's back. They stopped at the landscaped plants which blocked the view of the water. Naomi stood for a moment, pulled the leash a little tighter, bent Donna over even more.

Standing in the ankle high grass, bent almost double, her eyes on the foliage made black by the twilight, Donna wondered what was going on. *Why is Naomi being so rough? Is there that much hostility toward me? Or maybe there's something about having control over a helpless person that brings out the sadism.* Donna had a flicker of an image. In the quick daydream, she was in her current position, standing folded forward by the tug of the chain while Naomi beat her naked butt with a heavy dressage whip. It was a powerfully erotic thought, and Donna found herself aroused. She shifted her weight from one leg to another, trying to suppress the tingle.

I wonder if I'd be like this to her if our positions were reversed. Another flash image: Naomi naked with her hands cuffed behind her, a steel collar on her neck, her bare breasts with their dark nipples bouncing as she moved, the triangle of dark fluff exposed, the only covering for her vulnerable sex. Donna imagined Naomi's distressed, tear streaked face and the chain connecting Naomi's collared neck with Donna's controlling hand.

Of course I'd be like her. Anybody would, given a desirable captive and the freedom to do whatever you want.

Her legs trembled with arousal.

The walk back to the house was more leisurely and Donna was able stay upright, though Naomi didn't allow the chain to slacken and Donna was pulled along by the constant tug.

When they returned to the house, Paul was working at his desk. He looked up to see the two women. "How was your walk, Donna?"

"It was fun, sir."

"Naomi," Paul said, "you and Donna have messed around a little. How would you like to have Donna for the night?"

ঔ

Although Donna had been living in this giant stilt house for nearly a year, she hadn't really explored it. The guest bedrooms had been furnished by a decorator whom Paul had hired after the incident in which he and Donna had been forced to house several people who were hiding from potential assassins. Donna hadn't paid much attention to the guest rooms since that crisis, except to vacuum and dust them now and then.

They put Naomi up in a room that had a large window, of the size that used to be called a "picture window" in the days of tract houses in safe neighborhoods. It had a view of the Gulf, masked by mini-blinds. There was a heavy dresser backed by a large mirror, framed in elaborate wooden scrollwork. The bed was queen size, with a red bedspread and a headboard of heavy cherry wood, elaborately carved. The bedposts were lathed into a series of round knobs and were taller than Donna. On one side of the bed was an overstuffed chair upholstered in red leather, on the other was a night table and a lamp with a colored glass shade.

One accent wall was varnished cedar. The others had light bead board wainscoting and above that, real plaster painted a cheery yellow. There was a mirror perhaps eight feet wide and six feet tall mounted on one wall, beside the bed. Overhead, an ornate fan turned listlessly above a brass motor casing and lighting fixture.

On the wall opposite the mirror was a folding closet door and a door to the bathroom.

Once Naomi had locked the hallway door, she stepped up to Donna, put her arm around her, and gave her a long, open mouthed kiss. Donna was shocked to feel Naomi's probing tongue.

Naomi stepped back and looked appraisingly at Donna, put her hands on Donna's breasts, let them wander down Donna's body, groped Donna's sex and probed her lightly with a finger.

She stepped behind Donna and unlocked the handcuffs.

"Since you're the slave in this scenario," Naomi said, "you can put my things away. I'm going to hit the shower."

"You seem pretty serious about this," Donna commented.

Naomi looked startled. "Aren't you?"

Donna thought for a moment. "I'm surprised, that's all. Paul sprang this on me without any warning. I didn't know what to expect."

Naomi stepped back and gave her an appraising look. "Don't you want to do this? We don't have to."

Donna hesitated. "You and I have messed around a little, but never anything like this. But Paul wants it. If you want it, too, I'm game."

Naomi laughed and pinched Donna's nipple. "We've fantasized about doing this in front of men. Maybe it will come to that one day. Meanwhile, here we are."

"All right," Donna agreed. Her resolve was firm now.

"Paul called you a sex slave. Is that true?"

"Very much so," Donna said. But she rethought her answer. "I try to be anyway. But it's all on me. I'm afraid that if I don't play the part all the time, Paul will revert to his easygoing self."

Naomi laughed nervously. “Then I’ll be calling the shots tonight. Go ahead, put my stuff away. Turn the bed down, and stand beside it just like you would for Paul. I’ll be back in a few minutes.”

After she had finished the task, Donna stood with her back to the bed, facing the bathroom door. She kept her wrists crossed behind her, feet apart, her mouth open and her eyes straight ahead in a fixed stare. She was under discipline and didn’t need a guard to ensure that she maintained it.

Paul is really clever. How better to reinforce that he owns me than to lend me to someone? And what’s more humiliating than to be lent to my best friend? She searched her emotions. She didn’t particularly want to do this, but she didn’t object to it either. *I’m Paul’s to do with as he wants. He’s just making a point.* And, once she relaxed and set aside the analysis, she found that she was aroused…the discipline of standing in place, plus the humiliation of what was to come sent shivers through her belly and her groin.

Naomi always envied me, Donna mused. *Even though we’re best friends there has always been that little tinge of resentment. She sees me as the lucky one, with a well off father who could pay my way through college while she had to work her way through school.* Naomi had always envied Donna’s way with men, too. Naomi had married early and often…three men. Donna had gone from one paramour to another, easily acquiring men and dropping them right up until she had been snagged by Paul McCready.

So Donna’s arousal was heightened by the reversal of roles. Now the lucky girl, the one who had everything, was to be at the disposal of the one who had so envied her. *Here’s Naomi’s chance to act out her resentment. Paul handed me over to her for humiliation. He knows that I thrive on it. I hope Naomi isn’t all nicey nice.* Already Donna’s heart was pounding in the sweet thrill of sexual excitement.

Naomi was naked when she emerged from the bathroom and Donna was momentarily dazzled by her beauty. Her curly hair fell free. Her breasts, to Donna’s mind, were just the right size, with brown nipples that begged to be sucked. Her skin was a little darker than Donna’s and she had an all-over tan, interrupted by her black bush, which was neat and triangular, a perfect match for the surrounding skin. Donna had spent a lot of time with Naomi, both of them nude, lying in the sun or sipping drinks inside the house, or sometimes even falling asleep side by side. Donna had always admired Naomi's look…her soft curves and her solid legs. But she had never before allowed herself to *desire* her best friend.

It occurred to Donna that Naomi had desired her, and that Paul knew of this desire. *Maybe they set this up together.* Donna hoped that this was true, that they both thought of her as a sex toy, to be lent and borrowed for the asking.

When Naomi returned, she got into bed and lay on her back. Donna rested herself on an elbow and leaned over her. "I don't really know what to do," Donna said.

Naomi laughed. "You're a woman. You know where all the buttons are. Pretend that you're a man trying to get me aroused."

I can do this, Donna thought. She kissed Naomi on the lips, tentatively at first, but Donna was overcome by lust and the kiss became long and passionate, with Donna probing her tongue deep into Naomi's mouth, and Naomi responding in kind. Donna became voracious, pressing her mouth against Naomi's and exploring her teeth and cheeks and tongue. Donna came up for breath, lightly kissed Naomi's neck, then took one of Naomi's perfectly sized breasts in her mouth. Paul liked doing this to Donna, and now Donna understood why. All the while, her hand was on and in Naomi's sex, probing and rubbing. Naomi was moaning with pleasure.

Donna was aroused, hot with lust. *But I'm the sex slave here. I'm the one who's kept chained up, available for use.* This would be about Naomi's pleasure. Donna would end up lying in bed, her womb burning.

Donna brought her head down onto Naomi's abdomen, and lightly nipped her belly, using tongue and teeth at the edge of the pubic hair. All the while, her hand was stroking Naomi's sex, fondling the center of her pleasure, sliding moist fingers in and out of her.

Finally, Naomi gripped Donna's hand and pushed it away. "Take me all the way," she said. "Use your tongue."

ঙ্গে

As she was returning to the house after stowing Naomi's backpack, Naomi met her on the walk. Naomi embraced her, gave her a passionate kiss, and a rather thorough fondling that left Donna aroused. Donna handed her the car keys.

"You're very sweet," Naomi said as she kissed Donna's cheek. "We'll have to do this again soon."

"I'm sure we will," Donna replied.

Inside the house, Paul was sitting in his living room chair, the riding crop in his hand. He beckoned Donna to stand in front of him. He said nothing for a moment or so as he teased Donna's sex with the whip.

"So how did it go last night?" he finally asked her.

"It went very well, sir, once I got into the groove."

"Did you like it?"

That question threw Donna. She had delighted in the delicious degradation of being lent out for sex with her best friend. And she felt a childlike pride that she had performed well for Naomi and Paul, but she hadn't examined her feelings about the lovemaking itself.

"I don't know, sir," she finally said. "It was enjoyable enough I guess, but I was focused on pleasuring Naomi. I didn't get as much out of it."

"That's what Naomi said, too."

For some reason, Donna blushed.

"How did you feel about it?"

She thought for a moment. "At first I was…I don't know…shocked, maybe? that you would just turn me over to have sex with someone else."

"Do you object to that?"

"I don't have standing to object, sir."

Paul nodded. "You're right. You don't. In our current arrangement, you don't have standing to object to anything. How would you feel if I turned you over to other women?"

Donna shuddered, but she soldiered on. "My feelings would be irrelevant, sir. But I wouldn't mind. It would probably be easier to do it with someone that I don't know. And I wouldn't have as much of a problem getting started, since I know what to do now."

Paul smiled. “Maybe we’ll do that from time to time.” He noted her expression. “Problem?”

“I was wondering, sir. Will you be turning me over to other men?”

He sat back and stared at her. “I wasn’t planning on doing that, but if I did I would expect your complete compliance. Could I count on that?”

Her reaction was automatic. “I’m completely at your disposal sir. I will do whatever you wish with anyone you wish.”

He grinned. “You’re a brave girl, Donna.”

Donna was pleased. “Thank you, sir.”

He regarded her curiously. “Do you feel betrayed?”

Donna searched through her mind, trying to locate how she felt. “No, sir,” she finally said. “There has always been a sexual undertone in my friendship with Naomi. I’ve always thought she was a little bi and we always kidded each other about it.”

She hesitated. “It takes the friendship to a different plane. Always before, I was the wild girl and she was the one who was cautious and practical…and envious. Now she’s complicit. You put me on the spot, but she and I would probably have gotten together anyway.”

“So, you’re okay with it?”

She nodded. “Sure. Naomi and I have danced around this for a long time.”

She was silent as he stared expectantly at her. After a moment, she continued. “It was like that with you, sir, if you remember. I offered you everything, but you didn’t believe me.” She sighed. “Now that you know what I am, you’re a little harsher than I expected. But I love your restraints and your arbitrary humiliations. I know that you love me and that you’re so hard on me because you know that I need it.”

Paul nodded. “Donna, understand that Naomi is free and you’re not. Does it bother you that you’ve given up this much freedom?”

Donna took a deep breath. “Sometimes, sir, but I don’t dwell on it.”

“Turn around and take two steps forward.”

She obeyed. A few seconds later she felt the shock as the riding crop smacked into her upper thigh. She flexed one knee in reaction. After the stunning impact of the blow came the pain, and the heat spreading up into her buttocks. She stood there, hands clasped together.

"Put your hands behind your neck and lace your fingers together," Paul told her, his voice gentle. She obeyed. Another hard stroke, harder than the first. Her butt was on fire, and the core of the fire was at the very top of her thighs. She didn't move, but her eyes misted. She waited for the next one. One second, two seconds…

"Turn around," Paul ordered.

She did so, expecting to be struck on her belly or breasts. But Paul simply used the crop to prod her sex. She twitched as the stiff leather opened her fleshy hood and rubbed her clit.

She assayed her reaction. The first blow had been a shock, the second just painful. She relaxed her mind and absorbed the pain. Her butt *hurt.* She imagined what it would be like to be struck like this again and again…she felt the warmth in her ass, spreading to her groin. *This is way better than spanking.* The pain from each blow was sharp, focused, intense.

She liked the feeling she had the day after a good hard spanking. Her butt tingled and it hurt a little bit to sit. Ten or twenty blows from this thing, though, and she'd be standing all day. She savored the thought. She wanted more of this.

Paul tilted his head and studied her.

"Did you deserve that, Donna?" he asked.

Donna was the perfect slave concubine, Ba-el Shanah brought to earth. "If you believe I deserved it, my lord, then I did."

He smiled tolerantly. "No, Donna, I just did it because I felt like it. You don't *deserve* any of this. But that's what it means to be a slave. I can whip you whenever I get the urge. You can't avoid it by being good, and you can't provoke it by not being good. It's all up to me."

"My lord, I request permission to speak."

He shrugged. "Go ahead."

"I bought you the crop, my lord, so that you could beat me with it. I had hoped that you would use it for your own purposes.

When you're tense, or angry, or stressed out, please feel free to work me over with the whip. It is my honor to have you whip me."

His expression made her melt. *I can see the love in his eyes!*

"I don't think that would be good for you, little concubine," he said softly. "I'll give you a little smack now and then, but that's all you have to fear."

"I don't fear it, my lord. I crave it. Please punish me whenever you like."

Paul touched her cheek with the crop. "Donna, I don't need to punish you. The Deal is punitive enough. You never disobey me anyway. If I decide to spank you or whip you again, it will be because I feel like doing it."

He'll do whatever he wants to me. She felt a surge of warmth through her body. *Finally!*

"Do you agree to that?"

"I do, sir."

He looked her up and down imperiously, a warlord on his throne, inspecting his captive.

"You know, Donna, nothing stops you from getting in your car and driving away. You've got plenty of money. Why do you want this?"

She considered for a long time. "It's because I love you, sir. And I love being your slave. I'm all in with that."

He sighed. "But the slave thing was your idea. Why do you want it? Why slavery and not just the chains once in a while? And why do you like the chains so much?"

Why is he asking this now?

Donna thought for a moment. There was a whiff of anger at Paul for bringing her out of the moment, of ruining her feeling of being overpowered and helpless. "Sir, there is something about being naked, being restrained, that arouses me and keeps me aroused. When I'm driving home, I can hardly wait to get here, to get out of my clothes. When you put the chains on me, it's like getting into costume. When I'm helpless, when I'm chained and you pull me around on a leash…I don't know how to say this…" She sighed. "Naked, helpless… I don't have to be a grownup anymore. I don't even have to be human. It's the most erotic feeling!

"Even more, the knowledge that you *own* me, that you can overwhelm my will…God, sir, you really are my True Lord! Under this modern veneer, I really am just your slave girl. That's what I want to be. When I'm naked, and under your discipline, bound by your chains, I feel like myself. Donna Parker, the educated woman, the Sheriff, is somebody else, just a role I play. When I'm naked, when I can't use my hands, when I can't talk without permission, I'm stripped down to my basic self. No fakery, no defenses. Just me, Ba-el Shanah for real."

She was silent for a moment. *What else can I say? Why am I like this?*

Paul, wordless, regarded her. She couldn't read his thoughts.

"My lord," she continued unbidden, "I want to melt into you. I want to be an extension of your will, a glove on your hand."

Paul raised an eyebrow. Donna giggled. "Besides, sir, all this keeps me constantly horny."

Paul shrugged. "So this whole submission slave thing is just about keeping you hot for sex?"

Donna grinned. "I'm afraid that's true sir."

"That's interesting." He smiled mischievously. "Now, little slave girl, how would you like to spend the day? Blindfolded and chained to the wall out by the pool? Or put in shackles to sweep the walks and patios until it gets too dark to work?"

Donna sighed. She was relieved that the uncomfortable questioning was over. Now it was a question of how she was to be oppressed today. She dreaded both choices, but she loved the Deal, and she had agreed to such punitive treatment. She weighed both options but she couldn't decide. She would really like him to simply work her over with the riding crop until his arm got tired. Finally, she gave up: "It's entirely up to you, sir."

Paul shook his head. "Christ, you are so beautiful!" He laughed. "You know what, babe? It's hard for me to keep being mean to you. I'm in a nicey nice mood. Why don't you put on some clothes and we'll go for a drive. We can hit some restaurants, eat a little seafood, maybe catch a movie. You're a pretty accomplished sex slave, but sometimes I need you to be my little sweetie."

Donna felt a little tinge of sadness. There would be no more blows with the riding crop. She had hoped that he would whip her till her butt was sore. *But he's just too goddamn sweet!*

She sighed. "Paul, I don't know what I did to deserve having you. You make my head spin sometimes."

Chapter Thirteen: Deputy Gibbs Has a Bad Day

Donna Parker-McCready, Sheriff of Narvaez County, was zooming. She'd been subpoenaed to testify in Tampa in reference to a case that she'd worked two years ago, which had somehow developed into something in Hillsborough. Her Jeep was in the shop and she had asked Paul to take her by the SO to pick up her cruiser. He'd suggested that, instead, she sign out a car from the Conquest Security motor pool. This was her first inkling that Conquest even had a motor pool. When she saw the red 5.0 liter Mustang convertible, she'd fallen in love.

But en route she'd received a call from the State Attorney, telling her that the defendant had pled out, so her testimony would not be needed. So, she was in the city at 9:00 AM with nothing to do and nobody expecting her back for the rest of the day. She called Naomi.

Sometimes Naomi got grumpy when Donna called her in the morning, but Naomi was a nurse, and she happened to be off for one day in the middle of the week. "Sure, come on over," Naomi had said.

Donna had been worried that Naomi might have been creeped out by their recent tryst in Narvaez County. But the opposite was true.

When Donna came into the living room, Naomi stepped up, gave her a long passionate kiss, and ordered her to take her clothes off. Donna complied with a giggle. Naomi took her into the bedroom and had Donna make love to her. At Naomi's stern direction, Donna used her mouth to bring Naomi to climax. Then, Naomi produced the handcuffs, locked Donna's hands behind her back, and went to work on Donna. Afterward, both women glowed as they brunched at Starbucks.

Something else had suddenly started going right. The "naked Sheriff" publicity had more or less immunized Donna from scandal regarding her nudity. Twice in the past two weeks, Paul had brought home some business associates without warning. It was obvious that they had already been clued in to expect Donna to be naked. Donna was able to greet the guests then scuttle upstairs to dress before returning to serve drinks and snacks, and generally be a hostess.

Although the men, and one woman, stared at her, nobody indicated that the household was abnormal.

People expected to find her naked. They were fine with it. There was no need to worry about who was in the circle of acquaintances and who wasn't. Donna was, at heart, a shameless exhibitionist and she loved being naked and having people look at her. There would be no more humiliating her by threatening to show her naked to this or that person. She wouldn't have to scurry around and hide when Paul brought home guests.

Finally, Paul's talk after Naomi's last visit had clarified something for Donna. Donna was not going to be rewarded or punished for anything. Her treatment depended entirely on Paul's whims. There was no point getting stressed about meeting any goals, or wondering why she was, for example, blindfolded and chained to a wall. It was just Paul, playing with his sex toy. All she had to do was observe all the rules and restrictions, which she wouldn't dream of violating, and comply with all Paul's demands. She loved Paul's arrogant demands and the casual way in which he tormented her.

So she could just relax and enjoy whatever Paul decided to do to her.

Her only real issue with Paul was when he got too nicey nice.

So Donna was driving north on I-75, singing at the top of her voice along with the radio. It was a nice warm day and the top was down. She was wearing a white scarf to protect her hair, Ray Ban sunglasses, and a short, backless summer dress with nothing on underneath. It was as near as she could get to being naked, and she liked being naked. Of course, she was wearing shoes…cheap canvas boat shoes…and she'd rather be barefoot but, hey.

As Donna drove along she was feeling happy that she now had a sexual relationship with Naomi, one made safe because each woman had a male significant other. It occurred to Donna that she had been neglecting the girl-girl type of sex. She had spent her post pubescent life learning about men; how to please them, how to get pleasure from them. Donna considered herself very skilled with men. But she didn't know much about sex with women.

A competent sex slave should be able to do both. She idly wondered if she could get Paul to lend her to an experienced lesbian for, say, a month in order to learn all the techniques. She decided to ask him, just to see his reaction. She laughed as she drove along.

She began an elaborate fantasy in which she was a naked slave in a lesbian brothel, one in which some of the women were naked, but others wore floor length crinoline dresses and carried parasols. Her attention was focused on a detail, an elaborately enameled ceramic lamp, gold figures on a black background. The lamp was at eye level, so Donna deduced that she must be on her knees. Beyond the lamp, two naked women passed by, both wearing archaic curly hair styles and eyes that were made up to look unnaturally large. One of the naked women wore an obtrusive looking contraption: a wide leather strap that ran between her legs, and which was held up by a locked belt around her waist. At the groin the strap held a sort of bowl made of brass. Donna realized with a tingle of horror that this was a chastity belt, and the bowl, which was held painfully tight, was designed to make masturbation or manual stimulation impossible.

Donna, in the fantasy, was wearing nothing whatever, and was on her knees for the use of the women in the brothel. *I'm always naked in my dreams and fantasies. I wonder why that is?*

So Donna was on automatic, singing and driving, and fantasizing when she took the Harm Lake Road exit off the Interstate. This was a two lane back road through hilly country, the scenic route back to Ruffin.

There was a steep hill along the route, a favorite place to deploy a speed trap. Donna had worked it a few times herself when she was starting out. If you topped the hill at fifty-five, gravity would have you doing seventy by the time you reached the bottom of the grade. Donna tapped her brakes and slowed to forty mph before she started the descent.

At the bottom of the grade, she rolled along the long flat and accelerated to climb the next hill. She saw the blue light in her rearview mirror. She checked her speedometer. Fifty-seven.

She pulled over.

"Can I see your license and registration, ma'am?" the deputy asked as he rested his hand on her door.

Donna slid her macramé bag toward her and retrieved her wallet. She handed him the plastic folder that had the license, registration, and insurance card.

The deputy didn't seem to recognize her. *Not surprising the way I'm dressed.* She absent mindedly checked for his name. A shudder of fear tightened her belly. *He doesn't have a name tag!*

"Wait right here a minute, ma'am." The deputy walked back to his car. Donna took the opportunity to take out her cellphone and call dispatch. "Hi, this is Sheriff Parker-McCready, Narvaez One. I'm driving a POV and I've been stopped by one of our traffic officers. He's not wearing a name tag. I'm at the bottom of the big hill on Lake Harm Road. Can you tell me who's 10-15 with a traffic stop there?"

A frightening silence, then: "Ma'am, we don't have any officers 10-15 anywhere at this time."

Donna took a deep breath. "Okay, check the twenties of the units in this area. Then 10-21 the nearest units and dispatch them to this location 10-18 X. Understood?"

"10-4, Sheriff. We'll get 'em rolling."

She had just ordered dispatch to do a radio check for the locations of the deputies assigned to the area, then to telephone the nearest units and have them come to her location as quickly as possible without using lights or sirens.

She saw the deputy returning, aluminum clipboard case in hand. She quickly slid the phone back into her bag.

"Who were you calling, ma'am?" the deputy asked.

"I was telling my boyfriend that I'm running late."

He nodded, apparently satisfied. Donna looked him over. She made him to be about five-ten, buzz haircut that was growing out, broad shouldered and with forearms that showed he could lift serious weight. He was clean shaven, square jawed, a little wide around the middle. Mirrored sunglasses hid his eyes, but Donna could feel him staring at her.

She felt stupid. Her belt, with her holstered Glock, can of pepper spray, and Taser was neatly stashed under the passenger seat. She had her creds and badge in her bag and she was tempted to flash them. She decided to wait.

"Ma'am, I clocked you doing seventy-eight rolling down that hill. That's twenty three miles per hour over the speed limit. That's a two hundred and five dollar ticket. If you do traffic school, that knocks it down to a hundred and eighty."

"Okay," Donna replied hesitantly.

"And your insurance is expired. That'll be a hundred and fifty dollars to get it reinstated. And your driver's license will be suspended until that's taken care of."

"My insurance is not expired," Donna snapped.

"You'd best not argue with me, ma'am." Donna was impressed with the menacing tone. *I could be in some serious shit here.*

"That's a nice looking car. What are the monthly payments?"

So he didn't check the license and registration at all. She had no idea what the payments should be. She made something up. "Almost five hundred a month."

"You make enough money to cover that?"

"It's a strain," she said, making up a lie instantly. "I'm single and I'm a little behind on bills."

The cop brushed his hand through his hair and looked around. "You're looking at about three fifty in fines, ma'am, and loss of driving privileges for a couple of months. Can you afford that?"

"Not really," she said, affecting a pleading tone.

This is where things get dangerous.

"You're a good looking woman. Are you interested in working something out?"

Donna took a deep breath. "What did you have in mind?"

He walked around and got into the passenger seat. There was no locking him out of a convertible. "See those dirt tire tracks, ma'am? Just pull up there and follow those for a while. We'll stop and have a talk."

Donna looked around nervously. They were between two steep hills. Sheriff cruisers might be just over the hill, or they could still be miles away. There was no telling. She gulped and put the car into drive. Once she had pulled off the road and onto the dirt path, she was on a narrow trail through heavy brush. She worried about scraping the paint on the borrowed Mustang. *Like that's my biggest problem now!*

"This is far enough," he said. She stopped the car. He reached over and took the key from the ignition. As Donna watched, fascinated, he unbuckled his belt, unbuttoned his trousers, and pulled the zipper down.

"A man has needs," he explained patiently. "I'm a man and I just need some relief. If you'll take care of me, I won't write those tickets and you can be on your way. No fines, no points on your license. You're a single woman. By your car and the way you dress, you're a little wild. You probably do this all the time anyway."

So this is how he does it. Profiling. He's after a certain look, a certain kind of auto. And he's right. I bet most women that fit that profile wouldn't even bother reporting it. There's no proof. No evidence. What's the use of even filing a complaint?

"I've changed my mind. I'll take the ticket," Donna said.

His face reddened. He glared at her. "It's a little late for that."

He opened his pants further and his erection appeared, purplish and menacing. He crooked his arm and caught the back of Donna's head in his hand. He forced her toward him.

Donna waited till her face was close, and he was leaning toward her. She caught him on the bottom of the chin with a hard right uppercut. She heard his teeth clack together. He reflexively brought his hand to his face, freeing Donna to make a hard swing with her left hand. He saw that coming and blocked the blow, holding Donna's left wrist with both his hands.

Donna brought a right hook into his face. She wished she'd had a clear shot at his nose. She would have broken it and disabled her attacker. But his head was turned, so her knuckles caught him at the top of his cheek, on the bone just under the eye.

He jerked his head back, shocked.

"Get out of this car right now," Donna warned. "I'm not some fucking girlie girl."

He stared at her. Donna was amused to see the round red marks her knuckles had made in the already swelling upper cheek.

Without warning, he flicked a punch at her, catching her square in the forehead. She reeled. The world around her spun. He took advantage of the second or so of her disorientation to clap a cuff on her left wrist and wrap the chain around the steering wheel. He had plenty of strength in his left hand to force Donna's right inexorably toward the remaining shackle.

As her head cleared, she assessed the situation. *These aren't standard issue handcuffs. He's got at least twelve inches of chain. Plenty of length for a trick like this. He's thought this through. He's probably done it before.*

Donna was sitting in her car, her hands chained to the steering wheel. *Not a good position for oral sex. What's his next move?*

"You're not so tough, bitch," he said.

Donna said nothing.

"It would have been easy. All you had to do is suck my dick. You've probably had a dozen boyfriends and you did it for them every freaking day. Now look at you."

He produced a pair of EMT shears. He examined how her dress was held together, then cut through the sleeves, which let the backless garment collapse, revealing her breasts. He squeezed each one in turn and pinched the nipples. It occurred to Donna that she could turn away from him and face the steering wheel, which would make it harder to fondle her. But she was afraid to let him out of her sight.

He yanked on her hair. "You couldn't do it the easy way. Now you're going to get the whole nine yards."

Donna felt like crying, which enraged her. But she took slow breaths and tried to think clearly.

She wasn't afraid of being raped. She liked to have rough surprise sex with Paul, what she referred to in her mind as "grab and poke." She never used the term with Paul though, because no matter how dirty they played, he was surprisingly prissy about language. *Whatever.* Paul kept her furrows pretty well plowed. A rape probably wouldn't hurt her.

The issue was staying alive. This cop had passed up several chances to break it off. Until they actually started fighting, it would have been her word against his. Had she been what she appeared, the random passing motorist, there would be no record that he'd ever stopped her. *He probably isn't even on duty.* But the special handcuffs proved that he was willing to go the distance. Once you overpower and restrain your victim, and you're a cop, and you have a weapon, you're going down for a first degree felony…30 years. *So what's the downside of killing me?* He'd be betting that, without a witness, he wouldn't be caught. Versus the slight possibility that he would be not only caught but convicted and face life in prison or the death penalty. *Thirty years is as good as life anyway.*

He's going to kill me now. He's got no choice. But not before he gets his rocks off.

So her game was delay. Take the rape if necessary, but stall.

He hooked his arm under her thighs and lifted her legs free of the seat. He roughly swiveled her around so that her butt was on the center console, her torso twisted toward the steering wheel, and her legs pulled straight across the passenger seat. He was standing outside the car, the passenger door resting against his ass.

He pushed her dress up. "Bare pussy, huh? Well, none of this is going to be new to you."

He roughly pulled the destroyed dress off her. He stood up to take in the view. "I gotta tell you, bitch. This is a nice catch. We're going to have us some fun."

As he leaned in, she kicked him in the face. Once again, she didn't have a clean shot at his nose but she didn't miss it completely. His right nostril was trickling blood at a pretty good rate.

"There's some more DNA evidence, you fuck!" she screeched.

He was trembling with rage. So was she.

He leaned into the car again, and threw his heavy torso onto her kicking feet. He grabbed a leg in each hand, lifted up, and turned her completely over until she toppled over the door. Now she was caught outside the car and bent over the door, naked except for boat shoes, her arms crossed and chained to the steering wheel, with her rear raised and exposed.

He patiently walked around the car and stood behind her. He gave her a very hard slap on the butt.

"If you're done playing around, maybe we can get this over with," he said, amusement in his voice.

She felt his hand grope between her legs, felt his thumb work into her rear orifice and several fingers shove into her vagina. "How's it feel?" he taunted.

He squeezed. She felt the jolt of electricity pass through her body and she blacked out.

She heard a man's voice. "Get some bolt cutters over here."

She heard another voice. "Nathan Gibbs, you are under arrest, you sorry piece of shit."

After her officers had cut through the handcuff chain, a manic Donna Parker-McCready walked around for several minutes, naked except for her boat shoes and shackles. She directed the investigators to her destroyed dress, and tried to get them to retrieve her car keys so that she could get some clothing from the trunk. The search for the keys distracted the deputies, who were reduced to harsh questioning of Gibbs. They ignored Donna, who clearly wasn't quite with the program.

It wasn't until Whitey Ferris arrived and wrapped a gray NCSO blanket around her that Donna was corralled. Ferris verified that EMS was en route, then walked Donna down to the roadside and stood with her behind a police car until the ambulance rolled up. Ferris matter of factly explained that the patient had been raped, punched in the face, and had caught some of the voltage from a Taser. He and a woman paramedic rode sat in back with Donna. Whitey Ferris held her hand all the way to the hospital.

By the time she'd done the whole rape exam and the MRI and convinced the doctor that she was completely awake, alert and oriented times three and that it was safe to let her leave the hospital, it was after 4:00 pm. She was wearing hospital scrubs when Whitey Ferris brought her back to her office. She paid him no mind when she took them off and grabbed a uniform from a hanger. She remembered him when she heard the door close behind her. *Well, at least you finally got to see me naked,* she thought.

She was going to have Whitey take her home when her phone rang. "Sheriff, you might want to come back out to the scene. We've found something."

When she heard what it was, she called dispatch. "Call in Stu Wheldon, and have him spin me up a chopper."

ঔ

The handsome, graying Stu Wheldon was the Sheriff's Captain who headed up the Narvaez SO Aviation division. Wheldon was ex-

Army and had retired out after twenty years. He had been a helicopter pilot for most of that time and had seen action in Iraq, Afghanistan, and a few other not so famous places. He loved flying, bureaucracy not so much. His gig with Narvaez SO was perfect for a retirement job since he got plenty of time in the air and not a lot of management duty. He was one of three pilots who could fly the two OH58Cs or the one nearly identical Bell Jet Ranger. Donna couldn't tell one bird from the other. But a good leader lets the experts do their thing.

It took him twenty minutes to get his chopper into the air and another five to touch down in the open field between the SO building and a nearby stand of forest. He picked up Donna and they flew away, heading for Harm Lake Road.

Henry Klass had driven out to the scene to hang out with the two crime scene techs. Donna quickly got on the phone with him. "Let me know when you find the VIN number," she said.

"We've got a little clearing to do before we can get at it," Klass told her. "The brush is pretty thick out here."

"Be careful not to damage any evidence."

Klass's voice had an edge of humor. "I think they know their jobs, Sheriff."

"Understood, Henry. I'm just fretting."

She looked over at Stu Wheldon and laughed at herself. She was sizing him up, wondering how he'd be in bed. *If I didn't have this job to keep me busy, Paul would have to keep me in a brothel. I'm always thinking about sex.*

But she sobered quickly.

The tow truck driver was the one who'd seen it. As he was standing on the back of his truck, arranging the chains so that he could haul the Mustang onto the flat truck bed, he had noticed a taillight through a pile of dried brush. When the deputies checked it out, they'd discovered an early 90s Chrysler LeBaron. No tag. The windows had all been smashed. Rainwater had gotten into the car, damaging carpets and upholstery, bringing on the growth of mold, and degrading evidence. The car had been driven down an embankment into a shallow pit that seemed to have been used as an illegal dump site. Then, the car had been systematically covered with brush. From the air you could see where the brush had been cut and removed. Donna examined the site carefully as the OH58 orbited the site at treetop level. Klass looked up and waved at her.

"The VIN numbers match," Klass said into his cellphone.

Donna sighed. "I don't know how I feel about that, Henry. I'm glad we found the car, but…"

"I know what you mean, Sheriff."

From the air, everything was so close together. The wrecker with Donna's borrowed Mustang on its bed was less than a hundred feet from the car in which Shelley Lowndes had last been seen alive. *A few more minutes, and I could have been dead along with her.*

Stu Wheldon looked over at her. "What now, Sheriff?"

"As long as we have daylight, let's circle the area and looked for disturbed dirt. We've found the car. Now let's find the body."

଒

They didn't find the body. The next day there would be search dogs and the mobilization of volunteers to comb the mostly wooded area. But Stu Wheldon touched his helicopter down in the McCready gravel parking lot, let Donna off, and as soon as she had reached the walkway, took off for the Narvaez County Airport. It was after 10:00 and pitch black. Donna stripped off her clothes and hiked naked toward the house, activating the motion sensor lights as she walked. It was an odd effect, her nakedness being spotlighted every ten feet.

She walked up the dreary back stairs into the laundry room. Since the Crime Scene Unit had her gun and belt in the Mustang, she was only carrying her clothing. She threw her uniform into the hamper and walked out to where Paul McCready was waiting up for her, sitting and reading in his big chair.

The room was dark, lit only by the TV screen.

"My lord," she said, "I'm sorry I'm late. We got a break in a big case."

"It's all right, babe," Paul said. "You've got to do your job. Do you want to talk about it?"

"I don't think so, sir."

"Okay. Go get cleaned up."

As she started to leave, he suddenly said, “Hold it. What happened to your head?”

Donna knew that she had knuckle imprints on her forehead. She walked back over and stood in front of him and told him about the rape.

He stood up and put his arms around her. “Oh, baby, I am so sorry. Why don’t you go upstairs and shower and put on a gown or something.”

“Just because I had a bad day doesn’t mean you have to treat me like a girlie girl.”

He sat back down. “Donna.”

“Sir, my work and the deal are completely separate. What happens in one doesn’t affect the other.”

He looked up at her and she could see what he thought. He had the expression that she called “scathing.” It was his “cut the bullshit” expression. *I don’t know why everybody thinks he’s so taciturn. His eyes tell you everything. If he never talked at all, I could tell what he wants just by watching his eyes.*

Donna looked down at the floor and flexed her knee slightly, a sort of curtsy. “I’m sorry, sir. I understand that it’s up to you to decide whether I wear clothes or not. I’ll put something on.”

“We’ll suspend the deal for a while. You need a break.”

“Sir, I’m fine.”

“Donna, please humor your concerned husband.”

“Yes, sir.”

Great, she thought, annoyed, as she plodded toward the stairs. *God knows how many more days of nicey nice!*

Chapter Fourteen: Deputy Gibbs Has Another Bad Day

Long ago, the Sheriff of Narvaez County had been a man named Bill Sullivan. Sullivan was not a man in the normal sense. He had, in various guises, been the law in Narvaez for nearly two centuries. Donna's father had been a friend to Sheriff Sullivan and, when Donna had been a little girl, the Sheriff had bounced her on his knee and brought her candy when he visited.

Sullivan, like Donna's dad, worked for the McLaurys.

Donna knew nothing of Sullivan's movements through time, and she knew of Sullivan's problems with federal authorities only from second and third hand sources. The important thing she knew about him is that, when he had the Sheriff's headquarters built just a couple of years before he was pushed out and replaced by Bob Kessler, he had included a holding cell and an interrogation room.

The building had been remodeled twice since then, and the interrogation room was now tucked away behind a series of vacant offices and storage areas. To Donna's knowledge, it had been used only once during the reign of Sheriff Watson, and that was when Paul McCready had been sequestered there for an interview with an FBI hypnotist-psychologist.

Now, Nathan Gibbs, fresh from a night in an isolation cell at the county jail, was sitting in that room with its gray walls, gray floor, the gray table with the eye bolt driven through it, and the not very comfortable metal chairs. The Sheriff's cops hadn't chained his hands to the eye bolt. In fact, he was in "transportation restraints," which meant a waist chain and leg shackles as well as the handcuffs. The handcuffs could be attached to the waist chain, but once the deputies had him in the "aquarium," they had released his hands.

Donna admired the restraints. They didn't look as comfortable as hers, and certainly weren't as beautifully made. But the chains were heavier and she couldn't help but imagine herself naked in a transportation restraint set, shuffling past a…*Stop it!*

I don't know what's wrong with me. All this nicey nice is making me crazy!

Donna was standing in the little room behind the one way mirror. Whitey Ferris was beside her, along with Lu Herrera. Henry Klass, looking surprisingly imposing, sat across from the prisoner.

"What am I doing here?" Gibbs demanded.

"We wanted to have a little talk, and we thought that this was a little more cozy than the interview room at the jail." Klass's voice was neutral, almost conversational.

"You can't do that."

"Judge Simmons thinks we can."

Judge Simmons had once made the mistake of releasing a killer on bail, and the criminal had then held Donna at gunpoint. Paul McCready had emptied a .357 into the man, and an enraged Sheriff Watson had delivered a PR pasting on the Judge. Since then, Simmons had come to be very fond of Donna, and this guy Gibbs could count on no breaks from the judiciary.

"I want my lawyer."

Klass's smile was thin. "People in hell want ice water."

Gibbs looked shocked. He stammered for a moment, then said decisively, "I'm not saying anything more without an attorney."

"Mister Gibbs," Klass said, "we don't need you to talk. We caught you in the act. Half a dozen deputies saw you with your hand inside the victim. We have the dress you cut off her. We have the cuffs that you restrained her with. What are you? Thirty-eight? Thirty-nine? You'll be almost seventy years old by the time you get out of prison."

Donna smiled at the fear in Gibbs's face.

"What is it you want?"

"You've got nothing to lose by telling us about your other victims. Your life is over anyway. You're in here alone with no lawyer. We couldn't convict you based on anything you say here. Do the decent thing and let us give the families some peace."

"I don't know what you're talking about."

"Look," Klass said, his voice even. "You're done. We've got you for the rape. It's over. If you help us with…"

"There wasn't any frickin' rape. I stopped the woman for speeding and she offered to do something for me to make the ticket go away. It turns out that she was a little kinky, you know?"

"There are a lot of holes in your story, Mister Gibbs. But we aren't here to talk about this particular rape."

"Look, I know how it looks but the bitch just changed her mind."

Klass laughed. "Okay, you say that you pulled the Sheriff over for speeding and she agreed to let you fuck her to get out of a traffic ticket? I hope you go to trial. I'm going to love watching you tell that one to a jury."

"That bitch was Donna Parker?"

Klass's eyes narrowed. "The one who signs your paychecks, right. You're goddamn lucky she didn't kill you, because she's capable of it. And to be honest, Mister Gibbs, you'll be lucky if one of us doesn't kill you. I wouldn't mind putting a bullet in your head myself, except for all the paperwork. But if something happens to you, don't expect a lot of pissing and moaning from the public or from law enforcement. Do you get my drift?"

Herrera tapped Ferris's shoulder. "You're on."

Ferris walked around and went into the interrogation room. "It's okay, Henry, I got this." He pulled up a chair beside Klass.

Gibbs laughed. "I suppose this is the guy who's going to tell me how I can help myself. Bad cop good cop."

Klass laughed. "No, bad cop worse cop. Everybody knows that Thurgood here is a little sweet on the Sheriff. You done pissed him off, Mister Gibbs."

"Look, I didn't know that bitch was the…" Whitey reached across the table and slapped Gibbs hard on his already battered cheek.

"You will not talk about Sheriff Parker-McCready in that manner. Are you clear on that?"

Gibbs blinked, amazed.

"You've already got one of the most beat to shit mug shots I've ever seen," Klass told him. "It will take a lot more of this before anyone notices."

Tears began to well down Gibb's swollen and distorted face. "What do you guys want?"

"Not very much, really," Klass said. "All we want is a promise. Promise us that you will lead us to the body of Shelley Lowndes and that you will tell us in detail about your other victims and we will send you back to the Narvaez jail. Promise us that, and we'll get a legal aid attorney in to talk with you. The Sheriff, will send a recommendation to the State Attorney that she is open to cutting you a deal."

Gibbs thought about that. "Who is this Shelley Lowndes?"

"Oh, come on!" Whitey exclaimed. He stood up and turned around, disgust on his face.

Klass gazed at Gibbs for a moment. "Did you pay any attention to law enforcement at all when you were here? She's the missing woman from Citrus County we've been looking for. Maybe you should have asked her name before you killed her."

"Killed her?" Gibbs exclaimed. "I never killed anybody."

"You just have the worse luck in the world," Ferris exploded. "You pull over some woman and rape her and she turns out to be the Sheriff. You force her off to a secluded spot which just happens to be eighty feet from the car that Shelley Lowndes was driving when she was last seen alive. With that kind of luck, don't waste your money on the lottery."

Gibbs was openly weeping now. "Jesus!" he cried. "Oh, sweet Jesus!"

Donna turned to Herrera. "What are the chances that he's telling the truth?"

"I'm guessing slim and none," Herrera said.

Donna shook her head. "That wasn't a bad offer. Maybe he didn't understand how a victim asking for leniency would affect his case. If he'd gone for it, we'd have known that he killed the girl, but we couldn't have used it in court."

"Maybe he'll do a deal later. If he killed Shelley Lowndes, he likely killed others. He's definitely down with forcible rape."

Donna sighed. "Wrap this up and get that piece of shit back to lockup."

ଔ

Donna didn't know Estelle Alvarez, the Assistant State Attorney who was handling her rape case. Alvarez had been at the job four or five months and hadn't handled a major felony prosecution before. Alvarez looked to be in her early forties, was trim and attractive and moderately well dressed. She was wearing a blue, businesslike dress with a high collar and a skirt that reached below the knees. *I wouldn't have gone with the black rimmed glasses, maybe something less businesslike.* The woman was, to Donna's eye, a little pudgy around the waist. *She's probably had children.* Alvarez had honored Donna with a visit to Donna's office. Most crime victims had to show up and hang out in the lifeless waiting room at the SA's local headquarters.

"Are you open to a deal?" Alvarez asked.

"I could see a first degree on the rape and let him plead out anything he confesses to."

Alvarez sucked in a breath. "That will be a tough sell."

"We've got him dead to rights on the rape."

"I'd say we have about a seventy-five percent chance of a conviction if we go to trial."

"I would guess much better than that," Donna told her.

Alvarez shrugged. "It depends on the lawyer. If he gets a good attorney who mounts a full scale defense, he might have a year or two to contaminate the jury pool. You know: The naked Sheriff, entrapment. You had a badge and a gun…why did you agree to pull off the road with him? That sort of thing."

"Bottom line," Donna said firmly: "He wasn't supposed to be on duty. He stopped me at random. He didn't call the stop in. I called dispatch and requested backup. I fought with him. He cut off my clothes. He hit me and he stuck his fingers into me."

"Would you go for sexual battery as a second degree felony? He'd do fifteen years and still have some life left when he got out."

"Lawrence Singleton," Donna said.

Alvarez winced. Singleton was a California criminal who had been convicted of raping and then chopping off the arms of a sixteen year old girl in 1978. He'd served only nine years before being paroled in California. That state had resettled him in Florida and, in 1997, at the age of 69, Singleton had murdered a Tampa woman. Singleton was the classic cautionary tale about releasing violent felons who "have some life left."

"Sheriff," Alvarez said, "I know what you're going through. I'm being realistic. If we offer him a plea, it will save the state a lot of money and it will get him off the streets for sure. And he won't be able to get out on appeal."

"Assassination will always accompany robbery as long as both are punished by hanging…" Donna mused.

"Excuse me?"

"That's a loose paraphrase from the Marquis de Sade."

"You have some strange reading habits, Sheriff."

Donna laughed. "I don't like the concept. If he confesses to murder he does fifteen years, but if he denies it he does the whole thirty."

"The judicial system is what it is, Sheriff."

"If a rapist faces essentially the same sentence as a murderer, what's the incentive not to kill the victim?"

Alvarez said nothing.

Donna finally nodded. "I'm through philosophizing, Ms. Alvarez. I'll agree to a second degree felony if, and only if, he leads us to the body of Shelley Lowndes. Any deal other than that and I'll be on TV denouncing your office."

"I respect that, Sheriff."

"We're going to nail this to him, one way or another," Donna said.

ଔ

Donna went home to nicey nice, which meant that Paul McCready was treating her as a normal husband would treat a normal wife. In fact, he had made a nice supper for her of baked tilapia, hash browns and a perfectly delicious salad. Donna was wearing a very short loose fitting house dress, her concession to his requirement that she dress like a normal wife. She was barefoot and not wearing underwear.

How did I ever stand this for so long before?

She didn't know why she bridled so much at nicey nice. Paul was a perfectly lovely man and, left to himself, he would have spoiled and pampered her. Now that he had acquired some wealth, he was willing to buy her anything she wanted. She had a whole closet full of beautiful clothes and sometimes he even made her wear some of them.

She was looking forward to a week or more of going out to dinner, or to movies, or to festivals. He'd even spoken of a cocktail party this Friday, where she could relax and meet people and have fun.

But that wasn't what she craved. She wanted rough treatment. She wanted chains and blindfolds and sudden rough sex. Nicey nice was okay. She liked lying on the sofa and making out as well as anyone. But finally it bored her. Being blindfolded and chained to the wall was more exciting. Absent vision, she could slip away from this world and explore around in the Miasma. Being made to work outside in chains was interesting…doing a long repetitive chore while the hot sun beat down and made her sweat, or the chill evening air made her legs cold and her steel cuffs icy against her skin. Daydreaming and sweeping, hour after hour, enjoying the sweet humiliation. That was what she really craved.

If she had her way, her subjugation would go further. She imagined herself strung up and whipped and left to hang moaning, her arms tied above her head. She imagined being forced to service one man after another, or to be turned over to women for use. Even Paul, who knew her as well as anyone, would be shocked if he could really read her thoughts.

But Paul was being nicey nice. He felt bad about her handling by the rogue cop Gibbs, and he was making it up to her.

But Paul knew her and knew what she craved. Sooner or later, it would be back to the rules and the chains. It was killing her to wait.

"How much longer for the nicey nice?" she asked Paul. She took a bite of fish. It was very good. Paul was an excellent cook and when he made food for her it was delicious. But right now she would have preferred to be on her knees, eating cold glop scooped up with her fingers.

"Are you getting tired of it?" Paul asked, smiling.

"I am, sweetie. I know how you love me and all, but I really crave some rough handling. It's hard for me to focus when you haven't roughed me up and worn me out the night before."

"I thought that you needed a break from all that."

"Yes, but for how long?" She couldn't hide the frustration in her voice.

She thrilled to the steel in his. “That is up to me. The end of nicey nice will come when I decide that it’s time. It will be very sudden, very harsh, and you will get no warning.”

That cheered her up. “I’m glad to hear that, sweetie. Could I have some more orange juice?”

Chapter Fifteen: Other Women

Donna Parker-McCready was having a late lunch at the Fireside Inn with Sharon Becker. Donna liked Sharon, and Sharon had been over to the house a couple of times to hang out naked by the pool with Donna, while Sharon's equally naked boyfriend fixed drinks and worked on his tan. Donna loved checking out his equipment, which Sharon found amusing and which Dave Leeper thought was funny.

But Donna was also jealous of Sharon, simply because Sharon was slightly younger and Sharon was stunningly beautiful. It was not that Sharon worked with Paul McCready and that he obviously liked to look at her *because, what man wouldn't?* but also because Donna loved being at the center of attention among men, and Sharon was a serious rival for the center.

Sharon was knocking back a margarita. Donna envied her. Donna was bound by Paul's prohibition against alcohol and driving, and also by her own department policy. So Donna was sipping a sweet non-alcoholic concoction.

"So, Sharon, why did you want to see me?" Donna asked.

"No reason," Sharon said. "Paul asked me to give you a call. He was tied up and wanted to make sure you didn't have to eat by yourself."

Donna was touched. "That was sweet of him."

"He really does love you, Donna."

"I know," Donna said wistfully. It had been five weeks since Paul had gone into nicey nice mode, and he showed no sign of returning her to prisoner status. He pampered her and touched her whenever he had a chance, took her out nearly every night and in general was the perfect husband. Donna feared that she was seeing his natural self, and that his cruel domination was a passing aberration. Or, perhaps, he was lulling her into a happy normality, so that it would seem that much harsher when he put her back in chains.

She hoped for the latter.

"How's Dave?"

"Dave is fine. He and the McLaury's are working on something important, but I don't know what it is. I try to see him as much as I can because our time is almost up."

"Why, what do you mean?"

"Oh, Donna." Sharon sounded as though she were about to cry. "He was only here for seven years, and then he has to go back."

"Go back where?"

"Wherever it is he's from."

Donna shook her head, confused. "Where is he from?"

"He can't tell me."

What the hell? "Can you go with him?"

This time, Sharon did break into tears. "Oh, Donna! I thought I could handle it but I can't. I've been in love with him since I was seventeen. He's the only man I've ever loved."

Now Donna was blinking back tears. One of what Donna considered her own character flaws was that she was weepy. It was a girlie girl feature that she could not suppress. For lack of anything better to say, she asked: "How long do you have?"

"Till the middle of 2014." Sharon began sobbing again.

Donna reached across the table and held Sharon's hand. "That's still a lot of time. A lot can happen between now and then."

Sharon held up one hand, gesturing Donna to wait a second. She drained her drink in one long gulp. She waved at the waiter.

The waiter was a middle aged man named Joe, who was usually a bartender but was having to fill in since one of the servers was sick. "Another margarita, Miss?" he asked.

"Make it a double," Sharon told him.

Donna was envious. "I used to pound down drinks like that," she said. "But I got in trouble a couple of times and Paul cracked down on me."

Sharon took a deep breath and got herself under control. "That's interesting. You're two people, aren't you? There's no doubt who runs the SO, but I can tell that Paul runs your household."

Donna laughed. "How so?"

"Your nooners, for one thing. We know what you're doing when you have lunch in his office. You're the Sheriff of the county and you come in to service your husband at lunch time."

“Well,” Donna said reasonably, “he is my husband.”

“I wish I had a husband,” Sharon said. “I’d be like you. I’d go naked for him and come in for a BJ while he was at work. Just somebody who would love me and not go away.” She looked up and grinned. “You don’t suppose Paul would want to start a harem in 2015, do you?”

Donna laughed. “I never thought about it, but he could certainly handle one.”

“Sister wives,” Sharon said.

Donna considered the idea happily. Two women, that’s what Paul needed. One wife to be his slave and be kept naked in chains all the time. The other to get the benefit of his nicey nice side. *Best not fantasize too far in that direction. This could easily come true.*

“I hope the nooners aren’t upsetting anybody,” Donna said.

Sharon touched her hand. “Oh, no, Donna. When Paul has you over for lunch, everybody gets free food.”

They laughed about that, and talked dirty about men, and about movies and clothes. But then something occurred to Donna, a half forgotten rumor, reinforced a year or so ago when her husband had been turned away from a mysterious cabin in the forest.

Sharon,” she asked, “you said Dave wasn’t from around here and has to go back somewhere. Is he a time traveller?”

“Oh, Donna, he is,” a half sloshed Sharon answered. “But you can’t talk about that with anyone.”

❧

It was a 7:15 on a bright Saturday morning, and Donna was having breakfast with her husband. He had made her a fine omelette and there were toasted English muffins with peach jam. This was the sixth week of nicey nice and Donna was getting used to it.

She was wearing a cheery blue house dress that didn’t quite reach to mid-thigh. She wore nothing underneath it and was barefoot. She had developed an aversion to shoes.

“How is work going?” Paul asked between sips of fresh hot coffee.

“So, so. You know how it is. Things just flow along until something breaks.”

“How is the Gibbs case going?”

She looked up. She didn’t like to think about that one. She took a sip of coffee.

“I don’t know, sweetie. The SA has an offer on the table. Fifteen years on my rape and he pleads out of everything else. All he has to do is confess to all he’s done and lead us to the body of Shelley Lowndes.”

“He won’t take it?”

“No.”

“Why not?”

“Who knows? He’s willing to confess to the murder, but he won’t give us details and he won’t lead us to the body.”

“Maybe he doesn’t know where it is.”

That offhand comment hit Donna like a punch in the chest. “Why wouldn’t he?” she gasped.

Paul shrugged. “Maybe he didn’t do it.”

“Paul, we were right there, less than a hundred feet from Shelley’s car.”

“It doesn’t mean he did it.”

Donna felt her anger surge. “What are the chances that he’d set out to rape me less than a hundred feet from the last victim.”

Paul cocked his head and studied her. “Don’t get mad, Donna. I’m not criticizing you or telling you how to do your job. But what if it is just bad luck?”

“What are the odds, Paul?”

“That’s a good question. First, what are the odds that he would pull over a random car and try to rape the driver, and it would turn out to be the Sheriff? Astronomical, right? But, suppose that he was targeting a particular profile – a young pretty woman driving a hot convertible? Now, it comes down to the odds against the Sheriff being a pretty young woman driving a hot convertible during the time that he’s set up on Lake Harm Road. It’s still highly unlikely, but not ridiculously so.

“Now, what are the odds that he would take you down that road near where you found the Lowndes car? First, it’s almost inevitable that he'd take that particular track, once he had you. But as for the car: There are hundreds of places to dump a car, but that particular place is a pretty good one. It's hidden from the road. There's already a trash dump there. There are a lot of trees around so you'd have to be right over it to see it from the air. In my humble, no longer expert opinion, there's a good chance that somebody dumped the car there and Gibbs knew nothing about it. He took that dirt track because he was already right there."

Donna felt sick.

Paul said nothing for a few minutes. He sipped coffee, watched her face.

"Are you okay, Donna?"

"I'm fine, sweetie. I was just considering the possibility, that's all."

He nodded. "What do you have going this weekend?"

Donna's heart pounded. *The end of nicey nice?* She no longer knew how she felt about that. "I've got the weekend off. Henry is in charge."

"Do you have gas in your Jeep?"

"I just topped it off on the way home."

"Naomi asked if she could have you for the weekend. I said it was okay with me if it was okay with you."

"There's nothing going on at work, so I should have the weekend free. So, whatever you want me to do."

"I told her you'd be there about 9:30 this morning."

"I'll go pack, sir."

"No packing, Donna. You'll go as you are. Take your wallet with your car stuff and credit cards. Do not take any other personal items, not even a purse. Leave all your money here. You're just delivering yourself to her. Clear?"

Donna felt the unease and excitement as a warm feeling in her face and fluttering in her chest. "Yes, sir."

"Here is an envelope, Donna. It contains instructions to Naomi as to how you're to be stored when not in use." He handed it to her. "Take it and go. Right now."

ଔ

Donna did take her Glock and her badge. Paul had just waved her on as she had held those items up on her way to the laundry room. *Just delivering myself.*

On the drive down, she turned the Gibbs case over in her mind. In all the discussions about Gibbs, everyone had spoken in terms of "if he did it." But nobody really believed that Gibbs was innocent of the Shelley Lowndes disappearance. But what if he were? Paul's suggestion irritated Donna. If he were right, the SO needed to be going all out trying to solve the case. Negotiations with Gibbs's lawyers were a waste of time.

When she couldn't stand it anymore, Donna pulled off the road and called Henry Klass. She laid out the possibility that they were on the wrong track with Gibbs and asked him to pull the Lowndes file and "take another look at it." Klass couldn't hide the irritation in his voice. Not only was it useless extra effort, but he truly hated Gibbs.

Donna showed up at Naomi's doorstep holding her gun, phone, and wallet. Naomi laughed when she opened the door. "What did he do, kick you out of bed and send you down here?"

"He let me finish breakfast first," Donna replied.

"Come on in. Here, give me that stuff. I'll put it away for you."

Naomi took Donna's things into another room. She returned to where Donna was standing. She embraced Donna, and gave her a long deep kiss. Donna reciprocated, although she wasn't quite in the mood. The Gibbs case had distracted her.

Naomi pulled up Donna's dress and fingered her sex.

"This is for you," Donna said. She handed Naomi the envelope. "Paul said it's instructions on how I'm to be stored."

"Stored? Paul is getting to be a master of head games." Naomi opened the envelope and read it.

"Do you want to read it?" she asked Donna.

"It's addressed to you, so I don't think I'm supposed to."

"I see you're all in with Paul's game."

"It's my game, too."

"Well, it says that you're supposed to be naked, handcuffed, and blindfolded the whole time you're here, except when we're actually doing it or in bed. I'm supposed to take full advantage of you.

I'm supposed to keep you stimulated but not let you climax, and you're not supposed to be allowed to touch yourself."

Donna laughed. "That's Paul!" She pulled off her house dress. "I guess I won't be needing this."

Naomi stepped back and sighed. "You're really beautiful, Donna. In your little dress, looking like a waif, you were just so…poignant. Are you sure you want to do this?"

"I want what Paul wants," Donna said.

"We don't have to do what Paul wants," Naomi told her. "We can make out on our own terms, or we could just spend the day together. I agreed to this because I'm a little bi, and you and I have always talked about making out for the men. This is like that, but instead of watching us, Paul is using me in his head game with you. Are you okay with that?"

"Sure," Donna said. "I'm the one who offered to be Paul's slave. I'm following Paul's orders because I want to."

"Well," Naomi replied, "whatever floats your boat. I suppose if it were up to Paul, you'd already be cuffed on your knees in the bedroom, but that can wait. Let's have some tea and talk for a while, relax a little. I got you a nice little pair of fur lined handcuffs. Also a sexy sleep mask and a genuine nylon dog collar. You'll be the prettiest sex slave I know."

Donna laughed. "Naomi, you didn't have to go to all that trouble. You already bought me a whip."

"Secretly, I'm going to try to get Doug to let me wear that stuff."

"I didn't know you guys were into that sort of thing."

"What? You think you're the only one who's kinky? Who brings her girlfriend over to strip for her man?"

Donna frowned. "Naomi, you said you were okay with that."

Naomi laughed. "It made me jealous, but he could go to a strip club any time he wanted and I wouldn't know a thing about it, so I'm cool. But as for handcuffs, yeah, you know how it is. If you're a cop's girlfriend, you spend some time in cuffs."

Donna smiled knowingly. "It's always been that way for me."

"Come on, naked girl. Let's go to the kitchen and make some tea."

ଔ

Donna felt a little guilty as she came into the living room late Sunday afternoon. Naomi had been as strict as Paul could want Saturday and Saturday night, but on Sunday, after Donna had brought her to orgasm, Naomi had sat up in bed and said, "That was great. It will never replace what a man can do, but it felt really good. How are you doing?"

Donna had stood up. "I have to say, Paul's fingers are a lot bigger than yours, but you do have me worked up."

Naomi had laughed. "And you'll stay that way. Now I'm going to lend my borrowed sex slave some clothes and take her out on a date."

"But Paul said…"

Naomi had waved aside her objection. "Remember, you're the slave. You have to do what I want. I haven't been to the Lowry Park Zoo in a while."

ଔ

Paul was in his office behind the panel barrier. The dire wolves were sleeping in front of his desk.

"So, how'd it go?" he asked.

"Sir, I have a confession to make."

"Okay."

"Naomi took me to the zoo this afternoon. We just hung out. After Sunday morning, I wasn't blindfolded and naked like you wanted."

He smiled. "That's okay, babe. You were on loan to Naomi. You weren't to have a say in anything. She was in charge."

He leaned back and grin. "Besides, babe, you know I say that scary stuff just to get you going."

Donna nodded, relieved.

"So, are you sexually frustrated?"

"Naomi gave me a pretty thorough intimate massage before I left, so, yeah."

“Take off that dress, Donna.”

She complied immediately and stood with her hands behind her back.

He shook his head. “Donna, you are so fucking beautiful. It was killing me to be here without you. Turn around.”

She did. She heard him scoot his chair back and a few seconds later felt the steel on her wrists.

“Sir, does this mean that nicey nice is over?”

“Pretty much.”

“Thank God, sir. I felt like I was drowning in saccharin.”

“I think a good hard spanking will fix that.”

Donna beamed with delight. “Don’t go easy on me, sir. My ass hasn’t been smacked in a long time.”

“Don’t worry about that.” He took her arm and steered her toward his chair in the living room. As she stood, waiting for him to bend her over, she was already ecstatic in anticipation of his fingers digging into her passages between blows.

But, as she was bent over his knee waiting for the first blow to land, she couldn’t shake the vision of the car, nosed down into the garbage pit, the last remnant of Shelley Lowndes, the missing white girl.

Chapter Sixteen: Another Case

The meeting was in the Sheriff's office, which, more and more, was Donna's office. The "ego wall" had been cleared of Tommy Watson's certificates and photos, to be replaced by copies of Donna's college diplomas, certificates, awards from various civic groups, and a handful of photos of Donna with various civic leaders and business types.

Henry Klass, head of Major Crimes was there, as was Whitey Ferris, Director of CID. The subject: Nathan Gibbs.

"So how did it get into your head that Gibbs isn't guilty?" Klass asked.

"I was talking with Paul, and he suggested that if the Lowndes car were a coincidence, then Gibbs's behavior regarding the plea makes sense."

Klass shook his head. "Paul McCready! Are we ever going to get out from under that guy?"

Donna said nothing. She looked to Klass expectantly.

"Swear to God, I don't know how that guy got so connected. He just goes along, not seeming to do any work, not being friendly to anybody, and all the sudden he's in charge of everything." Klass caught himself. "I'm sorry, Sheriff. I know you're sleeping with him…"

"I am," Donna said, a hint of pride in her voice. "I'm married to him. I have certain specific needs and he fills them very well for me." She saw the hurt look on Ferris's face and decided not to chase that conversational train. "But let's not dwell on past personality conflicts when we could be developing new ones."

Ferris laughed and Klass made a gesture of surrender. "Okay," he said. "Enough of my bitching. I still like Gibbs for Lowndes."

"I've been looking at it with new eyes," Donna said. "I was understandably pissed at the guy, and that may have clouded my judgment. Suppose he was just a corrupt rapist cop. He stakes out a place where there is steady but sparse traffic, pulls over vulnerable looking women. He threatens them with a citation and offers them a way out of it. If one takes him up on it, no harm no foul. To both of them, it's a mutual agreeable transaction..." She saw Klass wince. "Agreeable in an economic sense, I mean.

"At what point does it escalate to murder? Say he pulls the woman off the road. She balks. He threatens her with force. She gives in. I'm guess that at that point, most women would give in. Even at that point, there's very little chance that he will get in trouble. The woman will know it's her word against his. She's had a very unpleasant experience, but making an accusation against a cop will be an even more unpleasant experience. So, even if he's using a little coercion, he's not risking very much.

"Say a woman puts up a fight. Now, he's in a position where he's looking at a forcible rape. But he hasn't thought it through. So far, he's just been getting blow jobs on the side of the road. He doesn't consider that a major crime. All of a sudden, he's looking at a first degree felony. His best move probably is to kill her, but that's a big mental step. And, it's complex. He has to hide the body and the car. How likely is it that he would get into an escalating situation like that and then repeat the offense a few weeks later, near the site of the first crime? Is he that stupid? If he is that stupid, how did he hide the body so we can't find it?"

Klass sighed. "Okay, we'll leave Lowndes open. Do you want to hear about the new case?"

"Go ahead."

Whitey Ferris spoke up. "The name is Rosalinda Nunez. She ran away from home...Columbus, Ohio...in July of 2011. She'd been living with her father but they weren't getting along. Her father thought she'd gone to live with her aunt in Pine Hills. Her aunt was expecting her but Rosalinda never showed up. Dad gets killed. He was collateral damage in a convenience store robbery in early 2012. The aunt never hears from Rosalinda, but doesn't say anything because the girl had an alcohol and drug problem and figures that she's run off with some guy.

"But, a week or so ago, the aunt runs into Rosalinda's best friend, who's living in Ruffin. It turns out that Rosalinda had showed up back in 2011 and stayed with the friend for about six weeks. The friend doesn't know what happened to her, and she still has

Rosalinda's stuff. The aunt hears about Lowndes and Rogie, and decides to report Rosalinda's disappearance."

"How old?" Donna asked.

"Rosalinda would have been seventeen, almost eighteen when she disappeared."

Donna counted on her fingers. "Okay, suppose a serial killer came to town in 2007, killed the woman who's now the construction site skeleton. Then he kills Rosalinda four years later. Then Shelley Lowndes, then Marilyn Rogie. A GUT."

"Or a stretch," Klass commented sourly.

"Any more leads on skeleton girl?" Donna asked.

Whitey Ferris answered. "I thought we had a live one with the Sheffield place, but it turned out to be nothing."

"Tell me about it," Donna said.

"Warren Sheffield, formerly did the Heating and AC stuff at Narvaez Regional. He owned ten acres a mile and a half from the construction site. Turns out he had a couple of sexual battery complaints, but no convictions."

"Sounds promising," Donna noted.

"But he's got an ironclad alibi. In 2007, he was doing time in Michigan on child porn charges."

"How about the year before? That's in our window."

"He was either on trial or in prison from September, 2005 on. He's still there. He didn't do it."

"Who lives there now?"

"Nobody. The wife and two kids lived there for a while. You know the wife. Virginia, the waitress at Molly's."

"Sure, I know her. She's supposed to be ultra-religious. How'd she get mixed up with a child porn type?"

Whitey shrugged. "Wives are the last to know."

Donna laughed. "As a wife, I hope that's not true." She sat forward. "Thanks for the briefing. I guess I don't have to tell you to check out Rosalinda. If she was underage and a boozer, she must have had some fake ID. See if you can track down what name was on it. Guys, we've got to solve one of these cases."

"Will do, Sheriff," Klass said.

Donna checked her watch. "Meeting's over, guys. I've got to meet my husband at his office for lunch."

ꕥ

This lunch was different. When Donna came through the office complex, she found everybody in the break room. The usually bare banquet tables were covered with white cloths and food was set up, banquet style on one of them. Sharon Becker waved at her from across the room. Donna started to go inside, but felt a powerful grip on her upper arm. "This way, Donna," she heard Paul say.

She was a little irritated as her pulled her back through the doorway and steered her down the hall, his hand still clamped on her arm.

They came into his office. There was a young, relatively pretty woman setting up food on Paul's desk. *What the hell is this?* The woman had dark hair, dark eyes, and a dark complexion. She was wearing a shiny silk dress decorated with figures reminiscent of Japanese lacquer paintings.

"This is Carla Montez," Paul said. "Ms. Montez is our new steward, a full time hostess. She makes sure that our meetings are catered and our clients get fed. Carla, this is my wife, Donna."

Carla smiled, showing unnaturally white teeth. "I'm pleased to meet you, Mrs. McCready."

"I'm pleased to meet you, Ms. Montez."

"Carla is fine. I'll just get out of your way now."

"Before you go, could you move the settings to my side of the desk? I like to have Donna beside me when I eat."

"Of course, Mister McCready." She quickly reset the Wedgewood style china.

After the woman had left, Donna said, "You're having lunch served on porcelain? That's really nice."

Paul locked the door. "It won't make much difference to you. You know the drill."

Donna did. She quickly removed her clothing and put it on the side chair, shoes and gun belt on top of it. Paul motioned her to his side of the desk, took hold of her shoulders, turned her around, and cuffed her hands behind her back. He motioned her to kneel.

One of Donna's favorite things was to be kneeling, naked and handcuffed, while Paul hand fed her. It was one of the first things that she'd revealed to Paul about herself when they first began their relationship. It had a profound effect on her, and she always felt elated after the ritual. She didn't really know why.

Her lunch was interrupted by the intercom. "Mister McCready?"

"I asked not to be disturbed, Ms. Wanamaker."

"I'm sorry, sir, but Sharon has a document she needs you to sign and the messenger is here."

Paul sighed. "Send her in."

He stood and lifted Donna to her feet and pointed to the bathroom. Donna scurried into the room and used her butt to close the door. She heard Paul unlock the office.

"What is this vital document?" he asked, a trifle sarcastically.

"The Portland proposal, sir. We're on a tight deadline."

"Hang on."

Donna could hear his chair move. "There are my signatures," he said after a few moments. "Anything else?"

"Where's Donna?"

"She's in the bathroom."

"And her clothes are out here? Got it."

"Aren't you on a deadline, Sharon?"

Donna heard the door lock. Paul came for her, roughly pulled her back over to his desk, and made her kneel. He continued hand feeding her the rather excellent Chinese food until she had enough, then used her mouth in another way.

Donna liked that, too. She liked oral sex in general, but the rough kind with hair pulling and rough probing of her throat always left her feeling stimulated and glowing, like she felt after a hard workout. *Endorphins, I guess.*

Without too many words being exchanged, she rested her cheek against his genitalia for a happy several minutes after he was spent, and then stood up at his command, so he could release her from her cuffs. She went back to the bathroom, got cleaned up, and the couple embraced, kissed, and fondled for another few minutes before she got dressed and headed out.

It had become a routine, and, for her, a very pleasant one. *I need a little rough handling in the middle of a slow day.*

As she was driving back to the Sheriff's headquarters, she received a text. At a red light, she checked it. It was from Danielle Travis.

Chapter Seventeen: Lunch With the Vampire

Danielle Travis was looking good. She was wearing a tight fitting longish dress with long sleeves, incongruous on a hot Florida day, sunglasses, and a broad brimmed straw hat. She put her bag on the table, took off her sunglasses, and smiled.

"It's nice and dark in here, Donna. It's quite comfortable for me."

"This is Paul's personal reserved table. The Fireside is the classiest place in Ruffin, which isn't saying much."

Donna examined Danielle Travis with a law officer's eye. The woman seemed to be young, in her mid-twenties probably, had a good figure, and thin, elegant hands. Her dark brown eyes were bright and friendly and set in an alabaster face that had the appearance of delicately carved statuary. Pale as she was, she was not pallorous or unhealthy. Donna looked for the telltale vampire teeth, but Danielle didn't appear to have that feature. Vampires had the power to obscure their appearance, but Donna was sure that she was seeing the real Danielle, as the woman's image was crisp and solid.

Danielle picked up a wine list. "You're very pretty, Donna, even in your uniform. Paul is right to keep you naked. Your body is exquisite."

Donna frowned. "If you say so."

"Michael thinks so, too. I mentioned you once and he said that you were stunningly beautiful."

That made Donna cringe. Michael Dalton was a vampire and an extremely prolific serial killer. Donna had trapped Dalton and the vampire Arianne in an ancient wood house and burned them both to death. Michael had recovered, and had enlisted the help of Paul McCready in bringing Arianne back from the dead. Paul's association with Michael Dalton was one of the issues between Paul and Donna that was folded into their bizarre relationship.

"Thank you, I guess," Donna replied crisply. "Why did you want to see me?"

Danielle smiled. "Straight to the point I see. Donna, I'm afraid I've gotten off on the wrong foot with you. I'd like us to be friends."

Donna glared into her face. "How many people have you killed?" she asked bluntly.

Danielle tipped her head back. "Oh, that again. I've honestly lost count. More than sixty."

"And you want me to overlook that detail? I'm a Sheriff, for God's sake."

Danielle studied the wine list for a moment. "It's not like you could convict me of any of them. My mentor was very accomplished. I wasn't like Michael, who was abandoned on his own and who did the best he could - in a messy and spectacular way."

"I'd like to try."

"None in Florida," Danielle said. "Except for that handful that Michael and I killed on your behalf, and we know that the authorities are covering those up. No, my victims are scattered over twenty states – falls, traffic accidents, suicides with notes- you get the picture. Those one horse jurisdictions wouldn't want to reopen their investigations even if you had some evidence and contacted them. I'm afraid I've gotten away with it."

Donna said nothing.

"I don't have to kill anybody anymore," Danielle persisted. "I'm a mature vampire. I'll even have those lovely fangs in a few years. A little blood donation now and then and I'll be fine."

Donna let out a long breath. "So, you want to be friends. Why, exactly?"

"The times I visited your house, I misjudged you. Male vampires I know like to keep their familiars naked. I was a familiar myself, once, so I know what it's like. I viewed you in that light, a naked slave, a familiar, a blood source. I treated you like that, I apologize. It wasn't clear to me that your apparent slavery is just a sex game between you and Paul. I see now that he really loves you. I'd seen you together before. I should have realized that."

Donna blinked and said nothing.

After an uncomfortable silence, Danielle spoke again. "I understand that you aren't in any way my inferior, Donna. And I need your help."

Why should I help you? Donna thought. But she said, “In what possible way can I be of help to you?”

“Since I learned about the Miasma, Donna, I’ve been thinking about ultimate issues. Life, death, what comes after. I was a young lawyer when I first met Michael. I did cocaine, drank, hooked up with guys. I was also a vampire familiar, although it took me a while to find that out. Without getting into details, I was about to be killed –erased, at any rate. Michael saved my life. But I never believed in Michael’s stories about dreams and the Miasma. I thought that there was nothing beyond this life. The only escape from death was vampirism. You can see that, right?”

Donna nodded, suspicious.

“But Paul crossed over into the Miasma and brought back Arianne. That changed everything. There really is something beyond. I’m wondering if I’ve made a mistake.”

“I don’t see how I can help you with that,” Donna said.

“If you’ll recall, Donna, I came to your house and interviewed you about all this. I had you *charmed* so you might not remember everything.”

“Okay.”

“And I questioned Paul about it that night at dinner…”

“In our relationship, Paul can impose a silence rule on me. That night I wasn’t allowed to speak unless asked a direct question. I kind of daydreamed through that conversation since I wasn’t allowed to take part.”

“That’s unfortunate.”

Donna shrugged. “It’s psychological conditioning. Keeping me silent, keeping me naked, keeping me chained, is all designed to make me more submissive, to separate me from everyone else and make it clear to me that I’m not free.”

Danielle looked at her in surprise. “And you enjoy that?”

“I suggested it. Understand that I *want* to be his slave. It took Paul a while to come around, that’s all. Of course, he had to be stricter than I was with myself. But back to the point.”

“Going over everything that I’ve learned from you and Paul, I now realize that you are the key. You really are the daughter of the Goddess, in some way that I’m not clear on yet. The Goddess created

Paul for you, or at least made him what he is and gave him his power for you."

Donna raised an eyebrow. "What power?"

"Donna, Paul has the blood of vampires. He has Michael's blood, which is a mixture of the blood of the oldest and most powerful vampires there are. But we of the Community believed that the effect of an infusion of vampire blood wears off if the vampire doesn't feed. Of course, we can't think of any cases of that happening. It's more or less legend. But Paul is getting stronger, because he has the power of the Goddess as well."

Donna half laughed. "Danielle, I'm the source of the Goddess story. Paul picked it up from me. But look at my life. I'm not the sanest person in the world."

"Your sexual fetishes don't define you, Donna."

"Danielle, I believe in the Goddess and I believe that the land of Koth exists and that the Miasma exists. But I also realize that all that might not be true. I'm an orphan, Danielle. My mother died when I was in my teens and my father died when I was in college. Don't you think it's possible that I imagined the Mother Goddess, an idealized immortal mother, and made her so real that Paul dreams her, too? And who is Paul, but the father that I craved? My real father was an easygoing liberal parent. I loved Paul because he had that same amused tolerant attitude my father had, but, in contrast to my father, I could see the steel underneath.

"Maybe Paul is just a guy, and I've just idealized him. I made him that perfect father who loves and tolerates me but has the strength that I wanted."

"That's an amazingly honest self-assessment, Donna, but you're forgetting one thing."

"What is that?"

"Paul crossed over into the Miasma and brought back Arianne."

The server arrived, apologizing profusely for not having noticed the women when they came in. Donna ordered soda water with lemon, and a BLT. Danielle ordered steak tartare. The server, a young woman who seemed to be high school age, noted that the Fireside had only recently started serving that dish, and that was in deference to Paul McCready. The order taken, Donna replied.

"You're right. Paul did bring back Arianne. That only proves that Arianne's spirit went somewhere and came back. It doesn't prove the other stuff."

Danielle laughed. "You're a very skeptical person, having seen what you've seen."

"My father was a scientist. I get it from him."

Danielle smiled. "Paul had a technique for reaching into the Miasma. He said that he learned it from you."

"I go there in my dreams," Donna said.

Danielle stared at her. "And when you're awake?"

Donna sighed. "When I'm awake, and there's nothing much going on, I can get into daydreaming so much that I go there. But Paul likes to chain me so I can't move, and blindfold me, and leave me somewhere by myself."

"That's a rather harsh punishment," Danielle remarked.

Donna shook her head. "No, Paul doesn't punish me for anything. He does things to me to keep me uncertain, off balance. More psychology. Anyway, blindfolded and alone and undisturbed, I go completely into the Miasma. I feel the cobblestones under my feet, smell the smells of sweat and urine and the fishy seaside smells, and the smell of cooking meat. I feel my arms, restrained by chains, and the wind on my skin, and the tug on my leash as I'm led through the streets. It is so real.

"Samuel Johnson, I think it was, was asked to prove that the world was real. If you remember, Bishop Berkeley's thesis was that we couldn't prove that the world wasn't a dream or an illusion. Johnson kicked a stone and said, 'I prove it thus.' Scientists ever after have defined reality by saying that it 'kicks back.' For me, Koth kicks back. I feel it."

Danielle touched Donna's hand. "I believe you, Donna. I believe that you are the daughter of the Goddess, and that the Goddess created Koth for you and Paul for you."

Donna didn't recoil from the vampire's touch. "That's a major leap of faith, Danielle."

"I know that the Goddess exists because she has made Paul so powerful."

Donna smiled tolerantly. "Paul has some power to *charm* because he has the vampire blood. And he's gotten rich very quickly, so now he has the power of wealth."

"Oh, no," Danielle said, "it's much more than that. Remember, I'm a vampire. I can see his chi."

ଔ

That evening, when she arrived home, Paul was already there. "I've been shopping," he said. He showed her a backpack-satchel he had bought for her to carry her clothes, belt and shoes when she stripped in the parking lot and had to carry everything inside. "A little easier than your tote bag," he told her. And he called the two pups, who had on new heavy leather collars, already adorned with their license and vaccination tags.

He produced an identical collar and showed her. "I got one to match, for you." He handed it to her. It had one large round tag, about three inches in diameter, engraved with the words: "Donna, owned by Paul McCready."

She laughed. "That's very sweet, my lord. Now you have collars for all your bitches."

He frowned. "I would have said 'pets.' But only one of them needs a leash. Come here."

He took her into his office and used standard handcuffs to hold her hands behind her back. He attached a leash to her collar. "Let's take my pets for a walk," he said.

Once outside, he walked her down the walk, across the gravel lot, and onto the sparse grass. The German shepherd pups were running and playing joyously.

"You know what, Donna," he said, "you need some play, too." He unshackled her hands and unlocked the leash. "Go play with the pups. Run. They'll chase you."

Donna was puzzled at first, but took off running. The dogs chased her, she wrestled with them, ran again. Sometimes they knocked her down and she rolled around in the sand scuffling with them. This continued until the dogs were panting and she was covered with sweat and sand and her hair was full of leaves. It was fun, running and rolling on the ground, all while naked. She hoped that he would set her loose to play more often.

He didn't cuff her hands but he clipped the leash to her collar and led her back to the house, the panting dogs running ahead eagerly.

Once inside, he took off her leash. She felt strange being in the living room with him without being in chains. *I feel almost naked*, she joked to herself. He walked over to his chair and sat, faced by Donna standing with her hands behind her back, and the dogs sitting on their haunches.

"Okay, everybody. Belly rubs," he said.

The dogs surprised Donna by rolling onto their backs, front paws tucked, hind legs spread and in the air. *When did he have time to teach them that?*

"You, too, Donna," he ordered.

She got onto her back quickly enough, but he had to help her flex her arms and tuck her hands, then to crook her knees, spread her legs and hold her feet in the air, so that she most resembled a dog in belly rub position.

He knelt between the two dogs and scratched their bellies for a while. Finally he dismissed them and turned his attention to Donna.

"How do you like belly rubs?" he asked.

"It feels nice, sir, but it's very embarrassing."

He laughed. "Slaves don't get embarrassed. You're not allowed any dignity."

She sighed. "I forget that sometimes."

"Well, get used to this. We'll be doing it more often."

She looked up at him, looked for the wavy disturbance that was the emanation of chi the vampires claimed to be able to see. She couldn't see anything except Paul, his outline stark against the background of the room.

She was in a strange place. Holding her legs in the air was uncomfortable, but Paul's fingers rubbing her lower belly gave her a powerfully erotic feeling. Like most of Paul's torments, it made her want to have sex with him. She relaxed and her mind became a dreamy null.

Chapter Eighteen: A Niche in Time

It was morning. Paul had fixed a breakfast of bacon, scrambled eggs, and grits. Donna, naked as always, walked into the kitchen and knelt on the floor. "I'm not a very good slave to you, my lord."

"Why do you say that, Donna?" Paul asked as he put some food onto his plate.

"You always cook for me, and I should be doing all that for you."

"I like cooking. Besides, don't I make you kneel on the floor and eat with your hands? That's pretty slave like."

"But I'm not doing anything for you, sir. You're still waiting on me."

"You seem to be depressed today, Donna. What's the matter?"

"It's nothing, sir. I'm whatever you want me to be."

He caught on. "It's that time of the month again, isn't it, Donna?"

"It is, my lord."

He laughed. "It's okay babe. Sit at the table with me. We can be nicey nice today."

Donna was relieved, but would never have admitted it. "You shouldn't have to adjust to me, my lord."

He got a plate for her and set her up with food, a coffee cup, and silverware. "Don't be ridiculous, Donna. What does the great lord of Koth do when his concubine Belshana is on the rag? Surely he accommodates her."

"I think they put her in a special tent, like in the Bible. Then he goes down to the kennels and pulls a backup girl out of a cage."

Paul burst out laughing. "That's what we'll do, then. Problem solved."

Donna laughed at that.

She had a question. "Remember the cabin you visited once, a long time ago? The one your guards wouldn't let you in."

He thought. "Jeez…that was a long time ago. Why?"

"Where is it?"

"You get to it from one of the forest trails off Gettes-Shaffer Road, the continuation of Forest Road. I'd have to think about it. I don't recall the directions offhand. Why?"

"I'm curious, that's all."

He sighed. "Okay. If you want to check it out, run it by Dan McLaury first. You don't want to screw with one of his projects and cause a problem."

"I will, sir."

McCready nodded, a little suspicious. "Are you okay, Donna?"

"I've had some cramps, that's all. I took a Motrin."

"Did you want to stay home from work? I can stay home and fix you soup and things."

She laughed. "Sir, for a slave driver, you're ridiculously sweet. But no, I'll be fine. I'm not up to an emergency booty call to Naomi, but I can work."

He looked stricken. "Oh, baby, you know we were just playing with you. Naomi doesn't have the heart to persecute you like I do anyway. I was just having some fun with your 'slave' thing."

"I know, sweetie. You don't persecute me. You let me be myself. Nobody else could do that for me. I love you for it."

"And I love you, babe. Why don't you finish eating and get some clothes on. I'll treat you like a normal wife for the next few days."

"Oh, no!" she said in mock horror. "Not more nicey nice!"

☙❧

Donna rather cynically encouraged Sharon Becker to have another margarita. It was easy to do at the back table of the Fireside in mid-afternoon, with the shadowy lighting and the rich wood paneling and the miscellaneous music providing the undertone. The story Sharon told her was unbelievable.

In the last year of the Twentieth Century, Sharon Becker, one of her girlfriends, and a teenage boy had gotten wasted and driven out to an old, supposedly haunted cabin in an area of the State Forest known as Witches Woods. It was called that because "…it's like the roach motel. People go in and they don't come out."

A man lived in the cabin, a well-built muscular man with white hair. His name was David Leeper. Sharon and her friends had gone into the cabin, and they had been transported to the Pliocene era, when the Gulf of Mexico lapped at the edge of what now was a cypress swamp around the cabin, twenty miles inland. She had seen mastodons and gomphotheres and giant carnivorous birds, a giant crocodile….Sharon caught herself.

"I'm not supposed to tell anybody this."

"It's okay," Donna cajoled her. "You've already told me this much."

"Well, Bobby and Betty and I got home. But later the cabin took Barney Kobe and Patty Kendall, Barry Rohm, and Betty. They were gone almost two years."

"Jesus!" Donna hissed. She knew that Patty Kendall had married Barry Rohm. It had been in the newspaper when it happened. *I hope their wedding went better than mine.* And Kobe, too. So there was this enormous secret that the most important people in the county knew about. *Dad told me that the McLaury's were investigating time travel. He lied. They had time travel and they were trying to figure out how to use it.*

So, at some point, the "older" white haired David Leeper had become the young stud who now lived with Sharon, and whose penis Donna liked to ogle when they were all naked out by the pool. And this version of David was going somewhere next year, so Sharon was already feeling devastated.

Donna pondered whether to press Sharon for more details, but decided that it would be best if Sharon didn't recall exactly what she'd said. She waved the server over and ordered another round of drinks. Sharon was getting another margarita and Donna was getting the non-alcoholic version.

Donna excused herself to go to the ladies room. Once there, she called Paul. "Sweetie, I'm having lunch with Sharon Becker. She asked me to tell you that she doesn't feel well and she won't make it back to work this afternoon."

"Tell her it's okay. She's a contractor anyway. She sets her own hours. Feeling better?"

"Much better, sir."

"Good, I'll see you later. Do you want to do dinner and a movie?"

"I'm just a slave, my lord. I have no choice in these matters."

He laughed. "Whatever, Donna. Check the listings and pick a movie you like."

"See you then, sweetie. Love you."

ଓଃ

Donna had left a reeling Sharon Becker in her bed in Pine Hills and returned to Ruffin after having spent over two hours at "lunch." She had barely gotten her office computer turned on when she got a telephone call from Whitey Ferris.

"Hey, pretty lady."

"Hey yourself, Whitey. What's up?"

"I just wanted to give you a heads up. The Forestry Service has been doing a controlled burn out here in the State Forest. Apparently, there was an abandoned car out here in the brush and it went up when the flames hit it."

"I suppose there was a body in it and that's why you called."

"That's right."

"Are you there?"

"I'm on my way. We have a couple of units on scene."

"Is there any place we can land a chopper?"

"Probably not. It's deep in the forest."

"Okay, I'll see if I can round up somebody and head out there. Give me directions when you find the place."

The question is, how long that body's been there. So, a dead body in the forest. And everybody I know has been lying to me all my life about what the McLaury's are up to and what my dad was doing for them. And I'm on the rag and it's all nicey nice at home. Could it get any better?

ଓଃ

The car was maybe a hundred yards off the forest road, a scar of red clay and limerock that cut through the woods for about seven miles. In summer, when it rained, Forest Road, aka Gettes-Schaffer

Road, was almost impassable, cut by rivulets into gullies and its low spots filled into deep ponds. But today, the road was passable and so Henry Klass was able to pilot his Interceptor along the dirt highway with only the occasional bone jarring bump.

The scene wasn't hard to find. A Forest Service fire vehicle, a Narvaez Fire Rescue pumper truck, three shiny clean Forest Service pickups and two Narvaez Sheriff's vehicles were already there. Whitey Ferris met them.

"The car was parked near some fallen trees and covered with brush," Whitey explained. "It was a controlled burn, and when the car went up, Forestry drove up and suppressed the fire."

"How much of the body is left?"

"The body is in the trunk," Ferris explained. "The vent went off and the Forestry people moved in. It's not like the movies. In a car fire, the tank vent flares first, and the car doesn't get totally involved until the seals melt on…"

"Dammit, Whitey, I've seen car fires before. The body, remember?"

Ferris looked shocked and hurt. Klass laughed. "It's okay, Lieutenant. You'll understand when you're married."

Donna blushed. "Henry's right. I'm sorry. Please don't take it personally."

"Anyway," Ferris said. He escorted them up to the burned car.

Donna examined the site. The tires were melted and the paint was blackened, but that was probably because the palm and palmetto brush had burned. The car itself was recognizable. She decided not to try the doors. *Leave that to the crime scene techs*. The trunk was open. Inside the trunk was a blackened skeleton.

"This is an old body," Donna said. "The fire didn't burn off all that flesh."

"No," Whitey answered. "Look at the legs. They're straight and the torso is folded over. Some of this ash here…" He leaned forward and, using a ballpoint pen, lifted up a section of ash on the femur, "…is a stocking or panty hose."

Donna nodded as he revealed the brown nylon fabric.

"No sign of any other clothes," he said. "But there is some burnt fabric on the neck. Maybe a ligature?"

Donna sighed. "What do you think?"

"I think that this is what remains of a female subject who was strangled and carried to the trunk and set down inside. The assailant set her straight down, so that she was sitting with her legs straightened. Then he folded her up at the waist and closed the trunk lid."

"We'll call in FDLE on this one," Donna said. "We need DNA and a bunch of other stuff that we can't do here. When they get the VIN number, we'll have something to work with."

"I've got that already," Ferris said. "There's a clear spot on the windshield."

"Run it when we get home." Donna looked around. They were standing within easy view of the road. "Why didn't anybody see this earlier?"

"Before the burn," Whitey said, "this area was all overgrown. Palmettos, grass, everything. Somebody had piled branches full of pine straw on top of the car. There would have been vines growing over it. It would just be a lump of trash to anybody driving by."

"How do you know about the pine straw?"

"Forestry guy told me. They washed it all off when they hosed down the fire."

Donna sighed as she looked at the deep ruts left by the brush trucks. "We aren't going to find much evidence around the scene, are we?"

"No, ma'am."

"Well, stand by here, Lieutenant, until some crime scene people get here. I'm heading back. Nothing I can do."

"Yes, ma'am," Ferris said sadly.

ঙ্গ

When she got home that evening, a little before six, she stripped in the parking lot and placed her things in the bag that Paul had bought her. She took the opportunity, there in the gravel lot, to insert a new tampon, and she put on the dog collar that Paul had given her. She trudged to the house, went up the back steps, went upstairs to the bedroom, and took a quick shower. She came back downstairs, hands behind her back, and went into Paul's office, where the two dogs were sitting.

"Hi, Sheriff," Paul said. He smiled at her. "I think this is a good time for you to be quiet. Don't speak until I tell you that you can."

She nodded her understanding.

He put on her waist chain and clipped her hands behind her back. He brought his hands along her body, squeezing her breasts, massaging her vulva, and making her shudder. "I think I'll take my pets for a walk," he said. He clipped a leash to her collar.

He let the dogs out first, then followed, with Donna bending forward as he tugged on the chain.

He walked her down the paved walk in silence, and across the gravel, and through the sandy lawn of the adjacent lot. She did not trail behind him, but he walked, grasping her leash at the point where his hand rested against her breasts. He walked a little fast, but she was accustomed to this by now. They reached the corner and he led her past the vacant house, and back to the mangrove barrier that blocked the view of the sea. Occasionally, Donder or Blitzen would come up and sniff at her, and look up for reassurance, then scamper off again. He walked her along the vegetation barrier, farther than he'd ever walked her before. Then he turned and headed back, passing their house and out into the vacant lot.

All the time he said nothing to her, and she, silenced by his order, said nothing to him. Sometimes he would tug a little harder on the chain, bending her forward, for no apparent reason. He walked her along the water's edge, which, along this lot, was demarcated by a crumbling seawall. It was still early evening, and she could see the gorgeous orange sunset reflecting in the Gulf water. He released his grip on her leash and stood beside her next to the seawall, his hand on her butt, and looked out to sea for several minutes. Then he pulled her to him and stroked her breasts as he kissed her, a long kiss with his tongue deep into her mouth and she flicking her tongue in response. Then he led her along the seawall, until he reached their boat slip, and their floating dock.

She wondered if anybody out on the water in a boat, or maybe camping on one of those tiny islands, could see her walking naked and chained. Maybe someone with binoculars, or one of those powerful bird watching telescopes?

The thought cheered her. Paul's mastery of her made her happy and she wished that she could show it to the world. It was a warm night and the breeze was up, blowing through her hair and tickling her loins, and caressing her whole body. She wished that she could grasp Paul's hand and hold it against her breast, but instead it rested there, a constant weight on her neck. The weight, Paul's steady tug guiding her forward, gave her a blissful, aroused feeling. She wondered what Paul had in store for her tonight.

He led her past the fence around their swimming pool, and around the side of the house, and through the screened off area, and to the backstairs. He said nothing to her, but tied her leash to the railing post and left her standing as he went back outside. For a moment, she felt a thrill of fear as she thought he might be leaving her tied there as he went away. But she heard him calling the dogs. A few minutes passed and screen door open. He went up the steps and let the dogs into the house. He came back for her.

Once inside, he led her to a rug and released her hands. "Belly rub," he called. The dogs came up to his feet and rolled onto their backs. "You, too, Donna," he said. "I want you to be as quick as the dogs."

She obeyed, her face burning with humiliation.

After he had finished rubbing her belly as she lay, feet in the air, he had her stand up.

"You can talk now," he said.

"Sir," she told him, "I thought that I was beyond embarrassment, but you have found my weakness."

He laughed. "I know. That's why you're going to have to practice again and again. But this was just an interruption of the nicey nice. Give me a kiss and go get ready. Or have you forgotten that we're going out to dinner?"

She gave him a kiss, the best she had, her hands groping his crotch. He broke away and smacked her on the butt. "On your way, little slave girl," he said.

She held up her arms, showing that she still had on the cuffs.

He removed them but left the waist chain.

ஐ

During dinner, Paul was so nice to her, and during the movie he held her hand. She felt like she was young again, and Paul was another boy trying to seduce her. She smiled at that thought. *I am so far beyond innocent! No seduction needed.* But she was caught up in the pretend, in the romantic fantasy. For a few hours, she forgot that she was Paul's slave, and she forgot about McLaury's time machine and about Danielle's quest for meaning and about the skeleton in the car.

When she got home, the only reminder of her status was when Paul ordered her to strip beside the car, and when he removed her waist chain in his office. But once he had beckoned her to bed, he was as gentle with her as, she imagined, he would have been if they were both teenagers after the prom, and he was introducing her to the Big Mystery.

Chapter Nineteen: The Skeleton in the Car

It took nearly four weeks to nail down the case of the skeleton in the car. The VIN led them directly to Dominic and Teresa Torricelli of Hauppauge, New York. The local authorities took a while, distracted as they were by the problems of hurricane recovery. But eventually they were able to determine that Teresa Torricelli, who had just turned twenty-six at the time, had run away from home late in 2010. She and husband Dominic had been married for three years.

Dominic was a transit worker who had never missed work and hadn't taken a vacation during the timeframe in question…That is, October, 2011, when Teresa had stopped paying her electric bills or showing up for work at her job in a Ruffin diner.

New York authorities had found a sister and were able to use her DNA to prove that the skeleton was, with a likelihood better than 99.9%, Teresa Torricelli.

So, the Narvaez Sheriff Department had a murder victim whose identity and approximate date of death was known. The logical prime suspect had already been ruled out.

All this investigation was done without any contribution from the Sheriff, Donna Parker-McCready. It was Henry Klass and Whitey Ferris, doing their routine jobs. Donna had been doing annoying administrative work, had gone to a major law enforcement conference, hobnobbed with local politicos, and generally been acting like an elected Sheriff. Nathan Gibbs was in jail, willing to cop to almost anything but unable or unwilling to provide details.

In her private life, Donna remained the part time sex slave of her annoyingly easy going husband. She had also had three opportunities to practice, with Naomi Spears, the art of pleasing women. Donna had been distracted. She had forgotten about the vampire Danielle Travis, and had tucked away her curiosity about Sharon Becker, the McLaurys, and her father's work on time travel.

Donna was the victim in the one crime that they could pin on Nathan Gibbs, the roadside rape of the County Sheriff. In her own mind, Donna had largely dismissed the seriousness of the charges, since he had only penetrated her with his fingers, and then only for a second or two before he'd been hit by the Taser. She had begun to come around to the idea to charging him with a second degree felony. But there was the possibility…

"What do we do with Nathan Gibbs?" Donna asked her two chief investigators, Henry Klass and Whitey Ferris. They were in a closed door meeting in the Sheriff's office, which had mutated even more into Donna's office, now brightened with photos of the Sheriff and her husband Paul, posing with the "dire wolves," Donna posing with Naomi and Doug Ackerman, and an enlarged scanned photo of her mother and father in their early years. There were roses on her desk as well, sent by her devoted husband. It felt like a violation to bring talk of rape and murder into such a homey atmosphere.

"I don't see the problem," Ferris said. "It's up to the State Attorney. He's as much as admitted to the Lowndes killing. If he doesn't want to play ball, let him do thirty years."

Klass frowned as he considered the question. "It doesn't matter," he said finally. "If he doesn't give us information on Lowndes, we can charge him if we're ever able to prove anything. Beyond nailing him to Lowndes, it isn't your problem."

Donna thought about that. Gibbs was big news in a county that had two five day a week newspapers. It would be bigger news when it came out that the Sheriff herself was the victim. The press already knew it, but there were laws and newspaper policies about revealing the identity of a rape victim. If Donna recommended that they throw the book at Gibbs, she would look vindictive. A recommendation for leniency would make her seem weak.

"The brush bothers me," she said.

Klass rolled his eyes. "Brush?"

"I don't know the man that well, but Gibbs doesn't strike me as the industrious type. I have a hard time visualizing him out cutting down scrub to cover a car. That takes planning. He hadn't really done a lot of planning when it came to my situation."

"I know Paul McCready was a good cop," Klass said. "his personality aside. But you're letting him get under your skin. Gibbs took you to less than a hundred feet of Lowndes's car. That's a fact. He's got to be our prime suspect."

"Do you think he did Torricelli?" Donna asked.

"I've got no idea," Klass said. "A body that old…"

"It was the same thing," Donna went on. "A car hidden by brush that had been cut and stacked to hide the car. It was almost a signature."

"We've considered that, of course," Ferris broke in. "But we've got zilch connecting Torricelli to anybody. Right now, I'm backgrounding Forestry employees. They're out there all the time and they never reported the car."

Donna rocked her chair. "I don't like the way we're focusing on Gibbs for Lowndes. I think we need to widen the net."

It surprised Donna when Ferris disagreed. "We're looking at everybody, Sheriff. But, with all due respect, you're not on top of this investigation. We are. We just aren't finding any other suspects."

"You haven't found her body, either," Donna said. "If Gibbs did it, we should be able to shake loose something about where the body might be."

Both Klass and Ferris looked away.

"How about the Monarch Estates body?" Donna asked.

"We've got zip on that, of course," Klass told her.

"Why 'of course?'"

Klass shook his head. "We're not magicians. We don't have an ID or a clue and the area was inhabited by transients for years. Anybody could have killed her."

"Does Gibbs look good for her?" Donna asked.

Klass, irritated, shook his head.

"You know," Ferris said, "the one thing that connects these killings is Highway Fifty."

Donna could see that. "Sure, one doer or gang of doers. They kill somebody in one place and dump the body somewhere along the east-west route, several miles off the main drag. So killings that are widely separated in terms of miles are basically along the same route."

The intercom sounded. "Sheriff, this is Sue in Dispatch. There's a firefight on Gettes Shaeffer Road."

ঙ৪ঌ

The gunfight was not a fight so much as a group of what were apparently Civil War re-enactors who had fired on a group of kids who had been riding down the dirt road on four wheel ATVs. One of the vehicles had lost a tire and the rider had fled into the brush. Not surprisingly, he had been abandoned by his comrades until half a dozen deputies had corralled the re-enactors.

Corporal Michael Ballantine reported off to Donna. "They were firing these antique muskets at us. I thought that they weren't loaded, but one of the balls hit Wilson's window."

"Did you return fire?" Donna asked.

"Warning shots into the dirt, ma'am. I know it's not policy, but…"

"A judgment call, Mike. Good work." Donna knew that this could have gotten bloody. Apparently, the re-enactors had formed a skirmish line with a third of the group firing while a third reloaded and another third stood up to fire. They had opened fire from more than a hundred yards away, with the deputies taking cover behind their cars. Three volleys had been fired before two other patrol cars arrived from near Ruffin. They had driven into the group from behind.

Policy was to meet lethal force with lethal force, aiming at the center of mass. No warning shots or aiming to wound. Unofficially, in Florida, Sheriffs would tell their people, "You shoot at a deputy, you die."

A young man approached Ballantine and Donna. Donna hated him on sight. He was thin, wore new Levis, a tee shirt with some rock band's decal, and was carrying a helmet painted with flames. "Excuse me," he said.

Ballantine frowned. "We'll be with you in a minute."

"Those fuckers shot out my tire and dinged my paint. Who's paying for that?"

Donna looked around. She saw a deputy whom she didn't immediately recognize and waved him over. She caught his name tag. Milks. She'd have to remember that. "Deputy, make sure you ticket all these ATV riders for riding on the public roads and riding in the forest. And arrange to have those pieces of shit impounded."

Milks grinned. "Yes, ma'am."

The youth started to say something but Milks caught his arm. "Best not to mouth off to the Sheriff," he said.

The SO had captured twenty very thin, hard bitten looking men. Most had teeth missing. All had scruffy beards and longish hair that was dirty and stringy. Some had high round billed caps, some had floppy broad brimmed hats. Donna noticed that none wore zippered trousers but instead wore overly loose pants made of heavy cloth, buttoned in front with brass buttons and held up by suspenders. The deputies had them lined up, their hands secured behind their backs with plastic cuffs.

Donna walked past the line of prisoners, then walked over to where their weapons had been stacked. She picked up one of the muskets. "I've never seen anything like it," she said. The gun looked like it had seen hard service. She noted the hammer and the strike plate and realized that she was looking at an antique. The stock of the gun was wood, scratched and barely varnished *maybe not varnished at all, maybe oiled and rubbed.* Some knives had been seized as well. They looked like butcher knives that had been heavily used. Some had wood handles, some bone. They did not look like the stereotyped edged weapon. There were a couple of swords, both of them curved sabers and, in comparison to the other weapons, very well maintained. There were flintlock pistols in braces, six of them. Donna picked one up and saw that it was charged, ready to cock and fire. She set it down carefully.

"What the hell is this?" Donna demanded. Ballantine shrugged.

She walked over to the line of ragged looking men. "Which one of you is in charge?" she demanded.

"I be in command of this unit," one man answered her. He was wearing a vaguely military style blue jacket with faded yellowish piping. "I am Gabriel Dawes, Colonel in the Army of the United States. Who might you be, madam?"

"I'm Donna Parker-McCready, the Sheriff of this county."

"Sheriff?" he repeated, confused. "Can you tell us where we be, madam? Where is it that women dress like men and Sheriffs command so many men?"

"You're in the Blackwater State Forest, Narvaez County, Florida."

He shook his head, trying to take it in. "Are we still then in Florida?"

Donna frowned. “Yes.”

Donna saw the fear and confusion in Dawes’s eyes. “What manner of carriages are these that no draft animals pull them?”

Donna put up a hand. “Let me ask the questions. Where are you from?”

“I have a commission from General Jackson commanding me to go south into Florida and raise a regiment. I found recruiting sparse in these parts, as there seemed so little white population…”

“Who is General Jackson?”

“Madame, he is the Governor of the two Floridas, headquartered in Pensacola.”

Donna closed her eyes to think. “Would that be Andrew Jackson?” she asked.

“That is his name, yes, madam.”

Donna tried to place the man’s accent, but couldn’t. “Andrew Jackson,” she said. “Okey dokey. This commission you say you have…is it a written document?”

“In the General’s own hand. Yes, madam.”

“Could I see it?”

“In my purse, madam.”

The purse, it turned out, was a round stiff sided leather bag that hung from a shoulder strap. The black leather was held together with thick leather cord stitched at half inch intervals. Donna found the document, a piece of rolled parchment. The ink was impressively black and not smudged, although there were places where the writer had made mistakes and scraped the ink away.

“It looks real,” Donna said to nobody in particular. She walked back over to Dawes. “What year is it?” she asked.

“Year, madam?”

“Yes, Colonel. What is the current year?”

“If I ken your question madam, it is the year of the Lord, 1821.”

Donna sucked in a breath. “I believe I see your problem, Colonel.” She paced over to Ballantine. “Split these men up into pairs for transport. I’ll call the jail and see if we can accommodate them.”

It turned out that the jail could not. But a quick conference with a Fish and Wildlife officer gave her the location of a place not far off the road where land had been cleared so that deer could graze. Donna moved the prisoners there and deployed half a dozen deputies to guard them. She then drove into Ruffin, where she bought out WalMart's supply of five man mountain tents. She returned to the forest site and set to work with her officers setting up the tents. She had also brought a back seat full of Wendy's food and half a dozen buckets from KFC.

"I hope this fast food doesn't give them heart attacks," she told Ballantine.

She considered calling Dan McLaury to demand an explanation, but decided to let him come to her. Instead she went home, hours late.

In her parking lot she stripped and went to her house, wearing nothing but her dog collar. Once inside, her husband humiliated her by giving her a belly rub. After she had gotten herself cleaned up, he had her lie face down on the floor. He used standard handcuffs to lock her hands behind her back and left her lie that way for about two hours, her breasts crushed against the floor, legs spread, right cheek against the wood, stark naked.

She loved this treatment, and this kind of harsh neglect usually had her aroused by the time Paul sent her up to bed. But tonight, not so much. As she lay on the floor listening to the TV, she recalled Sharon Becker's drunken story, and rumors about the McLaurys and information about the future. And most of all, she recalled Paul's account of going out to see the McLaury cabin and being refused admission by his own employees.

She knew what she would be doing tomorrow.

Chapter Twenty: Disappearing Buzzards

Donna had telephoned Leroi Adkins, the day shift commander, before she left for work. She was appalled to learn that attorney Barry Rohm had shown up at Donna's forest campsite already. He had arrived at 7:30 AM, armed with a writ of habeas corpus and a bus. *So where did he take them?* Donna had Rohm's cell number, but her calls went to voicemail. She decided to try talking with Judge Simmons, who had signed the writ.

She caught him in his chambers at 8:20, before the start of his court session.

"Sheriff, you can't set up a concentration camp in the woods. You should have known that."

"The jail couldn't house them, and they were totally disoriented. Think of it as temporary housing for a group of homeless people."

Simmons was running an oiled comb through his sparse white hair, examining the results in a mirror on his desk. "Mister Rohm's pleading was that these people were under arrest and that you were holding them illegally. If what you say is true, and that they were simply homeless, I don't see your problem. Mister Rohm has assured me that they will be well housed and cared for."

"There is the matter of them firing on my deputies."

The judge put his comb down and stood up. His black robe was hanging from a shelf behind him. He slipped it on. "I'd be perfectly willing to entertain a request for a bench warrant, Sheriff. But face it: You violated the Constitution by not properly arresting and charging those men."

Donna hesitated for a moment. She was tempted to tell the judge about the anachronistic nature of the men she had arrested and held. But she had strained his credulity before, or at least the FBI and Narvaez law enforcement had, when they had raised the possibility that the Judge's nephew had been killed by a vampire ghost. Now Simmons and everybody else in the county was convinced that the unexplained violence, hallucinations, and dementia that had plagued the county last winter had been caused by an escaped chemical weapon. She didn't know how the judge would handle a time travel story.

"Can you tell me where Barry took them? I'd be glad to go out there and re-arrest them."

"They were all released on their own recognizance," Simmons replied. "He didn't necessarily take them anywhere."

Donna sighed heavily. "Thank you, your honor."

Once outside the courthouse, Donna pulled her iPhone from her purse. She didn't have anything compelling on her calendar this morning. She called her inherited assistant, Barbara Caldwell, and asked if anything new had come up. No. She then called Stu Wheldon and asked him to meet her at the county airport.

ꕤ

Of the perks that Donna got from her position as Sheriff her favorite was her power to deploy a helicopter. During all her time as a deputy and an administrator, she had not had the opportunity to ride one of the department's three "birds." Now she could call in a pilot whenever she wanted. The only constraint was Darlene Martinez's eagle eye on the fuel costs in the monthly expense report.

Today, Donna wasn't worried about her Chief Financial Officer. She was sitting back in the tiny passenger seat, looking out over the county airport, her shoulder straps buckled and her sunglasses in place.

"Where are we headed?" Stu Wheldon asked as he brought the helicopter into the air.

"I want to do a flyover near the swamp, the area called Witches Wood," she said.

"What swamp?"

"The Blackwater River, in the State Forest."

"I've flown that area before. I don't know of any place called Witches Wood."

"It's apparently a local color name. What I'm interested in is a large fenced area with a big cabin in the middle, inside the boundaries of the State Forest."

"I know where that is. But it's McLaury property. Are you sure you want to do this?"

Jeez, does everybody in this county take orders from the McLaurys? "Yes, I want to do this. I have some questions about an incident that happened yesterday."

"You're the boss, ma'am."

I'm glad you think so, Donna thought. But she let her annoyance subside and concentrated on enjoying the ride, looking down on treetops and houses and flights of birds. She tried to see individual people on the ground but found that she couldn't bring them into focus.

The State Forest didn't look nearly as wild from the air. It was made up of oak and pine and gum, primarily, with the ground either brown with pine straw or green from palmetto. What made it look "civilized" was the network of forest trails…simply bare dirt…that threaded through the woods like veins on a leaf. The forest was, after all, a tree farm and deer raising facility. It was an artificial "nature."

When they saw the black water of the river, Donna knew that they were close. The pine and oak gave way to the feathery cypress along the river's edge, and then to a broad expanse of green cypress standing in the swamp. Slightly beyond, Donna could see the cabin and the cleared area surrounding it. There were vehicles on the ground and a roadway along the so far invisible fence.

"There it is," Wheldon said.

"I'd like to get as close a look as possible," Donna told him. "Can you make a couple of passes at treetop level?"

"I'll go as low as a hundred and fifty feet," Wheldon told her. "We don't want to buzz somebody's property."

Wheldon flew the chopper well away from the cabin and dropped altitude as he circled the site once, then brought the craft down to head across the area around the mystery cabin. As the chopper approached, a flock of vultures rose from the trees, apparently spooked by engine noise. Wheldon tipped the craft slightly to avoid flying into them. He slowed the helicopter into a sort of slow drift toward the target, the flock of vultures flapping themselves into the air and powering forward in front of them.

Donna watched in amazement as the birds, one by one, flew past the chain link fence and, one by one, vanished into thin air.

Wheldon banked to the left and pulled the chopper up, just short of the fence.

From perhaps two hundred feet up, they watched the flock of vultures. Half vanished in the air beyond the fence. The rest of the flock sensed that something was wrong and wheeled around.

Wheldon said nothing. He held the helicopter motionless for a moment, then rotated it around and headed away from the cabin.

When they were high in the air, well away from the forest, and the cars and houses below were toys, like the toy cars and houses in an electric train set, Wheldon shouted above the engine noise. "What the hell was that?"

Donna shook her head.

On the ground, Wheldon forgot his place in the chain of command.

"Sheriff, don't *ever* ask me to overfly something like that. I don't know what you're working on, but if it hadn't been for those buzzards, we'd be gone, too. You don't pay me enough for that kind of shit."

"I wasn't expecting that," Donna answered meekly.

Wheldon was partially mollified. "Well, look before you leap next time, Sheriff. There is too much weird stuff in this county for you to be going on joy rides over restricted areas. Maybe you need to talk to the McLaurys."

Donna was on the verge of anger. "Maybe so," she allowed. She was thinking, *Where can I find another pilot?*

ଔ

Barry Rohm wasn't much help. He'd finally returned Donna's call and explained that he'd been tied up in a settlement negotiation but that he could block out an hour for lunch. He wanted to stay near the court house, so Donna's favorite haunt, the Fireside, was out. Instead, the Sheriff and the big name attorney joined the lunch crowd at Molly's.

Rohm ordered the home style meat loaf. Donna ordered a luncheon salad.

"Yes," Rohm told her, "I got Colonel Dawes and his men ROR'd. You didn't have a right to hold them in a camp out in the woods."

"They were already camping in the woods," Donna argued. "I just arranged it so that they didn't hurt themselves or anybody else."

"Nevertheless, Sheriff, there is such a thing as the Constitution."

"There is also that pesky law against firing on law enforcement officers."

Rohm tipped his head back. "Okay. Colonel Dawes apologizes for that. If you'll send the bill for any damages to our firm…"

"There's the issue of assaulting my deputies."

"We'll be glad to reach a satisfactory settlement with them."

Donna couldn't believe what she was hearing. "You mean pay them off?"

Rohm frowned. "You have some objection to that?"

"Barry," she said, "this is a criminal offense!"

"All I ask is that you run it by your officers. I'm sure that they would rather get financial compensation than spend a lot of effort putting some confused men in jail."

"Suppose," Donna pressed, "I don't run it by my deputies. Suppose I want to prosecute?"

"Colonel Dawes and his men are out of your jurisdiction," Rohm told her. "You won't be able to find them."

"That's obstruction of justice," Donna said.

"Good luck penetrating attorney client privilege, Sheriff. As it is, since I was active in your campaign, it would be a conflict for my firm to represent those gentlemen. So, our firm's involvement will be ended if you turn down compensation. I won't even know which attorneys they're using, let alone where they are."

Donna squeezed her eyes shut in frustration. "Okay," she finally said, "how did you know about our arrest of those men? What is your connection with them?"

"Sheriff," Rohm responded, "let's just say that an interested party contacted us. But Colonel Dawes and I go way back."

"Back to 1821?"

Rohm's eyes narrowed. "What are you driving at?"

"I'm driving at your disappearance, along with Patty Kendall, Barney Kobe, and a woman named Betty Whitehall back in '02 and '04."

Rohm gave a deep sigh. "That again? What are you implying?"

"I'm implying that the McLaury family has a time machine in a cabin in the State Forest and that Colonel Dawes and his men somehow escaped from it."

Rohm's voice hardened. "Look, Sheriff, you're poking around in matters that are way over your head. Keep pursuing them and people will start to question your sanity."

Donna stared hard at Barry Rohm. He was wearing a tailored suit that cost thousands, a tailored silk shirt, a handmade tie. His dark, graying hair was impeccably styled. There had been times in the recent past when she had been face to face with him and nearly swooned from desire. But now she hated him.

She nodded her acceptance. "All right," she said, "I'll accept that Dawes and his men are off limits. But there are too many strange things going on in this county."

"Sheriffs have come and gone for two centuries," Rohm replied. "But the cabin has always been there. Keep that in mind."

ઉજ

Donna had cleared her schedule and headed north to Gainesville. By the time she arrived at Barney Kobe's institute it was almost 4:00 and she had squandered most of the day trying to track down the story of Colonel Gabriel Dawes and how he was connected to the McLaury family. Kobe listened to her account of the shootout, arrest, and disappearance and said to her, "I knew that sooner or later this would come back to haunt us. Let's go someplace quiet."

They took Donna's Jeep to a barbecue restaurant that served beer. Kobe found a booth near the door and they ordered lunch/supper, meaning big plates of pulled beef on open buns and an all you can eat salad. Kobe ordered a pitcher of beer.

"I've got to be careful not to drink too much," Donna warned. "I've got a long drive and my husband will beat my ass if I get a DUI."

Kobe laughed. "From what I've seen of you, you can beat his ass."

If only, Donna thought.

Kobe told her the story of the cabin…how three teenagers had discovered it just prior to the turn of the century, and had been missing for eighteen months. Of how Sheriff Kessler and Kobe had investigated the story told by one of the youths, Betty Whitehall. Of how Bob Kessler had summoned Barry Rohm, newly disabled and separated from the FBI, to work as a special deputy assigned to the case of the disappearing teens. Finally, Kobe told what he himself had experienced when he, Barry Rohm, Patty Kendall, Dave Leeper, and Betty Whitehall had found themselves trapped in an out of control time machine.

Kobe's story was spare and very short on detail. But Kobe, Rohm, *et al*, had indeed visited 1821 and met a would-be filibuster named Gabriel Dawes, along with his scruffy band of soldiers. Apparently Dawes and his group had gotten inside the cabin's effects field when a shift occurred, sending the men forward almost two centuries. Meanwhile, Kobe and his companions had gone deep into prehistory, and Kobe would not discuss that.

Donna listened to Kobe's carefully edited story as she picked at her salad and the pile of pulled pork. She cautiously sipped the beer. Very early in their relationship, Paul McCready had laid down the law about drinking and driving. Although she knew that Paul would never hurt her or punish her for anything, playful humiliations aside, she would not be able to face herself if she disappointed him on an issue this important. So, as Kobe became more effusive, Donna talked less and less.

By the time they were through eating, Donna had fleshed out her impression of the situation in Narvaez County. Dave Leeper was, in fact, a time traveler, a researcher whose origin was rather far in the future. So the cause of Sharon Becker's misery was that Dave would be returning to the future, where Sharon couldn't follow.

All the people involved in the early 2000s time travel incidents were now firmly established in their chosen professional fields and were doing quite well, underwritten by McLaury money. Barney Kobe had his PhD and his endowed professorship and research institute. Sharon Becker had been tutored and financed through law school and been selected as an associate with Johnson, Rose, McLaury and Rohm. Barry Rohm, of course, had been added to the law firm as a partner. Bob Kessler had gone on to the House of Representatives. Tommy Watson, his right hand man, had been appointed Sheriff.

It all made sense. The McLaurys were so wealthy and powerful because they were able to get reports from the future. The family had foreseen the Great Depression and were in position to buy up half the land in the county for pennies an acre. They had foreseen the freezes in the 1980s and gotten out of citrus just in time. They had bought high tech in the '80s and '90s, shorted it in 1999. They had shorted banks and housing in 2006. They had bought into all the stock market booms. They couldn't miss.

Now my husband is rich because he's got an in with these people. That's how he went from being a hired CEO to being a multimillionaire in less than a year. The knowledge made her sick. There was something dishonest and corrupt woven into the very basis of Narvaez County. Her father had been involved in it. Her husband was involved in it.

After she had dropped Kobe off and was headed south, Donna rolled the new information over. She was in a strange position. She herself was a millionaire since the recovery of the stock market had run up the value of the portfolios she'd inherited from her father. She was married to a very wealthy and powerful man. On paper, she was one of the wealthiest and most influential women in the county.

But she didn't have the usual accoutrements of wealth. She was, after all, a slave. She was not allowed to wear clothing or to move around freely. That she was kept in chains and led around on a leash surely freed her from the ethical implications of being part of such blatant, for want of a better term, insider trading.

But, of course, she was living her desired lifestyle on a seaside estate surrounded by a high wall, all of which was assembled due to her husband's inside deals. *So I'm guilty, too.* She would not have had the luxury of living under such oppression had Paul McCready not made some dubious bargains.

ଔଓ

Donna arrived home relatively late, almost 8:00 PM. It was nearly dark. She got out of the car, relaxed for a few moments, then took off all her clothes. She carefully stashed them in the pack that Paul had bought her, and then donned her leather dog collar with the tag that said that she was owned by Paul McCready. So, her bag slung over her shoulder, she walked stark naked to the house. She noticed that the stones no longer hurt her feet. The soles of her feet had gotten thick and callused from her being nearly constantly barefoot. It was dark enough that the motion sensor lights came on, one after another, as she hiked up the walk.

Paul had ordained that she must strip in the parking lot as an extra rule designed to humiliate her and emphasize her submissive position. But she had come to love it. When she took off her clothes, she also stripped away everything that had bothered her during the day. Free of her uniform and paraphernalia, she became new, a different person, ready to fit into the life she loved, the life in which she mimicked the slave concubine Ba-el Shanah. She always felt her spirits lift as she walked toward the house, ready to spend the evening naked, her hands made useless by steel shackles, her own volition pushed aside and replaced by that of her warlord master.

As she walked from the laundry room into the living room, she saw Paul standing behind the bar. “Good evening, my lord,” she called.

“Howdy, Sheriff,” he responded cheerfully. “Working late?”

“I was, sir. But I’m home now. If it pleases you, I’ll go shower and then come down to do your bidding.”

He smiled a broad smile. “Sounds good, babe. I’ll be waiting.”

ଔଓ

Donna, after her shower and some time spent drying and arranging her hair, painting her nails, and applying makeup, returned downstairs to find Paul in the kitchen. Per the house rules, she was naked and kept her hands behind her back. She walked up to Paul, close enough to push her breasts against his chest. He grasped the nape of her neck and pulled her to him for a long kiss.

She folded her legs so that she was standing on her knees. “I’m ready for use, my lord,” she said.

Paul tousled her hair, then put a hand under her arm to pull her to her feet. “Plenty of time for that later. Have you had dinner?”

Donna was surprised. Usually, satisfying Paul’s sexual needs was the first priority of the evening. “I went up to Gainesville to see Barney Kobe, sir. We went out to eat, but I didn’t eat much.”

“Are you hungry?”

Donna thought for a moment. “I could eat again, sir. That was several hours ago.”

“I fixed some pork chops and vegetables. Would you like some?”

“I would. Thank you, sir.”

“Have a seat at the table, Donna, and I’ll fix you a plate.”

Donna was perplexed. Nowhere was “the Deal” more obviously in effect than at mealtimes, when Paul got to dictate what she ate and under what circumstances. Usually, she had to eat while kneeling on the floor, using her fingers since forks and spoons were forbidden her. Tonight, though, Paul put out a full place setting with plate, napkins, and utensils. Such “nicey nice” was confusing and somewhat alarming.

She sat down at the opposite end of the table from Paul, where he had set her place.

As he sat, he asked, “Can I get you anything else?”

Donna decided to push her luck. “Might I have some wine, my lord?”

Paul laughed. “Sure, why not? White or red?”

“Sir, there is an open bottle of Chablis in the fridge.”

“Then you shall have it, my dear,” Paul replied, mocking her formality.

As he walked around the table to pour her wine, Donna realized that she was sitting with her legs crossed. She blushed with embarrassment and quickly moved, sitting with her knees spread.

Paul gently touched her face. “It’s okay, baby. There’s no rule against crossing your legs. You look very pretty sitting that way.”

Donna was confused for a moment, then decided to resume sitting with her legs crossed. Paul bent down and kissed her. He returned to his place at the head of the table.

“Permission to speak, my lord?” Donna ventured.

“Go ahead.”

“What’s the occasion, sir?”

“The occasion?”

“For the nicey nice, sir.”

Paul laughed. “Donna, you’re too sweet for me to persecute all the time. I just felt like being decent to you for a change.”

“It’s very disorienting, my lord.”

Paul spread his arms. “And yet, it’s my choice. By the terms of the deal, you have no say over how you are treated.”

“That’s true, my lord.”

“So you’ll have to face the fact that I love you and, every once in a while, I might feel like being nice to you for no reason whatsoever.”

Donna smiled happily. When Paul eased up on her because she was tired or not feeling well, she resented it. She felt that he was being condescending. It implied that she couldn’t handle the treatment that she’d agreed to. But when Paul was nice to her because he just couldn’t help himself, that was a different matter altogether.

She enjoyed the warm feeling of being loved and, by her standards, pampered.

Time to spoil it.

“Permission to speak, sir.”

“Donna, you’re free to speak as long as you’re not under the quiet rule.”

“Thank you, sir,” she said, suddenly somber. “Sir, I learned today that the McLaurys have access to a functioning time machine located in the State Forest.”

“I know that,” Paul said easily.

“Which leads me to believe, sir, that the McLaurys have access to economic and financial information from the future.”

Paul took a sip of water. “And?”

"That's how the McLaurys have become so wealthy. They know what is going to happen to the economy in advance."

"Donna, the McLaurys don't control the cabin. They don't have perfect information. They don't have the financial pages in advance. But the big movements, the events that go down in history…yes, they know about those."

"Have they shared that information with you?"

McCready sighed. "Donna, you know in your heart that they have."

Donna stared at him accusingly. "Paul, you have the vampire power of *charm* so you are always able to make your sales. Now you're telling me that you have advance information…insider information…about what the economy and the stock market are going to do? Is that how you got so rich so fast?"

"Of course it is, Donna. What did you think?"

Donna felt her jaw tremble. *I am not going to start crying!* "Sir, don't you think that you have an unfair advantage?"

McCready burst out laughing. "Unfair? Donna!"

"Unfair," she repeated, resolute.

"Do you know what's unfair, Donna? Getting my ass shipped off to Iraq and redeployed again and again, that's unfair. You want me to feel bad because I've got an advantage bidding on the same contract as some smarmy ass business school grad? Those guys were doing 'team building' exercises while I was getting my leg nailed back together at Ramstein. Fuck 'em! So what if I'm a little more persuasive than they are because I have some vampire blood. Deal with it!"

Donna had seldom seen Paul that agitated. She didn't know what to say.

"Tell you what, Donna. Finish eating and we'll talk about this."

Donna picked at her food. She had lost her appetite.

When she could eat no more, she told Paul that she was finished.

"Let's go out to the living room then," he said.

He sat on the sofa. "On your knees," he ordered.

Donna's heart sank. He often gave her orders in a brusque or harsh voice but that was pretend. Tonight, though, she could hear that he was angry. As much as she loved his pretend anger, she feared his real anger or, even worse, disappointment. Her whole being was dedicated to pleasing him.

She knelt in her display position with her knees spread wide, hands behind her back, toes touching. She made an effort to spread her knees extra wide. She stared straight ahead, let her mouth hang open. She would give him her best effort.

Paul chuckled. "No, Donna. That's a good display. But put your knees a little closer together and get comfortable. We're just going to talk."

"Sir, yes sir," she said.

He sighed. "Donna, things have just gone so much better for me when I decided to just take what was in front of me."

"How so, sir?"

"Start with the McLaurys. Early on, I got Dan to cut me in on some of their deals. Later, when I developed my *charm* and when I realized how the McLaurys got so wealthy, I got them to fund my buy-ins with bank loans. Borrow a million at two percent, cash out at ten percent, and you can get rich pretty quickly. So the McLaurys had inside information. How far do you suppose the SEC would pursue an insider trading complaint based on the McLaurys having a time machine?"

"I don't know, sir. But there is still an ethical question."

"It's not like the McLaurys would have stopped if I hadn't dealt myself in."

She thought about that. "I suppose not, sir."

"Besides, Donna, when I first met you, you were sitting on bank accounts worth three hundred thousand and a portfolio worth three hundred thousand, invested in Mitch McLaury's brokerage. Now your portfolio, two years later, is worth over a million. How do you think that happened?"

This was like a blow to her chest. "You mean…?"

"I mean you've gotten the same advantage that I've gotten. Only you didn't know it. Does that make it more ethical?"

Donna said nothing.

"So, Donna, I took a job where I was basically an employee…a two-fifty per year CEO, and I parlayed that into a multimillion dollar fortune. And I took a security company that was set up as a charity for burned out McLaury retainers, and I built it into a national powerhouse. I saw my opportunity and I took it."

He stared at her. She digested what he had said, then responded.

"I don't have a reaction yet, sir."

"Let's talk about you. Ever since we first started dating, you made it clear what you wanted. But I was being the nice guy. I accommodated you, played with you. I felt that I was protecting you from yourself. I was being ethical. You didn't appreciate that. You took it as weakness, insecurity…"

"I thought that you were very sweet, sir."

McCready laughed. "Well, when the dreams started, and I dreamed of Koth, and saw what you were dreaming, I got the picture. The girl wants to be a sex slave. You know what? It might be fun to have a sex slave. Now that I have one, I can tell you it is fun. What do you think?"

Donna blinked. "I…" It took her a moment to find words. "I love being your slave, sir."

He smiled at her. "That's good. I plan on taking full advantage of you in every possible way."

"I'm glad to hear that, sir."

"Now, Donna, the vampires. Let's start with one key fact: I am alive today because of Michael Dalton. That is a simple fact. When I chased him into a cave in order to kill him, he rescued me from drowning. When I was bleeding to death, *he gave me his blood* to save my life. When gangsters were trying to kill you, he and Danielle killed them first. I don't care what else these people did, or who else they killed, Michael and Danielle have been friends to me. So I was happy to help Michael bring back Arianne. And when Danielle got tired of working for Mankiew, I was happy to hire her. I know, dear lady, that this is the core issue between us. But they are my friends."

"Lady!" she scoffed. "Look at me."

He laughed. "What? You don't think a lady is ever naked and on her knees?"

"I'm a lot of things but I'm not a lady."

"What is Ba-el Shanah when she is clothed in red silk head to toe and seated beside her true lord at the banquet table?"

Donna decided not to pursue the point. "I won't debate the morality of dealing with the vampires. They are what they are. I even like Danielle, when I can set aside the thought of how many people she's killed."

"If I'd brought home a general instead of a vampire, you would have had no qualms about how many people he'd killed."

Donna thought about that. "That's true, sir. But I wouldn't have been so afraid of a general."

McCready shrugged. "I'm sorry about that. Are you still afraid of her?"

"Not as much, but I wouldn't want to piss her off. That's my main point, though, sir. The vampires are dangerous. Their reactions are so quick and they are so violent."

McCready's eyes narrowed. "Donna, I'm as dangerous as they are. Remember, I have Michael's blood. And it's getting stronger, not weaker."

"Maybe I should be afraid of you?"

"Maybe you should," McCready said somberly. "Here." He patted the couch beside him. "Lie here."

She got up on the sofa and lay on her side, her head resting on his thigh. He took her hands and had her clasp them together and hold them just under her chin. He checked his reach, and had her scoot until he could reach her breasts and belly and crotch. "We'll talk about ethics some more some other time," he said. "Right now, I want to sit here and watch TV while I'm molesting my woman."

Donna was ready for this. She felt defeated. She had brought up her moral objections to the means by which Paul McCready was becoming ever more wealthy and powerful, and he had rather thoroughly refuted them. *I didn't really think this through.* She had made a mistake, a mistake of the kind that Paul had stopped making. She had information. The question was how she could use the information.

She would have to confront Dan McLaury.

Beyond that, she wouldn't think about it anymore tonight. The key to being a Sheriff during the work day and a sex slave at home was compartmentalization. Tonight, she would lie on the sofa and focus on nothing but Paul's hands stroking her body.

Chapter Twenty-One: McLaury

Donna had come to work intent on a meeting with Dan McLaury. She called his secretary only to find that he was out for the day. Donna's next order of business was a 9:30 appointment with Sonia Taggart, the psychiatrist who held a contract with the Sheriff's Department for mental health and forensic psychiatry services. Taggart's office was a few miles east of Ruffin. Donna arrived early and had to wait in the reception area, paging through old magazines.

The issue that Donna wanted to discuss with Sonia was her reaction, or rather non-reaction, to her recent rape. Since the Gibbs incident, Donna had felt no change in her emotional life. She had written it off as just another on duty episode. Donna was worried that there was something deeper going on.

Sonia had been non-plussed. Her take was that Donna had become accustomed to rough handling in her sex life and that the power dynamics associated with rape were not in play, since Donna had set herself up more or less as bait, and had known that help was on the way.

Donna was fine with that explanation. "Face it, Donna, you're normal," Sonia had told her. "You don't really need therapy when you're not traumatized by an incident."

Nevertheless, the discussion had taken up the whole morning. Besides the discussion of the rape, which Donna had decided wasn't serious enough to warrant the term, Sonia had questioned her about details of her home life with Paul. Donna was happy to talk about that, particularly the new wrinkle in which Paul made her roll over as though she were a dog. Sonia seemed to be particularly interested in that, but Donna suspected that this was just gratuitous entertainment for the psychiatrist. However, Donna didn't mind entertaining her and so had a fun discussion about objectification.

By the time Donna got in to her office, it was 11:00. She put in a call to Dan McLaury's office but was told by his secretary that he was out and couldn't be reached. Donna's calls to his cell went to voicemail. *Time to think about lunch.*

She could have called Conquest Security to see if Paul wanted to eat with her, either at one of the local restaurants or in his office. When he didn't have time, he usually delegated lunch with Donna to Jerry Corbin or Sharon Becker. But Donna didn't want to appear pathetic by calling there too often. So, she reached out to her standby, Whitey Ferris.

At the Fireside, Ferris appeared sad.

"I finally broke it off with Shawna," he told her as they sat, sipping ice tea and waiting for their orders.

"That family thing finally broke her?"

"Yes, it did," he said, shaking his head.

Donna reached across the table and patted his hand. "It's okay, Whitey. It sounds like she wasn't right for you anyway. Keep looking. The world is full of women."

"It's not that easy to find one you like, though." He looked into Donna's eyes, and she melted.

I'd better get hold of myself. "You just have to keep looking, Whitey."

Ferris shook his head again. "There are a lot of pretty women out there, pretty lady. Not many like you, though."

Donna was touched. She took his hand, and held it with both hers. *I really, really like this man,* she thought. She wondered how Paul would react if she cheated on him. She would have to tell him. She could never bring herself to lie to him. Certainly, she had given Paul the power to punish her severely and he might do that…severely enough that she would not enjoy it. Or, it might shatter him. Beneath his arrogant warlord exterior, she knew, was the wounded man, the survivor with his memories of pain and his nightmares. She would hate herself if she reduced him to that again.

That's masochistic thinking. Focus on the real issue. "Oh, Whitey, I really do like you. But I'm already spoken for. I'd never cheat on my husband. You need to find a woman that you can love and make happy, and she'll make you happy." *Like Paul makes me happy,* she thought, suppressing an inappropriate giggle. She knew that a life with Whitey would be endless nicey nice. *Besides, I can hardly keep up with Paul. How could I handle another lover?*

"I guess you're right, ma'am. You can't blame a man for trying, though."

Donna laughed, delighted.

She refocused. "What's new with the missing women?"

"Nothing," Whitey told her. "We still like Gibbs for the Lowndes disappearance. There are enough similarities that we might could tie him to Torricelli if we had any kind of timeline. But there's no way he's on the hook for Marilyn Rogie."

Donna nodded.

Back in her office, in a meeting with Henry Klass and Whitey Ferris, Donna heard the same story. The roadside rapist, Nathan Gibbs, looked good for Lowndes, but only because of the circumstance that he had undertaken to rape Donna within a hundred feet of the Lowndes car.

"The question," Donna said, "is whether he's really that stupid. It's hard to believe that he is."

"He was stupid enough to rape passing motorists," Klass pointed out.

"Well," Donna answered, "he was sexually extorting passing motorists. The only violent rape we know about was his sexual assault on me. The sex for tickets scheme was really pretty low risk. It just got out of hand when he had me drive back there. I don't like him for Lowndes as much as you guys do."

Klass shook his head, disgusted. "Sheriff, inside your hard assed exterior, you're pretty soft hearted. Please don't go wobbly on this guy. He's not somebody you need to feel sorry for."

Donna's anger flared, but she caught herself. "Thank you for your frankness, Henry. It's just that no further evidence has turned up. The alternative hypothesis…that there is a serial killer working who is not Nathan Gibbs…is starting to look pretty likely to me."

"How so, Sheriff?" Klass asked.

"The State Attorney is offering him fifteen years of his life plus the chance to skate on at least one death penalty case if he leads us to the body. Why would he turn that down?"

"Maybe his lawyer wants more," Klass offered.

"Or maybe he doesn't know where the body is," Donna said.

Klass nodded slowly. “So you like one guy for everybody: The Monarch Estates skeleton, Nunez, Rogie, Torricelli, and Lowndes? If one guy did all those, he’s a dangerous guy.”

“I like one guy for Rogie and Lowndes,” Donna replied, “because of proximity in time. I like the same guy for Torricelli because of MO. I’m agnostic about the rest.”

Whitey Ferris finally spoke. “So, Sheriff, you’re saying that there is yet another serial killer operating in our jurisdiction? And Gibbs is what? Coincidence?”

“You guys are running the investigation,” Donna said. “I’m just throwing out my opinion.”

“That’s a goddam scary opinion,” Ferris muttered.

Donna gazed at Whitey sympathetically. She understood his discouragement. Whitey Ferris knew about the vampires.

෴

Donna took two other meetings that afternoon. One was with a committee of concerned citizens upset about speeding in a Pine Hills school zone. Donna wrote a memo to Leroi Adkins and Lu Herrera asking them to detail a patrol officer to the area for a while. The other was with the parents of one of the young men whose ATVs Donna had ordered seized after the incident in the forest. Donna told them where to go to file a form requesting the return of impounded property. She warned them that their son had violated the law and could end up not being able to get a driver license if he did it again.

It was after 4:00 when Estelle Alvarez returned her call.

“I’ve been rethinking my position on the Gibbs matter,” Donna told her. “I no longer have an objection to letting him cop to a second degree felony.”

“You realize you’ll lose your leverage on the Lowndes matter,” Alvarez replied.

“Frankly, Estelle, if he hasn’t led us to her by now, he probably doesn’t know where she is. If you put him in prison now, he’ll get the needle if we nail it to him later.”

She heard the Attorney sigh. “If we buckle on this, his lawyer will want more. He’ll offer to cop to a third degree. What’s your position on that?”

Donna was silent for a moment. After she turned the issue over in her mind, she answered: "Look, I would prefer not to be identified and I would prefer not to have a trial. But, if you need to bring him to trial, I'm okay with it. You have him dead to rights on sexual assault and you almost certainly can convict him. Do what you have to do. If he can't help us on Lowndes, I have no further interest in his case."

"I'll offer him second degree," Alvarez said. "If he won't take it, he goes to trial and gets thirty years."

After the conversation with Alvarez, Donna rocked back in her chair and closed her eyes. The phone rang. It was Daniel McLaury's secretary. Mister McLaury would be able to see Donna at 9:30 the following morning.

༻❀༺

When she came home, Donna saw that Paul McCready's Escalade was already parked in the gravel lot. She sighed. She was tired and she had hoped that she would have a little respite before Paul put her in chains. *I shouldn't think like that. This is what I wanted and what I asked him for.* She got out of her Jeep and removed her clothes. She carefully packed everything into the bag Paul had given her. She put on her leather collar and walked naked to the house.

She climbed the back steps to the laundry room and walked through the living room. Paul was standing at the bar. "Howdy, Sheriff," he called to her.

"Hello, my lord," she replied. She started toward the stairs.

"Just leave your bag there and go get your chains," Paul told her. "We're going to do something different this evening."

He put on her waist chain and wrist cuffs, and fastened her wrists together in front of her with a twelve inch chain. He attached a leash to her collar. "I want to play with my pets," he said.

He called the dogs, and let them out the front door. He went out, with Donna trailing behind.

On a lawn chair in the front lawn were three rubber chew toys made to vaguely resemble bones.

"We're going to play fetch," he explained to her. "you and the pups. I'll throw to the dogs and they'll go fetch. Or, I'll throw for you, and you have to run and fetch the toy. The rules are: You have to run flat out to the toy. You have to pick it up with your mouth, without using your hands. And, you have to run flat out to get it back. Stand on your knees."

So now I'm a dog? She dropped to her knees as instructed.

"When you return, you have to fold your arms and droop your hands like a dog begging. You hold the toy in your mouth until I take it from you. When I throw it again, you have to jump up and go after it." He took hold of her wrists and showed her how he wanted her to hold her arms.

He threw to the dogs first, while Donna waited on her knees. "This one's for you, Donna," he said. He threw the toy. He had a good arm and Donna had only a general idea of where the toy landed. She ran as fast as she could to the landing area, looked around frantically until she found it, and dropped to her hands and knees to grasp the toy in her mouth. She stood up and ran back as fast as she could. When she reached him, she folded her knees into the position he required. Paul took the toy from her mouth and threw it again.

They repeated this again and again. Donna had been tired before. Now she was exhausted, panting for breath. Paul left her standing on her knees, the toy between her teeth. He let her skip a few turns as he threw to the dogs. Finally, he took the toy and told her "fetch." He threw it into the weedy undeveloped lot, and she had to walk through grass and vines before she spotted it. Her teeth and lips scraped through sand as she grasped the toy in her mouth. She leaped up and ran back to Paul as fast as she could, only to have Paul twist the toy from her teeth and throw it away again.

Finally, Paul sat down in his lawn chair. "Okay, belly rubs," he said. By now, Donna knew to react instantly. The dogs immediately rolled over on their backs. Donna was only seconds slower, her hands tucked above her breasts, her legs folded and her feet in the air. She was lying in this perverse position, her back resting in the sand and sparse grass.

As usual, Paul rubbed the dogs first, then started with Donna. His belly scratching wandered a bit. He pinched her nipples and rubbed her pubis.

"Back to the house," he announced. The dogs headed back immediately. Donna was delayed as Paul clipped her leash to her collar.

In the driveway he stopped. "You need a little cleaning," he told her. He fastened her leash to a support post. He then got the garden hose.

The water was cold, and Paul used it to effect, hosing down her legs and torso, then blasting the stream of water into her face. Next he got personal, spraying at her groin and, when she turned to escape the impact of the high pressure hose against her delicate flesh, the crack of her butt. She screamed in delight, twisting to get away but held by the leash. As she screamed and giggled hysterically, Paul turned off the water, found a towel, and dried her off.

"Wasn't that more fun than a shower?" he asked.

"Sir, you are evil."

She laughed, and she thought *I wonder how many of my friends have this kind of fun?* She felt like a child again, playing until she was ready to drop, giggling and screaming. *It's undignified but who cares? I'm not allowed to have dignity anyway.* None of the women she knew would have tolerated being made to fetch like a dog. *But it's their loss.* She was happy, purring with joy.

Paul tugged on her leash, the signal to head inside.

He had her stand on her knees in front of the sofa, her hands in the dog/begging position, with a dog on either side of her. Then, he produced a sack of crackers from the kitchen and sat down on the sofa, offering crackers to the pups and to Donna. He teased her, holding the cracker to her mouth, then letting her overbalance as he drew it away. He would feed a dog, then Donna, then the other dog, until he tired of that.

"Donder, Blitzen, that's enough." The dogs obediently headed to the laundry room, their nails clicking on the floor.

He turned to Donna. "You make a pretty good dog," he commented.

"I'm glad that you're pleased, my lord."

He cocked his head to look at her. "You can sit back on your knees now."

"Thank you, sir." She assumed her spread knee display position, although her hands were chained in front of her.

"Let me see your hands," Paul ordered.

She stretched her arms out to him. He took her hands in his, and kissed each of her fingers in turn. "Have I ever told you that you have pretty hands?" he asked.

She thought for a moment. "I don't believe you have, my lord."

Donna didn't think that her hands were pretty. She kept her nails clipped short and used a clear lacquer polish. Her hands were wrinkled around the knuckle joints and were muscular for a woman. Donna didn't think that her hands looked feminine enough.

He kissed her hands again. "Very nice hands, Donna. It's a shame to keep them chained all the time. Stand up."

She stood.

"Step away and turn around."

She obeyed, not knowing what to expect.

"God, Donna," he said, "you're a work of art. I am so lucky to have you."

"And you do have me, my lord. I am your slave."

She was reminding him, in her subtle way, not to get too nicey nice with her. It was one thing for him to be nice once in a while. She didn't want him to lose his resolve to dominate and imprison her, though.

"Well, slave girl, I've had a long day. I say we get you out of your chains and up into bed. Let's see if you can do anything with those lovely hands of yours."

"Will there be smooching involved, my lord?"

"Probably so," he allowed.

"Your sex slave is at your command, my lord."

Donna was torn. She was tired and would much rather spend the next few hours smooching or reading or watching TV instead of kneeling in chains downstairs. On the other hand, she did not want Paul to start easing up on her. *But he did run me into the ground treating me like a dog, so he's not all that nice.*

"How would my sex slave like a sandwich before we go upstairs?"

"Whether and when your slave is fed is up to you, my lord."

Paul burst out laughing. "Okay, babe, come into the kitchen and get on your knees. I'll fix you something."

ↂ

In bed, Paul had Donna put her hands to use, lightly brushing his skin, teasing and squeezing him. "Your hands are very nice," he said. "But you know what I like best about you?"

"What is that, my lord?"

"It's your mouth, Donna. You have the most wonderful mouth. It's very pretty. Your lips are just the right size and just the right color. Your teeth are so even and white."

She giggled. "Is that all you like about my mouth, sir?"

"You're very skilled with it, too." He touched her cheek and had her open her mouth wide. He slid two fingers in and probed around, brushing along her cheek, pushing against the back of her throat. He grasped her tongue and pulled it forward, so that he held it with one hand while he prodded it with the other. Donna felt that as a weird sensation. The pinch of the thumb and forefinger produced a discomfort that was almost painful. But as he pulled and wiggled her tongue, she felt deliciously helpless. He released his grip and explored along the roof of her mouth. "A very nice mouth," he pronounced.

"Thank you, my lord," she muttered.

"Naomi likes it, too, I take it?"

"She does, sir. She likes to kiss as much as you do. And the other stuff, of course. I've gotten good at applying just the right amount of pressure with my lips and tongue and teeth to send her off into orgasm."

He chuckled. "You're very versatile."

"I try to be, sir. I was considering asking you to lend me to a lesbian so that I could develop my skills."

Paul burst out laughing. "Does Naomi think you need more work?" he finally asked.

"No, sir. But if I'm going to be a sex slave, I want to develop all aspects of the role."

He smiled. "Good idea. You never know when you're going to get traded to the other team."

"No, sir. But when I aspire to something, I try to master it. I want to be the best at what I do. I put everything I had into being a cop. I'm going to apply myself just as much to this. I want to be a very good sex slave, one you can be proud to show off or to lend out."

He laughed again. "We're lending you out, are we?"

"If you wished to do so, I would certainly obey you. I would want to make you proud."

He pulled her to him and stroked her back. "Donna, I don't know what to make of you. You're such a wild woman!"

She looked up at him. "I'm not wild at all, sir. I'm your obedient little piece of chattel, willing to do anything that you require. You won't find a woman more tame than me."

"I suppose that's one way of looking at it," he said.

"Sir, have I ever refused you anything, or even balked?"

"I have to admit that you haven't."

She grinned. "You see? I'm perfectly tamed. Why don't you make use of your tame woman?"

He smiled. "Let's see what your hands and your mouth can do, working together."

As Donna began kissing him, she thought about their banter. *We were kidding back and forth, but it's all true.*

಄ೋ

The next day, Donna felt puffy and her bottom was sore, as Paul had worn her out first by the game of fetch and later by "heavy use" in bed. She hadn't been able to roust herself for her morning exercises, so Paul had gone downstairs and made coffee. He had brought an insulated coffee pot back to the bedroom so that Donna could wake herself up.

She had snarled at the idea of breakfast in bed. "I'm the slave in this house," she'd argued. "It's my job to do the serving." She'd declined Paul's offer to let her use the elevator and had hiked down the stairs to the kitchen. She had plopped herself down on her knees on the tile, but Paul had ordered her to sit in the chair "like a human being."

"I thought that you were turning me into a dog," she'd grumbled.

"You'll be whatever I want you to be," he'd told her firmly.

Secretly she was relieved that he was going easy on her. After the extra vigorous love making, she had melted into the bed and she still felt woozy. She'd sat naked in the kitchen chair, legs crossed. She'd felt guilty as Paul served her a breakfast of omelette, bacon, and biscuits. She was not supposed to be pampered.

"I think we'll do normal breakfasts for a while," Paul said. "It's too much of a switch for you to go from eating with your fingers in the floor to being in charge of the Sheriff's Department."

"I thought that you wanted me to make these transitions without a hitch," she objected.

"But the deal is, how you are treated is up to me," he'd told her. "If you're going to be my property, I want you to function properly."

That was pretty close to an argument, she thought as she drove toward the McLaury office. *Either I've got to learn to control myself better, or Paul is going to have to crack down on me a little harder. If I'm going to have disputes with him over simple things, I might as well be a normal wife.*

ঔৣ

Daniel McLaury, his hair cut close in a flat top style, his pin striped shirt creased and crisp, his gold rimmed glasses shiny and clean, sat behind his desk and considered Donna Parker-McCready. His manner was easygoing.

"I always get a little worried when the Sheriff wants to talk to me," he joked. "What can I do for you, Donna? Or, I should say, Sheriff?"

Donna got right to the point. "It has come to my attention that you have a time machine on your property inside the State Forest."

He tipped his head and regarded her. "Forgive me. I had thought that you already knew about that."

"I had heard rumors, but I never knew…"

“Your father worked for us for many years. He didn’t tell you what we had?”

“I understood that you were researching time travel, and that he was trying to solve the question of whether there were Many Worlds, but I didn’t realize that you had a working time machine.”

McLaury chuckled. “If only. We don’t *have* a time machine. Somebody else does. What we have is the land around the time machine so that we can control access.”

“What’s the difference?”

“The time machine moves people, animals, and objects back and forth in time according to the wishes of whoever controls it. Humans can hitch a ride, but we have no control over it.”

“So what good is it?”

“We have managed to construct a sort of schedule of when it shifts and when it shifts to. We’re able to do a certain amount of historical research and our agents in the future can get some information back to us. So we’ve learned some things about the past and we have a certain foreknowledge.”

“Which you’ve used to make yourselves rich.”

McLaury shrugged. “You have to understand, Donna, that the family doesn’t use the time machine in order to make ourselves wealthy. We’ve made ourselves wealthy so that we can use the time machine.”

Donna shook her head. “What does that even mean?”

“It means that the McLaury family came to Narvaez County in order to keep the cabin…the time machine…from being discovered and to provide a system for gathering up and protecting time travellers. Colonel Dawes and his men, for example.”

“Speaking of which: Where are they?”

McLaury chuckled. “Let’s just say they’re not with us anymore. Hopefully, they’ll wake up in 1821 with severe hangovers.”

“How did they get outside your fence?”

“Good question. We don’t know. But the thread has to maintain position as the earth moves at thousands of miles an hour. I think probably drifted off by a few feet.”

“The thread?”

"That's what we call the constant line that threads through time and space…the beam that is the center of the effects field."

"Where is the McLaury family from?" Donna asked, overwhelmed by questions.

"My grandfather came from the future. That's all I know. Only Mitch and I even know about the cabin and the time travellers, but…"

"How about Dave Leeper? Where is he from?"

McLaury laughed. "Dave will be born about twenty years from now. On his first trip here, he was isolated in the cabin and got swept along on some interesting rides. This time, we gave him a job and he's been a big help to us. He would be an invaluable source of information about the late twenty-first century except…"

"Except what?"

"Well, unfortunately, he hasn't spent much time there. He's spent much of his time in what, to his people, is the past."

"Sharon Becker will be devastated when he leaves next year."

McLaury sighed. "Sharon thought that she was a sexual adventurer. She thought that she could shack up with Dave while he was here and then move on when he had to go back. But she got attached." He lifted his glasses and gave Donna a meaningful look. "We all get attached. I'm sorry for Sharon. If it's any consolation to you, on this time line, Dave returns in 2017 and settles down with Sharon, so that he lives much of his life in the era before he is born. But don't tell Sharon that. We don't know if we'll stay on this timeline."

"There are other timelines then?"

"I don't know," McLaury said. "That's an issue that your dad worked on. But we don't know. The concept comes from quantum mechanics, and physicists have ways of working around the question. But the philosophical issue remains. If there is only one timeline, then everything is already set. We know that the future already exists. Otherwise, there would be no time machine. The past is already set. So, if there is only one timeline, nothing we do makes any difference. The past and the future already exist."

"But if there are many timelines, then we don't really know the future."

"Correct," McLaury said. "So the advantage that the family has may turn out not to be an advantage at all."

"You didn't foresee Colonel Dawes arriving."

"For me to foresee that, I would have to send a message to my future self. Then my future self would have to get the message back to my past self. The workings of the cabin being what they are, the amount of information we can send backward in time is extremely limited."

Donna was silent for a moment.

"But you came to see me about something in particular," McLaury said. "What was it?"

Donna sighed. "I was shocked when I found out how Paul had gotten so rich so fast. Insider trading is against the law."

McLaury looked at her in surprise.

"Insider trading? As in information from the future?"

Donna nodded.

"Okay, if there is more than one timeline, and I'm pretty sure there is, we're still gambling. We do a little better than your average Wall Street broker, but we're still gambling. But the SEC would never try to make a case based on time travel as inside information."

"There's a moral issue," Donna said stubbornly.

McLaury smiled. "Donna, what would it take to make your moral qualms go away?"

Donna was shocked. "Are you offering me a bribe?"

"Why not? We've paid off everybody else. We've given Sharon a wonderful career. We've made Barry Rohm wealthy and powerful. Barney Kobe has a great academic career. Bob Kessler is in Congress. Lord knows, your husband has benefitted from his association with us. And you? We've made you pretty wealthy, and we've made you Sheriff…"

"Only after Paul turned the job down."

"Oh, no," McLaury said, "Paul was never going to be the Sheriff. We put him into that office so that you could resign to run. We knew that you would be the Sheriff of Narvaez County before you were even born."

Donna was incredulous. "What?"

McLaury nodded. "Oh, yes. Haven't you ever looked back at your career and wondered how the hell it happened? How you went from being a detective sergeant to being Sheriff in just two years? Have you ever wondered why I was so quick to pull Paul McCready, a clinically depressed former cop, out of his funk and put him in charge of a new corporation? Shit happens, Donna. But I make shit happen. So what is it you want?"

"In exchange for what?"

"Donna, I'm not trying to bribe you as a public official. Normal law enforcement doesn't fit into the situation with the cabin. But the McLaurys need the Sheriff to be cooperative. We need you to bury any incidents that come up in association with the cabin. I'm not talking about overlooking violations of the law. Just minimize talk about strange incidents, anachronisms, that sort of thing. You seem to have some qualms about how your husband has gotten so wealthy. We need you to forget about that and just accept that you're married to a very rich, very powerful man. We're not asking you to break the law, just to cooperate with us. What do you want from us in return?"

"How about I think of something and get back to you?" Donna asked.

☙❧

Donna Parker, naked except for her thick leather collar with its oversize dog tag, put her hands atop her head and slowly turned around. "Your sex toy is all clean, sir," she said.

"Turn around and put your hands behind your back," he ordered.

She obeyed, and felt the steel handcuffs against her wrists. She heard the click as he locked each one.

He reached around and squeezed her breast. "How was your day?" he asked.

"Busy," she said. "I learned a lot that I didn't know."

Chapter Twenty-Two: Dress Up

Weeks passed. Sheriff Parker-McCready became less and less involved in the frustrating investigation of the killings and disappearances. Without Gibbs, there were no leads, and Gibbs had become a dry hole, even for Lowndes case.

At home, Donna's role as a sex toy continued to evolve.

Without announcing anything to her, Paul had begun focusing on getting Donna outside and active. He continued walking her, along with the dogs. Sometimes her hands would be cuffed behind her back and, at some point in the walk, Paul would release her from the cuffs and the leash and send her off to frolic with the German shepherds. She loved this. At his urging, she would run flat out. The dogs would chase her and knock her down. She would roll on the ground and wrestle with the dogs, giggling and screaming with delight.

Or, Paul would play fetch with her, tossing the rubber bone into the distance for either Donna or the dogs to chase. Donna learned to do the dog pose perfectly, standing on her knees, her hands at nipple level and folded down. She learned to spring to her feet and take off running as soon as Paul took the toy from her mouth and threw it. Sometimes he would tease her and fake a throw. She would be thirty feet away by the time she realized she'd been fooled.

When he had run her to the point that she was staggering, he would leash her to the post and torment her with the high pressure hose. She found that hard to get used to, so she would always giggle and scream as the stream of water hit a sensitive body part. Afterward Paul would towel off his exhausted pet.

Sometimes after she had been run to exhaustion and hosed down, dried, and her hands clipped to her belly chain, he would take her back inside, hobble her legs, blindfold her, and command her to silence. She would kneel or lie on the floor in the blackness, her mind flashing from one image to another until she would settle into her true home, the land of Koth, where she was Belshana, the slave concubine and daughter of the Goddess. Sometimes the Mother Goddess would land beside her in the guise of a giant owl, and slowly transmute into the beautiful woman. They would walk unseen, both naked, among the ragged crowds on the streets of Koth.

Or, sometimes, Ba-el Shanah was in chains in the bed chamber of her true lord, the barbarian Paul of Koth, who would seize her and use her roughly, so that in the real, the shackled Donna would feel her womb wet and burning and she would hope desperately that Paul would decide to grab her and use her where she was, chained and helpless, or else take her upstairs and order her to bed.

Sometimes, though, he would clip her hands to her belly and take her for a walk, around the back of the house and along the seawall. There, his hand on her shoulder or on her butt, he would pull her to him and they would stand and watch the deep orange sky darken as the sun set on the Gulf of Mexico. She loved to watch the feathery red and orange bands droop below the purple and blue as the red rubber ball sun slowly descended, and merged with its reflection in the darkening sea. Sometimes she could make out boats and people on boats, far in the distance. Sometimes she would see a flock of birds, laboring across the sky in V shaped squadrons. She smelled the fish smell of the water and noticed the constant squawking of the birds and thought that she was in the best place she could be, with the best husband-owner she could have. Paul's hand on her ass gave her reassurance, and a feeling that she was wanted and, more, desired. She could not imagine a more pleasurable sensation, and she longed for him to lead her up to bed and take her, firmly and gently, as he always did after they walked out to the water, because it always put him in a gentle mood.

On weekends, he tried to find tasks for her: detailing the car, or sweeping the walk or weeding the extensive flower beds, all done naked with hands and feet chained. There was nothing hard or grueling, just menial tasks designed to remind her of her slavery. If there was time left before noon, he might walk her out to some remote place on the property, roll out a blanket, and leave her chained to a tree. She enjoyed this, too. With her arms firmly clamped behind her, there was nothing for her to do but sleep, or watch birds and insects and clouds, or daydream. Left to herself, she would have felt compelled to do some work or read, or watch TV. But, since Paul enforced this idleness, she could lie on her side and enjoy the sea breeze tickling her skin, and the sound of birds, and the gentle sunlight.

Sometimes, too, on weekends, Paul would have arranged for Naomi to visit. He would leave Donna handcuffed in Naomi's charge and find some excuse to be away for the afternoon or evening. Naomi was a demanding mistress until she was satisfied, and then they were best friends again, watching movies and eating popcorn, drinking a little too much wine. Or sometimes, Donna would put on clothes and she and Naomi would go out to eat, or go to a movie, or maybe one of the bars along 19. They would talk and gossip and have fun.

As he had warned, Paul had taken to making her breakfast in the morning, and requiring her to sit at the table and eat. Sometimes, if she got home late, he would cook dinner for her as well. Other times, he would require her to fix their dinner and then to wait table while he ate. Afterward, her cold food would be handed her in a metal bowl and she would eat it with her fingers while kneeling on the floor. Or, as was happening more often, he would fix her a plate of food and set it on the floor, cuff her wrists behind her back, and require her to eat without using her hands.

Donna felt that Paul had at last reached a happy medium. He had designed a life for her that was full of fun and play, while being restrictive and humiliating enough to fulfill her masochistic needs. Donna loved Paul wholeheartedly. And she knew, beyond doubt, that he loved her. Donna was, for the first time in her life, completely happy.

ઌ

Donna stood in the kitchen, her hands behind her back. Paul was away for the weekend and so there was no requirement that she keep her hands behind her, but she did so anyway, out of habit or of respect for her absent master. She was naked, except for the heavy leather collar and the metal ownership tag. She expected to remain naked until Monday morning, unless some law enforcement emergency arose. But there were few emergencies that would require the attention of the Sheriff, so she assumed that she would not wear clothing anytime during the weekend.

It was late morning and Donna was already feeling guilty because she hadn't done any work yet. She had just eaten breakfast...oatmeal which she had eaten without utensils while kneeling on the floor. She felt that, since she didn't need to be in Sheriff mode, she did not deserve to sit at the table and eat with a spoon. She was much sterner with herself than Paul was with her. She was in a good mood. She had treated herself to an extra cup of coffee, made the way she liked it with whole cream and honey. The day was bright. She thought that she might go out to the pool and lie in the sun. When the day got too warm for tanning, she planned to swim some laps. She had already done her morning exercises, which included ten laps around the oversize pool. She would try to do two more sets of ten today. This would make up for whatever torments Paul would have inflicted had he been present.

The gate buzzer sounded. Donna keyed the speaker. "Yes?"

"It's Danielle Travis. Paul sent me."

Donna's heart began to thump. In cold fact, she was afraid of Danielle. True, they had once had lunch together in a friendly manner, but that was out in public. The one time that Danielle had visited Donna by herself, the vampire had used *charm* to calm Donna down. And when Paul had brought Danielle by the house once, Donna had been terrified to the point of tears.

Donna's first impulse was to tell Danielle to come back later. But the vampire *was* working for Paul on some legal matter. And Danielle didn't need to lie to get into the compound. The ten foot wall would be no problem for her, nor would any of the door locks on the house. Donna sighed. *I hope she's telling the truth.* "Just a moment," Donna said into the speaker.

She pressed the switch that opened the gates.

Donna hastened to the living room, where she quickly donned the undersize bathrobe which was her emergency garment for greeting guests. She rousted the sleeping dogs, who were sprawled out in front of the sofa, and locked them in the laundry room.

When the doorbell rang, Donna was quick to open it.

Danielle was stylishly attired, in a dark red dress and high heels. Her hair was stacked atop her head and her face was carefully made up with just the right amount of blush to offset her unnaturally pale complexion. She strode past Donna into the house.

She handed Donna an envelope. "Read this," she said.

Donna tore the envelope open and read the message, which was hand written on quality stationery bearing the Conquest logo: "Donna, I have sent Danielle to you. You are to comply with any requests, orders, or suggestions that she makes. You are not to dispute or question anything that she wishes you to do. I expect your complete cooperation with her. Love you, Paul."

Donna went pale. She began trembling and felt tears welling in her eyes.

Danielle gazed at her, concerned. "Are you all right, Donna?"

Donna gulped. "Yes, I'm just surprised, that's all. Paul didn't say anything to me."

"I'm sorry," Danielle said in a solicitous tone, "I thought that I only needed to speak to Paul. I guess I should have run it by you before I came over."

"No…no," Donna replied quickly. "Whatever Paul wants me to do is fine."

"You're sure? You seem shaken."

"I'm fine," Donna said, her resolve returning. "If Paul wants me to do something, I'll do it."

Danielle smiled. "You two are so sweet. It's beautiful how much you love him." She stepped through the door and waved her hand.

"If you like, Donna, I can charm you so that you're less upset. I had hoped that we were over the fear thing, but I can see that you still don't feel safe with me."

Donna took a deep breath. "Danielle, I'm either safe with you or I'm not. Being hypnotized won't make any difference to the reality. Don't worry, I'll calm down."

To Donna's shock, a man entered the house. He looked to be in his mid-forties, had longish hair which hung away from his head in stringy twists. He was medium build and wore painter's pants and a tee shirt with horizontal blue stripes, reminding Donna of a character in a European art movie. He was carrying a camera tripod and a battered case.

"This is our photographer," Danielle said. "Al Campanelli, meet Donna." The man extended his hand. Donna held the bathrobe closed with her left hand as she used her right to return the handshake.

“Photographer?” Donna asked querulously.

“Yes,” Danielle replied. “I’ve brought some things for you to try on.” She looked around and then pointed to the far wall. Campanelli headed in that direction. “Ever since I first visited you, I’ve been bothered by the way Paul has been keeping you. I told him that a man as wealthy as he shouldn’t keep his sex toy naked all the time. And he shouldn’t send you out in a ratty bathrobe to meet people. He should dress you up, decorate you. Finally he agreed. Al is here to take pictures.”

Donna frowned. “What is it you want me to do?”

“First, get rid of that rag that you’re wearing. It’s an embarrassment. I’ve always hated it.”

Donna was confused. She looked from Danielle to the distant Campanelli, who had a deadpan expression. “Get rid of it?”

“Sure. Take it off. We’ve got other things for you to wear.”

Donna hesitated. She decided that she was, after all, a sex toy…a slave…and that she had told Paul that she would be fine with being lent out to others. How could she object to undressing in front of Danielle and this photographer? After all, Danielle had seen her naked twice before. And the photographer must have seen many naked women. She let the robe drop to the floor.

“Let’s find a place to set up,” Danielle said. They moved further into the living room.

Donna was shocked when two more men came through the door. They were both younger and wore jeans, sneaks, and tee shirts. One of the young men was blondish and had short neatly trimmed hair. The other seemed to be modeling himself on Campanelli. Each of them was carrying a steamer type trunk. “My assistants,” Campanelli said. “Don’t worry. They’ve seen it all before.”

As Donna blinked in bewilderment, Danielle explained. “Paul says that he wants to decorate you, not cover you up. So, I’ve had some designer friends of mine make some clothing that is pretty, but leaves your breasts and sex and ass exposed. It’s a little kinky, but we know about you and kink.”

Great! Donna thought. *Not just weird clothes, but photos of me in weird clothes. Well, this is what I signed up for: No freedom, no privacy, no dignity.*

Donna examined her feelings about being exposed, naked, to three strangers. She was, she decided, embarrassed but not in a major way. Along with her embarrassment was her pride that she was following Paul's instructions. She was elated that he had so much faith in her that he would send his command in a simple note, knowing that she would obey. So she was smiling as she stood at her at-ease position with feet apart and hands behind her back, watching the photography team set up their folding screen and drape, and positioning their reflective umbrellas next to the wall that separated the living room from Paul's office.

Danielle hauled one of the trunks around the barrier wall and motioned Donna to follow.

The first dress was predictable. It had a very tight bodice with an underwire structure that pushed Donna's exposed breasts up and outward. The skirt was floor length, but was cut away at the hips, so that Donna's sex was not only exposed but emphasized. Danielle produced some mules for Donna to wear, fussed with her hair and brushed her face with powder, then led her to the semicircle to be photographed in various poses.

Afterward, Danielle took Donna to the downstairs bathroom so that she could see herself in the mirror. Donna liked the look, and felt better about the project.

Other garments involved wide belts that held up "skirts" divided into two parts that were held in place by bands around her thighs. This style of clothing covered nothing but her legs above the knee, leaving her ass and crotch exposed. Various tops had cutaways to expose her breasts, or individual holes for each breast. Donna dutifully tried them all on and posed as instructed for the cameras. She posed standing, or one leg braced up on a chair, or kneeling, or resting on knees and elbows, exposed, the fabric trailing away. Sometimes, Danielle would stop the photographers in order to redo Donna's makeup, or to pin up her hair.

Some of the garments were photographed outdoors, which required fifteen and twenty minute breaks to set up.

Finally, when Donna had just finished an indoor shoot of a dark fake fur ensemble that covered her torso and thighs, Danielle motioned the fur covered Donna toward the living room door.

"Paul has asked us to photograph you naked in your chains," Danielle said to her. "That would mean you doing pretty graphic poses in front of these men. Also, of course, you'd be helpless in my presence, and we know how skittish you are about me. Paul knows this and he said that it's up to you. You can refuse if you want."

Donna closed her eyes and considered. She was inclined to refuse. If nothing else, she was tired. She had gotten up at 4:30 AM to exercise and it was now mid-afternoon. She had had no lunch and no breaks. She had stood in her at ease position during the setup interludes, so she hadn't even had a chance to rest her legs.

The photographers did seem creepy to her, although she found an odd satisfaction in obeying their disinterested commands. And she *was* afraid of Danielle. But if Danielle suddenly decided that it was time for a snack, Donna's free arms would be of little avail. It was, she concluded, no more dangerous to be chained in Danielle's presence, than it was to be free. "If that's what Paul wants, I'll do it, of course."

Donna was given the choice between having Danielle or one of the photographer assistants apply the oil that would give Donna's tan skin the glistening wet look so essential to quality porn. After a few moments of hesitation, Donna chose Danielle, and the preparations began.

Donna was aroused by the conflicting sensations…the gentle rubbing of Danielle's hands all over Donna's body, including the most erogenous areas, and the knowledge that Danielle was an extremely dangerous creature who had murdered more than five dozen people. The fear mixed with pleasure had Donna tingling with excitement and she wished that Paul were around for a quickie.

The nude bondage scenes were first shot in the living room, and then everything was moved out to the pool. By the end, they were having her pose outside the enclosure with the Gulf in the background. Donna was hoping that there would be no nearby boats.

At the end of the session, Danielle removed Donna's chains and motioned Donna to climb the back steps. Once inside, Danielle touched Donna's shoulder, startling her. "You did very well," Danielle said. "That took a lot of courage. Does Paul's approval mean that much to you?"

"It does," Donna replied.

Danielle smiled. "Paul has you impressively disciplined, Donna. I've seen how Paul is with you and there's no doubt that you love each other. I don't understand your relationship, but it's beautiful."

Donna didn't know how to respond, so she simply said, "Thank you."

"If I send the photography van away, could you give me a ride back to my motel?"

Donna felt a thrill of alarm, but answered, "Of course."

"Would you go with me to a restaurant or a bar, Donna? This isn't something Paul is requesting. It's me. I'd like to get to know you better."

"A nice restaurant," Donna said. "I'm starving. I haven't eaten since breakfast."

"Wherever you like."

"I'll have to wash off this grease," Donna told her. "And get some clothes on. Make yourself at home."

ઉ઼

They ended up at a restaurant along 19, a steakhouse and bar that had a piano player as live entertainment. A handful of very elderly people were clustered around the piano, singing drunken accompaniment to the very old hit songs. "Time is passing this place by," Donna noted. "The new elderly are the Boomers, and this isn't their music."

"Time passes," Danielle said. "Soon the Boomers will be on their way out, then Generation X, and then the Millennials. One generation after another, down the memory hole."

Donna laughed. "You're a bundle of joy, Danielle."

Donna was feeling good. She was wearing a low cut blue dress and heels, dressed for a night out. Donna would have preferred a more lively spot but, as Sheriff, she didn't want to be seen partying at a loud bar. But she was out of the house and out with people, albeit very geriatric people.

"Forgive me," Danielle said, "I'm in a melancholy mood."

"Try to cheer up," Donna told her. "This isn't the liveliest place on the strip, but still…"

The waiter, a thin dark haired youth in an off red uniform jacket and ruffled shirt, brought their orders. Both had ordered Porterhouse steaks. Donna's was medium while Danielle's was extra rare. Donna dug into her salad while Danielle shoved hers aside.

"If you're a member of the Community, going out to eat has a certain lack of variety," Danielle complained.

Donna tipped her head and regarded the vampire. "You can't do vegetables. Can you eat chicken or fish?"

Danielle shrugged. "I can eat protein, generally. I can even still handle peanut butter, but not the bread or jelly."

"I guess you thought it would be worth the sacrifice," Donna said.

"As I said before, it finally boiled down to this or death."

Donna took a sip of wine. "So here we are, Danielle. Tell me: What was the deal with the clothes?"

"It was like I said. I suggested to Paul that he dress you up, get you some show clothing. I thought that it was a waste to have such a good looking slave and not decorate her a bit."

Donna laughed with delight. "Decorate me? Do they have what…some sort of affair like a dog show where I can be paraded around?"

"I'm sure that you could find something like that."

"Maybe we could have one at the Narvaez Fairgrounds," Donna suggested, giggling.

"A charity fund raiser? Yes," Danielle said, smiling, getting into the game.

Donna settled back. "Why is it that you want to know me?" she asked. "Why did you come see me that first time?"

"First, I like you," Danielle replied. "Even when you were terrified of me, you've always been decent to me. And, I'm fascinated by you and Paul and the Miasma."

"So, you're fascinated by Paul?"

"Yes, I am. Paul has a certain attraction…"

"I think it's called *charm*," Donna said.

"Oh, no. I first met him when he walked into our hideout in Citrus County, long before he took on Michael's blood. He wasn't afraid of us at all. If you'd ever seen Darren in vampire mode, you'd get what I'm saying. But I liked Paul then. And Michael liked him, even though Paul had done his best to kill Michael."

"So, Paul is attractive to vampires. How do I fit in?"

"I've told you before: You can enter the Miasma. Paul believes that you are the daughter of the Mother Goddess. You told me that, too, when I visited your house."

"So, if I am?"

"I would like to speak with the Mother Goddess."

Donna frowned. "I don't know if I can do that?"

"Why not?"

Donna sighed. "I go to the Miasma when I'm asleep, or when I'm in a deep daydream, an almost hypnotic state. I don't know how to bring other people there."

Danielle sat back, disappointed. "Can you talk to her?"

"Maybe." Donna thought for a moment. "When I want to send her a message, whether I'm in the real world or in Koth, I send her a sample of what I need. I sent her some of the Great Lord's semen when I asked her to give me a man in the real world. I sent some of his blood when I asked her to save his life. Sometimes I write a thank you note on a piece of paper and send it…"

"How do you send it?"

"In Koth, I burn it on the altar of the unknown gods. In the real, I burn it in my incense holder on my owl sculpture."

Danielle's eyes widened. "So, if I wrote something, you could send it to her?"

"I could try. No guarantees."

"What do I have to do to gain her favor?"

Donna frowned. "She is a goddess. There's no way to bribe her or to affect her attitude about anything. She likes some people and not others. There's no way to change that."

Danielle looked disappointed. "But she liked Paul."

"She did," Donna said. "But I think that she built Paul, for me."

Danielle laughed. "That's so sweet…egotistical, but sweet."

Donna got serious. “I’ll tell you what, Danielle. Write out what it is you want to say to the Mother Goddess and I will try to send it to her. The message has to be small, though. I’m burning it in that incense holder.”

“I’ll do that. I’ll get it to you tomorrow.”

Donna nodded. “There’s something that you can do for me,” she said.

“What is that?”

“There have been a number of unexplained disappearances in the County…”

“Donna, surely you don’t think that I had anything to do with them.”

Donna shook her head. “No, the timeline doesn’t fit you. But I need to know if there is another vampire operating around here.”

“I doubt it,” Danielle said. “Because of what you did to Michael and Arianne, and the fact that many people here realize that we exist, the Community has stayed well clear of this region.”

“Is that a definite no?”

Danielle sighed. “I wouldn’t rule out a new vampire…one operating like Michael did, without Community support. But it isn’t likely. There aren’t that many of us, and even fewer want to reproduce. An experienced vampire would disguise the killings as something else. My guess would be that you have a serial killer.”

“If a vampire were operating here, could you detect it?”

“I would be able to recognize his chi if I saw him, but that would be the only way.”

“Danielle,” Donna said, “you’ve only seen me at home, when I was in my slave mode. But I am a serious person, and I’m the Sheriff of this county. I’m asking you in that role: Will you help me with this?”

“Hunting a fellow vampire, you mean?”

“Hunting a killer, whether he’s a vampire or not.”

Danielle thought about that. “Donna, I would so like us to be friends. And, I do have a great deal of free time. The legal work here comes in dribs and drabs. I don’t know what you have in mind, but if there isn’t too much day time involved, I’m game.”

ଔ

Paul came home in the middle of Sunday afternoon. Donna was waiting in her display position, kneeling on the living room floor, knees spread wide, hands behind her back. The dire wolves ran to the door and greeted him, as Donna stayed in front of the sofa, her eyes straight ahead and her mouth open.

Paul paused to handle the dogs a bit before he walked over to Donna. He ruffled her hair for a moment, then seized her ponytail and pulled her head backward. He fondled her breast with one hand, then bent down and kissed her. He stood up.

"Belly rub," he called out. The dogs raced to his feet and rolled onto their backs. Donna was caught by surprise.

Paul arched an eyebrow at the still kneeling girl. "Belly rub," he repeated. This time Donna assumed the humiliating position, her wrists folded beside her breasts, her legs crooked with her feet off the ground. Paul rubbed each of his pets in turn.

"That's enough," Paul said. The two dogs quickly sat up. Donna rolled over onto her hands and knees. "Not you," he said. "You forgot your training, Donna. Back in position."

Annoyed, Donna rolled onto her back and put her feet into the air. "Stay that way," Paul ordered.

He walked to the front door and returned with a briefcase. He sat down on the couch and opened the case. "Okay, Donna, next command. Beg."

The dogs sat up on their haunches and moved their front paws. Paul rewarded each of them with a dog biscuit. Donna was standing on her knees, her mouth open and her hands folded in front of her. Paul popped a dog biscuit into her mouth.

She was startled. She held the biscuit in her mouth for a moment, decided that she was intended to actually eat it, and so bit down. It was relatively big, so she had some difficulty working it into her mouth and chewing it, but she managed.

"How does it taste, Donna?"

She was surprised to be asked a direct question. "Sir…it isn't a bad taste. It isn't good, either. It's pretty tasteless, really."

"Pleasant or unpleasant?"

"I'd have to say unpleasant, sir. It's like eating cardboard."

"That's what I thought, too. It's made of wheat and soy flour. High protein but no sugar or salt. It's designed to be edible by humans and dogs, but edible is the best you can say for it."

"Where did you get them, sir?"

"I had them made by a baker in San Francisco, especially for you. You'll get used to them. You're going to be eating a lot of them."

She sucked in her breath. "If it pleases you, my lord."

He laughed. "It does. The dogs seem to like them. And notice the dog bone shape…very haute cuisine."

"Yes, sir," she said.

"Well, fetch me your leash. I have some disks to watch."

"Handcuffs, sir?"

He shrugged. "No, just your leash. You can kneel here by the couch while I watch TV. Danielle will be over later."

Donna felt her heart race. "Danielle, sir?"

"Yes, Danielle. You need to get used to her coming over here. She's working closely with me on this California project. But tonight, she's going to help you model the costumes you tried on. I'm going to look at these disks and decide which ones I want to see. Now, go get your leash."

His voice was slightly grumpy, which distressed Donna. She'd already screwed up getting into the belly rub position, and now this. *I'm becoming incompetent as a sex slave. That's pretty bad.* She hastened to get the leash.

She knelt with her back to the sofa. Paul tugged on the leash until she was leaning backwards with her shoulders resting against the cushion. Since she was kneeling, it was an awkward and uncomfortable position, but his grip on the leash left her no room to readjust herself, so she stayed leaning back, straining her neck to see the TV screen.

The disks contained one high def picture after another of Donna in outfits that highlighted her sexual parts. At first, Donna was embarrassed, as well as being uncomfortable from the way she was kneeling. But soon she began examining the photos as though they were pictures of some other woman, some anonymous model. The physical discomfort and the embarrassment were forgotten. *I look pretty damn good!* She had never been photographed this way before. She loved her oversized breasts, highlighted by the cleverly designed clothing. She found her bare pubis beautiful, too, and admired the delicate flesh between her thighs. *It's interesting to see myself as the men see me...like Naomi sees me.* She giggled at an interior joke: *I think I'm falling in love with myself.*

When she saw herself photographed nude, in chains, she gasped in astonishment. She was perfect. Her long legs were exquisitely carved muscle, her abdomen tight, with muscles defined. Her ribs were barely noticeable traces on her torso, and her breasts hung against her chest, the nipples large and rubbery. She strained against the leash for a better view. She saw herself posed hands over her head, on her knees...on her elbows and knees taken from all angles...lying spread eagled on a towel by the pool. A perfect body, well displayed, tanned and oiled.

She smiled at her expressions: sometimes smiling, her face sometimes crinkled into a frown or a look of distress. Danielle had coached her on the facial expressions. Danielle had known what she was doing.

Donna couldn't recall if Paul had imposed silence on her. She decided to take a chance.

"Permission to speak, sir."

A chuckle. "What is it, Donna?"

"What will you do with the pictures, my lord?"

"I thought I'd put them up on a website."

Donna knew that he was teasing. "No, really, sir."

"We'll keep them," he said. "When you're old and wrinkly we'll take them out and look at them and you can remember what a knockout you used to be."

That touched her. It made her sad as well. "You won't kick me out when I'm too old to be a sex slave?"

A sad laugh. "No, Donna. I'm going to keep you around forever. You're a work of art. You'll be my beautiful antique."

"Permission to stand up and kiss you, sir?"

He laughed. "Granted."

She stood and kissed his forehead. He pulled her to him and she ended up lying sprawled out atop him on the sofa, engaged in her favorite thing, smooching.

It was near dusk when Danielle arrived, dressed in a short, tight red dress *blood red* with a scoop neckline, her hair pinned up, and wearing red high heels. A naked Donna opened the door for her.

Danielle paused to make small talk with Paul while Donna stood in her at-ease position, hands behind her back. Danielle then led Donna to the closet where the fetish clothing was stored and began the show.

Donna was first exhibited in what Danielle described as a replacement for the terry cloth bathrobe, It was a red satin garment that was loose and billowing above the belt line, so that it was almost impossible for Donna to move without flashing a boob. Below the belt, the garment was split in the middle. As the dress only reached to mid-thigh, short of standing with her feet together, Donna could not avoid showing her crotch and her ass.

"Danielle, that is perfect," Paul raved. "It looks like it came directly from Koth."

Danielle was sleek and elegant. Her heavy mascara and the patch of bright blush on each side of her porcelain face made her look doll-like. She smiled. "I gave the designer your description and she came up with this. It achieves your purpose, I think, of exposing your slave while pretending to cover her."

"It does. Walk around a little more, Donna."

Donna did so, exaggerating the flounce in her hips as she walked.

"Beautiful," Paul said. "You'll wear this for any guests you don't go nude for."

Donna smiled but didn't reply.

The next outfit was a cape. Getting into this involved removing the dog collar and replacing it with a loosely fitting steel hoop around Donna's neck. The cape was hung on rings, like a shower curtain. Fastened in front, the cape formed a knee length cone around Donna's body, and the fabric above the hoop covered her face to just under her eyes. The ensemble included a round cap and clog type heels, all in matching off-pink. Danielle made her parade in front of the sofa.

"Dressed like this," Danielle pointed out, "she's unrecognizable. You can walk her around anywhere with her hands cuffed behind her and no one will know. This is how you move your naked woman from place to place in public."

"It looks like it would work," Paul commented off handedly.

"And when we unhook the front…" Danielle unclipped the catch and the garment fell open, exposing Donna's nudity.

Paul sighed. "That's a dramatic effect."

This made Donna uneasy. Paul had never before spoken of taking her anyplace else to be shown naked. *Is this Paul, or just Danielle?*

The next dresses to be shown were short house frocks that were fastened full length with snaps. One of the dresses snapped in front, the other in back. They were strapless, held up by elastic at the top. That meant that the dresses could be completely removed, even if Donna's hands were cuffed. It also meant that the dress could be completely unsnapped and pulled open, exposing the body underneath. The best feature though, as Danielle took pains to demonstrate, was that, by releasing a couple of snaps, Donna's hands could be clipped to her waist chain through the dress. Paul liked that feature. He had Donna parade around, modeling each dress with her hands appropriately cuffed.

After Danielle had gotten Donna out of the chains and the frock, Paul said, "That's enough for tonight. We'll have Donna show the others from time to time. Drink, Danielle?"

"I think so, yes."

"Donna, why don't you get comfortable next to my chair? Don't worry about your hands."

Donna understood that to mean that she was to kneel with her knees together and her hands on her thighs until further notice. Paul went to the bar. "What would you like, Danielle?" he called.

"Scotch and soda," Danielle replied.

"That sounds good. Donna, you'll be having the same thing. Me? I'm going with a martini."

He mixed the drinks for Donna and Danielle before he returned to make his own.

Paul and Danielle spent a couple of hours of animated conversation about the ins and outs of Conquest Security and its operations in California. Donna, naked except for her dog collar, knelt wordlessly, leaning her head against the chair while Paul absent mindedly stroked her head and brushed her face with his fingers. She nursed her drink and tried to follow the conversation, but realized that she didn't know enough about Paul's business to keep up.

And why should I? I'm just his sex slave, his pet. She looked inside herself for a reaction to this truth, but she had none. It was simply her reality.

Chapter Twenty-Three: A Breakthrough

Al Cadbury had been investigating the Teresa Torricelli case, and he was making progress. He'd obtained the employment records, such as they were, of the people who had worked in that restaurant during 2010 and 2011. Then he had begun patiently tracking people down. Many of the people had left the state and couldn't be tracked, at least not in the short run. Others had relocated to other parts of Florida. The Sheriff had raised no objections to Cadbury going to other jurisdictions to trace leads, as long as he checked in with the local authorities.

In a trailer in rural Volusia County, he discovered that Teresa Torricelli had been living with a man at the time of her disappearance. "No," the former waitress told him, "she never said the name." That had set Cadbury's heart racing.

He stopped working on his other cases and devoted his efforts to chasing Torricelli leads. Lieutenant Ferris redistributed the workload to Richard Dykes and Corrine Greene, absorbing a great deal of bitching in the process. But Cadbury was free to drive all over central Florida contacting folks who had been fellow employees of the slain woman.

Finally, in north Tampa, he ran into a carpenter who'd done some restaurant work during a slack time. "I knew Teresa, sure," Mark Kane had told him. "Yeah, she was shacked up with Bob Elledge. I think he might have had a job…Oh, yeah! He was an electrician, worked for a contractor. Got laid off a lot. Yeah, Teresa was banging him all summer."

"How about fall?"

"Fall, too. But they were having trouble by then."

"What kind of trouble?"

"I don't know. But I saw a lot less of Teresa and a lot more of Bob. He and I used to drink a lot of beer and shoot a lot of pool by the end of summer. That means he wasn't home banging his hottie."

"When did you see him last?"

Kane shrugged. "Hell, I don't know. Two or three weeks ago. Ran into him in that pizza joint on Lutz-Lake Fern Road."

"Where does he live now?"

"He said he's still hanging in Narvaez County, working off and on."

Whitey Ferris stood silently, hands together, as Al Cadbury reported all this to the Sheriff.

"That's good work," Donna told him. "And he might still be in our jurisdiction. That's amazing."

"So we find him," Whitey Ferris said firmly.

"Try to find him quietly. If he finds out we're after him, he'll flee the state."

"I'm on it," Cadbury said, determination in his voice.

He left the office.

When Ferris closed the door, Donna said, "Al does good work. I underestimated him."

"How's that?" Ferris asked.

"To tell you the truth, Whitey, I like big strong men who keep themselves in shape. Sergeant Cadbury is a little fat and I applied a lot of stereotypes: lazy, dumb, that sort of thing. I was prejudiced, Whitey. I abhor that in myself."

"You're the one who promoted Cadbury in the first place. I've never noticed any prejudice in you."

"Says the big strong man." Whitey grinned at that. "But prejudice cuts both ways. I've gotten a lot of mileage out of being a dumb blonde."

"Nobody thinks you're dumb now."

Donna made a half smile. "I'm sure that there are many people who think that they're smarter than I am, and that they could do this job better than I can. So, I think you're wrong."

"No, they're wrong," Whitey responded.

⁂

The Sheriff of Narvaez County sat back in her chair and assessed her situation. She was utterly reliant on other people: Klass, Whitey Ferris, Cadbury, to close this case. *These cases.* The boyfriend looked good for Teresa Torricelli now, but what if he wasn't the guy?

What if all the cases were done by one subject, a serial killer? What if each of the cases had a separate perpetrator?

Starting with zilch, Whitey Ferris and Al Cadbury had made progress in one of the cases that had puzzled the department. Teresa Torricelli's live in boyfriend was a viable suspect and was possibly somewhere where they could get at him. If they could wrap up Torricelli…*it would be good to wrap up Torricelli, but what are the odds that this electrician did all the others? I've got a person of interest in the Torricelli case, but on the others, I've got nothing.*

Chapter Twenty-Four: The Dire Wolves

It was a bright Saturday morning. Donna, wearing nothing but her dog collar, was sitting at the kitchen table eating the breakfast that Paul had prepared for her. She felt good. The sun was already bright and she could see the tops of the trees through the broad kitchen window. She felt rather guilty that she was sitting at the table to eat, even though she was not going to be working today. But that was Paul's call, and Paul seemed to enjoy having her sit next to him at breakfast. He liked to squeeze her breast sometimes, or use a napkin to clean food from above her lip. Donna enjoyed this attention, and enjoyed the unfamiliar sensation of sitting cross legged and eating with a fork.

They didn't have much conversation. Paul was looking through some papers, and Donna could no longer talk with him about internal Sheriff business anyway. But their relationship really wasn't built on conversation. She was to him as Ba-el Shanah was to Paul of Koth: his possession. When she and Paul did talk, it was either meaningful, or it was teasing banter. She did not hunger for banal trivia between them.

When she had finished eating, Paul stood up and took the dishes from the table. He returned and set down a small plate.

"Something new today, Donna. Take off everything but your collar and your ear studs."

"I'm not wearing anything, my lord."

He laughed. "Your wedding rings, your hair band, any hair pins that you have. Anything artificial."

Puzzled, she complied. She dropped her engagement and wedding rings onto the plate. She undid her hair, so that it fell over her shoulders in a tangle.

"Is this what you want, sir?"

He nodded. "It is. I've got some things to work on, Donna, and I want to have the house to myself for the next six to eight hours. So, I'm putting my pets outdoors."

Donna got the picture. "That includes me?"

"Correct. In the future, I won't bother to explain. I'll just put you out. But today, since this is the first time: You and the dogs will stay outside until I call you in with the whistle. I don't want you hanging around the house. You have nine acres to roam around on. Get well away from here."

Donna couldn't hold back her protest. "What am I supposed to do outside?"

Paul shrugged. "The dogs manage to keep themselves entertained. You don't seem to mind being chained up outside. Why would you object to being set free out there?"

Donna started to argue, but decided not to waste her breath. This was, after all, well within their agreement.

Once she was outside, looking up the front steps, she was at a loss. The two dogs gazed up at the naked human, seeking guidance. Donna wiped her hands on her bare thighs and looked around. The dogs, finding no wisdom, scampered off. Donna considered her situation. *I'm naked and I'm outside.* She didn't know why this alarmed her. She didn't mind at all when Paul led her out in chains and hitched her to a tree. Possibly that was because his leaving her helpless implied an obligation on his part to check on her from time to time, to bring her water or more insect repellant. *To pay attention to me.* Even from afar. Now she was on her own.

But what do I need, really? Water, certainly. But there were hose bibs all over the property. She was in no danger of dehydration. A bathroom? *Well, nine acres...* She would be embarrassed, but only to herself. There would be nobody watching. She would need shade, but there were numerous trees as well as an entire empty stilt house on the next lot over. She was safe in that respect. If she were still outside in mid-afternoon, it would be dangerously hot. But as long as she kept hydrated and took advantage of the shade, she would be okay.

She wondered if she was supposed to obey the rule that she keep her hands behind her back. Paul hadn't said anything to her about that. But she had been so faithful in her observance of that rule that she didn't know what to do with her hands anyway, so she set out walking along the wall, her wrists crossed behind her. The dogs saw her and joined her for a while, but then raced off when they saw something move in the distance.

She crossed the gravel parking area first, to snoop around the empty house. This would be a perfect base of operations in the hot afternoon, with its expanse of concrete underneath the high rise house. The place had a swimming pool, although it was much smaller than the pool at the main house. Donna checked it out. The pool was clean and sparkling. *Paul must have some sort of maintenance crew to work on this place.* Probably the pool service that maintained the large pool also did this one. Donna had never noticed.

I really have been a prisoner here, Donna thought as she walked along the saltwater tolerant foliage that blocked the ground level view of the sea. But then she remembered all the time she had spent at home while Paul was away. She could have gone exploring any time she wanted, but she hadn't. *Maybe deep down I didn't want to go out naked by myself.* Of course, only her word kept her nude while Paul was away. Paul's demands had made a deeper psychological impact on her than she had thought.

As she wandered along the property, she came to the line where the foliage thinned and she was walking along the exposed seawall. She felt vulnerable, as she was now visible from the Gulf. She could see a small catamaran beached on one of the islands, could even see people walking around. She wondered if they could see her, and could see that she was naked, and knew who she was. She dismissed the idea…unless they had telescopes. But they were just picknickers, walking around oblivious.

She saw a big pelican sitting on a post sticking out of the water. She leaned forward to get a better look, and was conscious of her boobs swaying. She smiled. *Like udders. I'm just all about boobs.* In a quick flash of longing she wished that Paul was here to take one of her breasts in his mouth. Or maybe Naomi could do it. Or one of them on each breast. *I'm so bad! I can't even look at a pelican without getting horny.* She was conscious of the breeze caressing her skin, and she took the opportunity to touch herself, and opened her flesh so the breeze could caress where it really mattered.

Aroused, she put her hands back where they belonged and skipped along happily.

She walked all the way across the undeveloped lot, which was a tangle of woods and vines and weeds separated from the seawall by a relatively clear sand path. Donna proceeded nervously, afraid that at any time someone on a boat would get close enough to see her. She came to where the great gray wall ended, hard against the old seawall, braced up by an enormous triangular buttress.

Donna held on to the buttress as she worked her way along the top of the sea wall. She was really exposed now. Her ass would be visible against the gray wall for miles. She saw that the wall ended in a long triangular buttress running onto the beach, perpendicular to the side brace. Stymied, she worked her way back, scratching her belly on the rough concrete.

She looked down. The water was deep, maybe deep enough that she could get into the water without too much walking on the jagged rip rap. She decided to give it a shot. *What's the worst that could happen? A cut foot?* The waves were lapping about three feet below her. She carefully lowered herself, scraping her ass across the edge of the seawall. She found her footing on the rocks and then plunged forward. She was in about four feet of water. Elated, she began swimming.

She swam about fifty feet, then stood up, and carefully walked back to the slimy concrete wall. With some difficulty, she climbed back up. She scraped her nipples and knees and the inside of her leg getting out of the water, but once out she was ecstatic. She was on the other side of the wall! She was free. Feeling good, she decided to push it. She sat on her butt at the edge of the wall, with her arms around her drawn up legs.

She smiled with joy. She sat and watched the silvery fish shimmer by below her. She saw a lonely needlefish. In the distance she could see the water roiled by a school of mullet. A small open motorboat passed by a few hundred feet away, close enough to wave. Donna waved back happily.

She didn't know why being outside the wall made her so happy. Maybe Paul's chains and restrictions had oppressed her more than she'd realized. Not that she would hesitate to return and throw herself under his control, but right now freedom was invigorating. She stood up. *True, I'm basically a wild animal right now, but I'm not in chains.* She looked around. Far in the distance she could see houses. *I wonder if they can see me. Who cares?* She knew that there were no other houses on this little spit of land, a remnant of a 1970s dredge and fill operation that had been halted by a court order. For decades, development had been prohibited until the McLaurys had lubricated the regulatory machinery. She was on an overgrown, undeveloped lot. She decided to cross it.

She came to the street, and looked to her right and saw the long forbidding gray monstrosity that was Paul McCready's wall, built to be her prison. She smiled grimly and crossed the street.

On the other side of the street was a forest of palmetto and, as she walked a little further, a mire. It was a watery expanse of black muck covered with chest high grass. As she walked, she found that the grass was sharp edged and cut her skin. She was sinking into the muck. The black, sticky stuff came up to her knees, sometimes mid-thigh as she struggled forward. Suction made it hard to raise her feet, and her footprints rapidly filled with water. Meanwhile, her legs were crisscrossed with tiny lacerations.

To her relief, she found herself at the edge of a grass covered, tree lined, sand ridge. She took a few deep breaths and climbed it, pushing aside vines and low plants as she went. When she reached the top, she heard a car in the distance. She realized with a shock that she was standing next to Shoal Line Boulevard. To her left she could see the bar and marina. To the right there was more swamp. Dismayed, she scurried back down the ridge.

She sat down for a while and listened as the cars went past. She was on a section of fill that had been dumped here to protect Shoal Line Boulevard from being washed away in a high tide. She was basically in a coastal marsh that had been dug up and filled in places so that people could build and do business in the Gulf.

There was no help for it but to trudge back through the muck. She was a little more fearful this time. She now realized that she could fall and get seriously stuck, maybe even die. But, difficult as the return was, she didn't regret her excursion. Paul had told her to go explore, and she had.

She crossed the lot next to the wall. As she stood on the seawall, a figure covered with black muck, with muck even in her long stringy hair, she held her hands behind her back. A boat raced along, not a hundred yards away. She could see the kid steering…white tee shirt, white billed cap. She could see the brunette sitting up behind him, hair controlled by a wide pink band, wide sunglasses. Donna smiled. She didn't know if they'd seen her. She didn't care.

She was so covered with sawgrass cuts and scrapes from clambering over concrete that she didn't care if she cut herself on the rocks, too. She backed up, took a few running steps, and leaped as far out as she could into the water.

She felt the water force itself into her nose, tasted the brine. She saw the brown of the sea and the globules of light as she broke the surface. She blinked, and blew her nose, and backstroked past Paul's boat slip and his floating dock. She found a safe looking place and got out of the water.

She hoped she hadn't missed Paul's signal. She whistled and the two shepherds loped up to her. So far, she'd gotten away with it. The German shepherds trailing her, she went to the unoccupied house, found a garden hose, and treated herself to a long drink of lukewarm water. She hosed herself off and then she squatted in the grass to take care of *that* business. Finally, she opened the gate to the pool fence and jumped into the cool fresh water. Donder and Blitzen stood on the cool deck and stared down at her with interest.

This is great! No relentless, drudging swimming of laps. Just hanging out in the water. She swam to the bottom and glided along, shaking her head side to side to clean her hair. She splashed. She tried out the various swimming styles she knew. *Freedom!*

When she was tired of swimming, she got out of the pool and went into the shade under the house. She lay on her side, her bare skin against the cool concrete. After a few moments, the dogs joined her for a snooze.

She was awakened by a yelp from one of the dogs. After a few seconds of getting oriented as to where she was and what she was doing, she heard the whistle. She stood up and began running toward the house as fast as she could go.

When she arrived, panting for breath, Paul laughed. The two dogs were on their best behavior, sitting on their haunches and looking up at him, devotion in their eyes. Donna realized that she must look like a crazy woman.

“I see one of you has been a bad dog,” he said. He motioned Donna to him and had her turn around. “A little property damage, I see.”

Donna’s heart sank. “My lord, I have a confession to make.”

She felt him clamp the cuffs onto her wrists.

“Let’s hear it,” he said.

“My lord, I swam around the wall and left the property. I crossed the street and the swamp all the way to Shoal Line.”

“Okay,” Paul said. He fastened the leash to her collar.

“My lord, if you’re angry…”

Paul shrugged. “I’m not the one who’s a public official. I’m not the one who would have to explain to the voters why I was running around naked.”

“My lord, I’m sorry.”

“It doesn’t bother me,” he said. “If you regret it, it’s on you. Come here.”

He had her kneel, her breasts and belly pushed against the support post. He fixed the leash so that she had less than twelve inches of chain between her neck and the giant timber. He checked the chain for slack, and when he was satisfied that she almost none, he gave her a dog biscuit and patted her on the head. She worked the biscuit into her mouth, feeling foolish as she chewed it.

“Time to give my pets a bath,” he said.

She stayed chained against the post as he procured a bucket, a roll of garden hose, and other paraphernalia for bathing the dogs. She couldn’t watch the process, but sometimes a spray of water would strike her back, making her shudder from the sudden cold. She could hear Paul reassuring the dogs, heard the splashing sound, the whoosh of the hose, and the sounds of him vigorously toweling each dog in turn. Finally: “All done, guys. Let’s get in the house.”

She heard him clomping up the front steps, followed by the clicking of the dogs’ claws against the wood.

After what she estimated as fifteen or twenty minutes, he returned to her.

He pulled her ponytail so that the neck chain was taut. “You’ve been a bad girl,” he said, “so this might be a little painful.”

He released her from the neck chain, removed the handcuffs and took off her collar. "We'll have to dry this on the fan tonight. Tomorrow, you'll need to oil it before you wear it again."

Her heart sank. He was angry after all. "I'm sorry, sir."

He touched her lip. That was a signal that she wasn't allowed to talk.

He had her stretch out her arm. He produced a bottle and poured liquid onto a cloth. He rubbed her arm with it. As the liquid came in contact with the grass cuts, she felt a stinging sensation. At first, the pain shocked her but as he did her other arm, and then her legs and hips, she felt her whole body burning. She found the stinging sensation enjoyable. She watched, mute, as he rubbed her down.

"Does it sting?"

She made a serious face and nodded her head vigorously.

He smiled. "That was the antiseptic. Now for your bath."

He started with her hair, soaking it with the hose, then applying shampoo, followed by a long rinse with cold high pressure water. Next he did her body, with soap and a rough scrub brush. He examined the dozens of cuts and scrapes and decided that they had all been thoroughly irrigated and were unlikely to get infected. He reapplied the antiseptic. He talked softly to her the whole time, as to a skittish animal.

The next step was to order her to her hands and knees. She had always found this position, which had her ample breasts hanging free, to be deliciously humiliating. He sponged her body with bath oil, focusing especially on those loose breasts, and on her bottom. The sensations made her shudder. To have a man bathe her in this manner was erotic, but out on the driveway, in broad daylight…she could barely stand it.

He spent a long time toweling her off. His treatment of her hair was rough and prolonged and left it a tangled mess. But, when he began rubbing down her body she became so aroused that, except for her exquisite discipline, she would have been reduced to begging him to take her right there and then.

Instead, she was the obedient slave who said nothing when he ordered her into the house.

Inside, she felt completely naked without chains or her collar. Although Paul had never imbued the collar with any ritual significance, Donna felt the need to wear it as a sign of her servility. She carried it with her and put it on as soon as she got home. Except for when she was lying out in the sun, or bathing, she wore it all the time, even in bed. It felt very strange to be nude at home without it on her neck.

"Go upstairs and get your hair under control," Paul told her. "When you're through, come back with either your laptop or your iPad. Also, pick out a book to read. Bring your phone, of course."

She returned, hair dried and ponytail in place, holding her iPad, iPhone, and a romance novel. Paul smiled when he saw the title.

Paul set the electronics on his desk and had her do her ritual turn to show that she was clean. He produced the steel collar and clamped it around her neck. She hadn't worn it for a while, and she was surprised at its weight, and how much it restricted the up and down movement of her head. Paul then put her into her custom stainless steel cuffs and connected her wrists with an eight inch chain.

He had her kneel on knees and elbows in front of his desk then ran a chain to an eyebolt in the floor. Her neck chained to the eyebolt, she was unable to rise any further than half an arm's length from the floor.

Paul gave her a dog biscuit. As she chewed it, he told her, "I have some things to do, so I'll be in and out of the office. You'll be here six or eight hours. This is just an ordinary dog leash, so you can get loose. You're on the honor system. You'll have to let yourself loose, then hook yourself back up. You're allowed to do that once, one bathroom break. I expect you to behave. That means you stay here, don't talk, and keep yourself entertained. Are we clear?"

Donna grinned and nodded her agreement.

He placed three dog biscuits on the floor in front of her and walked away.

Donna took a moment to reflect on her situation. She had drunk plenty of water during her outdoor escapade, so water wasn't a concern for now. It was clear that she wasn't going to get any lunch. *Too bad.* She was slightly hungry but thinking about it would make it worse. *Apparently the dog biscuits are supposed to be lunch.* She could tell time on the iPad so she knew when to schedule her bathroom break: about three and a half hours in. She'd try to hold it for four. She could drink water from the sink at that time, too. Paul had taken her phone, so he'd be screening calls. If the SO needed her for anything, he'd let her loose.

So I'm fine. Everything's all taken care of. Compared to other times when Paul had chained her up for hours, this wasn't bad at all.

ઉૹ

As Donna lay stretched out on the floor, propped up on her elbow, reading, Paul came into the room and stepped behind her. He knelt down, pressing a knee into her buttocks. He took hold of her upper arms and lifted them, removing her support. As she lay, her breasts and cheek flat against the floor, he quickly unhooked her wrists, brought her hands behind her back, and fastened the cuffs together. He released the neck chain and helped her to her feet. Next came the waist chain and a leash. Gripping the leash where it hooked to the collar, Paul led his captive into the kitchen.

He had prepared a pretty good meal: rice mixed with melted cheese topped with chopped chicken breast, asparagus tips, and broccoli. He placed a plate on the floor for her and maneuvered her into a kneeling position so that she could tip forward and eat, using only her mouth. She enjoyed this. It was degrading, which Donna found erotic, and the food was still hot. She knew to lick the plate clean when she was finished. Only when she was satisfied that not a morsel remained on the plate did she raise her head. Paul grasped her shoulders and pulled her into an upright kneeling position. He dabbed her face with a cloth, then held a bottle of water so that she could drink. Donna had been seriously hungry. It was past the normal dinner time, so the good hot meal made her happy, and she felt a warm glow of love for Paul. *I'm such a good little slave.*

Paul took the plate away and helped her to her feet. "Time to walk my pets," he said.

Donna was surprised. She had been reading her book and so had lost track of time, but she knew that it was late. She was not in a position to question, though. First, the deal was that she had to do whatever he demanded. Moreover, she was still under the quiet rule and was not allowed to speak. But she was not surprised when Paul opened the front door and the dogs ran off into blackness. His hand gripped high up on the leash, Paul carefully led her down the dimly lit steps.

They walked at a comfortable pace, which was rare. Paul was taller than she and so she usually had to hurry a bit to keep up with his stride. She was glad that he was slowing up for her, but she also felt a little guilty about getting that kind of consideration. She thought that her status meant that she was not entitled to any allowances. As they were about twenty feet up the walk, the first motion sensor light kicked on. "You're free to speak now," Paul told her.

"I can't think of anything to say, my lord."

She saw his amused smile. "Well, babe, how do you feel? Are you happy?"

"I am, my lord."

She heard him sigh. She apparently wasn't giving him the information he wanted.

"How about your day, Donna? How did it go?"

"I like the way you kept me on that short leash for so long. I got to read and snooze, but I was never really comfortable and I wasn't free. And the way you took me straight from that to being chained like I am now…very professional."

She heard his chuckle. "Professional?"

"I felt like a real prisoner, sir. No freedom and rough, impersonal handling. No room for resistance, no coaxing. I liked it."

"How about the rest of the day?"

She felt her gut tense. "I'm sorry that I escaped from the compound, sir."

He laughed. "No, you're not. I could make you sorry, I suppose, but I don't really care about it. Pets get out of the fence sometimes. Are you going to do it again?"

"No, my lord," Donna responded quickly. "I'll be a good little pet from now on."

He laughed. "I'm sure you will, Donna. Any questions? Any complaints?"

"I have no standing to complain, sir."

"You can complain, Donna. I just don't have to pay any attention."

"What's the deal with Danielle and the clothes, sir?"

"Is that a complaint?"

"It's a question, sir."

"Danielle is a strange girl and she didn't know how to take you. She likes you, but her view of how you and I relate comes from her understanding of vampires and their familiars. She was a familiar herself, once, you know. When she understood that you weren't a familiar in the vampire way, she tried another category, the BDSM scene. She thought maybe you were that kind of slave. She thought that it would be nice if you had some sexy clothes to show off at S&M clubs and scene parties. It sounded fun to me, so I got her a credit card and told her to go to it."

Donna looked up, amazed. "What?"

Paul sighed. "Danielle's out on her own, Donna. Her only real friend among the vampires was Michael Dalton. He's setting up a new identity, though, so they've had to cool off their relationship. Danielle was practicing law as an associate in San Francisco, and not happy with it. I ran into her out there and she asked if I could help her out. I retained her law firm on condition that they detail Danielle to Florida to work with my firm. It worked out."

"What does that have to do with the clothes?"

Paul shrugged. "Danielle is lonely and she's bored. I figured that if she wanted to play dress up with you, it might cheer her up. It did, actually."

"Playing dress-up is pretty girlie girl."

"Danielle is, surprisingly, a girlie girl. If she hadn't gotten caught up in the vampire scene, she probably would have gotten married and settled down. She gets misty eyed when she talks about children. She met you and thought that I wasn't treating you very well. She thought that you might be a happier slave if you were decorated and displayed."

"I like my slavery straight up," Donna said, "simple and brutal. Keep me naked, keep me chained. Don't let me see, don't let me talk. Don't let me use my arms. Make me helpless and turn me into a sex machine. Then do anything you want to me."

Paul laughed. "There's our hard core Donna. But you'll wear those costumes when I tell you to, because you don't get choices like that."

He heard her angry exhalation.

"You know, Donna, I do put a lot of effort into our…relationship. Your role as a sex slave is very simple. You stay chained so that you're helpless and you're available for sex in any manner at any time. So I could just keep you prisoner. That might be intense for you, but it wouldn't be that interesting to me. And even you'd get tired of it after a while, when it got routine. I don't want to torture you, or whip you, or think up bondage predicaments. So what do I do?"

"You should listen to Naomi. She thinks I should have slave tattoos and wear corsets and bridles all the time. She thinks I ought to be whipped once a week."

Paul laughed. "She should get her own sex slave. But to me, you're a piece of fine art. You have a perfect body and a perfect face, and beautiful skin. I don't want to see you covered with marks. So no whipping for you. No marks. Corset and bridle? You see that in porn that women write. I'm not into that. I want you wearing nothing but enough chains to keep you helpless."

"Danielle thinks that I should replace my wedding rings with a slave ring."

"That's neither here nor there, Donna. But I've got your number."

"Sir?"

"You like obedience, and you like humiliation. What's more of a challenge than having a vampire who scares you show up with a bunch of kinky clothes?"

"Don't forget the creepy photographers that got to see me naked."

"Donna, you're the one who dreams of being displayed naked in a cage. How could you object to a few photographers?"

"Good point," she agreed.

"Anyway, here's how it's going to go. What you initially offered freely is now mandatory. The nudity, the display positions, the chains, and the loss of speech, keep you constantly humiliated and servile.

"I want you *feeling* humiliated constantly and I want you deeply and instinctively submissive. I want no resistance from you. You are not free, and you need to always be conscious of that. We need to constantly reinforce your servility. It's just a matter of finding new ways to humiliate you."

"Is that why you've demoted me to be a dog?"

He laughed. "I think that's it's a promotion. I like dogs. But I'll bet you didn't see it coming. You thought that you'd just be a sex slave like Ba-el Shanah. But this is different. You really are mortified by the belly rubs and the begging. I can see that it's an effort for you to comply."

"But I do comply, sir. And I'm getting used to it."

"Yes, you are, Donna. So we'll pick it up as time goes on. But you see what's happening. We've been playing all this time, but now your psychology is changing. You're becoming more and more servile. More enslaved. You're becoming what we both want."

They were at the end of the walk and conversation ceased as Paul led her through the gravel parking lot in the dark. "One of these days I'll have to put you out here with a rake and have you smooth this out," Paul remarked.

By the time they reached the other side of the gravel area, the motion sensor lights were blinking off. Soon they were standing in perfect darkness.

Paul pressed on, and Donna realized that his night vision was much better than hers. She felt exposed. She was naked with her arms tightly clamped, in the pitch black. She looked up for encouragement, but the sky was black. There were not even stars.

Well away from the gravel, she complained that she had to use the bathroom. Paul stopped and let her squat in the grass. *Speaking of humiliation.* When she stood up, a tug on her leash set her walking again.

This led her to muse about being treated as a dog.

Perhaps in the future, instead of trips to the bathroom, she would be walked on a leash. Or maybe even just told to go outside. The prospect only mildly alarmed her. Of course, there were other possibilities: being made to communicate with barks and whines; being made to stay on all fours. She liked the last two ideas, but decided not to suggest them to Paul. It was his job to impose things on her, her job to comply. She hoped that he wouldn't get someone to make specialty dog food for her. The tasteless dog biscuits were enough. But the dog biscuits were evidence that he didn't mind spending some of his money on new ways to humiliate her.

The prospect of a dog's life made an enjoyable fantasy. She was also pleased that Paul was consciously and systematically enslaving her. It was certainly working. She was already completely his creature. Once the clothes came off, her role as an intelligent and independent woman fell away, and she became the helpless sex toy, lost in worlds of fantasy and, in each one, pathetically eager to please her master. *My harsh master. I really want him to be stern with me.*

She was disappointed with his view on whipping her. She'd really craved that. *But maybe he'll come around.* If marking her was his concern, maybe he'd go for paddling her, or using a flogger. If he didn't want to do it himself, maybe they could find someone else who would. That thought left her purring.

Paul broke her reverie. "Nothing to say, Donna?"

She had thought of something. "Sir, I'm very happy that you're working to make me more compliant and submissive. I want you to break my will and make me completely subordinate to your wishes. But I have money, clothes, and a car. Real slaves have nothing. Real slaves live in fear of punishment. If you aren't willing to punish me, you can't compel me. The only reason I'm your slave is because I want to be. So, we really are just playing."

He laughed. "I could always sick the dire wolves on you."

It was her turn to laugh. "Oh, yeah, that's really scary."

He dropped her leash and grasped her shoulders, turning her around. "Walk forward six steps," he ordered.

Puzzled, she counted off the paces.

Suddenly she heard violent snarling and growling. A furry weight slammed into her legs. She was knocked down and fell hard on her hip. Big clawed feet dug into her chest, just above her breasts. A huge face, barely visible, was inches above her, snarling fiercely, barking loud enough to make her ears ring. She heard the teeth clack together, could smell the rotted meat smell of a carnivore's breath. She felt teeth clamp onto her ankle and begin to shake her leg back and forth. She felt the panic rise. Her limbs tensed. She couldn't catch her breath, and her chest felt like it was about to burst. *I'm fucking helpless! God! The dogs are going to hurt me really bad.* There was a monster on top of her and she couldn't even bring her hands up to resist. She lost control. She screamed.

She heard a hand clap. "Donder, Blitzen: That's enough."

She heard the unseen beasts pad away in the darkness.

Paul put his hands under her arms and pulled her up. "You okay?" he asked.

"Jesus Christ, Paul!" She was furious, and shaking with anger and terror. She took some deep breaths to calm down. *I will not lose my temper with my master!*

"I learned the basics from Michael Dalton," Paul explained, "...from the memories that came with his blood. He learned to control a dog. I've improved on that. With these guys, it's simple. They're shepherds. You're a sheep. It isn't hard to get them to keep you where you're supposed to be. Just a little bit of *charm* and they're perfect guards for my little pet.

"They're not full grown yet. When they are, they'll weigh more than eighty pounds each. I will teach them to bite without breaking your skin. They'll be able to walk you, making you stay on the track, nipping your ass if you don't keep up speed. I'll be able to order you into a position and have them walk around, snarling, ready to jump you if you try to move."

"Shit!"

"So, Donna, are you afraid of me yet?"

She didn't answer. She took more gasping breaths.

"Come on back to the house, babe, and I'll show you something else."

Donna was relieved when they reached the paved walk and the lights started coming on as they passed. Once inside the house she finally felt safe. The two dogs, who had just earned their label as dire wolves, were once again tame and friendly and even licked Donna's leg and a more inappropriate body area before Paul sent them to the laundry room. He beckoned Donna over to stand in front of his chair. He stood outside the furniture area, about twenty feet away.

"Watch this," he said.

Donna was puzzled. She didn't know what he was referring to. But she began to feel a little aroused, and smiled. *I guess having the shit scared out of me makes me horny.*

Paul watched her, interested. She began to feel more aroused, began to feel wet. She was starting to feel embarrassed because Paul could see her arousal. But it became more intense, an irresistible urge to touch herself, to rub her crotch, to try to relieve that insistent nagging stimulation.

But she could do nothing. Her wrists were crossed and clipped tight against her back. She was getting desperate. She looked around for something solid that she could straddle and rub against. *I can't stand this! Maybe the coffee table.* She started toward it, but the fierce need made her suddenly unable to walk. She dropped to her knees, her eyes flooding with tears. She dropped over onto her side, crooked one leg and rocked herself side to side, crying unashamedly, howling with need.

Another feeling. Now the stimulation that she craved. She rolled onto her back, oblivious to the discomfort in her shoulders. She braced against the floor and thrust herself upward to meet the phantom stimulus. She rocked her hips side to side, felt the orgasm take her, and take her. Minute after minute after minute, the pleasure filling her belly, radiating in waves through her chest and her face, tensing her legs until she was on her back with her legs out straight, feet pointed out, toes curled. She was screaming in pleasure. The orgasm rocked her, ravaged her. Her breathing became fast deep gasps. The floor was glossed by her sweat everywhere around her.

Still the orgasm continued until she could no longer hold her legs up, and her head rolled to one side. The sensation was still there but her muscles could no longer sustain it. Slowly, the waves of pleasure subsided, and she lay in her puddle of sweat, exhausted and breathless.

Paul walked over and stood above her.

"Wasn't that a good trick? Danielle taught me how to do that."

Donna was wide eyed and gasping. "Christ, Paul!"

"You can't even object. You specifically agreed that I could do this to you."

She shook her head. She was too exhausted to speak.

Paul stood over her, watching her with clinical interest. When he thought that she had recovered sufficiently, he helped her to her feet. He knelt and examined her leg as she rested her weight on his shoulder.

"The dog broke the skin on your ankle," he said. "You've got some claw marks on your tits. That place where you fell on your hip looks like it will bruise. That and all the cuts from earlier, and my work of art is all marked up."

"I'm sorry," she said wearily.

He helped her walk back to his office where he kept the keys. She sank to her knees while he was removing the cuffs.

"Poor baby," he said as he leaned down and kissed her. "We've completely worn you out." He stood back up. "I think I'll make you sleep in the belly chain and collar. But I'll take them off long enough to get you cleaned up. Let's go on upstairs."

He helped her to her feet, but her legs gave out. He caught her before she fell.

"I can't walk," she said, and she began crying.

He maneuvered her past the office doorway. "No problem," he said. He bent down and pulled her forward across his shoulder. "I'll carry you." He stood and started toward the elevator.

"What you've learned today," he said as he bore her across the living room, "is that we're not just playing. And you *are* under my control.

Chapter Twenty-Five: A Little Help From My Friends

Sheriff Donna Parker-McCready leaned back in her office chair and mused about the weekend. She put her feet on the desk and considered her shoes. It was so weird to be dressed, with panties and slacks and socks and even heavy shoes laced to her feet. It was like being in disguise.

On Sunday, Paul had had a brief episode of nicey-nice and taken her to breakfast. Then he'd had her put on a bikini and, over that, a shirt and shorts, and driven her to Clearwater Beach to splash around in the waves of the Gulf of Mexico, where the water was emerald green and warm as soup. Afterward, a little random shopping so Donna could buy souvenir knick knacks she'd never look at again, then to a pleasant seafood restaurant where Donna had blackened grouper, and a salad, and two…two!...sweet drinks with umbrellas. Paul had treated her like a pampered mistress the day after he had scared the shit out of her and left her physically exhausted.

For all his scary talk, Paul is pretty nice to me. He's not a big teddy bear, but he is loveable.

A movie, a nice dinner, and he had brought her home to strip naked beside the car. Still in nicey nice mode, he hadn't chained her, so when it was time to walk the pets, her hands were free. He'd sent her to fetch her leash, and she did. She had returned to him on all fours, holding the leash in her mouth. He'd laughed, patted her on the head, and fed her a dog biscuit before heading her for the door, still on hands and knees. A sharp tug on the leash had brought her to her feet, and he'd cuffed her hands behind her.

When he had set her free to run and play with the dogs, she had done so. But she'd spent more time than usual on the ground. When the playful dogs knocked her down, she had wrestled with them, rolled over, and stayed on her hands and knees…lunging at them, growling at them, imitating barking at them. When Paul called her back, she'd stayed on all fours for the hundred feet back to where he was standing. Then she'd stood on her knees in begging position. Paul had laughed and given her a dog biscuit. *If he wants me to be a dog, I'll be a fricking dog.*

She was going to be on all fours a lot now. *I wonder where that will lead.*

She hadn't yet processed Paul's demonstration of his power over her. She'd decided though, that she was not going to get out of line, and she was going to tighten up on her compliance with his orders to assume particular positions, or to dance for him, or to fetch something for him. *No slack. No lollygagging. I'm going to be his little machine*.

The intercom sounded.

"Sheriff, I have a Miss Travis on the phone for you." Donna shook her head. Thoughts about her home life had been infiltrating into her work life. *Can't have that.* She picked up the phone. "Sheriff Parker."

"Hi, Donna. This is Danielle. I wonder if you'd mind if I dropped by your office."

"If you mean now, it's fine. I don't have anything on for the next two hours."

"I'll be right over. Thanks."

Danielle arrived fifteen minutes later, wearing a black, suitable for business skirt, a ruffled white blouse, and a sleeveless jacket. Donna took her feet off the desk and motioned for Danielle to come in.

"Sheriff," Danielle greeted her.

Donna rose and shook her hand. "Ms. Travis. To what do we owe this visit?"

"We haven't spoken since…"

"Since you used me for a Barbie doll?"

Danielle looked down in disappointment. "You were angry about that. I'm sorry."

Donna laughed. "It's not your fault. Paul sprang it on me as part of his head game."

"I didn't know…"

"Paul is entitled to do whatever he wishes with his slave," Donna said. "It's none of my business, really. I just comply."

Danielle raised an eyebrow. "That's a very strange attitude."

"It's what we are," Donna said. "I'll admit that I was uncomfortable, but only because I was surprised. I didn't like all the costumes, but some of them were quite nice. I especially like the satin greeting robe. And the photographs were beautiful. So, thank you, Danielle."

Danielle shook her head, confused. "So we're cool?"

"Well," Donna said, "you are a vampire, so we're not *that* cool. But I've talked about you with Paul, and he's starting to convince me. As he pointed out, if he were working with a general, I wouldn't be worried about the guy's death toll."

"That's an interesting way to look at it."

"It isn't a perfect analogy, but let's not worry about my qualms. You're wondering about your note?"

"My prayer," Danielle said.

Donna nodded soberly. "I burned it in my incense burner. That's all I can do. We'll have to wait and see if she appears to you."

"Thank you," Danielle told her. "I sincerely appreciate this. I know how hard it is for you to overcome your…feelings."

Donna shrugged.

"So, how are you and Paul getting along now?"

Donna gave a tight smile. "He seems to want me to be a dog, now."

"Really?"

Donna told her about the belly rubs and the dog biscuits. Danielle cracked up with laughter. "Just talking with you and Paul, nobody would know you two are this crazy."

"Now you know," Donna said.

"How far will you go with it?"

"As far as Paul wants to take it. Like I said, I have no standing to object to anything. If he wants me to be a dog, I'll be a dog."

There was a knock on the door. "Come in," Donna called.

Whitey Ferris came through the door. He froze when he saw Danielle.

"I believe that you've met Danielle Travis," Donna said.

Danielle stood. "It's nice to see you again, Lieutenant," Danielle said. She extended her hand. Whitey shook it.

"It's nice to see you, too," Whitey replied, obviously lying. "Sheriff, we've got a standoff out by Harm Lake Road."

"What kind of standoff?"

"We have half a dozen deputies backing up Al Cadbury at a ranch about a mile off Harm Lake, just this side of the county line. He went out to talk to Bob Elledge."

"Who's Bob Elledge?"

Whitey rolled his eyes. "It turns out that Bob Elledge is the dude who was shacking up with Teresa Torricelli. Al Cadbury traced him to this ranch and went out to talk to the dude. But apparently a bunch of weirdos is holed up there, and they won't let him in without a warrant. They're brandishing weapons from behind cover inside the property."

Donna shook her head. "They don't have to let us in. The guy won't even come to the gate and talk?"

"Apparently not."

"Do you think they would let us in if we obtained a material witness warrant?"

"Beats me. I'm not the expert on weirdo."

Danielle suppressed a giggle.

"I hope shooting doesn't break out. Where is this place?"

"I don't know. Dispatch has the info."

"I guess Dispatch is doing this by phone? I didn't hear any radio traffic." Donna kept a scanner at low volume and mostly ignored it.

"I didn't know anything until Dispatch called my cell."

Donna nodded. "I think I'm going out there and take a look. Maybe I can get things calmed down."

"Do you want me to go with you, Sheriff?" Whitey asked.

"No, I'm hoping that the weirdos won't be so hostile to a woman." *And weirdos are probably racists.*

Donna turned to Danielle. "Danielle, do you want to come with?"

"Sure," Danielle replied. "I've got nothing going till late afternoon."

ଓଃ

Donna was violating her own policy about civilian ride-alongs. Danielle hadn't filled out any of the requisite paperwork and hadn't passed any background check. That concern flickered through Donna's mind as she turned off the paved road onto the unmarked dirt trail that Dispatch had assured her led to the Bedford Ranch. Donna didn't know the place. It was probably one of the surviving cattle operations that dotted the agriculturally zoned parts of the county. The scene wasn't hard to find. There were a string of police cruisers lining the narrow sand road.

Donna walked up to Leroi Adkins, the shift commander. Adkins was a middle aged African American whose flat top white hair made him look, as Paul had once remarked, like a walking brush. He wore black rimmed eyeglasses and had a pear shaped body. His appearance always made Donna smile.

She introduced Danielle and listened to Adkins report.

"Where are our guys?" Donna asked.

"They're forward along the drive. The gate is about a hundred feet away from here."

Donna nodded. Her view of the scene was blocked by brush. She walked forward on the sand road, careful to stay behind the cruisers for cover. Behind the scrub was a large cleared area along the drive. At the end of the drive there was a metal rail fence and gate. Beyond the fence, three men loitered, carrying rifles. *Hunting rifles, not assault rifles. A good sign.* Between the gate and the open pasture was a long flattop berm. *A bad sign.*

She saw one deputy crouched behind a stand of oak saplings, his pistol drawn and aimed at the three ranch people. She couldn't see anyone else.

She walked back to where Danielle and Adkins were standing. "I don't like this," she said. "We don't have eyes on everybody. There's a good chance that we'll lose people if shooting starts. Let's back off. If we need to crash the place, we'll bring in the Tac Team and run our APC through that gate."

Adkins didn't quite get her drift. "You're saying you want us to pull out?"

"Yes," Donna said. "In good order. The most forward guys back out first. The guys behind them will cover."

"Yes, sir…I mean yes, ma'am, Sheriff." Adkins stepped away and spoke into his mobile.

Soon there were eight deputies, some armed with AR-15s, some with riot guns, standing in a cluster beyond the line of cars. Donna walked up to them. "I'm going to drive up there and see if they'll listen to me. Get in position to respond if I call you or if there are gunshots."

There was silence, then Adkins shouted. "You heard the Sheriff. Get in line, ready to deploy."

Donna headed for her cruiser. She was surprised when Danielle got into the passenger seat beside her.

As Donna drove up the short driveway, she looked around. She didn't like the tactical situation. A roughly fifty foot strip of land had been cleared and mowed along the fence line. Between the sand road and the cleared area was perhaps another fifty feet of oak scrub…small trees, most about as thick as a man's arm. Poor cover. Sixty or seventy feet beyond the fence was a berm, maybe eight feet high and two hundred feet long, with an opening for the driveway. Donna couldn't see a purpose for the berm except as defensive cover. Somebody who would spend the time and money to build something like that must have been pre-planning a battle.

Or maybe he has a naked sex slave he doesn't want seen from the road.

She stopped the car and stepped out. It annoyed her to see Danielle get out of the car, too. Donna looked at the three men beyond the gate. Two hung back, their rifles pointed at the ground. The third approached the gate. Donna liked his looks. He was in his mid to late twenties; was tall, broad shouldered, flat bellied, had greasy straight black hair, and a short well-trimmed beard. He wore faded jeans and a damp wrinkled blue shirt which was open down to his belt line. His skin glistened with sweat. The bill of his ballcap was tipped back and he had a big smile on his face. His short carbine rested on his shoulder.

Get me a little drunk and I'd do him.

Donna walked up to the gate. "Are you the owner of this ranch?"

"What happened, darlin'?" Donna was impressed with his Deep South drawl. She liked Southern accents. "The he-men gave up and they sent in the pussy brigade?"

"I'm the Sheriff of this county. It is my understanding that Bob Elledge is staying here."

"Whether he is or he ain't, you're not getting onto this property."

Donna sighed. "If we want to get onto this property, we will call and get a warrant. Then, we will bring in a SWAT team and a helicopter. We'll burn the house down and shoot anybody who runs out of it. If you follow the news, you'll know that's how I'll handle it."

The man laughed and spit on the ground. "She-yit! You're a tough talking little honey, aren't you."

Donna's face reddened.

The man laughed again. "You're not going to get a warrant. You can't get a warrant to talk to somebody. And who you gonna serve it on, anyway? So talk bad all you want. You're out there. We're in here."

Danielle, in stocking feet, stepped beside Donna. "Do you want me to handle this, Sheriff?"

Donna blinked, caught off guard.

"So what are you going to do?" the man taunted.

In a flash, Danielle had jumped the fence. The subject had just enough time to bring his gun off his shoulder. Danielle seized it by the barrel and smashed it onto the fence rail. The carbine broke in half. Danielle threw the man onto the ground. He looked up in terror as Danielle knelt, her knee on his chest.

The other two men sprang into action. They stepped forward and pointed their rifles at Danielle. Donna had been stunned into passivity. Now she drew her Glock.

No need. Danielle turned toward the men and gave them a withering glare. They dropped their firearms into the dirt and took off running along the fence.

As Donna watched in horror, Danielle flicked open a butterfly knife. She held up the rifleman's wrist and made a cut. Blood poured from the incision. Danielle bent down and clamped her mouth onto the bloody wrist.

It took Donna a few moments to overcome her disbelief. She climbed over the fence and walked over to Danielle, her pistol pointed and ready to fire.

"Jesus Christ, Danielle!"

Danielle held up a hand, motioning her to wait.

Donna stood, both hands on her Glock, trembling, while Danielle finished. "You can't do that, Danielle," she said. "I'm going to have to arrest you."

Danielle stood and used the back of her hand to wipe blood from her mouth. "A girl's got to eat," she said.

"Still…"

"You're not going to arrest me, because he won't file charges." She turned to the man, who was now sitting up. "You okay, hon? Did you want to press charges against me?"

The man grinned. "No way. That felt good."

"See," Danielle said. She stood up and confidently paced through the opening in the berm. "Nobody here except cows," she called. "Go get the car."

Seriously rattled, Donna opened the gates and walked back to the cruiser.

ঔ

The main ranch house was a worn two story building with a covered front porch and rust streaked tin roofing. Donna and Danielle were met on the front porch by an elderly man wearing a straw hat, a yellowing tee shirt, and bib overalls with one strap dangling. He looked at the two women with rheumy eyes. He seemed to be far gone into confusion. "We're here to see Bob Elledge," Donna announced.

"Inside," he said in a throaty voice. Donna took that as an invitation to enter.

The house was not well-maintained, although it did have some modern features. The front door, for example, had a steel casing for the cheery light blue steel door, a model straight from Lowes or Home Depot. There was shiny bead board wainscoting, but the varnish was worn from the hardwood floors. Donna had her gun drawn, pointed down, her elbows against her chest. She proceeded slowly past the staircase, down a long dingy foyer.

At the end of the hallway was a large room, worn wood floors covered with bright area rugs. Several men were lounging on worn sofas watching a large screen television.

"Which one of you is Bob Elledge?" Donna demanded loudly.

A young man stood up. He was in his late twenties, early thirties. He was wearing worn khakis and a square cut checked shirt that wasn't tucked in. He seemed pale for somebody who lived on a ranch. His light brown hair was curly and needed combing. "I am." He said. He was grinning until he saw Donna's pistol. "Whoa, what's this?"

"We want you to come with us. We want to take you in for questioning in regard to a homicide."

He raised his hands. "Sure, no problem. But I don't know anything. You don't have to shoot me."

"Turn around and put your hands behind your back. When he complied, Donna holstered her weapon and took out the handcuffs.

"That isn't necessary. I'll come in peacefully."

"It's just a precaution, sir."

"What the hell," Elledge said. "You can't be too careful nowadays."

When Donna reached the sand road and the cluster of deputies, she let Elledge out of the car. She motioned to Al Cadbury. "Here he is. He's been cooperative so far. I haven't read him his rights yet. Do it before you start out."

Cadbury, a pudgy man who was sensitive to heat, was sweating profusely. Donna was worried about him. "You okay, Sergeant?"

"I'll be fine as soon as I get some AC."

Donna laughed.

Danielle got out of the car, stood up, and looked around. Leroi Adkins walked up to her. He stared at the hand sized bloodstain on her blouse. "What happened to you?"

"Nosebleed," she said.

ઉ૪૭

The first few minutes of the drive back were taken up by Donna's obligatory rant about drinking blood during police calls. "I'm sorry, Sheriff," Danielle told her. "But it's been a couple of weeks, and there was an opportunity."

"So you have to drink blood, what? Every two weeks."

"About," Danielle said.

"What happens if you don't?"

"You feel hungrier and hungrier. It bothers you just a little at first. Then the hunger grows until, finally, you're so desperate that the need is uncontrollable. That's when we're dangerous, Donna. But if we just charm a person once in a while and nip a little of their blood, we're just like everybody else."

"What about the owners of the blood?"

"They experience it as a pleasurable event. Most of the time, we do it along with sex. If you're like me, just starting out, you do a one night stand once in a while. The older vampires usually develop familiars. Michael, for example, is very good at getting a circle of people who are addicted to him."

"Women?"

"Sure. Michael is male."

"That's why you broke up?"

Danielle sighed. "Partly. But Michael was setting himself up in Malibu. I was a drudge for a law firm in San Francisco. We couldn't see each other enough to maintain a relationship."

Donna shook her head.

"Screwing men just for their blood…that doesn't sound like a very satisfactory life."

"It's better than not screwing men at all. What's your motivation for screwing Paul?"

Donna was thrown by the question. "Sex. He's a great lover."

"How about the other stuff? I bet you could have sex with him without the bondage, without being his slave."

Donna sighed. "We did that for a long time. But this is a need I have. There is something inside me that makes me need to be humiliated and enslaved. Paul understands it and he does what I need him to do."

"It all boils down to a penis, doesn't it?"

"Excuse me?"

"If a woman wants to have a normal life…a family, children…she needs to attract somebody with a penis to make that happen. If she's lucky, she finds the one. If she's less lucky, she becomes a single mother. If she's not lucky, she stays single and gets laid occasionally, until she's not attractive any more. She spends her middle and old age alone and bitter. In your case, you had these burning needs. But you had to find a person with a penis to fulfill them for you. Otherwise you would have been dissatisfied and frustrated your whole life."

Donna considered this.

"What happened to you, Danielle?"

"Law school. Working as an associate and making the billable hours quota. You can't meet anyone that way…you can't get to know anyone that way. I was in my late twenties still doing one night stands. It got worse. I was working for a vampire who kept me *charmed* and anemic. Eventually, the *charm* didn't quite work. I was still under compulsion, but I knew what was going on. Maybe they closed up the bite marks with vampire blood a little too often and I developed some immunity. If it weren't for Michael, I would either be dead or wandering around some city with my personality erased."

Donna was shocked. "I didn't realize…"

"If I could go back and start again, I wouldn't have gone to law school. I'd have gone into something else and gotten married in my early twenties. I'd have a house and children by now."

"You don't want eternal life?"

"Look at me, Donna! I'm a freaking ghost. Twenty minutes in the sun and my skin is sunburned. I can't eat a freaking pizza! I'll never have a family. I'll never even have a husband. I'm a freak. I live at the edge of humanity. Vampires don't have a culture. There's no vampire civilization, no vampire scientists or vampire artists. There are humans…all that stuff is human. And I'm not human."

Donna was shocked to see bloody tears stream down Danielle's face.

Danielle continued: "I read a book once. It was an old book called *On the Beach*. It was about people in Australia after a nuclear war had destroyed the Northern Hemisphere. Fallout had spread around the world and the characters were waiting for it to arrive. They were the last people on earth and they were waiting for a slow, painful death. The book was so sad I couldn't finish it.

"That's how it will end for me, Donna. Me and a few vampires. Alone, in an empty world. That's eternal life."

Donna said nothing.

"That's why I need to see the Mother Goddess, Donna. I need to know if there is something else beyond this life. That's why I so want you to be my friend. Donna, I am so fucking alone!"

ᴄᴚᴐ

Bob Elledge was a tough nut to crack. Donna had just finished a slightly late talk to a Rotary Club luncheon, and the detectives were still trying to get something from Elledge.

"Fucking psychopath," Klass told her as she came into the little room behind the mirror. "He is smooth."

"So just tell us what you did to Teresa," Cadbury was conducting the interrogation, with Whitey Ferris by his side.

"I didn't do anything to Teresa. I shacked up with her for a while, that's all."

"You didn't get curious when you didn't hear from her for month after month?"

"No, man," Elledge replied. "We were broke up. I didn't expect to hear from her."

"I understand," Cadbury said unctuously. "You're breaking up, you're arguing. It gets physical, you lose control. It's not really your fault…"

"Damn right it's not my fault. Because I didn't do anything to her."

Cadbury sighed. "You're not helping yourself here."

"Look," Elledge said, "I understand what you're doing. You guys are looking for whoever killed Teresa, and I'm an old boyfriend and you're taking a run at me. But I didn't do it. You're wasting your time. And mine."

"Goddammit!" Whitey exploded. "Don't tell us how to do our jobs." He slammed the table for emphasis. "You were pissed because your girlfriend was breaking up with you, you couldn't take it, so you killed her. You're not unique. It's an old story. We've heard it dozens of times. You can help yourself, tell us what happened, and your side of the story goes on the record. The State Attorney might cut you a deal. Otherwise, we're going to take our time, build the evidence, and you'll get the death penalty without anybody hearing your side of things."

Elledge was not intimidated. "I'd tell you a story, if I had one. But I don't. Teresa and I broke up. I moved out of her crib. I haven't seen nor heard of her since."

"Look," Cadbury said, "we've got four witnesses who will testify that you told them on separate occasions that you were going to kill Teresa Torricelli."

"No, you don't," Elledge said simply.

Donna suppressed a laugh.

"So," Whitey demanded, "if you didn't kill her, who did?"

Elledge shrugged. "Dunno. I didn't know she was dead until you dudes told me."

"If you're so innocent, why wouldn't they let us into the compound to talk to you?" Cadbury asked.

"It's not a compound. It's a ranch. They're all into this patriot thing…the Constitution, that old timey stuff, you know. They're especially big on the Fourth Amendment. But if they'd told me you were there, I would have come out."

Donna could see Whitey wrinkle his face in frustration.

"Can you account for your whereabouts in October, 2011?" Whitey asked.

"2011? Shit, who remembers? Can you tell me where you were in some month in 2011?"

"We're asking the questions," Whitey said.

Elledge thought for a moment. "2011, 2011…wait, I was in the UP in October."

"Where the hell is UP?"

"Michigan. The Upper Penninsula. I was working for Wyles Electric. They sent me up to help finish a project they'd fallen behind on."

"Bullshit!" Cadbury said. "You need to be union to do electrical work in Michigan."

"I'm in the IBEW," Elledge said. "My card's in my billfold."

"Check it out," Donna said to Klass.

"When did you supposedly do this work?" Cadbury demanded.

"September sixteen to December first."

Whitey closed his eyes. "Do you need a break?"

"I'm good," Elledge replied, "but if you guys…"

"We'll just wait for a few minutes," Whitey said.

Klass didn't take long. "I gave Wyles a call. They operate in five states. They verified Elledge's employment and that he was working in Michigan September through November, 2011. They're faxing the payroll records."

Donna keyed the speaker mike. "Guys, the Michigan story checks out."

Elledge grinned. "So, can I go now?"

Whitey nodded and Elledge stood.

"One more thing," Whitey said suddenly. "Why did you break up with Teresa?"

Elledge shrugged. "She was banging this other dude. I don't share, you know."

"Who was this other dude?" Whitey asked wearily.

"Some hardass cop. Some simple ass name…let me think." Whitey fidgeted. "Oh, yeah. Gibbs, his name was. Nathan Gibbs."

ශ්‍ර

Donna's last bit of work for the day was to give a little talk to a 5:30 criminal justice class at the community college. The class had gone a little over, and she didn't get home until almost 7:30. As she walked into the living room, naked except for her dog collar, she heard Paul call out, "Howdy, Sheriff."

Donna looked around at saw him standing beside the bar. She paused to see if there would be any deviation from the routine. "Go on and get cleaned up," Paul told her dismissively.

Today, Donna had learned something about Paul. She had brought Danielle Travis back to the Sheriff's Office, let her clean up in

Donna's personal bathroom, and lent her a white shirt to replace her bloody blouse. She had actually felt sympathetic to Danielle, and had understood her pain. *But Paul has always been sympathetic to her. He always saw her humanity.* Something clicked. Jerry Corbin had once told her something that Paul had never told her: That Corbin had shown up at Conquest Security, crippled, homeless, and unbathed. Paul had given him $3000 and the use of a car so that he could find a place to stay and get cleaned up enough for Paul to legitimately hire him. Donna had attributed that to Paul's solidarity with another Iraq veteran. *But really, Paul is just a very kind man.*

He was compassionate toward people whom others despised: A homeless war veteran, a vampire…*a crazy masochistic woman.* She suddenly understood the depth of Paul's love for her, that he would go to such lengths to meet her needs. *I didn't really understand him.*

When she returned downstairs, she put her hands atop her head and did her pirouette. "Your sex toy is all clean and ready for use."

Paul smiled and stepped toward her. She placed her hands behind her back and assumed her at-ease pose. "Long day today, Donna?"

She stepped forward and dropped to her knees. She unzipped his pants. "Shall I take care of your needs first, my lord?"

He patted her on the head. "If we're going to do that, let me sit down on the sofa. She waited until he had sat down, then got down on all fours and crawled to him. She unzipped him, gave his member a couple of squeezes, and then plunged it into her mouth. She gave it her best effort and it didn't take long for him to finish, and she took her time releasing him. She sat back on her heels.

He leaned forward and patted her head. "That was one of your best efforts. Why are you so frisky tonight, Donna?"

"Sir, I decided that I've been slacking off in my sex slave duties. From here on, I'm going all out to be the best slave possible."

He smiled. He reached into his shirt pocket and produced a dog biscuit. She grinned as she chewed it.

"That's good. I'll make sure you maintain the effort. Stand up and turn around."

She obeyed, and he cuffed her hands behind her. He attached the leash, blindfolded her, then grasped her shoulders and had her turn back and forth until she was disoriented. He got a rough, tight grip on her upper arm and led her away.

When they stopped, he said, “I’ve come to see the advantages of very short leashes. They allow for more professional handling, as you put it. Get on your knees and sit back on your heels. Keep your knees together.”

She did as he told her. “I’m going to bend you all the way forward,” he said. She allowed him to push her shoulders forward until her forehead was touching the floor. She felt him attach the leash.

“In my spare time, I’ve been putting eyebolts throughout the house, so there will be lots of convenient places to chain you.”

He walked away. She found that she could lift her head no more than three inches from the floor. Her torso was folded tight against her thighs, a nice display position, she realized. Someone approaching would see the arch of her back, her slightly raised ass, and the soles of her feet. She wondered how long she would remain here. *However long he wants.* She sighed and relaxed, and lapsed into daydreaming. She was not physically comfortable, but she loved the unyielding restraints.

He returned to get her after what she felt to be a short time. He guided her through the house until she felt cool tile against her feet. She knew that she was in the kitchen. He stopped, released the handcuffs, removed the leash, and finally took off the blindfold.

She saw two places set at the table.

“Why doesn’t my best possible sex slave sit at the table and have dinner with me, and tell me about her day.”

Chapter Twenty-Six: Sweet Dreams

Donna wakes up in a brightly lit room. She is naked, and lying on a hard floor. The floor, she sees, is dark red ceramic tile. She looks up to see that the wall is made of cinder blocks, painted a glossy gray. She realizes that she is completely naked. She is in a cell.

The cell is no wider than a queen sized bed. She can spread her arms and touch each opposite wall. It is slightly longer than she is tall. Lying stretched out, she can touch her feet to the wall beside the dark gray steel door. Perhaps two feet past her head is a Turkish toilet, rising inches out of the floor. So the cell is about five feet by eight feet. There is no cot, nor blanket, or anything she can use to cover herself.

The ceiling of the cell is high above her. It appears to be made of cast concrete. The marks from the forms are still visible under the gray paint. There are fluorescent light fixtures with bare bright tubes, and in each corner there are video cameras pointed down...big, obvious cameras painted dull beige, the lenses set back in metal shades to protect against glare.

She has no idea where she is, or why she is here. But she is confined in a very small cell, and whoever put her here is watching her.

She lies in a fetal position, her body pressed against the hard tile, full of fear and trying to remember. She recalls nothing. She begins to cry.

She lies there crying for a long time.

She hears the frightening noise of the door lock, and the whining screech of the hinges of the heavy door. People walk in and stand around her. At first, all she sees is their boots. But looking up, she sees that they are wearing blue uniforms with patent leather belts that hold keys and pepper gas tubes and stun guns. They have police style caps. Two of them, the men, are wearing mirrored sunglasses and carry long wooden batons. The third is a woman with short blonde hair and blue, hate filled eyes. She carries an instrument which is a flexible stick wound with leather and with a wide triangular leather flap at the end.

Donna straightens up when the woman strikes her bottom with the leather weapon. "Get up, you lazy slut!" the woman hisses. Donna starts to rise but one of the men kicks her hard in the ribs with the side of his boot. The other grasps her hair and pulls her up to her knees. The woman sneers and slaps the leather tool into Donna's breasts.

One of the men grabs a hank of her hair and uses it to steer her as they muscle her out of the cell.

Beyond the cell door is another room, larger than the cell itself. There are eyebolts in the walls, and from some of them cuffs hang on chains. There is a metal chair, and a metal stool against one wall. There is a yellow garden hose rolled up and connected to a spigot. There are coils of nylon rope next to it. The room is made of block and painted a dark red, almost brown. There are no cameras here. She is sick with fear.

"Bend the bitch over," the woman commands. One man holds her shoulders so that her butt is higher than her head. The woman slaps her hard across the ass with the leather weapon. One of the men prods her vulva with his baton, sliding it against her opening. Donna is crying uncontrollably. They wrap a heavy chain around her waist. They straighten her up, put cuffs on her wrists, and lock her wrists to the chain against her belly. They cuff her legs and give her enough chain that she can walk if they hold her upright.

"You've got a visitor, you useless whore," the woman tells her.

Outside the room is a long hallway, with blue steel doors every few feet. They manhandle her down the hallway to a big room. There is a big reinforced window on the wall beside the door. Otherwise, the room is dull gray block with a floor covered in chipped yellowing white vinyl. There is a gray table in the center of the room. There is one metal chair on one side of the table, two chairs on the other side.

They sit her in the chair and leave the room.

There is a door that Donna hadn't previously seen on the other side of the room. It opens. A woman walks in. She is short and very shapely, with large breasts and beautifully sculpted legs. Her hair is light brown and cascades in waves down to her waist. She is nude. Her pubic hair is very light brown and sparse, a discreet round patch above her sex. The woman's face is round and gentle, her lips thick and sensuous, her eyes wide and brown.

This is not her usual aspect, but it is the Mother Goddess.

The Goddess remains standing.

"Hello, Ba-el Shanah," the Goddess says.

Donna tips her head forward. "My mother."

"You are far from Koth, my daughter, and far from the real. In this world, you are called Donna. Is that correct?"

"I don't know, my mother. I am dreaming."

"So you are, my daughter."

"It isn't a nice dream, my Mother."

"You are a captive in all the worlds, Donna. Do they treat you worse here than in Koth?"

"In Koth and in the real, my lord is Paul. I thrive on his torments."

The Goddess touches Donna's face, and Donna feels the warmth and love spread through her body, cell by cell. "If you keep spinning this world, my daughter, you will eventually create Paul here, too."

"I don't like this world, my Mother."

The Goddess smiles, and love radiates from her face. "I see that. But we are here for a reason. We will dwell here but a short time."

The door opens and a woman enters. She is wearing a dark red knee-length cocktail dress with a square neckline. She has on red shoes with five inch heels. She is pale, an ivory carving come to life. The rouge on her face and the blue makeup around her eyes makes her look like an antique porcelain doll. She carries a red patent leather purse.

The woman takes a seat across from Donna. "Hello, Danielle," the standing Goddess says.

Danielle looks around. "Where is this? Who are you?"

"I am called, by some, Antala. I am the Mother of Worlds."

"The Mother Goddess?"

"Yes," the Goddess replies.

"Why are you naked?"

The Goddess laughs, and the sound is beautiful, like the chirping of birds in the morning. "What need do I have of clothing, Danielle? I am the wind, and the rain, and the sunshine, and the cold. I am pure thought, and this form is pure thought. I assume it so that you can see me."

"Why are we here?"

"You asked my daughter to arrange a meeting. We are in this place, because we are in Donna's dream. My daughter, Donna, loves captivity and prisons. She makes worlds where she is a captive or a slave."

"Are we in the Miasma?"

"Everything, Danielle, is in the Miasma, even the real. But this is a dream world that Donna has made."

"It will be gone when she wakes up?"

The Goddess took time to consider. "Danielle, Donna is my daughter and she is a maker of worlds. In the real, when someone creates something, she starts at the beginning and works forward. In the Miasma, there is no beginning and no end. To create, one starts in the middle. To create a world, you start with a scene, an instant in time. Donna was in a cell. Why? If she likes, she can go back and create an account of how she got there. Then the guards...who are they, where did they come from? So, she creates from the middle. If she wishes to spend more time in this world, she can develop it, and it will go on and on, with its creator constantly creating the past. But if she awakes and forgets the dream, the world will go away."

"I don't like this world," Danielle grumps.

The Goddess smiles. "Donna?"

"I don't like it, either," Donna says.

Now they are on a great marble floor. In front of them, in the distance, is a gazebo, a pitched tile roof held up by fluted stone columns. Behind them is the carved stone balustrade. It is night. A giant orange moon dominates the sky, so close that the wrinkles of mountain ranges and the debris around craters is clearly visible.

The Goddess is different, too. She is in her usual form, tall and thin with carved legs and broad shoulders and flowing, nearly black hair. She is wearing a buckskin tunic that hangs a third of the way down her thighs, barely providing modesty.

Danielle still wears her red dress. Donna is still naked, her hands chained against her belly, her feet hobbled. "Better?" the Goddess asks.

"Why is Donna still chained and naked?" Danielle asks.

"It is Donna's dream," the Goddess replies. "Donna?"

The chains vanish, and Donna finds herself in the red satin greeting gown that Danielle chose for her in the real. Donna can't move without showing a breast, or parting the skirt to uncover her ass and her sex. But Donna likes it, as does Danielle.

The familiar dark haired women appear, their ample breasts jiggling as they carry out the stone table. The women are young with olive skin and doe eyes. They have ropes tied around their waists from which hang small rough woven hemp aprons that conceal their sex. They are otherwise nude. Chairs appear magically. The Goddess sits at the end of the table. Donna sits with the balustrade behind her. Danielle sits facing her.

"What is this place?" Danielle asks.

The Goddess smiles. "This is the island between the worlds," she says. "It was built by my daughter, Donna, whose true name in all the worlds is Ba-el Shanah. If you would dwell in the Miasma, you will find yourself in a quilt of worlds, one bleeding into another. Or, the Miasma is an endless set of island worlds, with endless nothing between them. It's a trick, you see. If you see nothing between the worlds, you can move from one to the other without effort, as does my daughter, Donna-Ba-el Shanah. But if you see nothing *you fall into the endless sea of nothingness, true death.*

"The Miasma seethes with all the thoughts of all the people who ever were and whoever will be. The strong can make worlds from nothingness and live there for a time. The weak dissipate into incoherent waves of thought. Am I answering your questions, Danielle?"

"If Donna is your daughter, and creates worlds, why is she a slave in all the worlds she creates?"

"When I say that she is my daughter, I am saying that I created her especially for myself. But she also created me. I would have no presence in the real, except for my daughter. I am thought, you see, and her thought gives me this form. I am always with her, because I live inside her. But we are different facets of the same being. I am thought and I am perfect freedom. She loves the life of a captive, and prefers to dwell in chains and slavery.

"But I would not abandon my daughter to cruel and malicious masters. I have made for her a True Lord, a strong master who

subjugates her and overrides her will, who keeps her chained and enslaved. But he also loves her and protects her and honors her. He owns her, but in doing so, he allows her to own him. He is her master and she his slave in all the worlds. Their love is eternal."

"What about me?" Danielle asks. "Will I live eternally in the Miasma?"

"Ultimately, all beings are thought and thought is eternal. In the real, you are a vampire and the offspring of the vetala. In the Miasma, you will be something else in whatever world you dwell. You will not be Danielle Travis, the vampire, but you will be a conscious being. If you can find your way to this place, this island among the worlds, you can move between worlds as my daughter does, as the gods do. Would you drink the purple wine of life so that you can return here whenever you wish?"

"I will do it," Danielle says.

Big glazed ceramic mugs appear from nowhere on the table. A young woman, naked except for her loin clout, carries a huge pitcher to the table, but pours the wine without effort.

The Goddess holds up her mug. "This wine is nectar, made from pomegranate seeds, which are the magic of return. If you drink this wine and you are dead, you return here but cannot reenter the real. But if you drink it when you are alive in the real, this stone island is your gateway to the Miasma. Drink, Danielle, and you can always return to Ba-el Shanah's stone island."

The Goddess and Donna drink from their cups. Danielle hesitates but then, holding the mug with both hands, gulps the nectar down.

Donna finds herself in blackness. She realizes that she is lying down and, in a few moments, discovers that she is in a bed. She feels along her body and discovers that she is naked. But then, she feels her neck. She is wearing a thick collar, leather, with a metal disk in front. She remembers now. She is in the real and she is Donna. She blindly reaches around until she touches the man under the sheet beside her. This is her true lord, Paul McCready in the real, Paul of Koth in her favorite dream world. The Goddess created this man to humiliate and enslave her daughter Donna, but also to love and to cherish her. Donna is his slave, and loves him without bound.

She raises the sheet and snuggles against him, his butt resting against her crotch and belly, her breasts flat against his back. She loves the collar that shows that she is his slave. And she loves him. She is so filled with love for him that she begins to cry.

ଔଓ

After a nice dinner, which Donna had eaten using utensils and sitting at the table, Paul had taken Donna outside for a game of fetch. When both she and the dogs were exhausted, he gave her a dog biscuit and had her walk back to the house on hands and knees at the end of a leash. She finished the evening blindfolded with her hands cuffed behind her and kneeling, face to the floor, restrained by a short chain.

Paul released the neck chain and helped her stand. "Ready for bed, little concubine?"

She laughed as he uncuffed her hands. Still blindfolded, she found his shoulders and stood on tiptoes to kiss him. "My lord, if it pleases you, may I have an hour alone upstairs before we go to bed?"

"Why?"

"I want to pray to the Mother Goddess."

"Sure," Paul said. "Just ring my cellphone when you're ready."

She gave him a quick kiss. "You are such a good master!"

Upstairs, she took out the gold medallion with the sapphire center and hung it on her neck. She lit the incense cone in the bowl at the feet of the ceramic owl. Lacking any other ritual, she knelt in front of the chest, her knees together and hands behind her back. She closed her eyes and waited until the colorful images dissipated and she was looking into blackness. She felt the cobblestones beneath her feet, and the breeze from the great owl's wings tickling her face.

Chapter Twenty- Seven: Revelations

"What's the deal on Nathan Gibbs?" Donna asked, as Whitey Ferris closed the door to her office.

"The State Attorney let him plead to a second degree felony on your assault. They've already sent him to Stark."

"That's odd. Alvarez never got back to me."

"You didn't catch that our people transported him? It should have been in the daily report."

Donna sighed. "I must have been slacking off, Lieutenant. Can we tie him to Torricelli?"

"Al Cadbury has half a dozen witnesses who claim that he dated her, but tying him to the murder is another story. We aren't there yet."

"We'll need to question him."

Whitey shook his head. "We'll have to set it up with the prison people. Plus, we have to get hold of his lawyer and fit it into his schedule. It's not going to happen soon enough."

"God dammit, Whitey, we're so close on this. Tie him to Torricelli, maybe we can shake loose Shelley Lowndes."

"I thought that you didn't like him for Lowndes."

"If he killed Torricelli, Lowndes is a lot more likely."

"He won't roll over on a capital offense."

Donna frowned. "I know. That would take a deal. He turned down the last offer, which would have let him take fifteen years for however many murders. What would it take to get some information out of him?"

"Nothing that's legal," Whitey responded. "But he didn't do Marilyn Rogie, and we can't link him to the Monarch Estates skeleton. At best you clear two murders.

"Two murders is pretty frickin' good, Whitey."

"If we can scare up some evidence."

Donna sighed. "Darlene Martinez and her crew in Administration are saying we're spending too much on travel, tracking down witnesses."

Whitey shrugged. "Well, they're wrong. What are you doing for lunch?"

"I've got to visit a high school at ten, so I'm doing lunch a little late. I'm meeting Danielle Travis at the Fireside at one, if you want to join us."

"The devil woman?"

Donna laughed. "Yeah, that one. But she likes you, so, seriously, if you can break free, please have lunch with us."

Ferris rolled his eyes. "Pretty lady, you get me involved in the strangest shit. Okay, if I can hold out till one, I'll be there."

☙❧

"Danielle, this is Lieutenant Ferris. I believe that you know each other."

"Yes, I remember the Lieutenant."

"My friends call me Whitey," Ferris said.

Danielle's eyes widened as she looked over the hulking African American. There was mirth in her eyes. "I can see why. My friends call me Cruella."

Whitey sat down beside Donna. Donna was aroused by his closeness. She felt his hip resting against her and blushed slightly.

"I'm looking for friends, Sergeant," Danielle said. "Would you like to be my friend?"

Whitey smiled. "Do I have to call you Cruella?"

"Not really. I'm Danielle…or Danny, or Dan. Why are you called Whitey?"

"Blacky just doesn't have the same ironic ring," Ferris said.

Danielle laughed. "Really, I'm curious. But if you'd rather not…"

"My mother's name was White. My full name is Thurgood White Ferris. If you're going to make a nickname out of that, Whitey is as good as you can do."

Danielle nodded. "I guess you're right." She held up a menu. "What looks good?"

Donna was fighting the urge to squeeze Whitey's thigh. "I'm always up for a salad in the afternoon," Donna said. "Paul usually makes such heavy dinners."

Whitey cocked his head. "Paul does the cooking?"

"Most of the time," Donna said.

"She's Paul's pet," Danielle offered. "He keeps her on a short leash, but he pampers her."

Ferris frowned.

"An accurate description of my home life," Donna concurred. She smiled mysteriously, recalling Paul's leash.

The server came and took their order. Donna asked for her usual: a salad and sparkling water. Ferris ordered a steak with all the sides. Danielle ordered a Porterhouse "as rare as you can get it."

"Danielle and I have been dreaming," Donna said. "We're going to compare notes to make sure that it was the same dream…in other words, that we were really in the Miasma. I know it is boring for you, but it will only take a few moments."

Ferris's eyes widened with mounting shock as Donna and the vampire exchanged details of the dream.

Finally, Donna said, "That's it, Danielle. It was the same dream. We were in the Miasma together. Is that what you wanted?"

"I have so many questions," Danielle answered. "It's like, that was just the start…"

"You can go back to my stone island in your dreams or, if you like, when you're awake and have the time to get yourself into a trance. Start there, find worlds that you like. Maybe you can even visit Koth."

"I'll try it," Danielle said. "Just to know that there's something else…"

Their order arrived and they began to eat in silence.

Finally, Danielle spoke: "Lieutenant Ferris, how do you feel about dating white women."

"I like white women just fine," he replied.

"How about *very* white women?"

Ferris put his fork down and eyed her. "I'd have to think about that. Would you drink my blood?"

Danielle laughed. "So, you know what I am? No, Whitey, I wouldn't. Not unless you wanted me to."

"But you could make me want it."

"I could, but I wouldn't. I'm a very ethical vampire."

Whitey took another bite of steak.

"Come on, Lieutenant, I'm hitting on you."

Donna looked from one to the other, not sure what was going on.

"Suppose I did ask you out, Danielle. What would happen?"

She sat back. "You're a shrewd bargainer, Lieutenant. Okay, you would find out that I'm easy, almost desperate. Dinner and a movie and you've got me. I give very good head, and I'm a dynamite fuck. If we click, great. If not, I'll leave you alone."

"You're the most forward girl I've ever met," Ferris said.

You should have seen me when I first went out with Paul, Donna thought.

"You're in love with Donna Parker, I can see that," Danielle persisted. "And she's very fond of you. Get a couple of drinks into her, and she would go to bed with you. But you will never pry her away from Paul. If you fuck her, you will hurt her."

A somber Whitey Ferris looked down at the woman sitting next to him. Donna nodded sadly, tears brimming in her eyes. "She's right," Donna whispered.

Ferris took a deep breath.

Danielle spoke. "Whitey, you may find this hard to believe, but I am very lonely. If you won't be my lover, at least be my friend."

Ferris nodded. "Give me your digits," he said.

ଔ

Back at her office, Whitey Ferris was apologetic. "Was it true what she said, about you and me?"

Donna grinned, wistful. "Yes, Whitey, it was. If you could have seen it, we probably would have slept together by now."

He shook his head. "Damn! If I'd known that…a couple of drinks, huh?"

"That would have done it."

"Would it really have hurt you that bad?"

Donna nodded. "Probably. I would have to tell Paul…I can't lie to him. I don't know how he would react."

"I understand," Whitey said. "Damn, girl! I couldn't close my eyes without seeing you…and you not respectable at all. I'm ashamed at the way I thought about you."

"Seeing me naked and available, I take it?"

"Yeah. To say the least."

"Whitey, everybody fantasizes. Actually, I'm flattered that you have sexual fantasies about me. I'll let you in on a little secret: That's why I have salads for lunch and I work out every day, so men will fantasize about me. That's okay. I fantasize, too. Tell me, is your dick really fourteen inches long?"

Whitey laughed. "White lady, it's more like eighteen inches."

Donna doubled forward, laughing.

When she recovered, she asked, "Do you think you'll get along with Danielle? After all, she's a devil woman."

"What I've learned from hanging with you and Paul is that things are a lot more complicated than the old good versus the devil stories. Evil lives in people. Danielle has done evil things, but she's not necessarily more evil than anybody else."

Donna thought about that. "You're remarkably broadminded, Whitey."

"Aren't you the one who was giving me lectures about prejudice?"

Donna made a face. "You're right."

"The way I see it," Whitey said, "I know two dangerous women. The devil woman is less dangerous than you are."

Donna giggled. "Probably so. But don't feel that you have to stop fantasizing. I'm proud to go naked in your fantasies."

"Don't worry, pretty lady. You'll be there."

"Friends, Whitey?"

Whitey pushed his fist to her. "Friends always, pretty lady."

ଔ

Donna was sitting back in her chair, feet on her desk, talking on the phone with Danielle. She was looking at a photo of herself, dressed in shorts and a cut-off top, posing with Donder and Blitzen when they were pups. *Funny how things work out.*

"I hope you're not offended that I cut in on you and Lieutenant Ferris," Danielle said.

"It was rude, Danielle, but I'm not offended. You saw your opening and you made your move. And you were right about us."

"He burns for you, Donna. I may not be able to make him love me, but I can give him a good fuck. You can't do that for him, not really."

"You're right, Danielle. I can't. I hope that this works for both of you." *Especially for him.*

Danielle sighed. "Do you know why Paul won't drink blood and become a full vampire?"

What's this about? "Because he's not up to murdering five dozen people?"

"There's that," Danielle said. "But I think he could get past that. He was killing people for George Bush, for God's sake. No, it's the dogs. He loves dogs, and he has outlived every dog he's had so far. He was grief stricken for months each time. He said that, if he were to convert, he would lose you like he did his dogs, one after another. He told me that he couldn't stand to keep living while you withered up with age and died. He would rather die than live without you."

"I didn't know that," Donna said, as tears flooded her eyes.

"Arianne outlived many, many lovers," Danielle went on. "Over time, it wore her down. She became vicious and bitter. But she got to know love, if only for a human lifetime. I want love, Donna. I want a man to snuggle up against in bed, and to take me out at night. I just want what humans want. You can't begrudge me that."

"I don't," Donna said.

☙❧

That evening, Donna was standing beside the kitchen counter being prepared for the evening. She was naked. She had on leather leg cuffs and her ankles were connected by a sixteen inch chain. Her wrists were crossed, locked behind her with metal cuffs and fastened to the chain around her waist. A leash dangled from her leather collar. She knew, from seeing the sleep mask on the table, that her world was about to go dark. As always, there was a tingle in her groin and moisture between her legs as she wondered what Paul was about to do to her.

She was telling Paul about the lunch.

"So Danielle saw it, too?"

"Did you know how he felt about me?" she asked, then hastily, "sir."

Paul smiled. "I could see how you felt…feel about him. I could guess that it was mutual. You're a very attractive woman, Donna."

"Thank you my lord. If I had slept with him, what would you have done?"

He shrugged. "I don't know. Pets do escape the fence sometimes."

"But how would you react, sir?"

He thought for a moment. "You know, Donna, a man doesn't know himself that well, not really. I can't say how I'd react."

"Under the deal, sir, you would have the right to punish me, physically punish me, as severely as you choose."

Paul gave a bitter laugh. "Donna, if you fuck around on me, the deal is broken. Whatever else happens, there won't be any physical punishment."

She blinked, feeling a little angry.

"Have you ever slept with Danielle?"

Paul was surprised. "No, Donna…"

"You two seem to know each other awfully well."

Paul tipped his head back. "You're jealous, Donna? No, Danielle and I work together and we've become friends. But no, we aren't lovers. I like her. She has a nice side, but she couldn't tempt me away from you."

"Would you sleep with Naomi if you had the chance?"

Paul raised an eyebrow. "For a slave concubine, you're getting a little pushy."

"Sir, I'm sorry. I forgot my place. My lord, would you sleep with Naomi if you had the chance?"

He shook his head.

"My lord, she's always wanted you, you know. She's always talked about threesomes…me, her, and you. You share me with her, but it's really you she wants."

Paul sighed. “Don’t you think I know that, Donna?”

“I wouldn’t mind sharing you with her.”

Paul put his hands on her shoulders. “I would never cheat on you, Donna.”

“It wouldn’t be cheating, Paul. I am your slave. I’m just property. You’re free to do whatever you like. Sir, you can’t cheat on property.”

Paul gave a brief laugh. “Donna, I think you’re taking the deal a little too seriously.”

Donna broke character. “Paul, how can you say that to me? Look at me! I’m stark naked. I’m naked for two thirds of my life! I go for days without putting on clothes. I spend hours chained to the floor every fricking night. I pretend to be a dog for you… a dog for Christ’s sake! for hours at a time. *Now* you tell me I’m taking the deal too seriously?”

Paul stared at her, amazed. He unclipped the leash.

“No, sir, I don’t want you to let me loose. I am serious about the deal. I want you to be serious, too. I want you to restrict me more, humiliate me more. Treat me exactly like a dog, if that’s what you want. Chain my arms and legs to the floor, too. I want you to crush me.”

Paul shook his head. He grasped her chin and pushed it up so that she was looking into his face. “You know what, babe, I don’t feel like doing this. I feel more like going out for dinner and catching a movie with my wife. So that’s what we’ll do. Turn around.”

“Nicey nice, sir? That’s what you’re offering? Nicey nice?”

“A break, Donna, for somebody who’s been playing a role a little too long.”

❧

In her office the next day, Donna reflected that Paul had been right. Masochism was one thing. Insanity was another. Thank the Mother Goddess that Paul loved her and understood her enough to keep her from going over the edge.

Donna felt good about her relationship with Paul. She decided to work harder on the dog thing. She liked the amused smile on Paul’s face when she returned on all fours with the rubber toy, or when she sat up to beg for one of those awful dog biscuits. It was fun for her, and entertaining for him. *I'll get better at it, do more.* She'd had a nice time the previous night, being treated like a sweetheart instead of a chained animal. *Maybe I shouldn't be so prickly about nicey nice. Any other woman would be happy to have a man like Paul treat her like a queen.*

She felt good about her job, too. It was a matter of time before Whitey Ferris and Al Cadbury nailed the Torricelli murder to the corrupt cop, Nathan Gibbs. She was now sure that he'd killed Shelley Lowndes, too. If she could prove it, great. But even if her people couldn't prove that he'd killed Lowndes, she had already put the son of a bitch in prison. That was not nothing.

The Monarch Estates skeleton bothered her. It wasn't Linda Hannity, so it was unlikely that Nathan Gibbs had killed her. She wished Whitey had never brought it up. It was an old case, and there was only the barest possibility that it was connected to Torricelli, or Lowndes, or Rogie. Shit! *Not even the barest possibility. No possibility at all.*

She remembered an issue that she had forgotten to address. She found a number on her cell and pressed "dial." When the receptionist answered, Donna said, "Hello, this is Sheriff McCready. Is Dan McLaury available?"

As she passed Whitey Ferris on the way out, she told him: "I'm attending to some important business. I'll be out the rest of the day, but you can reach me by phone if you need me."

Chapter Twenty-Eight: Called Out

They had made love again, gently and romantically this time, an hour or so later, in their bed. Donna lay with her head on Paul's belly and played with his spent penis. "Poor little guy. A few minutes he was so big and proud."

"Show some respect," Paul told her. "That little guy is your true master."

She giggled. "And yours, my lord. If it weren't for that little guy, you wouldn't be paying for your giant wall and your useless slave girl."

He laughed. "I keep the dogs, and they're pretty useless. So maybe I'd keep you anyway."

"Yes," she said, "I'm a very nice dog."

"You are," he replied. "You're the only one I let sleep on the bed."

"Do you still like the deal, my lord?"

"Of course I do. Why do you ask?"

"You seem to be backing away from it…giving me more freedom, being nicer to me."

"I love you, Donna. I love to tease and torment you, but I don't want to push you off the edge. Since I love you, it's hard for me to be cruel to you all the time."

"You're never cruel to me, sir. You always treat me with respect. You never yell at me or call me names."

"But I do put you in chains."

"I love that, sir. I love the feel of steel on my wrists, and knowing that you can do anything to me that you want. I love the pull of the leash on my neck. That isn't cruelty at all. That is the ultimate thrill…the best foreplay there is."

"But too much of it isn't good for you, little concubine."

She sighed. "What happened to keeping me constantly humiliated and servile? What happened to breaking my will?"

"Scary talk is part of the game."

"But you showed me that you could control the dogs, and that you could control me with *charm*. You really are my master."

"I can do a lot of things. But it doesn't mean I will do them. You're a sweet little slave, Donna. But you're still you. I'll never crush your spirit."

She gave a frustrated sigh. "Whatever. Even if you are too soft hearted for a slave master you're the best lover out there. If I ever lose you, I'll need four boyfriends to replace you."

"And a dog trainer," he pointed out.

She burst out laughing.

༺༻

Donna was wakened from a sound sleep by the ringing of her iPhone. She frantically fumbled under the bed until she got it into her hands. She brought it out and the light from the screen illuminated the room. It was SO Dispatch. She listened for a while and then stood up. She punched Paul in the arm. "Sweetie, that was work. I've got to go in."

Paul looked up, blinking in the dim light. "What?"

"Work," she explained patiently. "The Sheriff's Office. I've got to go in to work."

"Okay, babe. See you tomorrow."

༺༻

Donna was wearing jeans, sneaks, a tee shirt, and a gun belt when she arrived at the scene, a national chain motel near the intersection of 19 and 50, across from the water slide attraction. The deputies didn't recognize her until she flashed her badge and repeated her name twice.

The deputy at the door to the motel room, a guy named Jenkins, did recognize her. "Sorry, to get you out of bed, Sheriff. This lady says she's a friend of yours and insisted that we call you."

There were two cops standing between Donna and the subject, who was sitting on the bed. One of them turned around, and Donna could see the dark haired woman in the sheer nightgown. "Danielle? What the hell happened?"

Jenkins, a thick waisted fortyish veteran, spoke up: "The call came in as a confused subject running around, bleeding. When we got here, we found him in the courtyard. Definitely Signal 20. He claimed this lady tried to eat him. We did find a butterfly knife on the bed."

"Eat him?"

"Not that way," Jenkins, red faced, hastily replied. "Cut him up and eat him, like a cannibal."

Donna frowned. "This woman is an attorney. She works for my husband and she's a friend of mine. What happened, Danielle?"

Danielle seemed properly embarrassed. "Donna, you know how it is. I had a little too much wine down in the motel bar, and this guy picked me up. We came up to his room, had sex, and fell asleep. I woke up when he started screaming. There was blood all over the bed."

"Where is he now?" Donna asked.

"EMS took him," Jenkins said. "He had a laceration on his wrist that might need stitches. And he might be on drugs or something."

"So, what's the plan?" She quickly scanned his name tag. "Corporal Jenkins?"

"She says that this is her knife," another deputy said, holding up the bloody weapon.

"It is," Donna said. "I've seen it before. She carries it in her purse."

"There might be drugs in the room."

Donna frowned. "Does Danielle appear to be on drugs in your opinion?"

"No, ma'am," Jenkins said.

"Dump Danielle's purse out on the dresser." One of the deputies did so.

"Any drugs?"

"Apparently not, ma'am, the deputy said." She could see him opening a compact as he spoke."

"Okay, was she wearing pants?"

"A dress, ma'am."

"Any drugs in her clothing?"

"No, ma'am."

"Corporal," Donna said, "I take it you're the senior officer on the scene. What do you want to do?"

"Ma'am, since she's a friend of yours…"

"No, sir," Donna cut in. "Forget that. As you see it, what do we need to do?"

Jenkins sighed. "The victim basically accused the subject of assault, but his consciousness is obtunded. I'm inclined to wait until his head clears and see if he wants to pursue charges. I personally don't find it credible that his injuries were caused by Ms. Travis."

"You have her contact info?"

"Yes, ma'am."

"I'll take Ms. Travis home. She's been drinking and it isn't safe for her to drive. She can pick up her car tomorrow."

"That sounds like a good resolution, Sheriff."

ଔ

Danielle, still wearing her nightie and wrapped in an NCSO blanket, sat on her sofa. She was always pale, but now she looked unhealthily so. Her eyes lacked luster. She was holding a mug of tea that Donna had made for her.

"This place must look like a dump to you, Donna."

"No, it's a nice place, Danielle. It's a hell of a lot nicer than the rabbit hutch I lived in before I shacked up with Paul."

"I suck at housekeeping."

"Thank God for the house cleaning service Paul hired. If it weren't for them, you'd need a front end loader to get through the clutter."

"I've got to go out again, Donna." Danielle's voice was pitiful.

Donna sighed. "I don't think that's a good idea right now. What the hell happened?"

"I was desperate, got in a hurry. I started before I got him completely glammed."

"Is your *charm* weaker when you're hungry?"

Danielle looked up, her eyes wide and miserable. "I don't know, Donna. Maybe."

Donna counted back. "That guy at the gate…was that the last time you fed?"

Danielle nodded.

"Almost three weeks ago. Are you going to be all right?"

"Donna, it's like drug withdrawal. The longer I go, the more desperate I get, the less human I get. If I don't feed soon, I'll be like Michael when he was starting out…I won't be able to help myself. I'm afraid I might kill somebody."

"I can't let you go back out there."

Danielle's voice was miserable. "Donna, you aren't able to stop me."

Donna shook her head. She held out her left arm. "I can't believe I'm doing this, but here."

There was amazement in Danielle's eyes. "Donna, are you serious?"

"How much blood do you need?"

"You have very strong chi, Donna."

"It must be the goddess blood," Donna said. "How much blood? I have to be able to drive home."

"About like a blood bank donation, probably less."

"Okay, do you have a clean knife?"

Danielle made a tinkling laugh. "I do, Donna. A surgical scalpel. Sit down and I'll charm you so you don't feel any pain."

"No, I want to have a clear head. Besides, I like pain."

Danielle stared at her for a moment. "Maybe you do."

Donna felt the scalpel slice into her wrist. She flinched at the pain, but then felt a tingle of excitement in her groin. *Maybe there is something to this pain-pleasure stuff…Or maybe I'm just a freak.* She relaxed and, lacking anything better to do, stroked the kneeling vampire's hair as Danielle sucked at her arm. There was a solid lump of pain in her wrist…not distressing, easily endured.

Finally, Danielle looked up at her and showed blood-yellowed teeth surrounded by blood smeared lips. "I'm done. Thank you, Donna." She stayed on her knees as she wrapped gauze around the incision. She bent the elbow up and had Donna hold pressure on the wound.

"Hold on, I'll cut myself and drip some vampire blood on it to speed the healing."

"I think I'll do Steri-Strips at home," Donna replied. "Forgive me, but I'm a little squeamish about vampire blood."

Danielle laughed. “Don’t be silly. Here.” She made a cut in her index finger, brushed Donna’s hand aside, and dripped blood onto the wound.

“I don’t know how to thank you, Donna,” Danielle said.

Donna shook her head. “Just don’t expect me to do this every two weeks, Danielle. You need to take care of yourself.”

“I will, Donna. Why don’t you lie down on the sofa until you’re sure you’re okay. I’ll see if I can find you some orange juice.”

Donna lay down and stretched out her legs. *The things I do to protect the citizens of Narvaez County!*

Chapter Twenty-Nine: Another Narvaez County Sunday

Donna was lying naked atop the bed, her golden hair undone and spread across her shoulders and under her shoulder. Her left arm hung off the side and her hand was on the floor. She was sound asleep. She felt Paul's hand on her back.

"Are you okay, babe?"

She slipped into semi-consciousness. "I'm okay, sweetie."

She heard Paul say, "It's okay, babe. You can sleep in."

"What time is it?" she asked sleepily.

"A little after eight."

She rose up to sit on the side of the bed. "I've got to get up."

"I'll make you some coffee," Paul said.

When she heard the elevator moving, she toppled over sideways and went back to sleep.

She was still sleeping on her side with her legs drawn up and her hands between her knees when Paul returned with the coffee. He had made it just the way she liked it, lightened with whole cream and sweetened with honey. She forced herself to sit up and sip it.

He's babying me, like I'm some kind of girlie girl. She suppressed her annoyance and smiled and said, "Thank you, sir. You're such a sweet master."

"I'll be downstairs fixing your breakfast," he said.

When she heard the elevator depart, she drank down the cooling coffee and forced herself to stand. *Worst hangover I've ever had, without drinking.* She forced herself to stand and walk to the bathroom.

After she had used the commode, she sat there, trying to get up the energy to move. *How much sleep did I get?* She started adding. Her day yesterday had started at 4:30 AM, and Paul had given her no rest. She'd detailed the car and prepared the meal for the guests, and stayed up after dark to be ordered around and groped. *And I gave Paul two blowjobs and fucked him twice, all since 4:30 yesterday morning.* She shook her head. She'd gotten less than an hour of sleep before the call to Danielle's assistance. She'd gotten home after 4:00. *No wonder I'm beat. I could justify going back to bed.* She got up from the commode and started toward the bed. *No, I can't. I'm a slave and slaves don't get to sleep in.* She turned around and stepped into the shower. *Except Paul was bluffing, and we've just been playing, after all.*

After the shower, and after her hair was dry, she felt better. Her face still felt puffy and the lights were too bright but she felt better. She put on her dog collar and trudged down the steps. She stumbled once and had to catch herself.

When she sat down at the kitchen table and Paul put the beautiful omelette in front of her, she felt like throwing up. Paul sat across from her and watched her eat. Her head was clearing a little, as the food dispersed into her system. She was only a little nauseous now.

"What happened to your wrist?" Paul asked.

She held up her arm and examined her wrist as though she'd never seen it before. Just a little three inch gauze wrapped and taped. "Oh, Danielle had a problem with feeding and the deputies were called. I took her home, and I gave her a little blood so she wouldn't get in more trouble."

Paul was incredulous. "You let a vampire suck your blood?"

Donna was caught off guard by his raised voice. "It was Danielle, and she was getting sick."

"I can't believe you'd do something like that! Are you insane?"

Donna flared. "Do not talk to me in that tone of voice. I'm the Sheriff of this fucking county, and as Sheriff, I did what needed to be done. You may be the master here, but you don't have shit to say about what I do as Sheriff!"

Paul physically stepped back. "I'll send her back to California tomorrow," he said quietly.

"For what? Being a vampire? You knew all about her when you hired her. How is it better for her to be a vampire in California than here? And we owe her. That gang would have killed us if she and Michael Dalton hadn't killed them first."

Donna looked up at him with a prim smile. She could see that he was furious. He was breathing fast and his face was red.

"That was poor judgment, Donna," he said softly.

"It was my judgment, Paul. I stand by it."

Paul sighed. "We can't afford for her to get in trouble here. She needs to go back. And that's my judgment."

Donna's eyes narrowed. "Paul, she's my friend."

Paul stared at her. There had been no pleading in her voice.

He sighed. "Fine! But keep an eye on her. We can't afford to have her going off the tracks."

"This is a good omelette," Donna said, to ease the tension.

"Maybe after breakfast you should sleep a couple of hours," Paul said. "You look a little tired."

"Paul, don't baby me, I'm fine."

"Still…"

"Paul, I'm a slave. I'm not some little girlie girl. If you want to break a slave, you pressure her when she's tired and worn out. That's when the pressure works the best."

"Fine, you're a slave. Your master wants you to take care of yourself."

"All right…I'm taking care of myself." There was a sneer in her voice.

"I don't want you to get sick."

"I know, I know. My master wants me to be his little kitten."

"You're going too far, Donna."

"Too far?" she screeched. "Because I don't want to be treated like a fricking girlie girl?"

Paul arched an eyebrow. She could see that he was furious. There was a lump of fear in her gut. "Donna Parker, get out of that chair and get on your knees. And get those hands behind your back."

The fear and the arousal was delicious. In seconds, she was on her knees on the tile, hands behind her back, mouth open, staring straight ahead.

"Now," Paul said, "I want you to take a few seconds and get that insolence out of your voice. You will apologize to me, and your tone of voice will be respectful. You will observe the speech formalities."

Uh oh, I've screwed up big time. She took a series of deep breaths. "My lord, I am very sorry for being disrespectful and arguing with you. I beg your forgiveness and I accept your punishment, sir."

"That's better, Donna. You're the Sheriff but I am the master of the house. In matters of our relationship, you will obey me and you will be respectful when you speak to me. Are we clear?"

"Sir, I understand, sir."

Donna's heart was racing. *That's more like it.*

"Stand up," he said. She stood, keeping her hands behind her back.

"What do you have on tap for the day?" he asked.

"Sir, I have nothing scheduled. I'm at your disposal, sir."

"This looks like a good day to put my pets outside. Put your rings and your hair band on the table and get out of here. Now."

As she followed the dogs down the back steps, she decided that this was an improvement. A year ago, Paul would have ignored her snippiness. Now he had the confidence to shut her down. But as she walked out onto the driveway, she was in a pissy mood. Last night, he had walked back his scary talk about breaking her, and keeping her humiliated and servile. She hadn't realized how much his threat had weighed on her until the threat was gone. Whenever she had come home, she had felt a tension in her groin, like she had to pee, fearing what Paul would do to her next. She had felt like a genuine slave, trapped and hopeless. But he had just told her that he hadn't really meant it. So that fear that she had so cherished was now gone. They were just playing.

Of course, if I piss him off enough, he might change his mind and use that charm. That hopeful thought was quickly extinguished. *But if I got too hard to handle, he'd probably just cancel the deal.*

The weather was warm and damp. The wind was blowing, the sky was gray, and rain was almost certain. *Great! I provoked Paul into putting me out in the rain. I wouldn't be surprised if he left me out till dark...all night, even.* There were worse things, of course. And she could get out of the rain under the empty house. *I can make this fun if I change my attitude.* Still, she was annoyed at Paul's weakness. *He sucks as a sadist. Underneath he's all nicey nice. If I were a man like Paul, and I had a slave girl like me, I would keep her terrified. And if she ever smarted off to me like I did to Paul, that little bitch would have a sore butt for a long, long time!*

As she walked down the walkway toward the gravel parking area, her legs felt heavy. A big raindrop struck her shoulder. *Great! It's about to start.* She stumbled and she didn't feel good.

I got myself into this, so I'd better get something out of it. She decided to cross the parking lot and hang out for a while in the big grassy area where Paul always took her to play with the dogs. She wondered how big the area was. *From the gravel to the driveway of the empty house, more than the distance from our house to the gravel Maybe two hundred and fifty feet.* She felt a band of tension above her eyes, the prelude to a headache.

One of the things Donna aspired to do was to be able to move faster on her hands and knees. She wanted Paul to be able to take her out on a leash and have her keep up with his normal walking pace while she was on all fours. She wanted to perfect her dog imitation, so that Paul could treat her exactly like a dog if he chose. Of course, she would never be fast enough to run like the real dogs. And she didn't think she would be able to walk the entire wall on hands and knees. But a few hundred feet…

So, when she reached the other side of the gravel lot, she dropped to her hands and knees and began scurrying as fast as she could. Her plan was to cross the grassy area, turn around at the driveway, and come back. She would repeat this again and again until she collapsed.

She felt better on all fours, actually. But the big raindrops were coming down more frequently. *It's not really raining yet.* She kept crawling along. *I'm going to get sick running around like this in the rain, with no sleep.* She noticed that her hair was wet and getting dirty because it was dragging on the ground. *Well, if Paul wants to make his slave girl sick, that's on him.*

She didn't quite make it halfway across the clearing before the dogs saw her. They thought this was great fun…running up, barking, running away and circling back. Donna was annoyed, but then realized that this was an opportunity to improve her dog behavior. She ducked down until her chin was resting on her hands, her boobs were touching the grass, and her ass was in the air. When the dogs came close to her face, she would jump up suddenly and bark. The dogs loved it. She improved her act by growling menacingly as her chin was at ground level, then giving a blood curdling yelp as she straightened her arms and leapt up.

It was full on raining now, but Donna didn't care. She felt good and she was having fun. The dire wolves were soaked. Donna's hair was a dirty wet mop. It was pouring down rain and there was thunder.

She wondered vaguely if Paul would call them in, and whether she would hear the whistle if he did. But there was no reason to worry about his pets being out in the rain. They could seek shelter under the empty house if they wanted. The worst thing about rain is getting your clothes wet and sticky. But Donna was naked, and she was fine with the feel of lukewarm water beating against her skin.

The dogs suddenly turned and ran toward the house. Donna couldn't hear the whistle, but she knew what had caused them to turn tail. She stood up and ran at breakneck speed toward Paul's home, enjoying the unfamiliar feel of rain beating hard against her face and breasts.

As soon as she got through the aluminum door and under the house, Paul handed her a towel and her cellphone.

She was toweling her hair as she took the phone.

"Sheriff, this is Dan McLaury. We've been working on your request from the other day, and we think you should come by the office and see what we've got."

"Right now?" Donna asked.

"If you can, Sheriff. We have a limited slice of time to work with."

"It will be about an hour. I've been…working…outside and I'm soaked."

She turned to Paul. "This is important, I've got to go."

"Donna, baby, do what you've got to do."

ଓଃ

They were in a part of Conquistador engineering that Donna had never seen before. It was a big room filled with drafting tables, touch screen computer tables, and whiteboard stands. McLaury ushered Donna in and introduced her to a tall, sandy haired, very muscular man. Donna estimated him to be on the young side of forty.

"Sheriff, meet Bill Sullivan. Bill, if you'll recall, was the Sheriff before Bob Kessler."

Donna's eyes narrowed. *What's he trying to pull?* She shook the man's hand. "I would have expected an older man."

Sullivan smiled. "I was older when I saw you last, Donna. I used to come over to your house, and you'd climb up on my lap. I was older when I saw you at your dad's funeral."

Donna carefully examined the man's face. The man she remembered was older, much older. But the resemblance was there.

"Sheriff Sullivan comes from a place where age comes and goes," McLaury explained.

Donna nodded soberly.

"I work closely with the McLaurys," Sullivan explained. "You know about the cabin. The role of the McLaury family is to protect the cabin…that's why they need you, Sheriff…and to shelter time travelers between jumps. They help with shelter, contemporary money, vehicles, that sort of thing. My people ride the cabin. We're not just observers. We make things happen. There are several of my people in your department. Hell, I've been Sheriff myself off and on since the 1800s. My people are in the business community in this county, and I've got agents around the country."

"Why?" Donna asked.

"To help things along, to make things fit. For example, one of your predecessors stumbled into the cabin and went back in time. We found it necessary to render him unconscious. Then, back in 1962, we had to install propane gas service and a defective stove in the cabin to make it look like he'd been overcome by gas forty years later."

Donna didn't know what to say.

"Which brings us to your problem. You needed witnesses to a murder that took place in 2006 or 2007. Do you understand the difficulties?"

Donna shook her head.

"Suppose we could launch you, for example, back to 2006. Then what do you do? You witness your murder and then live to 2013. Now there are two Donna Parker's in the world. And will be. See the problem?"

"Yes," Donna said.

"So, if we put you back in 2006, we have to get you back from 2006, or at least send you somewhere else where there isn't another copy of you. Ideally, you'd come back to where you started."

"Right," Donna agreed.

"But we don't control the cabin. What we have is a partial record of its movements. It turns out that we can't send anybody back to 2006. At a precise date and time in 2014, the cabin will shift whoever is in it back in time to April, 2005. In December, 2005, the cabin will make a shift that brings the passenger back to 2017."

Donna blinked and tried to follow this. "So this person will cease to exist between 2005 and 2017?"

"Correct," Sullivan said. "Except that, in the relatively remote future, he will double back to April, 2007, which is why he is here in the first place. So, he appears in 2007, lives here until 2014, returns in 2017, and, at some point in the remote future, he gets carried to an earlier date."

Donna shook her head. "How do you know all this?"

"Because it has already happened," Sullivan said. "My people in the future have a history of the cabin's stops and starts. What I have, and what Dan doesn't have, is a record of who was in the cabin when it shifted, and what they were doing."

"Bottom line," McLaury cut in, "the guy we're talking about will leave next year, when the cabin makes a leap to 2005. He will install a surveillance device aimed at the site where you found the skeleton. The device will monitor the site and it should at least record the burial."

"So this device will run from 2005 to what, 2008?"

"Correct."

"Do we have to watch the entire two years of tape?"

"It's not a tape, but no. We have a device that's programed to isolate the segments we need. Processing the memory stick will take a few weeks, of course."

A thought struck her. "It's Dave Leeper you're talking about, isn't it. That's why Dave has to leave Sharon next year."

"That's right," McLaury admitted.

"No," Donna said fiercely. "It's not worth breaking Sharon's heart to solve a cold case."

McLaury smiled gently. “Donna, if Dave hadn’t already done this, he never would have appeared in 2007. You can’t change it.”

“Come here,” Sullivan said. He led her to a work table with a slanted Formica surface. He lifted the top. Inside was a three foot wide cluster of laurel oak branches. Sullivan lifted it. “This is what you’re going to be looking for, Sheriff. It will be near the top of one of the laurel oak trees across the road from the burial site. He rotated the branches and Donna could see a thin rod that held four metal tubes, each about an inch long. “This is the camera array. Notice that there is a little spool of metal tape down here.” He moved some leaves. “When it’s time to retrieve the cameras, the tape will unfold to form a metal streamer two feet long, so you can see the assembly. Although this is very realistic, the whole assembly is artificial. Remove the whole cluster and bring it to us.”

“I have an aerial photo of the area with the tree circled. It’s up to you to figure out how to get it down.”

Donna began counting dates. “So you can’t even start this process until sometime next year?”

“Correct,” McLaury said.

She sighed. *Will I still be Sheriff when this thing is ready?* “So, when will this thing be ready to be picked up? My term of office only runs to 2016.”

“You can pick it up now,” Sullivan said. “It’s been there since 2005.”

⁂

Danielle Travis sounded sleepy.

“Danielle, I am so sorry that I didn’t come and pick you up. I had a fight with Paul this morning, and then I got a break in a murder case, and…”

Donna was driving toward Danielle’s house, iPhone in hand.

“It’s fine, Donna. I’m a vampire, remember? I’d rather sleep in the day anyway. I wasn’t planning on going anywhere.”

“I’m working on a big case and I need to go look at some evidence. Would you like to ride along with me to do that before we pick up your car?”

"Sure," Danielle said cheerily. "How should I dress?"

"Outdoor clothes," Donna said. "We may have to do some walking."

ଔ

Danielle was wearing a short sleeved shirt and jeans. She would put on her outdoor clothes if she had to get out of the car. Her outdoor wear for a late afternoon in Florida, with a temperature in the nineties and the humidity near saturation, was a long sleeved cotton shirt, a straw hat, dark sunglasses, and work gloves. She had also brought a bottle of sun block for her face.

"He's really sweet," Danielle said. "He calls me 'devil woman.' I think he's still scared of me, though. We've slept together twice. He's pretty good, but he doesn't have the stamina Michael had."

Donna smiled dreamily as she thought about Paul's stamina. *One thing about vampires and their blood...* "Do you think you have a future?" she asked.

"I think Whitey and I will kick it for a while at least. Right now the poor guy's just grateful for the sex. When that wears off, we'll see."

"You're not a very optimistic person, Danielle."

Danielle laughed. "I'm not, Donna. In the Community, as far as I can tell, none of us are."

"What was your fight about?" Danielle asked.

Donna told her.

"I was afraid of that," Danielle said. "But you defended me?"

"I did," Donna said. "I decided that, after all, we are friends. I'll have to set aside all the people you killed, I guess. I don't know what Paul did in Iraq, but he gives me the impression that he's not proud of all of it. I don't ask about it. I won't ask you about your crimes, either."

"I appreciate that," Danielle told her. "I can't express how much I appreciate it. I'm sorry that I caused a fight between you and Paul."

"It was just an argument over you. The fight was over whether I should go back to bed and catch up on my sleep."

Danielle laughed. "That master-slave thing is a little beyond you, isn't it. When you're at home, you do make the most loveable, docile slave. But away from home, with your clothes on, you're pretty bossy…even kind of a bitch sometimes. I think that's the real you."

"I'm split in that way. I want to run things, but I'm submissive sexually. It's more than just the sex. For some reason, I love the chains and I love being ordered around." She sighed. "But you're two people, too. When you're at my house, you're an arrogant, cold blooded bitch. But when I see you out in the world, you're very nice. And after I got to know you, I realized that you're really pretty needy."

Danielle smiled. "It must be that yin and yang thing the Buddhists are always yammering about. I think arrogance comes from being a vampire. Predators are naturally arrogant. The needy part is all Danielle."

"You're all right, though," Donna said. "I like having somebody else treating me like an inferior being when I'm being Paul's slave. It reinforces the game."

Danielle laughed. "Glad to be of help."

ꕥ

Donna drove her cruiser along the dirt roads. *Without GPS I'd be lost right now.* But she found the location without a problem. On the right side of the limerock road she could see the house that had been built after the murder and, through the stand of trees in front of it, the lawn which had grown atop the grave. A backhoe operator had been digging a burn pit. *Amazing luck that he picked just that spot to dig.* She reconsidered. *But it was a big burn pit.* And a lot of digging went into building that house. *They might have found it anyway.*

Donna pulled in to the barely discernible driveway. It was a nice property and the house was well off the road. She inched the car along until she was beside the big oak trees at the edge of the lawn.

Donna stopped the car and got out. She walked a little further down the drive until she had a clear view of the tree line. She reached into her pants pocket and found the device Bill Sullivan had given her. It was a black plastic square half the size of a domino, with a red dot printed on the center. As Sullivan had instructed her, she gripped the square so that her thumb was directly on the dot. She squeezed. High in the third tree down, a shining streamer unfurled and clung to the branch below. The plastic square crumbled into dust between her fingers.

She walked back to the car and knocked on the window. When Danielle rolled the window down, Donna said, “Get out.”

It took Danielle several minutes to suit up. It was a hot, muggy day. Donna thought that it might rain later. Danielle was dressed like an autumn gardener someplace in the Midwest.

A car came down the driveway. It was a charcoal Honda Accord driven by a fiftyish man with fat cheeks and red hair. He stopped to ask what was going on. Donna flashed her badge. “This is a murder investigation,” she said.

“Is it about that skeleton they found when they built the house?”

“That’s right,” Donna told him.

He drove on back to the house, a stucco two story construction with big pillars on the front portico. When she was sure he’d gone inside, Donna turned to Daniel. “Can you climb up there?”

Danielle turned, surprised. “Seriously, Donna? That’s why you brought me out here?”

“It’s okay if you can’t do it. It’s just that it would save bringing a ladder truck out here and tearing up these people’s yard.”

“What’s up there?”

Donna explained.

“I’ll have to put sunscreen on my feet, but I can do it.”

Danielle was as good as her word. They walked to the tree and Danielle took off her shoes. After she had oiled the top of her feet, she took a few paces back into the lawn, and then made a running jump to reach the lowest branch, which was a good ten feet overhead. With monkey like agility, she clambered from one branch to another until she was near the camera array, resting her feet on two inch thick branches fifty feet above the ground.

It took a few moments to loosen the unwieldy device, and then she let it drop fluttering to the ground.

She climbed down enough to find a long limb strong enough to hold her full weight. She inched out onto the bough until it began to flex visibly, then straddled the limb. She rolled under, so that she was hanging from her hands. She let go, and came crashing feet first into the dirt thirty feet below. Her knees buckled dramatically, absorbing the impact.

She stood up, brushed her hands together, and stepped up to Donna. "Did I look as good as Kate Beckinsale?" she asked.

"Your form was as good, but Kate had better clothes," Donna replied.

"You just like Kate's fetish costume. You should have Paul buy you a corset."

Donna smiled but didn't reply. She was fumbling with the artificial foliage. She picked up the camera array and the fake oak branch camouflage, and stuck it in the trunk of her cruiser.

ଔ

After Donna had dropped off Danielle at the motel where she had left her car, and after she had returned the camera array off at the McLaury facility, she went home. She was in a good mood. She took off her clothes beside the car, stuck her clothing and equipment in the bag, and strode happily up to the house. She greeted Paul in the living room…he was standing at the bar…and went upstairs. She bathed, dried herself off, and went downstairs.

She did her little twirl. "Your slave concubine is all clean, my lord."

"Well, after this morning I don't know how much of a slave you are, but I can probably still get some use out of you as a concubine."

Donna's heart sank. *He's still pissed about this morning.* She walked up to him and dropped to her knees. "Would you like to use my mouth, my lord?"

He smiled and patted her head. "Get up, Donna." This had never happened before. Her heart started to pound.

"Let's hold off on the slave concubine thing until you've had some sleep."

"My lord," she protested, "it's still daylight."

"Donna," he said, his voice imperious, "get your ass upstairs and into bed right now. I'll be up for a few more hours. When I come up to bed, you'd better be sleeping."

She started to argue, but thought better of it. Her hands still behind her back, she turned to go. A hard smack on her bare butt sped her along.

She was crushed. It had been such a good day in her Sheriff work. Now her true lord was angry at her. She felt a little panic. What would she do if Paul kicked her out? She couldn't imagine another lover.

But as she trudged up the stairs, her good mood returned. *He could never find another girl like me. We may just be playing, but I really am an exquisitely trained sex slave.* She giggled. *None of my friends would do for a guy what I do for him. They think I'm crazy. Let's see him find another chick that will let him lock her up in chains and have her be ready to screw any time, any place he wants to stick it. Let alone eat fricking dog biscuits!* She was safe. *Paul can grump all he wants. He'll never leave me.*

That thought kept her happy and, since she really was exhausted, she fell asleep smiling.

Chapter Thirty: Killers

When Billy Sheffield was ten years old, he had done something to his brother Ricky. Billy couldn't remember exactly what he'd done, but it was probably something like Dad had done to him, the thing that might get sent Dad away to the bad place if anybody told. By the age of ten, of course, Billy realized that the bad place was prison. Billy didn't want to go to prison.

But Ricky was a tattletale. For a whole day, Ricky had taunted him: "I'm going to tell Mom. I'm going to tell the policeman at school, and they'll send you to the bad place." The little six year old twerp! Billy hated Ricky anyway. Whenever any adults came over, they made a big fuss over Ricky, and his stupid first grade drawings. They listened to him read, for crissake! They paid attention to Ricky, who was such a show-off. Whenever Mom brought the church people over, they spent half a damn hour paying attention to the stupid, mouthy first grader. They ignored Billy. They positively disliked the oldest, Dave. Dave was twelve and by now everybody knew that Dave was stupid.

Billy knew that if Ricky said he was going to tell, he would. Mom had always told them that being a tattletale was the worst thing there was. Billy and Dave knew not to be tattletales. Tattletales were snitches and nobody liked snitches. Those police might ask you about Daddy's pictures, but don't tell them anything. The police will pretend to like you and pretend to be your friends, but if you tell them anything, they'll take you away and put you in a bad place. But Ricky would tell the police about Dad's pictures if he found out about them. If you hit Ricky, or took his cookie, or did any stupid thing at all, he would tell. Sooner or later, Ricky was going to get Dad sent to prison. But right now, Billy was the one in danger if he didn't do something.

Ricky is stupid. Ricky had just spent the last hour taunting Billy that he was going to tell, and that Billy was going to the bad place. But the stupid little kid followed Billy like a puppy dog, as Billy walked down the gravel road, as Billy walked into the park, as Billy walked out onto the moss covered boat pier at the edge of the lake. There was a railing along the pier. There was an old aluminum canoe with the boat cushions floating in two inches of water. There was a wooden paddle in the canoe. The other paddle was on the dock leaning on the railing.

Billy looked around. There were boats far away out in the gray lake. It was a cool Michigan day and the water was choppy from the brisk wind. Although people fished off this pier, nobody was out today. Not on the pier, not in the park. The water at the end of the dock was deep, over a man's head. Billy's ten year old mind hatched a plan.

At the end of the pier, Billy lay flat on his belly on the soggy wood. He stared intently into the water.

"Whatcha looking at?" stupid Ricky asked, like the stupid first grader he was.

"Nothing."

"What is it?" Ricky asked, in a first grade frustrated whine.

"Nothing."

Ricky angrily walked out and stood, his foot, clad in a red canvas shoe, right next to Billy's right arm.

"Babies can't look," Billy told him.

"Uh huh," Ricky said. He leaned forward to peer into the water.

It took the slightest movement of Billy's arm to tip the overbalanced child into the lake.

Ricky couldn't swim.

But he was close to the posts and cross beams under the dock. Even thrashing around with his hands out of the water, the stupid kid might get to safety. Billy stood up and grabbed the canoe paddle. He held it like a pool cue, rested it on the edge of the dock, and slid it forward, to slam into Ricky's chest. Rick gasped and shot backward.

Ricky had by now realized that he had to lean into the water and use his arms to move forward, but each time he moved toward the dock, Billy used the canoe paddle to push him away. Ricky was screaming now, his little face red with fear and rage. "Billy, I'm gonna tell!"

Billy was enjoying himself now, letting Ricky grab the paddle and be towed forward, only to have the slippery blade lifted upward and out of his hands as Billy simply used the edge of the dock as a fulcrum to lever it out of the water.

Finally, the child was tired enough that he couldn't resist the weight as Billy rested the paddle blade against Ricky's shoulder and held him under. Soon, there was no resistance. Billy raised the paddle blade and Ricky's lifeless body tipped backward and floated away. Billy watched, fascinated, as it bobbed on the waves.

He was startled to hear a huge splash as somebody dived into the water. Billy turned to see a boat not fifty feet away. He had been so intent on killing his brother that he hadn't heard the five horse motor as the boater came to the rescue.

It was an older man who pulled Rick from the water and began CPR. There was a woman in the boat and she was on the cellphone. Billy felt sick. They had seen him trying to kill his brother.

Billy walked back and forth as the man continued CPR. Once in a while, the man would raise his head and shout, "Where's that ambulance?"

Eventually, the man gave up. Billy's little brother was lying on his back on the planks, his skin very pale and crisscrossed with light blue veins. His reddish hair was wet and plastered against his forehead. His eyes stared up, lifeless, like a baby doll. *Bet you don't tell nobody jack shit now.* But Billy knew that he was still going to prison, for killing his brother. That was murder and they sent you to prison for a long time for that. Billy felt oddly exhilarated but the thought of prison was a weight in his gut.

He thought of running away, but they would find him. *Maybe the man won't tell,* he hoped, thinking wishfully. The ambulance arrived, along with the police. Billy heard the ambulance driver explain that they had been tied up by a traffic accident.

The policeman, who seemed to Billy to be an enormous man, walked up to Billy. "What happened?" he asked.

Billy felt that he was going to pee his pants.

"I was out on the lake when I saw it," the unsuccessful rescuer cut in. "The little guy fell in. This one…" he pointed at Billy "…tried to reach him with that canoe paddle, but the little guy wouldn't grab on. By the time I crossed the lake and got here…" His voice trailed off.

The policeman crouched down so that he was at Billy's eye level. "Is that what happened, son?"

Yes, that's it! That's what happened.

"Yeah," Billy replied with a long sigh, his whole body relaxing in relief. "I tried to get Ricky but he wouldn't grab on."

The policeman gave Billy a ride home. Billy's mother was hysterical for a while, but eventually hugged Billy to her and clutched him against her hip. For weeks afterward, the church people would come over and pray for Billy, and give him gifts, and take him places. In school, they let him out of class to talk to a counselor. The counselor was very interested in Billy's feelings, whether he had nightmares, did he miss his brother? She was careful to reassure Billy that Ricky's death was not his fault. Billy was quick to pick up what she wanted to hear and he played the part of a deeply traumatized grade schooler. Mom was especially solicitous and it was months before she raised her voice to him about anything. He sometimes caught her watching him, and she looked as though she were about to cry.

Dad was different. One day, they were in town, walking along the sidewalk beside the slow moving cars. Dad had his hand on Billy's shoulder. "Ricky was kind of a tattletale, wasn't he, Billy"

Billy was afraid to say anything. He just nodded.

"The grown up word for tattletale is snitch, Billy."

"Snitch," Billy repeated.

"The worst thing in the world is a snitch, Billy. If something bad happens to a snitch, it's for the best."

Billy pondered that.

Billy spent the next year or so as, alternatively, the hero who had desperately tried to save his drowning brother or as the victim of a terrible childhood trauma.

Puberty was still in Billy's future. But whenever he was lying in bed and thought about Ricky's lifeless body, a strange feeling went through his pee pee and it stiffened.

Billy had learned two things: It feels good to kill people. And dead people can't snitch.

ଔ

Billy was twelve when the Sheffields moved to Florida. The FBI and the Michigan authorities had finally caught on to the father's child porn hobby. But the move didn't help Dad's legal situation. The Florida cops took Dad away and sent him to Michigan anyway. So Billy's mother, Virginia, the naïve churchgoer, became a fixture in the Northwest Baptist Church and a popular server at Molly's, the favorite restaurant of the courthouse lawyers and staffers. Billy and his brother went to school. School was easy for Billy. He did his homework in minutes and so had a lot of free time. To Davy, though, school was a lot like a prison. He ditched it whenever he could.

Billy found a high school kid who was willing to sell him drugs. By the time he was thirteen, Billy was very popular and had plenty of money by middle school standards since he resold marijuana, and X, and various other drugs as opportunity arose. At fourteen, he had pubic hair and a teenager's desire. The girls, though, weren't interested in a punk middle schooler…at least not the girls who might be likely to want sex. That type of girl smoked cigarettes and had cellphones and wiggled their asses for the older guys, the guys who could drive and had cars.

Billy was good looking enough. He had blondish hair and piercing blue eyes. He worked out, because he had some ambitions that required physical strength. Still, being not yet full grown, he looked scrawny and *young*. But, he was a little over six feet tall and pretty strong. The high school kids who tried to push him around regretted it. He knew how to take care of himself.

ଔଓ

The woman's name was Rachel Sternberg. She had just turned thirty years old, but she refused to recognize that catastrophic fact. For the past six years she had been married and living in a small house in Moundview, Minnesota. The house was small, twelve hundred square feet, but had four tiny bedrooms and a basement with almost as much square footage as the house. There was a pool table and an old sofa and a widescreen TV downstairs, so her husband could pretend he had his own sports bar. He had various beer paraphernalia and sports team pennant tacked up on the cheaply paneled wall.

But Rachel had had the revelation. Her youth was circling the drain and she had spent most of it here in this old neighborhood of aging bungalows on tiny lawns. Looking back, high school had been fun and her young adult life had been fun, but all that had suddenly come to a halt when she got married and moved into this nice house in this quiet neighborhood. She had suddenly realized that this was it. Her husband Dan was nice enough but one day she had awakened and gone into the kitchen and found a sink full of dishes. *This is my whole life!* She had a job as a cashier, but Dan was the breadwinner. He thought of her as a wife, and took her to see his folks on Sunday, and to the movies or to go bowling on Saturdays, and he expected her to cook dinner for him on weekdays and to keep the house clean.

What's the point of it all? It was the same thing every day, day after day, until what? She was never going to get anywhere. At best, she'd eventually have a nicer car and a bigger house to take care of. She tried to remember when she'd last had fun. That summer before she'd gotten married, when she'd gone down to Florida to visit her cousin. That was fun…smoking dope and making out with the shirtless guys in their mud bogging trucks on Glisson Lake, out in the woods.

Rachel went into her bedroom and took off her clothes and took a long hard look at herself. She still had a good body. She looked good, with her long brown hair and brown eyes. Her face was showing a little wear but she was still *young.*

She still had some time left before she faded into middle age. She had time for some fun and for a new start. *Goddamn, I need a new start!*

She and Dan had a joint account. One Monday morning while he was at work, she took a cab to the bank and withdrew eight thousand dollars, their life savings. She bought a plane ticket to Tampa. Once in Tampa, she needed a way to get around, so she found a dealership that sold Honda bikes. She spent a little less than four grand on a 250 cc Honda Rebel, a helmet, and a leather jacket and panniers. She loaded her stuff on her bike and headed north on 41. She stopped at a Walmart in Narvaez County and bought a tent, a camp stove, and a sleeping bag. She was going to camp at Glisson Lake.

She was shocked when she arrived at Glisson Lake and there was nobody there.

Worse, what had been an uninhabited woods crisscrossed by limerock roads was now only partially wooded and was dotted with homes of various design and quality. In some places, the woods were gone, replaced by stupidly large lawns and houses every five hundred feet. But she found a place in the forest to camp and she stayed there for several days. Eventually she needed food, so she took her bike down to 19 to a convenience store.

That's where she met that cute middle schooler named Billy. He had walked all the way to the highway. She gave him a ride home on the back of her bike. She took it slow because she was overloading her bike, but they made it to his house okay. Standing in front of his house, she found out that he had some grass. He went inside and returned with a backpack. She produced two twenties and a ten, and he gave her a nickel bag. A mutually beneficial commercial relationship had begun.

Billie, though, wanted more than another customer for his chronic. He had more people wanting dope than he had product, anyway. What he wanted was sex. He wanted to take a girl's clothes off, look over her naked body and finally to have his way with her. He didn't fantasize about the girl wanting him. The junior high girls had pretty much convinced him that wouldn't happen any time soon. He wanted to be in a position to compel a girl to give him what he wanted.

Billie had a thing for brunettes. He liked Rachel's long dark hair, and he knew that she'd been married before. She wouldn't mind having sex, not like those junior high girls. She might mind him not having a car, though. So he devised a plan.

He kept dealing to Rachel. Now that she was camped out in the woods, in a county of suburban sprawl and no city, and highways and strip malls and rural homesteads and small scrub forests, Rachel became stuck. She was the homeless chick in the woods. She'd take her bike down to Glisson Lake and wash off in the mornings. Billy found out about that and surprised her there. She didn't mind Billy seeing her naked and sometimes she would be stoned enough to make out with him. But he wanted more.

He scored some downs.

His dealer friend sold him a dozen brown tablets for eighty bucks. Billy thought it was probably a rip-off but he didn't care. He tried one pill himself. He slept like a log for sixteen hours…missed a day of school, in fact. Whatever these brown pills were, they were definitely depressants. They were for real. The next step was to get Rachel to take them.

It wasn't hard. Before her marriage to straight arrow Dan, Rachel had loved getting down. To please her parents and land Dan, she had done the Minnesota Nice imitation. She'd even started going to church. But she liked the redneck culture of central Florida, which was about big trucks and guns and drugs and girls who didn't mind skinny dipping and taking their tops off at parties. What made that easy was grass and X. She wasn't adverse to the relaxed, stumbling high she used to get from downers.

"I don't have them with me," Billy explained. "I've got them stashed. I got to hide them from the 'rents."

Rachel liked this kid's easy drawl…It was a Midwestern accent stretched out and mutated by living in the South. She liked his looks, too. She had an idle fantasy about initiating him into the mysteries of sex. She could tell that the kid had a crush on her. If he weren't so young…but who would ever know?

Billy didn't have to convince her to take him to the spot he'd selected. She was perfectly willing to drive along with him weighting down her bike. When they stopped, it was Rachel who knew to pull the bike into the woods so that it couldn't be seen from the road.

They sat on a tattered blue blanket that Billy had spread out beforehand. They were in a small damp clearing of leaves and pine straw over gray sand. There were big trees nearby that kept the area shaded and suppressed the undergrowth. Billy could hear the constant undertone of insects and birds. He could see jet contrails crisscrossed in the pale blue sky. "It's a nice day," Rachel said. "It's a good day to get high and lie back and look at clouds." She took a swig of wine and handed it to Billy.

He took a hit. He didn't like wine. Too sweet. He liked beer, and he liked vodka or whiskey mixed in cola. *But wine is what we've got.* He took out the baggie and unwrapped the tissue paper inside. He handed two of the brown pills to Rachel. "I don't know what these are," he said. "The guy I bought them from says they're downs."

Rachel held up one pill and examined it. "Looks like roofies."

Billy flushed, embarrassed.

Rachel noticed. "That's cool, Billy. I don't mind. Roofies are cool. They're downs." She gave him a knowing smile. She knew why a guy might feed her roofies. Or thought she did. She was cool with it.

After half a bottle of wine and two of those brown pills, Rachel was feeling pretty good. She was having fun making out with this good looking ninth grader. She felt wild and incredibly debauched. When he opened up her shirt, it was just a natural progression. And she helpfully lifted her ass off the ground so he could pull down her jeans. She giggled as he tickled her, and she readily allowed him to tie her hands in front of her. And then she passed out.

When she woke up, she wasn't sure what was wrong. She couldn't move. Then she realized that her hands were tied together and pulled up over her head, so her arms rested against her cheeks and kept her from turning her head side to side. There was tension on her arms. She tried to move and realized that her arms were tied to something above her head. She wanted to shake her head side to side to clear it, but she couldn't. After a few moments she got the picture. She was lying on a blanket looking up at dead branches and leaves and a deep blue sky. There was something pulling on her left leg, and she realized that it was tied to something and was pulled straight out. She tried to flex her right leg, but it was tied, too, just not as tight. She realized in terror that she wasn't wearing any clothing.

She was spread-eagled, naked, in the woods.

She raised her head up and was able to see a little more. She saw the boy standing about ten feet away. "Billy," she called out, a little fear in her voice. "You can untie me now."

Billy walked over and stood next to her face. She looked up past those long blue denim legs to his bare chest and his distant face.

"You'll tell," Billy said, his voice flat.

"No," she reassured him. "There's nothing to tell. We just made love and got a little kinky."

He shook his head and walked away.

She tried to buck against the ropes but could do no more than raise her butt off the ground. She was stretched that tight.

"Please, Billy," she begged. "Don't leave me like this."

She couldn't see him. She couldn't hear him. She screamed.

When he returned to her field of vision, he had on his shirt.

Billy had foreseen this problem. He had picked up one of those foam rubber stress balls with the name of the bank stenciled onto it. "Shut up," he said, his voice menacing.

She started to scream, but she saw what he had in mind. Her eyes wide in terror, she clinched her jaw shut. Billy regarded her with what seemed to be clinical curiosity. Her breaths came in ragged, choked gasps. Her nose was runny and her chest was tight from panic.

Billy knelt down and pinched her breast, and dug his fingers into her crotch. She made a suppressed screech of protest. Billy's smile was cruel. He pinched her nose.

She squirmed and bucked, but couldn't lose the relentless pressure that was blocking her access to air. Finally, she opened her mouth to gasp for breath and Billy stuffed the sponge into the gap. She couldn't close her jaws again. Billy got his fingers over her lower teeth and exerted an irresistible downward pressure. With his other hand, he slid the entire sponge ball into her mouth, so that the whole thing was behind her teeth.

A few inches of duct tape and he was finished. She could still make noise, but she could no longer speak and she for sure couldn't scream.

Billy looked down at his handiwork and grinned. "Don't worry, Rachel. I'll be back in a little while."

She heard the crunch of the leaves as he walked away.

ଔ

Later on, Billy would reflect that he should never have told Davey about Rachel. He could have come back and let her loose and she almost certainly would not have reported her rape. After all, what was she doing out in the woods doing drugs with a minor? There was no way she could tell what had happened without making trouble for herself. Billy could have told her that it had been a joke.

But that was older Billy. Fourteen year old Billy couldn't think something like that through, and he couldn't keep his mouth shut. So he took Davey to see the naked girl tied to the trees.

It was almost dark by then. He and Davey took turns screwing the bound woman as she grunted and hissed, unable to do more because of the gag. Davey stood up and realized some other possibilities. He took off his belt and started beating the helpless woman, laughing as she flinched, stopping to piss on her face. He worked her thighs and her breasts, then pounded her abdomen savagely. He was laughing and bellowing like a jackass.

That was when Billy stopped him. Davey's noises might attract attention. Billy felt nothing for the woman, except fascination with her wide, horrified eyes. By now it was getting dark and he could barely make out the wide pink welts on the woman's body, except where they had broken the skin in narrow dark red cuts.

She'll tell now for sure. We're going to have to kill her.

He didn't want Davey there when he slashed her throat. He would come back later.

ଓଃ୭

That plan was thwarted because he couldn't shake Davy the next day. Finally he gave up and let Davy come with him to check on Rachel. Billy had a hunting knife in his belt.

"You look like shit!" Billy said to her when he saw her. "You smell like it, too." Her body was covered with cuts and deep black bruises, not to mention dozens of red bumps where the mosquitos had gotten her. There were ants all over her, too, the little black ants that are everywhere in Florida, and which make those painful itchy bites that turn into little pustules.

"No way I'm screwing that," Billy announced. He turned to go.

Davy took the opportunity to channel his brutal self. He kicked her a few times hard in the ribcage, then took his boot and kicked her hard in the crotch a couple of times. She made a choking sound as he did that. A random kick at her hip, and then in the face, and Davy was ready to head back.

The next morning they returned with shovels. She was mercifully already dead and crawling with blue bottle flies. They could smell the stench of fecal matter fifty feet before they reached her.

Billy was relieved. The plan had been to kill her with the shovels and then bury her. Davy was a little too loud when he got to beating her. Now they just had to dig a hole.

Billy wanted to bury her "six feet under" according to tradition. That was hard because the sand kept caving in. Eventually they had a hole about that deep, but it was a pit about ten feet across, more like a crater than a grave. Billy and Davy rolled the naked mass of insect covered meat into the pit and began covering it up. Later on, Billy would come back and collect all the evidence…the clothing and the wine bottle and the blanket and the strip of tape and the sponge…stick it into the saddlebags on the bike, and roll the bike away.

This all happened on Labor Day weekend, 2007. The body would be discovered in the waning days of 2009. Rachel Sternburg was the first of Billy Sheffield's murders. She was the skeleton in Monarch Estates.

ଔ

Billie didn't kill anybody for a long time after that. There was that one time, in his junior year, when he'd gone out with a classmate of his named Rita Calabreze. She had sneaked out to see him and nobody knew that she was with him. He'd driven her way out into the country and they got out and made out on a blanket on the other side of a fence off Highway 19. But the bitch didn't want to put out. Billy had been wearing a string tie, which turned out to be just what he needed. Once he'd made it into a noose around her neck, she overcame all her inhibitions. When they both had come, Billy just didn't release her. He kept twisting and twisting until she stopped breathing.

He carried her back to the car, wrapped in the blanket. They were conveniently near a coastal marsh in Citrus County, near Chassawitzka and she was conveniently naked. He carried her out into the muck and rolled her out of the blanket. The body was half covered with water where it fell. *Not a lot of pedestrian traffic out here*. He burned her clothing and handbag later. He knew enough not to steal anything that could link him to her, so he only kept the sixty dollars in cash that she was carrying in her purse. In the acidic water, the body would break down very rapidly, even aside from the fact that it would be eaten by scavengers like buzzards and crabs. The body was never found. Rita became a perpetual missing person, a permanent nagging heartbreak to those who had loved her..

But Billy noted the attention that a missing teen ager caused in the high school and the community. He didn't like the cops interviewing everybody who knew her, which included him. And he didn't like being forced to keep repeating pious inanities whenever somebody mentioned her name. *She's gone. Why don't you bitches deal with it?*

He learned a couple of things to add to his sum of knowledge: Dead people don't talk. He knew that already. The easiest way to control a bitch is to have a noose around her neck. The easiest way to make her dead is to just keep twisting that noose. And the corollaries: Don't kill people you know, or the cops will come around asking questions. And, kill people who are new to the area and don't have friends here. Finally, if there is no body, the whole thing blows over after a while.

He now had the requisite knowledge to be a prolific serial killer.

☙❧

When Billy was eighteen years old and done with high school, his mother came to him holding a cellphone. "Billy, what the hell is this?" she demanded.

Billy had been sitting in front of the TV, absent mindedly smoking a joint. He looked up at his mother, who was now well into middle age, thick waisted, big assed, in an overly long dress and fuzzy slippers. Her mostly gray hair straggled down her back, despite the off center hair band she was wearing. Her eyes were gray, and angry.

Billy looked at the screen and felt sick. It was a picture of him, age fourteen, standing over the naked body of Rachel what's her name, the blue nylon rope clearly visible on her ankle.

Billy didn't know what to say.

When did that stupid shit take that picture?

Mom waited for a few moments, and when Billy said nothing, she broke the silence. "You can't take pictures, Billy. Your dad took pictures and that's how they got him."

Billy stammered. "I…I didn't take any pictures, Mom."

"Don't you think I know that?" she hissed. "You're in them. And this is Davy's phone."

Billy stared at her, open mouthed.

"I love Davy, but he's simple. He doesn't have the sense that God gave a jackass. Don't let that boy take pictures."

Billy started to stammer something, but Mom cut him off. "You're smart, Billy. You know what you have to do. Davy's a dumbass. I'm sorry, but it's true. If the cops ever get hold of him, he'll roll over like a dog after a flea bath." She put her hand on his shoulder and looked into his eyes. "We both know what happened to Ricky." Billy blanched. Mom gave him a meaningful stare. "Davy's stupid as a cement block, but he's my boy. I don't want him to end up like Ricky. You take care of him, Billy. Don't let him get anything on you."

At that moment, Davy became a weight that Billy had to haul with him ever after.

ଓଃ

Billy didn't have to kill that many women. He was tall and handsome and easygoing, and when he hung around the local clubs and bars, he could usually find a chick to go off with him. He had a real ID that he'd lifted from this guy once, and with that he could get served in a bar and rent a motel room. He had enough money from dealing and from off and on work at Garrison's Salvage Yard to show a chick a good time. Women were easy for him.

He had an instinct for picking off the vulnerable women. He would sit at a table and watch the bar. If there were three women who had gone out together, only two would be engaged in conversation. On one end of the string of three women, one of the girls would be left out, leaning forward toward the back of her friend's head, trying to keep up with the talk. Billy would sidle up to the bar beside that one, say a few things to her, offer to buy her a drink, then peel her away from her friends to his table. Then he would do the interview.

If the girl was local and had contacts in the community, he would take her to a motel and have sex with her. They almost always went. It was good PR, got his name around as a cool guy who had drugs and was a good lay. If she wasn't local, he might tie her up, get a little rough with her. She'd probably be embarrassed to tell her friends and certainly the cops would pay no attention if she complained. Even if they did, it's not like she had his real name.

The prize was the woman sitting at the bar or the table alone. There was about a one in three chance that she was from up north, and had just left her husband or boyfriend and had come to Florida because it was the furthest away from home she could get. That chick would get the full treatment. There were a shitload of empty and abandoned buildings in Narvaez County, and there she would end up. He'd show her the knife, and she would take off her clothes and agree to whatever Billy wanted on the vain hope that he would let her leave the derelict building alive.

But, inevitably, there would come the cord around the neck, and the gurgling as she tried to scream, the bulging eyes, then nothing. Billy killed three women that way before his twentieth birthday.

Davy wrecked it all, though.

One morning he trailed Billy as Billy drove out to an abandoned building, where he was cleaning up after the previous evening. As Billy rolled the naked body out of the sheet of Visqueen, Davy appeared. Billy's first impulse, the correct one, probably, was to kill Davy with the shovel and roll him into the ground on top of the dead girl. But Billy was held back by what Mom would say. So he explained. From then on, he and Davy were partners.

Davy wasn't *ugly.* He had short dark hair and slightly pudgy cheeks that made his eyes look small, reminding Billy of a pig. He was presentable enough, though *especially if the chick is drunk.* But Davy was simple, and prone to say inappropriate things and tell fart jokes to girls he was trying to impress. Davy had never had any success with women, and the only time he'd ever dipped his wick was when he'd raped the hapless Rachel what's her name. Davy was simple, and he had a simple rage inside him.

So a division of labor came about. Billy would capture the women, take them to some building or other, take his pleasure with them, and then Davy would take over. After Davy was through, if the chick wasn't dead from the beating and the choking, Billy would put her out of her misery with his loop of quarter inch nylon cord.

After his second operation involving Davy, Billy bought himself a .22 pistol. He never threatened a chick with a gun. *The bitch might grab it and shoot you with it.* That eight inch hunting knife with the bone saw teeth and the big blood groove was intimidating enough. The pistol was for Davy, just in case he got out of hand. If he did, and Mom couldn't handle it…*Well, I guess I'll have to shoot her, too.*

He never got around to shooting Davy, though.

☙

Sara Nichols was a hard case. She'd grown up in foster care because her mother had been convicted of aggravated battery. The elder Ms. Nichols had been shacking up with an African American who had not been faithful. One day, as he was sitting in the bathtub, Ms. Nichols had dumped a can of Drano onto his crotch, back in the days when Drano was made from lye.

After a token hundred and eighty days in jail, the elder Ms. Nichols had violated probation by tracking down the (white) woman who had been the object of her boyfriend's affection. Ms. Nichols had worked in the groves during times of personal financial crisis, and so owned a razor sharp curved fruit knife. She had used that to carve up the other woman's face.

That had gotten her five years in the Florida prison system.

Sara idealized her mother. And Mom had given her some useful advice such as: "Let the bitch know that if she tells the cops who you are, you're coming back for her when you get out." And: "Don't put up with any shit from those bitches. Cut 'em up." Sara had taken that advice to heart.

Sara was a little heavily built, with broad shoulders and a thick waist. Her square jaw gave her face a masculine look, and one eye seemed to be slightly lower than another. She was an object of ridicule to all the hawt girls in high school, who constantly taunted her, or bumped into her and knocked her books from her hand. They walked around talking on their cellphones or to each other and sneered when Sara passed by. Sara hung with the guys…not the cool guys but the thugs and troublemakers. Here's what she knew about the other girls: She friggin' hated them.

So, twenty-three year old Sara was knocking back brewskis with a couple of ball capped rednecks when she happened upon Davy Sheffield. She regaled him with her fantasies of cutting off nipples and noses, and "…cutting off her fucking tit and stuffing it in her mouth." Davy and Sara had something in common. Pretty soon, she was Sara Sheffield and Billy had another partner.

Now, a new procedure. Billy would bring the girls and Davy would come in to bust them up a bit while he got his rocks off. When Davy was done, Sara would begin her work with her inherited fruit knife and a pair of lineman's pliers. She worked slowly and deliberately, smiling while she watched the horrified eyes as she showed the bitch a severed finger, or a slice of genitalia, or a chunk of breast with nipple attached. She particularly liked it when the bitch gave up hope, or tried to pass out. Eventually, Sara would demand that Billy find her places where she wouldn't need to leave the bitches gagged, because she loved to hear their begging and their screams.

After disappearing a couple of women in Narvaez County, they took a trip to California, stopping in small town bars along the way. Fourteen dead girls later, they arrived in San Bernardino.

The only time Billy ever killed anybody with his pistol was when he walked into the house that Davy and Sara had burglarized. The goal had been to steal some food and some money, but there had been a woman there. Davy and Sara had reduced her to a gutted, bloody pile who was still screaming and howling when Billy showed up to see what was taking so long. He put four bullets into the bitch's head to shut her up. When he saw the cold, stupid hatred in Sara's eyes as she looked up at him, he was tempted to shoot her, too.

He'd tilted his head and considered. If he killed Sara, Davy would be pissed…at least until his dim brain forgot about her. *What would Davy do, here in California with his wife dead?* Best not take the chance.

They caught Davy within a day. He and Sara had been in a bar and they'd been running their mouths. Miraculously, they hadn't mentioned Billy to anybody. Investigators discovered that Davy had been involved in an altercation in some other bar at the time the police believed the murder had been committed. Davy had something of an alibi. *Another fight, another police report!* Billy realized that he couldn't trust those two on their own. He couldn't abandon them, either, because they would eventually nark him out. He couldn't kill them, because that would land at his doorstep, too. The only choice was to go home.

He didn't like that, either. It turned out that Davy could only have an erection when he had just beaten a woman to within an inch or so of death. And the lovely Sara Sheffield would not tolerate a flaccid Davy Sheffield. If one person scared the two brothers, it was Sara Sheffield.

Billy Sheffield was a smooth talking, intelligent psychopath who could commit murder, or not. Left to himself, he would have run up a respectable death toll and possibly never been caught, or even noticed. But he was now entrained to two people who were both criminally insane and of limited intelligence. He was going to have to step it up.

Chapter Thirty-One: Good Questions

Sheriff Donna Parker-McCready was sitting at the reserved McCready table at the back of the Fireside restaurant, sipping on a non-alcoholic margarita. She was wearing sneaks and shorts and a button shirt, along with her gun belt. She had spent the morning at the firing range sharpening up her shooting skills. She was in a good mood.

On Friday, she and Paul had had the talk. After sending her to bed without her supper at the beginning of the week, Paul had treated her like an ordinary wife, no matter how naked she was nor how much she had spread her knees in her display position. He'd made her sit at the table to eat and persisted in having normal conversations with her. It wasn't exactly nicey nice, but it had been driving her nuts. Deep down, she knew that he wasn't going to make her abandon the deal, because *who could resist having me as a sex slave?* But being in a normal life wasn't the burden on him that it was for her. He could hold out longer. She shuddered to remember the five weeks of nicey-nice.

But he had sat in his big chair with her standing in front of him naked, hands behind her back. "Do you want to talk?" he'd asked.

"If you wish, sir," she'd said in her best slave way.

"Well, do you still want the deal?"

"I do, sir. Yes, sir."

"Okay, look, Donna. I'm not trying to break you or crush you. I want to make sure that you get enough rest and stay healthy. Can you accept that without whining?"

"I can, sir."

"I don't want to hear any more complaining about being a girlie girl. If I want you to be a girlie girl, that's what you'll be. Do you agree?"

"Sir, I'll be whatever you want me to be, sir."

"Okay, Donna, the deal is back on. On your knees."

She'd spent Saturday wearing only her leather collar and waist chain, on the decks outside the house, washing the vast acreage of windows. She'd spent Sunday in chains, with an embellishment. He had mounted eyebolts on the wall in the stairwell. To switch her chains from front to back, she would raise her hands over her head, to have them attached to the wall. He would hook her collar to the wall with a six inch chain. Then, he could release one hand and attach it to her waist behind her before he brought down the other hand. At no time in the process were both hands free. She had spent twelve hours with her hands bound. She had never felt so controlled.

She derived a pleasure from having him control her, like the pleasure one gets from being in something like a marching band, where disciplined precision is necessary. Or the pleasure one gets from accomplishing a difficult dance step or yoga posture. There was something about being drilled in assuming positions on the floor, or imitating a dog, or obeying his command to offer a particular variant on sex, that made her happy.

She loved having him control her, being helpless with his hands on her.

Monday, she had been a dog…playing fetch, learning to speak, begging for treats, and staying on her hands and knees the whole evening. The dog game had been humiliating at first but she had gotten beyond the delicious embarrassment and thrown herself into it. She had become a very disciplined and accomplished dog for her true lord and master. She was proud of how she had molded her behavior to fit his requirements. She had come to love being on all fours along with the dire wolves and doing their tricks along with them. It was fun for her and she loved to watch Paul's face as he gave her dog commands and gave her dog biscuits as treats. It was tremendously entertaining to him. *A slave has no dignity. Dignity is overrated anyway. What am I for, except entertainment for my true lord?*

She wondered how normal women could endure a normal life, staying upright and dressed and unchained all the time. *My own life is so much fun. How can they stand the same old thing?*

Naomi was meeting her for lunch.

Naomi couldn't stay long. She had come up to do some more work on her house and planned to drive home before dark. Donna regaled her with tales of her latest to-do with Paul.

Naomi, except for her occasional make out sessions with Donna, was pretty normal sexually. But she loved hearing about Donna's life with Paul.

"A dog?" Naomi said. "Don't let him find out about ponygirls."

Donna laughed. "That might be fun, too. But there are other ways to have fun. You'll have to get with Paul and schedule another make out session."

"I don't think so," Naomi replied. "I think I'm more comfortable being your friend, not Paul's extension. How about we stay friends and, if making out happens, it happens."

Donna's smile was thin, but she saw Naomi's point. "Okay," she agreed, but quickly changed the subject. "So what's up with you and Doug?"

Naomi sighed. "He's talking about a transfer. If that happens, I don't know about our relationship. I don't know if I'll follow him."

"Do you love him?" Donna asked, her hand on Naomi's wrist.

"Oh, who knows? I'm very fond of him, and I'd be devastated without him."

"There you go," Donna said. "Will he marry you?"

"He hints about it all the time. But he hasn't asked outright, and I don't know what I would say."

Donna felt sad. She would miss Naomi if she followed Doug to wherever the transfer would take her.

"It's good to be married," Donna said. "To have someone who loves you that you can come home to."

"Says the girl who's on her first marriage."

Donna laughed. "And my last. Nobody but Paul could accommodate my little eccentricities."

Naomi shrugged. "I'm sure you could find somebody. Paul has a particular personality, though. It would be hard to find somebody else like that."

"Plus, Paul loves me completely. I've never believed that about any other man."

Naomi laughed. "Of course he does. He loves dogs."

Both women giggled.

As Naomi was rising to leave, Donna spotted Whitey Ferris walking back toward her table. "See you later, Naomi," Donna said hastily. Naomi gathered up her bag and was headed out. "Lieutenant Ferris, what's up?"

"I was just out here by myself with nobody to eat with. I thought I'd check and see if the pretty white lady was here."

Donna laughed. "That's sweet, Whitey. How are you and Danielle making out?"

"We've been hitting it off on weekends. Not much action week nights, though. That husband of yours works her ass off."

Donna smiled. "Have a seat. Order something. My treat."

"You don't have to do that."

"I've got a rich husband. I've got more money than I know what to do with."

Whitey shrugged. When the server came, Whitey insisted that he get a separate check. "I'm going up to Stark tomorrow to see Gibbs," he said. "I don't know why. The son of a bitch won't tell us anything."

"Who's going?"

"Al Cadbury and me."

Donna nodded. "He probably won't talk. But let him know that we're looking at him hard for Torricelli. Maybe we can get an outline of a deal."

Whitey leaned back and looked down at her. "Sheriff, I've got a problem with Gibbs as the doer."

"What's that?"

Whitey gestured with both hands. "I like him for Lowndes, because he could snatch her off the side of the road, do whatever, hide her car and leave in his cruiser. But how did he leave if he did Torricelli?"

Donna sipped her drink. "Good question. I thought about that at first, but I decided that was one of those things we'd find out later."

"Except that it's a pretty important question."

Donna tilted her head. "You're thinking two people?"

Whitey nodded. "An accomplice, yeah."

Donna thought about that. "Shit! Did Gibbs have any friends?"

Whitey shook his head. "I don't know. Somebody who would help you pull a rape and murder…that's a damn good friend."

"Mmm," Donna muttered. "You don't think Gibbs had that kind of friends?"

"He seems like kind of a dick to me," Whitey said. "Not the kind of guy you like."

"That was my impression, too. But I might be biased, considering."

What if he's not the guy? All this work for nothing! The real doer might be still out there.

They didn't talk about business for the rest of the lunch. But after they were through, and both went back to work, Donna was uneasy. If Gibbs wasn't the killer of Lowndes and Torricelli, who was? If Gibbs was just one of two, who was the other killer? *Up to now it's been academic. We had Gibbs, we just had to nail him to it. Now there might still be lives at stake.*

ʊɜɛʊ

That evening, Billy met a dancer in a Pasco County strip club. He liked her because she had long dark hair, which made her his type. He had the touch with brunettes, could get them to do what he wanted. Blondes tended to blow him off. The chick was hard up for cash and Billy offered her five hundred dollars to do a private party for him and a couple of friends. He gave her a hundred to show his good faith. He picked her up after 2:00 AM when the club closed. She woke up naked on a plywood floor, her hands numb from being tied with zip ties, her feet bound with rope and held off the floor by a line to the bare timber rafter. There was a little square of daylight high up on the wall. There was a loud rumble of heavy machinery coming from outside.

She yelled for help, and eventually tried screaming.

She would do her best screaming after a day in this position without food and water. That's when the party would really begin.

Chapter Thirty-Two: Hunters

Henry Klass watched the video with growing disbelief. "Where in the hell did you get this?" he finally asked.

"That's the hard part," the Sheriff said. "I can't tell you and we can't use these DVDs to make our case."

"You're telling me that you have the murder on video, and you can't use it?" Klass's voice was quiet but incredulous.

"Not only that," Donna said, "we can't let anybody know we've got it."

Klass looked like he was about to speak, but Donna held up a warning finger. "Here it comes," she said.

The two perpetrators walked away from the nude woman tethered on the ground. One of them looked up, almost directly into the camera.

"He's just a kid!" Whitey Ferris exclaimed.

"Not a very nice kid," Donna said. "He apparently drugged that woman, tied her up and raped her."

"His friend beat the living shit out of her, too," Whitey said. "Those are two not-nice people."

"They'll look a lot different today. They're both young. I had stills made of the best shots, had them blocked and enhanced. We may be able to use them with face recognition technology, but we'll have to be discrete. When we catch these two, we can't let the defense know that we have this video."

"Why not?" Klass demanded.

Donna hesitated. "I obtained access to some very secret technology. The major condition was that I never reveal the source."

"Oh, come on!" Klass said, "We're trying to solve a murder. What kind of secrecy has priority over that?"

Whitey thought that he knew. "Her father was a scientist," he mused. "He worked for the space program."

That stopped Klass. He gave Donna a meaningful look. "Oh."

Donna nodded.

"Anyway," Donna said, "here's where we need to focus." She ejected the DVD from her computer and put in another one. There was a disk menu and she selected the scene labeled "motorcycle." It showed the smaller of the two youths pushing the victim's motorcycle out of the woods.

"This woman died hard," Donna said. "She lay out there for two days. I watched the whole thing…I've been screening these videos for a week. On the third day they buried her. But the motorcycle…if we could find that, we could ID the vic."

"The kid probably stole it," Whitey said. "He probably rode it for the next few years."

"Maybe," Donna said. "But that would have increased his exposure. One traffic stop, one nosy parent. What would he do about a tag? I think that he stashed it somewhere, got rid of it. I want a thorough search for that bike. I want door to door interviews asking about it. I want Glisson Lake taped off and divers in the water. I want that bike found. Henry, can you organize that?"

Klass shrugged.

"Lieutenant Ferris, I'm going to give you the pictures I've got. Pull the high school yearbooks and start looking for a match to those photos." She noted Ferris's expression. "It has to be you, Lieutenant. I don't want knowledge of this video going outside this office – the three of us. Are we clear?"

ଔଷ

Things moved relatively quickly. On a Monday morning, the dive team succeeded in attaching enough floats to the motorcycle to bring it from its resting place, at the bottom of a sixty foot deep sinkhole in the middle of Glisson Lake. Most of the leatherwork on the rusted ruin had rotted away, but a few days later a Minnesota driver license belonging to a Rachel Sternburg was found on the bottom, about thirty feet from where the bike had been. Unfortunately, the smaller print on the license was corroded away and they had only a partial DL number. When the crime scene techs finally obtained an identification number from the rusted bike, they were able to trace it to the dealership in Tampa. It had been bought by Rachel Sternburg in 2007. The Honda rebel had belonged to Rachel Sternburg and Rachel Sternburg's ID had been floated out into the lake somehow and sunk.

There was a sizeable probability that Rachel Sternburg had come to her end somewhere nearby. A few emails back and forth to Minnesota and arrangements were made to work out a DNA comparison between known blood relatives of Rachel Sternburg and the Monarch Estates skeleton.

By that time, Whitey Ferris had found a few students he liked. The one he liked best was named William (Billy) Sheffield, who first appeared in a 2008 yearbook. He was a dead ringer for the "satellite photo," and his family had owned property in Monarch Estates. He also had a brother, whose pictures weren't in the yearbook. Piling on: His father was a convicted sex offender.

Donna shook her head. "That makes him twenty years old now. How about his brother? He'd be about twenty-two. Do you think he's the other doer?"

Whitey was in Donna's office, sitting across from her. "I'd say that's a good possibility. Do you want to bring them in?"

Donna shook her head. "Remember, we don't have anything we can use. We've got a video that nobody can know we have, and that's it. Try to locate him, though. Locate and tail him."

Narcotics and Vice had intelligence that Billy Sheffield was in the area somewhere, but they had no home address nor any idea how to find him. Donna, Klass, and Ferris, were frustrated. They'd identified the vic and a strong suspect for the killing, but they couldn't find him and they couldn't use the only evidence they had to convict him.

Nevertheless, just identifying the victim was a tremendous accomplishment.

ঔঌ

That Friday night, in a loud country music club that had dim lights, a live band, and a dance floor, Billy hustled another young woman, a nineteen year old named Rose Garrett. She'd been charmed by the handsome young man who had plenty of money, and weed, and who had promised that he had a stash of MDMA back at his place. Rose Garrett had run away from her Newark, Ohio, home and had never tried ecstasy. So, she followed Billy Sheffield out into the parking lot and, in the moist hot air of a Florida night, stood in front of a payday loan store and kissed the cute Southern boy for a few minutes. She eagerly climbed into his big pickup and sat beside him, slipping out of her shoulder strap to lean against him as he drove. Billy's place was cool, but basic. He had Goodwill quality furniture and a coffee table made of plywood nailed to 2'by4' legs. She sat on the rug beside him and smoked some weed and did some pills that Billy told her were E. She woke up on an unfinished plywood floor, hands and feet bound, next to something that had an unpleasant smell that was wrapped in a six foot long roll of thick plastic.

Her parents would spend a great deal of money to find her. But she'd been using a driver license and credit cards that she'd stolen from a purse in a restaurant bathroom in Georgia. Nobody knew that she had ever been to Narvaez County.

ꕥ

Satisfied that they were close to closing the Monarch Estates case, the Narvaez Sheriff Department turned its attention to two more recent cases, those of Shelley Lowndes and Teresa Torricelli. Sheriff Parker-McCready believed that it was a near certainty that the corrupt cop, Nathan Gibbs, had killed Shelley Lowndes, but she had no physical evidence. If he'd killed Lowndes, he'd almost certainly killed Teresa Torricelli. He'd dated her, and the concealment of the vehicles was the same in both cases. He'd either killed them both, or he was the unluckiest victim of coincidence on record.

Donna, however, was Sheriff of the whole department. So, when one of her female officers shot and wounded a high school football star, she had to go into full damage control mode. The situation was made worse by the fact that the shooting victim had been charged for battery on a law enforcement officer while he was fighting for his life in the hospital. And, the press was in an uproar because the charges were in the public record police report while the fact that a deputy had shot the young man was not. FDLE would be investigating. Buzz Collins, the Tea Party Republican whom Donna had defeated in the primary, was on the attack.

So Donna was tied up with public relations for a good two weeks. She was out of her office meeting with politicians and lawyers during the day, and with small citizen groups in the evening. Although the deal was on, Paul didn't bother to chain her up or make her pretend to be a dog in the evenings. She was too stressed and she wasn't getting home until late, when all she wanted was some quick lovemaking in the bed, and then sleep.

The net result was that the Sheriff's Department settled for $250,000 and an agreement to be responsible for all medical bills. Donna got the State Attorney to quietly drop the battery charge. She couldn't fire the deputy involved, but Donna made it clear that the woman had no future as a field deputy, and found her a job with the Bailiff's Office.

Only after this was resolved did she take a briefing from Ferris and Cadbury about their prison interview with Nathan Gibbs.

"The guy is in complete denial," Ferris told her. "His lawyer was nibbling at a deal, but Gibbs said no. He insisted he didn't do it."

Donna leaned back and stretched her neck as far as she could. She sighed. "Doesn't he get that he's looking at the death penalty?"

"He probably gets that we don't have shit for evidence," Cadbury said.

Donna shook her head. "Ain't it the truth? We've got a serious suspect in the Monarch Estates case and we can't use the only evidence we've got. We know goddamn well that Gibbs killed Shelley Lowndes and Teresa Torricelli and we can't touch him."

"There is more in the Monarch Estates case," Ferris said.

Cadbury looked from one to the other, confused. Donna noticed. "Sergeant, we're getting into a sensitive area – need to know only. Could you step outside, please?"

After Cadbury left the room, Donna asked wearily, "So, what is it?"

"In the summer of 2010, David Sheffield and his wife Sara were held in San Bernardino in connection with a burglary and murder there."

Donna perked up. "Really?"

"Yes, that showed up when I did a search on VICAP. It seems that some items from the burglary were found in David's car. But the time of the murder was well documented, and it turned out that David had been arrested in an altercation at the time the murder was taking place.

"What about Sara?"

"She had a story about how the stuff came into her possession. They let them both go. The killing is still unsolved."

"David would have been what? Nineteen or twenty?" Donna tapped her pen on the desk. "What about Billy? He would be seventeen or eighteen. Do you think he would have been up to something like that?" She paused. "Did Billy Sheffield go to California?"

"We don't know. I interviewed the mother and she clammed up. The California authorities don't know anything about him."

"Could he have done this?"

"It was a particularly brutal murder – tortured, mutilated, and shot in the head. But the Monarch Estates killing was brutal, too."

"If these guys were involved in the California murder, we're looking at a pair of serial killers. We've got to nail these two."

"You won't get any argument from me," Whitey said.

Chapter Thirty-Three: Koth Justice

The witch Ay-el Danah stands in the hall of the Great Lord, Paul of Koth. Ay-el Danah has abnormally pale skin, from life in the dark recesses of the temple of Zis, the Lord of the Underworld. Her face is painted in the style of the ladies of the day, except that she has no need to whiten her face, but only to paint around her eyes with dark henna and to color her lips with dye from the red berry. She is covered from neck to feet by the black robe of a priestess of the Dark Lord Zis.

The Lord Koth has a bearskin wrapped around his shoulders but otherwise wears only a skirt made of leather strips, and heavy hand made boots. The Lord Koth is tall and heavily muscled with enormous hands and fingers the size of broomsticks. His chest is muscled by great slabs of flesh, and his arms are like tree trunks. Behind him, sitting on their haunches, are his dire wolves, one black and one salt and pepper, a wolf at each of his shoulders. Kneeling at his feet is his precious slave concubine, Ba-el Shanah, the daughter of the Mother Goddess.

Ba-el Shanah is a coltish woman, slim and tall and possessed of generous breasts, the nipples rouged with chalk stained with red berry. But she is tiny next to the Great Lord. Ba-el Shanah is naked except for the red sash around her waist and the red scarf, held on her head by a metal hoop. Red is the color of harlots and concubines, and slaves of that class are not permitted to cover themselves. Except that, at certain occasions of state, the Great Lord dresses his possession in scarlet silk dresses head to toe so that she may sit as a lady, albeit one wearing the colors of a pleasure slave.

Ba-el Shanah, besides her silk scarves, wears golden cuffs on her wrists and ankles and a gold torq around her neck. Her hands are chained in front of her with a long chain connecting her wrist cuffs. The lord holds a leather leash that is tied to the gold torq that decorates her neck. She is his prize possession and his mastery of her is a basis for his power, for it shows that the Mother Goddess trusts him to rule her daughter.

As Ba-el Shanah, the daughter of the Mother Goddess, was captured and sold into slavery when Tug overran Shenzi, so Ay-el

Danah, a favorite of the Dark Lord Zis, has fallen into enemy hands because Koth conquered Tug. But Koth is an enemy of the Dark Lord. Paul of Koth has slain the son of Zis, and has wounded the Dark Lord and sent him back to the Underworld.

All men love the Mother Goddess. The Lord Koth hates the Dark Lord Zis.

The Great Lord looks down from his raised throne. Below him stands Ay-el Danah. Behind her are half a dozen Koth guards, short spears ready. Standing against the wall is the executioner, leaning his weight on his great sword, a massive bronze implement that is four feet long and eight inches wide at its widest part.

"Are you Ay-el Danah?" the Great Lord thunders.

The priestess is unafraid. "I am, my lord."

"You are Ay-el Danah, the high priestess of the Dark Lord Zis?"

"Yes, my lord."

Paul of Koth leans forward. "The Dark Lord's son slaughtered my family. The Dark Lord fought on the side of Tug when Tug and its vassal Shenzi came to invade my lands. Tug is mine now, and Shenzi. I have vowed to erase the worship of the Dark Lord Zis, so that none may call him from the Underworld to walk upon the Earth. I will erase his worship and exterminate his cult."

"My lord, if I may speak..."

"Woman, hold your tongue! You weren't brought to me for trial. You are a consort of Zis. There is nothing to try. You have come to hear me sentence you to death. You will die this day, within the hour. Your head will rot on a pike, and your body buried in the dirt so that you may return to your master, Zis."

"My lord, may I ask one mercy?"

Paul raises an eyebrow. "Did you grant mercy to those whose blood you drank before you threw them into the pit?"

"I did not, my lord."

"Why should I grant you mercy?"

The woman takes a deep breath. "My lord, I abjure the Dark Lord and would join the Mother Goddess. Please do not put me in the ground. Burn my body so that my smoke will go to the Paradise of Mist."

The Lord's answer was a near growl. "You would have me pollute the Paradise of Mist with the soul of a consort of Zis?"

"My lord..."

"Lady, here is my sentence. We will throw you into a pit of wolves, and your mist can find its own way."

"My lord, I beg you..."

Paul ignores her plea, and the soldiers and the executioner approach her.

"Wait!" Ba-el Shanah cries. "Don't kill her."

Paul gazes down at his golden haired concubine. "Slave, do you dare countermand your true lord's order?"

"I speak on behalf of my mother," Ba-el Shanah replies firmly.

Koth motions his soldiers to stop. "She is the true oracle of the Mother Goddess," he explains apologetically.

Then to Ba-el Shanah: "What is it that the Mother Goddess wishes?"

"My Mother bids you spare the life of Ay-el Danah."

"She is a witch, a priestess of the Dark Lord!" Paul rises to his feet in rage.

Ba-el Shanah does not back down. "My Mother says that you may punish the lady Ay-el Danah in this life, but you may not slay her. And upon her death, her smoke must rise to the Mist Paradise where my Mother may welcome her."

The Great Lord resumes his seat. "All right, foreign bitch," he says to Ba-el Shanah, "how does the Mother Goddess say that I may punish the witch?"

"It is the will of the Mother that you take Ay-el Danah into slavery. Take away her noble name, take away her clothing, and send her to the kennels for a month to be taught the arts of the concubine. After that, she is to wear the red silks and no other clothing and be sold, a slave concubine or a brothel whore."

Paul of Koth shakes his head.

"Are you certain that this is what the Mother wants?"

"I and my Mother are one. She speaks through me."

The Great Lord sighs. "All right. Ay-el Danah, you are dead by my decree. Your noble name is ended. Ay-el Danah is no more. You who stand before me are the remnant of that lady. You are the slave

Danah, of Tug, until your new master gives you another name. Guards, remove her robe."

The guards brush her hands out of the way and unwrap the robe, leaving her white and naked.

"Burn the rag," Paul orders.

He turns his attention back to Danah. "You are to be branded with a criminal's mark, to show that you are enslaved for crime, and are not a prize of war. You will never be freed. If you survive your owner, his heirs must claim you, and if not, you're to be resold. When you are too old to function as a concubine, you will be put to work in the fields or the mines."

He notes Ba-el Shanah's disapproval. "If the Mother thinks that's too harsh, she's welcome to come and get her sooner." Then to Danah: "If my concubine, the daughter of the Goddess, had not been so specific, I would send you to the mines right now, if I spared your life in the first place. But the Mother herself has asked for mercy. So you will be a pleasure slave and, when you are dead, your body will be burned and you can enter the Mist Paradise."

The naked woman slumps to her knees, her hands folded in front of her. "Thank you, my lord. Thank you, Ba-el Shanah."

"Somebody put her in chains and get her out of here," Paul of Koth orders, disgust in his voice.

Donna woke up suddenly but found herself in blackness. She started to raise her head, but found that her motion was limited by something tugging at her neck. He hands were behind her back and she couldn't budge them. *Damn! Paul has me on a short leash again.* She was uncomfortable since her breasts and hip bones were mashed against the floor. She found that she could roll sideways and hold herself on her side by flexing one leg and bracing against the floor. She stayed in that precarious position until there was a sharp slap on her butt.

She felt strong hands straighten her leg and roll her back into a prone position. "I didn't say you could get comfortable," she heard Paul say. He positioned her legs so that they were fully extended and spread apart.

"I want to see those knees straight and those toes pointed all the way out, slave girl. I want you to stay in this position until your punishment is over."

Donna dedicated herself to following her true lord's directions. Her breasts were uncomfortable and her shoulders and neck were beginning to hurt. Locking her legs in position became painful fairly soon as well. But that was what her true lord wanted to impose, so she would gladly bear it.

Eventually, he came and unlocked the collar chain and helped her to her knees. "So, slave girl," he asked as he removed her blindfold, "have you been punished enough?"

"If you think I have, my lord, I have. Permission to ask a question, sir?"

"Go ahead."

"Why am I being punished, sir?"

Paul grinned. "Don't you think you deserved it?"

"I deserve whatever you impose, sir."

"Well, Donna, I've found that you're only happy when you've had some hardship imposed on you. Are you happy now?"

"Yes, sir."

"So, what do you have to say to me?"

"My lord, thank you for punishing me, sir."

"Let's get you on your feet. You've got work to do. We're having a party tonight."

Donna was instantly on guard. "What kind of party, sir?"

"The kind where you wear clothes and pretend to be Donna McCready, the County Sheriff. So let's get these chains off, get you dressed, and put you to work."

❧

"So I'm a slave in Koth, now?" Danielle complained, between sips of her drink. "That's the best you could do?"

"Welcome to the Bronze Age, Danielle," Donna replied.

They were sitting at a hastily assembled picnic table on the poolside patio. It was a pretty large party with important people attending. Henry Klass was there with his wife. Whitey Ferris had brought Danielle. Dan McLaury and former Sheriff Tom Watson were there, as was Barry Rohm and his wife Patty. Doug Ackerman and Naomi had called to say that they were on their way, as had Sharon Becker and Dave Leeper.

"The Bronze Age is one thing. Getting branded though…that hurt."

"I woke up before we got to that point," Donna said. "If you're doing things in Koth while I'm awake, you must really be there."

"As a branded slave," Danielle grumped.

"It's not so bad. I'm a slave there, too. In the Bronze Age, women are either slaves or they're wives, which is pretty much the same thing. A concubine is the cushiest slave job. Make the best of it."

"A lifetime of slavery," Danielle said, "some justice system you've got there."

"Better than spending the rest of your life on death row, which is what would happen if they brought you to trial here. Better than a needle full of poison in your arm."

"You've got a point," Danielle admitted.

Whitey Ferris came over and sat beside them. "I'm getting another drink," Donna announced. "Anybody else?"

Whitey and Danielle demurred.

Donna headed for the Tiki bar that Paul had set up under the overhang of the house. She ran into Dan McLaury. McLaury was carrying a plate of barbecue in one hand and a drink in the other and he had no female escort in sight. "Where are you sitting, Dan?" Donna asked.

Donna smiled when she noted that McLaury was staring hungrily at her. She was wearing a skort with a hemline well above her knees, and the most basic possible top, a piece of cloth that covered her breasts, held up by a piece of elastic around her back and a string tie around her neck. She spoke again. "Dan?"

"Over there." He indicated an empty picnic table. "But get yourself something to eat and come join me."

Donna found her way to the barbecue, where Carla Montez was standing at a table ladling food. A man whom Donna didn't know was supervising the grill. Donna got a plate of pulled pork and salad, went to the bar for a drink refill, and found her way to McLaury's table.

"Eating alone, Dan? I'm surprised," she said as she sat down across from him.

"I'm afraid I have an off putting demeanor," McLaury answered with a shrug. "What's new with you?"

"Same old same old," Donna replied.

"Did the DVDs help you?"

"Some," Donna said. "I'm pretty sure that we've identified the killers, but we haven't found them yet and we've got zilch for evidence, except for the video."

"Which you can't use. I hope you're not showing it around."

"It's on a need to know basis, Dan. Only my top people, Henry Klass and Whitey Ferris know we have it."

"I hope you didn't tell them where you got the videos."

Donna smiled. "I led them to believe that it was secret satellite footage."

McLaury suppressed a laugh. "If they were rocket scientists they wouldn't be cops. Where do you go from here?"

Donna sighed. "Good question. I need to find the subjects and question them. Without acknowledging the videos, I can't get a search warrant or a bench warrant. I need to pressure the subjects and their associates – get something I can use to pry this thing open."

"I have faith in you, Sheriff. You'll crack it."

"Do you know that for sure?"

McLaury chuckled. "No, Sheriff, my information is a little more granular than that. But based on what I know of your character, you won't stop until you have these guys in jail."

"That's true."

"By the way, you look outstanding tonight."

"Thank you, but I should warn you that I'm married."

McLaury laughed. "Don't I know it! And trying to steal Paul McCready's wife would have serious negative consequences."

Really? Donna longed to press for more detail, but restrained herself. Instead she asked, "Do you think that the video of the murder justifies tearing Dave Leeper away from Sharon."

"Dave has his own agenda, Sheriff. It just happens that it coincided with yours this once. It's not your fault that Sharon's going to lose her boyfriend for a while."

"I have felt guilty about it," Donna admitted. "I've become very fond of them both."

"They are nice people," McLaury said. "And they'll live happily ever after, eventually."

A man and woman whom Donna didn't know came up to the table and introduced themselves. McLaury introduced Sheriff Donna. Donna listened to the conversation for a while, then excused herself and returned to hang out with Danielle and Whitey Ferris. She looked around for Paul, but he seemed to be in an intense conversation with some business associates.

ଔଓ

The next day, after her morning concubine duties, Donna wound up naked, in wrist chain and hobble, working as a household slave cleaning up after the party. She always enjoyed working in chains because that was as close as she could get to real slavery as it existed in Koth. And something about the humiliation left her deeply satisfied.

But she kept thinking back to her brief conversation with Daniel McLaury. She was ninety-nine percent certain who had killed Rachel Sternburg, the Monarch Estates victim. But her department had been spinning its wheels for weeks.

Maybe I'm not a good Sheriff. Maybe this is all I'm good for. Maybe I should quit, and just be Paul's slave. I could be naked all the time, and Paul could work me and fuck me and I'd never have to feel bad because I can't bring justice for people I don't even know.

Chapter Thirty-Four: Under Pressure

I don't need this shit, Billy Mansfield thought. His brother, Davey, was being *that way* again. Davey needed fresh meat, and he was demanding that Billy provide it.

"You can't do a girl every couple of months," Billy explained patiently. "People notice. The cops'll realize you're out there. You make mistakes, leave clues. You've got to be patient, space it out."

"That's easy for you to say," Davey sneered. "You can get women. All you've got to do is go into a bar, flash some money and that big smile and you've got them eating out of your hand. Not everybody can do that."

"You've got Sara," Billy pointed out.

Davey glared. "You know I can't get it up without some beating."

Billy closed his eyes and shook his head. "If that's true, why worry? If you can't get it up, you don't need to get off."

"You don't know Sara," Davey said miserably. "She wants it all the time, but I can't get it up for her. And when I've got this dead fish on my crotch and she's all hot, she gets pissed."

Billy understood that. Sara was scary. Disappoint that bitch and she was likely to cut it off. Davey had done a lot of stupid destructive things in his life, but hooking up with Sara had to be the worst.

He's a fucking anchor, Billy thought. Billy realized now that he need never have killed another woman after Rachel what's her name if it hadn't been for Davey. *Like Davey said, I can get girls.* Billy could have found himself one or more women and settled into a life of man to girl sex if it weren't for Davey. But Davey couldn't attract women, and when he'd finally found one, she was worse than Davey. Dave liked to beat on the bitches. Sara liked to cut women, mutilate them. She liked to make them scream.

Sara's crazy torture obsession had nearly got them caught in California. She must have cut on that bitch for three or four hours before Billy put an end to it. Fortunately, Davey hadn't had the attention span to hang out for the whole thing. If Davey hadn't gotten in trouble in that bar across town, he and Sara would have been toast. And Billy wondered how long Davey could have lasted in police custody before he implicated his brother. *Probably about ten minutes.*

That was the worst part. Davey couldn't keep his mouth shut. If he were ever caught, he'd give up Billy in a heartbeat. And the way he drank beer and bragged, it was probably a matter of time before somebody took Davey's loony boasts seriously, and called the cops.

My best move is to shoot him right now. Except for Mom. And the fact that crazy Sara would drop a dime.

Billy sighed. "We can't keep doing this, Davey. Something's got to change."

"Just one more time," Davey insisted. "Bring us a girl and you can leave. No harm no foul."

"That's a stupid thing to say," Billy said.

"We need a girl, Billy. Just drop her off. That's all you gotta do. I'll whip her with my belt and Sara will cut chunks off her for a while, and then we'll fuck. By the time Sara gets desperate again, you can figure something out."

What I'll figure out is how to kill the both of you insane fuckers and get away with it.

Billy sighed. Davey had to go. If Davey weren't so hopelessly stupid, they could split up. Billy would leave the area and Davey could do whatever. But Davey was too stupid to even deal dope. Billy was supporting him. They had that gig at the junkyard but that was pocket money. Davey couldn't live on that. If Davey tried anything criminal, he'd get caught. If he got caught, he'd give up Billy. Simple as that. *Davey has to die.*

But it's got to be smooth...it's got to look like an accident. Then Sara has to go. This will take timing, preparation. Patience.

Billy was a firm believer in that old Dylan phrase: "To live outside the law you must be honest." Billy understood that he was a psychopath and a dangerous criminal. He wasn't proud of that but he wasn't ashamed, either. He liked to pick up women and hurt them. But he didn't like to hurt them the way that Davey did. A lot of women liked the kind of hurt Billy liked: pulled hair, rough handling, choking. And Billy could be smooth, too. He didn't need to hurt women in order to get off. Billy could imitate a normal person.

Davey couldn't. If people found out what Davey really was…

Billy nodded. "Okay, Davey. One more time. Tonight around midnight. Meet me at the shed.

ઉ૪

It was a typical motel lounge, with realistic looking dark wood paneling, a dark chair rail, dark carpeting and dim lights. What would have passed for atmosphere was disrupted by the square ceiling tiles and visible sprinkler heads. Soft generic music played, almost unnoticeable. There was the bar and an expanse of tables, mostly empty. People tended to be clustered in groups of four or more, apparently there on some kind of business that they were nattering about.

Billy liked motel lounges because they were usually quiet and the people there didn't know each other. Sometimes you could work a club and separate a woman from her group and lure her away, but for a quick pickup, a motel was the place to go. Almost by definition the women there weren't local. On the other hand they were older and might be missed sooner. But a single woman in a motel bar was probably trolling for a guy. Billy could be in and out in minimum time.

This particular motel bar had a fair number of women. There were the usual groups of three or four business types sitting at tables or at the bar. There were a bunch of single men, mostly older and heavier. That made Billy feel good. He would stand out from the competition. He looked around, made the tour of the lady's tables. He got into a couple of decent conversations, but the groups blew him off.

But then, jackpot! A woman strode into the lounge, walked up to the bar and ordered a drink. She took it to an empty table in the corner. This chick was hot! She radiated sexuality. She was thin with cute perky breasts and long dark hair. She was looking to get picked up and practically advertising that fact! She was minimally dressed…showing the goods…a short, low cut cocktail dress. Billy ambled over to her table.

"Hi. I haven't seen you here before."

"That's not surprising. This is a motel. I don't live around here."

"Do you mind if I join you?"

She looked up at him, appraising. "Sure, why not? You're cute enough."

She's a little older than me, Bill thought. *Not naïve. She's here to get laid.*

Billy sat down. "So, what do you like to do?" he asked.

She grinned mischievously. "I like movies, dancing. I like horseback riding. But do you know what I really like?"

"No," Billy said.

"I like fucking," she said in a conspiratorial whisper, "But my boyfriend's not here, so I'm out of luck."

Billy smiled. "I could help you out with that, doll."

She looked up at him with her best seductive expression. He leaned close to her and could smell the whiskey on her breath. "Could you? You're a good looking guy, and I'm easy."

"We could go to my place," Billy suggested. "I've got booze and some good weed there."

"That sounds good. Are you ready now?"

"I sure am," Billy drawled.

She stood up. Billy had his hand on her waist as they headed for the door.

"My name's Billy," he said. "What's yours?"

"Oh, me? I'm Danielle."

ଓଃ

Donna lay in bed, her head resting on the chest of her True Lord, listening to the loud thump-thump…thump-thump of his mighty heart. In this world, the real, she sometimes forgot that he really was her true lord, created by the Goddess to be her master. Paul was extraordinarily human, and he was very kind to her, although he liked to keep her in chains and set her to do humiliating tasks. He was playful, and his playfulness made him seem harmless and innocuous, but he was not.

This evening, he had been in a *mood* and he had taken it out on her. As soon as he had gotten home and removed his coat and tie, he had made her kneel and made use of her mouth. After that, he had put his naked concubine in chains and attached her leash to a cabinet door in the kitchen, where she knelt while he cooked dinner, a very nice meal of baked fish, rice, and mixed vegetables. He'd helped her kneel in position and bend over so that she could eat from her plate on the floor while he sat at the table and ate his own supper.

After that, he took her to the living room where he had her stand on her knees facing the wall while he watched the news. Then, he'd bent her over the arm of the sofa to take her from behind.

When she was able to stand again, he'd made her dance for him, a long series of belly dances that went on for an hour and a half. He didn't let her stop until she was staggering. He'd helped her to the sofa, where he bent her over his knee and gave her a long, hard spanking that was interspersed with plenty of groping penetration until she was once again trembling with desire. He laid her on her back on the floor and let her go to work. After he had spent himself and she was screaming in pleasure, he stood up, threw her over his shoulder, and carried her upstairs.

This was what Donna lived for: to be completely dominated, forced to perform, and screwed until she couldn't sit up. Once in bed, her desire had returned, and Paul was equal to it. By now she realized that her lust was driven by vampire magic but she didn't care. She wanted him in her. She used her hands and mouth and body to bring him pleasure, to arouse him, so that he would grip her hair and throw her onto her back and use her once again.

When Paul, exhausted, released his *charm,* Donna was liquid. She felt that she would be absorbed into the bed linens, would become a puddle. But she did not. She lay exhausted with her head on his chest and his strong arm clutching her to him, her breasts mashed against his belly. "Thank you, Mother Goddess," she whispered again and again.

She would do anything for Paul, obey any command. The leash, the chains, the dog biscuits and the rubber toy, all were just right because Paul demanded them. It was right that he denied her freedom, or blindfolded her, or made her act like a dog. She was his. It was easy to forget that, to imagine that they were playing. But she was his in all the worlds. And, when he chose to take advantage of his ownership of her, as he had tonight, she could not resist his possession of her. Nor did she want to resist. She wanted to be overwhelmed and mastered. She craved it, like food or oxygen.

This is where I was made to be, lying exhausted against my true lord. I love him beyond love, respect him beyond respect. In the morning I'll find new ways to abase myself, new rituals to perform for him. I'll show him that I'm his perfect slave, his property.

She fell asleep.

ꕥ

She was awakened by a hand on her shoulder, shaking her. She brushed the hand away. "Leave me alone," she mumbled.

"It's your phone," she heard a voice say. "It's Dispatch."

She said something incoherent.

She heard a voice. "Hello…no, this is Paul McCready. She's asleep. Is it important?"

She felt a hand on each shoulder now, shaking her violently. "Get up, Donna, it's Dispatch."

"God dammit, Paul! Leave me alone!"

She heard him laugh. "Get up, little concubine. You've got to go to work."

"Paul, I'm so tired…"

"Baby, come on! I'll make you some coffee."

"No…"

She felt his hand make a fist in her hair and pull. "Ouch!" she protested.

"Baby, wake up and answer the phone. If it's not important you can go back to sleep."

"All right." She sat up. Paul handed the phone to her.

"Yes, this is Sheriff McCready." She sounded almost conscious. "Okay, I'll be right there."

She handed the phone to Paul and fell sideways onto the bed.

"Okay, time to get up," Paul said firmly. He gripped under her arms and lifted her to her feet. Once she was standing, he grasped her left arm and frog marched her into the bathroom. He shoved her into the shower and turned on the cold water. Donna screeched in protest.

"You told Dispatch you'd be right there," Paul said. "Either get your shit together or call them back and tell her you can't make it."

"It's Danielle," Donna told him.

"Great," Paul replied, shaking his head. "Get dressed. I'll make you some coffee."

ʚɞ

The shower and Paul's coffee had roused Donna into wakefulness. Paul's coffee "will put hair on your chest" when fresh. But this was left over from morning, and was not only strong as hell but old. The taste, even with cream and honey, was disgusting. But it would damn sure wake you up.

By the time Donna drove up to the scene, where six SO cruisers were parked with their blue lights flashing, she was wired. The scene was an old single wide mobile home and a few sheds, made of either block or lumber. Half a dozen deputies were clustered around one concrete block shed.

Danielle Travis was standing among the cops, her hands cuffed behind her and a gray NCSO blanket covering her.

A deputy walked up to her. It was Corporal Jenkins. "This friend of yours seems to have a way of finding trouble," Jenkins said.

"What happened?"

"Maybe she'll tell you," Jenkins said. "There's a seven in the shed. Your friend says she won't talk to anybody but you."

"Let me look at the scene first," Donna said, businesslike.

"Suit yourself," Jenkins said.

She walked past Danielle and the deputies and ducked under the crime scene tape.

The shed was about ten by twelve feet and was lit by an old fashioned trouble light – an incandescent bulb in a wire cage, hanging from a bent nail and plugged into a square metal electrical fixture. The light was right beside the door. The seven was on the other side of the door, to Donna's left, a dead woman with short blonde hair. Donna didn't touch anything. She had a AA battery mini-Mag in her belt. She took it out and examined the body.

Donna couldn't tell much about the face. It seemed to have been rammed into the wall with great force. There was a smear of blood down the wall and the body was in a folded pile below the smear. One side of the face had been flattened. One forearm was broken into a right angle, so that the ulna and radius looked like broken sticks pushing through the gory flesh. *Damn near amputated.*

Donna had once helped move a dead motorcyclist. The body had felt "squishy" because the major bones were all broken. She imagined that this body would be like that. There was a considerable pool of blood under the corpse, and some had spread toward the door. The homicide investigations deputies would be puzzled about the mechanism of injury here, but Donna understood what had happened. *The poor bitch startled Danielle, or scared her. This is the result.*

Donna tried to find out as much information as she could without touching the body, but there wasn't much. Denim shorts, a bra, floral pattern top of some sort, red canvas shoes. There was a curved knife on the floor a few feet from the dead woman, and a pair of lineman's pliers beside an extended leg.

Donna went back outside and walked up Jenkins. "Who did you call besides me?" she asked, a little sharply.

"I asked Dispatch to call the homicide team on call."

Donna whipped out her cellphone and speed dialed Dispatch. "Hi, Lori? This is Sheriff McCready. 10-22 the homicide investigator. Keep the crime scene team rolling and roust Henry Klass and Whitey Ferris."

Jenkins was startled. "Why is this different from any other homicide?" he demanded. "I know she's a friend of yours, but…"

"That's ten thirty traffic, corporal. There is some shit going on that you don't know about. Are we clear?"

Jenkins was shocked. "Whatever you say, Sheriff."

"Okay, just so we're clear. Now I need to talk with Danielle alone."

Donna had Jenkins take the cuffs off Danielle and then walked Danielle to her Jeep. Donna helped Danielle in, then got into the driver seat. "Do you have any clothes at Whitey's house?" Donna asked.

"I've got a suitcase there."

Donna speed dialed Whitey. "This is Sheriff McCready," she said when Ferris answered.

"All right. It's the middle of the night, Sheriff. I'm coming as fast as I…"

"Danielle is on scene. She needs clothing. Bring her suitcase with you."

"What happened? Is she okay?"

Donna laughed harshly. "What do you think? Danielle's okay, but the other subject is Signal Seven."

"I'll be right there, Sheriff."

Donna clicked off and turned to Danielle. "So, what happened?"

"The dude that your people are looking for, Billy Sheffield? I was hunting at the motel bar, and saw him walking from table to table, hitting on women."

"How did you know about him?"

"Whitey had a sheaf of pictures. The guy was a little older, but it sure looked like him. So, I turned on the old *charm* and lured him to my table."

Donna shuddered. "If we're right about that guy, he's a stone killer, Danielle."

"What am I, chopped liver?"

"Good point."

"So anyway, I got him to take me home."

"Which is where?"

"Gulfview Acres. It was a shack, a two room house on acreage. It wasn't a bad place, but it was home made."

"Can you take us there?"

"Yes."

"Okay," Donna pressed, "what happened next?"

"We had sex. Then, while I was naked in bed, Billy got up and came back with a big hunting knife and some cable ties. He rolled me over and zip tied my hands. He put all my stuff in a big plastic trash bag, wrapped a sheet around me, and took me to his truck. He said we were going someplace else, and if I didn't resist I'd be okay. He threw my stuff in the truck bed and we came out here. He walked me out to this shed, threw me down on the concrete, and left."

"So Billy left. Who is the dead woman?"

Danielle smiled. "Let me tell the story. After Billy left, this other dude came in. He had a big heavy belt. He hit me with it a few times. I got tired of that, so I *charmed* him enough to make him lose interest. He walked away, and I heard him say, 'She's all yours. I'll be back to take her to the junkyard.' Then this woman came in. So far, I'd been going along with them because nobody had actually done anything that could hurt me.

"But this woman knelt down beside me, and the next thing I knew, she'd dug a knife into the side of my breast. I broke the zip ties and backhanded her. She went flying into the wall."

Donna nodded. "Were you able to feed before she died?"

Danielle shrugged. "A girl's got to eat. I was able to get some blood and some chi before she faded. I'm good for the next couple of weeks."

Donna let out a long sigh. "Okay, Danielle, when Whitey gets here, I'm going to send you to the hospital for a rape kit. I'm taking the position that, although the first sexual encounter was consensual, everything that happened after that was a sexual assault. That way I can arrest Billy Sheffield for sexual assault and hold him."

"I take it that you're keeping my stuff?"

"Where is it?"

"In the plastic bag beside the door. That's where I found my cellphone."

"You didn't get your clothes?"

"I thought you might need them as evidence. I just got my cellphone and called."

"Good thinking. The clothes per se aren't significant, but the fact that they were packed in a trash bag might indicate state of mind."

Donna reflected for a moment. "There's no vehicle around here. So the man was coming back to pick up the woman and, presumably, you. Did you find out anything more about this junkyard?"

"No, that's all anybody said. Billy brought me here and left me for those two."

Donna nodded. "Do you think Whitey will be cool with all this?"

Danielle smiled. “I have a way of making Whitey not mad at me.”

“Not *charm*, I hope.”

“Donna, you’d use it, too, if you could.”

Donna reflected back on what Paul had been able to get her to do, using his *charm.* “I probably would,” Donna admitted.

ଔ

By the time Whitey Ferris got Danielle dressed and took her to the hospital, Henry Klass and Lu Herrera were both on scene. “Who was that chick?” Klass asked. “Why did you call out Whitey and me?”

“Her name is Danielle Travis,” Donna explained. “She’s an attorney from San Francisco. She’s a friend of mine and she’s doing some work for Paul. And Lieutenant Ferris is dating her.”

“What happened to the seven? She looks likes she got hit by a truck.”

“Apparently she stuck a knife into Danielle, and Danielle slammed her into the wall.”

“What?” Klass exclaimed his disbelief.

Donna shrugged. “Soft bones.”

Klass wasn’t satisfied. “If she and Whitey have a relationship, he should be walled off from this case. Somebody else should take her to the hospital and take her statement.”

“He’s right,” Lu Herrera chimed in.

“But I think Lieutenant Ferris is the perfect choice for the job.”

“I’m just the Shift Commander,” Herrera said. “But it isn’t standard procedure to let officers with emotional attachments work a case.”

Klass agreed. “I’m head of Major Crimes and I don’t think it’s good procedure either.”

“And yet,” Donna said coolly, “for some reason the county voters decided that I should make the decisions around here.”

“Well, there’s my official objection,” Klass said.

Donna laughed. “Henry, you’re so serious. See me tomorrow about taking the Captain’s exam, before you piss me off and I change my mind. Meanwhile, I’m turning the scene over to you and Lu and the crime scene techs, whenever they get here. I'm heading home. I'm beat."

After Donna had pulled out of the long driveway and was piloting her Jeep down the long dirt road back to the highway, a thought crossed her mind. *I wonder if that was a literal junkyard?* She pulled off the road and opened up her laptop.

ℭℜ

From her mapping program, Donna had discovered that the nearest place that might be called a junkyard was Garrison's Auto Salvage, which was a mile and a half from the trailer and sheds she'd just left. Donna vaguely recalled passing by the place once, a long time ago. It had seemed to be several acres of junk cars, visible from the road through field wire fencing on its side boundaries. The front, of course, was blocked from view by eight foot high green sheet metal fencing. An eight foot tall steel rail gate secured the entrance.

As Donna drove past, she was startled to see the gate open and lights on in the slope roofed concrete structure that served as the front office.

Donna drove about a quarter mile and pulled over. She checked the time on her cellphone. She muttered a curse because she'd forgotten her heavy duty digital watch, regulation wear for her deputies. It was 3:18 AM.

Might as well go for it. She radioed Dispatch, gave them the junkyard's location, and advised that she would be checking out the open gate. She wanted backup 10-18X; no sirens. She turned her Jeep around, proceeded back to the open gate at crawl speed, and drove into the junkyard.

She pulled the Jeep to the very front of the building, stepped out, and unsnapped the retaining strap on her holster. Her right hand on her pistol, ready to draw, she opened the door of the building. There was a small area between the entrance and the counter…a handful of rusty lawn chairs, a gumball machine, all on chipped and dimpled floor tile of the sort that predated vinyl. The counter was rough wood and behind it were rows of shelving perpendicular to the front. There was a man standing between shelves. He looked young but weather beaten, pudgy cheeks, deep set brown eyes, short dark hair, He was wearing jeans and a checked cotton shirt hanging open to reveal his white tee shirt.

He looked at her without surprise. “We’re closed, ma’am,” he said.

Donna blinked. When she didn’t go away, he walked up to the counter and stared at her. “It’s after hours, ma’am. Did you need something?”

“I’m the county Sheriff,” she said. “We had a report of some suspicious activity in the area. I was wondering if you’d seen anything?”

The man looked surprised. *Is it possible he didn’t notice my uniform and my gunbelt?*

“Sorry ma’am, I was just doing inventory. But no, I ain’t seen nothing.”

The ain’t is an affectation. He doesn’t always talk like that. “Could somebody have slipped in here without you noticing?” she asked.

The man laughed. “Could be. I’ve been back here this whole time.”

Donna decided to push it. “Do you mind if I look around?”

The man grinned. “If you’ve got nothing better to do, knock yourself out.”

“Thank you,” Donna said. *He sure is cooperative for a bad guy. Probably the wrong junkyard.* She wondered what time it was. There was a round wall clock on the side wall. It read 3:45. *Who knows how accurate it is?* Again she wished she’d brought her watch.

The man returned to staring intently at the boxes on his shelves. Donna stepped outside.

The area was pretty well lit around the building and there were lights on posts out among the junk cars, but the place was otherwise dark and gloomy. Donna took out her miniMag and held it in her left hand, keeping her right hand on her Glock. She paced along the side of the building, which was illuminated by lights on the walls, and shined her flashlight into the gloom behind the building. There was a freezer chest with multiple locks *somebody’s venison,* a big open top drink cooler, some random tires leaned against the wall. That was about all she could see. I'm not going to find anything. *Maybe we can send some investigators here tomorrow.*

But, aside from the fact that the guy was working at night, there was nothing suspicious here. And the guy had been completely cooperative. *Usually, when you interrupt somebody working late they're meaner than a...*A clutch of fear gripped her chest. *Why doesn't this junkyard have a dog?*

*Of course, that's a stereotype, but still...*Donna had just about decided to turn back, but now decided to broaden her search. She walked out to the edge of the cleared area, all the way back to where the junked cars were stacked. She shined her light into the gaps between the cars. Then she saw it, the little mound of light brown fur.

She slipped along the narrow pathway, wrecked cars on either side of her.

It was a German shepherd, dead, half a dozen small red holes in its side, its head flattened in a pool of black fluid in the dirt.

Who shot the guard dog and why? Now she was seriously afraid. She took a couple of deep breaths. The blood puddle was darkening and forming a crust. The dog had been dead awhile, possibly hours. *Still!*

Her heart thumping, Donna walked straight back to the unlit back of the building. The freezer was big. And it was held shut by four separate padlocked hasps. The suspiciously late hours, the dead dog, and the locked freezer now took on a sinister significance. She keyed the mike and called Dispatch. "Narvaez One?"

"Go ahead, One."

"ETA on backup?"

"Fifty and Bush Mill Road," the responding deputy answered.

God dammit! There are half a dozen patrol cops on scene a mile and a half away! Standing around with their thumbs up their asses. Donna decided not to embarrass anybody though. The deputy should be there in less than ten minutes.

"Ten four," she said.

She walked up to the freezer and examined it by flashlight.

Four padlocks. That's a lot of fricking security for frozen meat. Is meat theft a big deal in this neighborhood? She crouched, examining the rust and paint carefully. By now, she realized that she was looking for blood stains. *Why'd they shoot the dog? Was he digging where he wasn't supposed to be?*

She saw several suspicious spots on the front of the freezer but this was a junkyard and there all kinds of liquids that could make dark stains. She stood up and aimed her light at the flat lid of the appliance. It was remarkably clean, like someone had rubbed it down.

Donna was bent slightly over the freezer, her back to the lighted side of the store. She caught movement in her peripheral vision. She straightened up. There was a figure a few feet from her, holding a breaker bar like he would hold a baseball bat, raised slightly off his shoulder, ready to swing.

Had he swung, he could have caught Donna in the side of her head, smashing her skull. But he took a fraction of a second to raise the weapon higher, so that he could bring it down on top of her. That fraction of a second was all it took. Before she formed the conscious intention, Donna raised her pistol and fired three shots, so fast that she heard one continuous boom.

The first shot struck the assailant in the abdomen. An autopsy would reveal that the bullet destroyed the abdominal aorta, causing a massive hemorrhage and immediate loss of blood pressure. The second shot entered the top of the man's skull as he folded forward. It exited out the neck. The third shot missed entirely and was lost among the junk.

Donna was knocked to her knees as the five foot breaker bar struck her lower leg and clanked onto the ground.

Donna fell back on her butt, gasping for breath. *Holy shit!*

She got her hyperventilation and trembling under control, stood, and stepped forward, holding her pistol with both hands. She knelt, scooped up her flashlight, and held it with her mouth. *This guy is dead. Deader'n a snake, as they say.* She resisted the urge to start laughing.

"Narvaez One," she said into her collar mike.

"Go ahead, One." It was Lori Collins, the night Dispatch supervisor.

"I'm 10-10 at an officer involved shooting. The subject is Signal Seven. I don't know if the scene is secure. I need backup 10-18. I'm at Garrison's Salvage Yard…"

"Ten-four, One. We have your twenty."

Donna could already hear the sirens.

About damn time!

"Narvaez Two, 10-97." It was Henry Klass.

ঔ

"You're the Sheriff now, you don't need to be out running calls," Klass scolded.

"Well, excuse me. I thought I had backup two minutes away." She felt like unloading on somebody, but Klass was just a man, being protective. So she was conciliatory. "Anyway, the guy was cooperative. I didn't see any danger."

"Do we know who he is?" Klass asked.

"No," Donna said. "He was standing behind the counter. He said he was here doing inventory. He invited me to look around."

"He was going to kill a cop? He must have known there'd be backup on the way."

"Maybe he's just stupid," Donna said. "The question is why would he want to kill a cop?"

By this time, Lu Herrera had walked over to stand beside Klass and Donna. "I posted Corporal Jenkins at the gate to keep everybody out," he explained. "Half the force is out here."

"Sure, now they are," Donna said bitterly. "I could have used them twenty minutes ago."

Herrera shrugged. "You know how it is when an officer is in trouble. They're walking along the fence line, though, in case there is somebody else out there. I guess we just wait for the crime scene techs."

"Let's open the freezer," Donna said. "That's what I was checking out when he sneaked up behind me."

"Open it with what?" Herrera asked. "Unless you know where they keys are."

"There is a bolt cutter beside my tool box in my Jeep," Donna replied. "If you'll go get it…"

"That's not a good idea," Klass interjected. "It's a warrantless search. You won't be able to use what you find."

"Which will only matter if we go after the owner of the place," Donna said.

"I have to object," Klass answered firmly.

"Lu, would you please go get my bolt cutter? Or do you need a Supreme Court ruling, too?"

Herrera shook his head and headed around the building.

At least somebody remembers who he works for.

"Why do you carry a bolt cutter?" Herrera asked as he snipped through the first padlock.

"Auto crashes," Donna said. "I might want to cut a battery cable or a steering wheel."

They were quiet as Herrera cut through the padlocks one by one. When the last lock was broken, Herrera raised the freezer lid with the heel of his hand.

Inside was a big roll of heavy plastic sheeting. Herrera got his arm under one end and lifted. "It's definitely a body," he said.

Donna pulled her cellphone from her pocket. "I'm going to roust a judge and get us a search warrant," she announced.

Chapter Thirty-Five: The Shit List

"I guess I'm on your shit list now," Henry Klass said as he sat down in front of Donna's desk.

Donna laughed. "Henry, if I had a shit list I'd spend all my time updating it and I'd never get anything done. What do you need?"

"Your lawyer friend IDed your dead subject as the guy who beat her with his belt earlier. We haven't found out who he, or the seven in shed, are, though."

Donna nodded. "Good work. No DLs on either of them? Nothing?"

"Nope."

"How are we doing at the scene?"

"We're going to roust the whole place. I've sent for cadaver dogs and I've got some folks from the FD out there with ground penetrating radar. We've found one relatively fresh body near the dead dog. It looks like your guess was right. The dog was probably digging at the grave and they killed it to keep it from exposing the body."

"Okay. Who owns the place?"

Klass gave a harsh laugh. "Garrison's Salvage is owned by a guy named Jim Garrison, oddly enough. We haven't located him yet. We've got an address for him though, but his neighbors say he's never there. They say he looks to be about eighty years old."

"So maybe he's no longer running the place. Any records?"

"Records," Klass scoffed. "That's a good one. Whatever those people are into won't be in that rat's nest they call an office."

"Well," Donna said, "Danielle picked out Billy Sheffield because of Whitey's sheaf of photos. I'm pretty sure the first guy was Billy. I'm guessing that the guy I shot was David Sheffield. We'll need DNA."

"The Sheffields aren't in CODIS."

"Virginia Sheffield works at Molly's," Donna pointed out.

Klass nodded. "That's a possibility. How are you holding up, Sheriff?"

"The FDLE interviewer was pretty sympathetic. I think that the state will call it a clean shoot. I had to borrow Paul's Glock. The state has my gun. And I'll be going to see Sonia Taggart for a psych eval when things level off. But emotionally, I'm fine. The bad guy is dead and I'm not, as Paul used to say."

Klass shook his head. "You're more stable than most men I know."

Donna laughed. "That's not saying much." She looked up. "So, Henry, how late are you working tonight?"

"Unless you have an objection, as long as it takes to run down Billy Sheffield or find out he's out of the area."

"Same here," Donna said. "It's almost six. I'll buy you dinner."

"Molly's?"

"No, I don't want to run into Virginia Sheffield the day after I shot her son. The Fireside."

"You're on," Klass said.

ଔ

As she sat at the table across from Henry Klass, Donna reflected on her day. It had been 4:30 AM by the time she'd gotten home. Paul had whipped up some breakfast for her while she showered. She'd eaten a quick breakfast and then knelt beside his chair. "I'm ready for use, my lord," she'd told him.

Paul had pulled her to her feet. "You're ready for bed, little concubine. Go on upstairs."

"I'm fine, Paul," she'd insisted. "Let me get you taken care of, and I'll go back in to work."

He'd spun her around, bent her over his knee, and given her a hard smack on the butt. "No back talk, slave girl. Get your ass upstairs. Call in and tell them you won't be in until afternoon. Then go to bed. I'll be up in a little bit to check, and you'd better be asleep."

"Yes, sir," she agreed, but not quickly enough to avoid another smack.

She loved it that he felt free to physically overpower her. Truth be told, if she'd been living alone, she would have called in for the next couple of days, until she ran out of wine. She was happy to have him give her orders and enforce them. His mastery of her made her a better cop.

So she'd quickly fallen asleep, her butt burning. By noon, when Paul had awakened her, the shooting was a distant memory, like a movie or something that had happened to somebody else. She had sat in the kitchen, nude, eating the salad Paul had made for her. She'd felt recharged. Paul had sent her up to get dressed after a quick kiss and some fondling of her breasts.

I am so fricking lucky.

The Florida Department of Law Enforcement would be no problem. The body in the freezer had clinched it for her. The Sheriff had personally followed a lead given by a kidnap victim, and it had led her to two murder victims. Her shooting of the unknown assailant fit right in. FDLE took her firearm for testing, and it would be months before they cranked out a report. But she was home free.

"I want to promote you to Captain," Donna absent-mindly said to Klass. "Just take the exam and it's a done deal."

"Thank you, Sheriff. As soon as we clear this up."

"Take a few days off and study," she said. "We've got this. I doubt that Billy Sheffield is still in our jurisdiction. Lab work and VICAP will finish this up for us."

The next day, Donna went to Judge McClure to tell him that she had probable cause to believe that there might be human remains buried on the property where Danielle had been taken. He signed a search warrant that allowed Donna to excavate that property.

Weeks would pass before the junkyard excavation was finished. They found a set of skeletal remains there. On the trailer property they found two sets of skeletons.

DNA results came in. The corpse that the dog had tried to dig up turned out to be Marilyn Rogie. They couldn't ID the corpse in the freezer.

Five sets of remains and only one ID. This just keeps getting harder.

ଔ

Paul didn't go into nicey nice mode this time. For a couple of days he showed her extra consideration, but after she got her mental health clearance from Sonia, he kept his concubine naked and properly chained. If anything, he was even more strict. Even when she was not chained, he did not allow her to move about without permission, and he imposed the silent rule on her most of the time. Often he did not communicate with her, but rather grabbed her arm and maneuvered her to where he wished her to go.

Donna, of course, loved this. For her, the more coercion the better. And she loved rough handling. She was no longer squeamish about *charm,* either. The fact that her husband could use *charm* to drive her into a frenzy had the same effect on her as fear of physical force did…it added a constant underlying tension to her psyche, ready to turn into intense sexual craving at the slightest provocation.

Under restriction when she wasn't physically bound, and on a short leash when she was, Donna lived her home life in a buzz of warm helplessness. She was the tool, the implement of her true lord.

Billy Sheffield, meantime, was hunted. Ty Rodriguez led a Tac Team raid on Sheffield's last known address, as identified by Danielle Travis. They turned up two pounds of grass and a couple of hundred oxycontin tablets, but Billy was long gone. Ty Rodriguez was also in charge of Narcotics/Vice and he had his narks working the bars and the hangouts looking for Billy. No luck.

One day. Donna was having lunch at Molly's with Danielle Travis and Whitey Ferris. Donna had been shopping and was wearing a summer dress, hat, and sandals. Whitey was in a short sleeved shirt. Their server was Virginia Sheffield.

"Are you ready to order?" Virginia asked.

On impulse, Donna fished out her badge. "I'd like to ask you a few questions," she said.

Virginia Sheffield was middle aged, broad at the hips. She was wearing a black patterned yellow dress under a white apron.

"I've got nothing to say," she snapped.

Donna watched her eyes. "We have a body at the morgue that we can't identify," she said. "We believe that it is your son, David. Have you heard from David recently?"

"I'm not saying anything without my lawyer," Ms. Sheffield snapped.

"Why would you need an attorney, Ms. Sheffield? We're just trying to identify a body."

The woman turned and pulled off her apron. "I don't have to tell you anything."

"Would you give us a DNA sample?" Donna asked sweetly.

Ms. Sheffield stormed to the back of the restaurant.

"I'm guessing it will be a while before we get to order," Whitey said.

"She knows something," Donna said. "I want to roust her. Find out everything you can, and get me grounds for a search warrant."

Chapter Thirty-Six: Birthday Girl

The case of the unidentified bodies settled into the background. Donna had personally given Marilyn Rogie's parents the bad news, and to her disgust, found herself weeping with them. Buzz Collins, whom Donna had defeated in the Republican primary, frantically shifted position. When the news broke that the Sheriff had killed a man, Collins had let loose a statement about the overly aggressive SO under Donna Parker-McCready. When the rest of the story came out, he criticized Donna for not acting sooner, and for being unable to locate her prime suspect. Meanwhile, David Sheffield was identified by a match with his father's DNA, which was on the national database because the man was in the Michigan criminal justice system. Sara Nichols Sheffield was identified, more or less, by default.

So the crime of the year was in temporary remission by the time Donna turned thirty-two.

The birthday party was the largest event that had ever been held behind Paul's wall on the waterside estate. There was an open bar in the living room and one by the pool. The guest list included dozens of employees and clients of Conquest Security, most of whom Donna didn't know. And, of course, every off duty Sheriff's Department employee, with a reception for the evening shift people in the afternoon. Most of the mucky mucks from the Republican Party were there, as well as the entire County Commission.

It was after 1:00 AM by the time the last guests left and the catering service finished cleaning up. Paul, Doug Ackerman, Dave Leeper, and Jerry Corbin, adjourned to the poolside patio to smoke cigars. Naomi Spears, Sharon Becker, and Donna stayed in the kitchen and indulged in some margaritas for a while, then decided to join the men. Sharon and Naomi sat in lawn chairs opposite the men, their dresses hiked as they sat cross legged. Everyone knew Donna's situation, so Paul had her kneel beside his chair, her hands behind her back, her knees spread wide, and her skirt pulled all the way up her thighs.

Paul held his cigar with one hand and stroked Donna's neck with the other.

After an hour, Sharon and Dave left, followed by Jerry Corbin. Naomi stood up and pulled on Doug Ackerman's arm. "Come on, we've got to go so Donna can get her birthday spanking." She bent down and kissed Donna on the lips as she passed.

"I'll see you out," Paul said. "Stay, Donna."

Donna stayed where she was. Alone, late at night. There was a bright moon and the clouds glowed overhead. The reflection of the torchieres flickered in the water. The night was bittersweet. She'd had fun, had been allowed to drink a little more than usual and so her head was spinning slightly. *But I'm getting old.* Thirty-two was close to thirty-five, the beginning of middle age and near the decision point as to whether or not to ever have children. So she closed her eyes and breathed in the salt air, slightly redolent of chlorine. She decided that, all in all, she was happy. *I'm not thirty-five yet. There's still time to have fun.* What would she do when she was old? Maybe return to school and get an advanced degree. She imagined herself teaching, wearing scholarly tortoise shell eyeglasses and a long dress and sweater. She smiled at the image.

She felt Paul's hand on her shoulder.

"Everybody's gone, little concubine. Get out of your clothes."

She started to stand, but his hand held her in place. She understood that she was to strip while kneeling. She did so quickly.

"Watch those hands," he warned. She quickly crossed her wrists behind her back. He stood beside her for a while. The night had been pleasantly cool. Now that she was naked, she felt cold.

"All fours into the living room," he ordered. She obeyed, scuffing her knees as she crawled across the concrete. When she reached the back stairs she started to stand and was surprised when the weight of his hand on her shoulder forced her back to her knees. She was going to have to climb the steps on all fours.

He's the boss. She began climbing.

She opened the door to the laundry room and the two dogs were in her face, snorting and licking. She wedged her way past them and crawled to the door, then on into the living room. Paul followed. She and the dogs stopped in front of Paul's chair. He stood, amused, and gave each of them a dog biscuit.

"Donder, Blitzen," he said. "Let's go outside."

The dogs bounded for the front door and Paul let them out into the darkness.

"You're due for a birthday spanking," Paul said in a warning tone.

"My lord, I know that I am, sir."

"How hard a spanking would you like?" he asked.

"I have no choice in the matter, my lord. I'm at your disposal."

"Humor me," he said.

She sighed. "You know me, sir. I want a good hard spanking that will keep my butt sore for days. So, as hard as you can spank, my lord."

He laughed. "Okay, slave girl. That's what you'll get. Come on into the kitchen."

She crawled across the hardwood into the tiled kitchen. Paul sat on a kitchen chair and motioned her to bend over his knee. He positioned her arms so that each hand gripped above the opposite elbow, keeping her arms well out of the way. He tucked her knees in, so that her butt was sticking out and her weight rested in his lap.

"Don't move your arms, or we'll start over."

"Yes, my lord," she said.

The humiliation of crawling all that distance had left her aroused and wet. Now, bent over his knee, her rigid self-discipline keeping her helpless, she was smoldering with desire.

She was shocked by the first blow. She felt the stunning impact as his hand smacked against her skin, and the burning sensation spread, leaving her butt tingling. *His hand is as big as my ass,* she thought with wonder. "That's one," he said, mockery in his voice. "You count, and don't lose track." The next smack stung more than the first. She gasped at the explosion of pain.

He made her count each blow. He struck her butt hard, and he didn't take breaks to fondle her. He varied the speed…a long rest period would be followed by half a dozen hard smacks in rapid succession. The pleasurable tingling between blows gave way to numbness, so that each smack now simply hurt. All the time she was bent over, unresisting, each hand clasping just above the opposite elbow. She couldn't even think of struggling. Had her arms and legs been tied in place she would not have been more thoroughly immobilized.

This seriously hurts! She thought with wonder. But she felt a grim pride in her own obedience, that she was bearing her True Lord's torment without complaint. Still, she was relieved when she finally counted off "thirty-two." She relaxed.

She felt a hard smack. "And one to grow on," Paul said.

He made her stand up.

He looked up at her. "You're crying," he remarked.

Tears had been flowing from her eyes. Now she began sobbing, too. This was the routine she hated. She was upset with herself for crying, which made her cry even more.

He regarded her with curiosity. "Do you have anything to say?"

She began bawling. He smiled.

"Try that again, little concubine." He used his finger to wipe a tear from her cheek.

"My lord," she choked out. "Thank you for spanking me, sir. Please punish me further if you wish, sir."

"That wasn't punishment," he said gently. "That was just a birthday spanking. Turn around."

She obeyed. He ran his hand along her buttocks. "It looks pretty red. I think you may end up with some bruises on your butt."

She broke into sobs.

"What was that?" he asked.

"I'm proud to wear your bruises, sir," she said between sniffles.

Maybe, she thought, *he's finally figured out that I'm not some girlie girl.* She half smiled at the thought of more punishing future treatment.

He stood up and lifted her chin with his fingers. "You're a brave girl, Donna. I've got to confess that I like to make you cry once in a while. I used to feel guilty about that, but I know that you like it, too."

"I do, my lord."

"But it isn't good for either of us if we do this too often." He ran his hand along her belly. "There's still more torment for you tonight, Donna, so stand in the corner until I tell you to move. You can finish crying there."

He guided her to the corner beside the kitchen door, showed her how he wanted her to stand, leaning so that her breasts were pushing against the wall.

She stood there sniffling as Paul went somewhere else.

Standing alone in the corner, she considered her situation. Paul hadn't bothered to tie her hands for the spanking. He knew her. She was so much *his* that she could not have imagined moving her hands to protect her butt. Her desire to comply with his rule was so strong that, even when he was away she always kept her hands behind her back.

They were almost one, now, master and slave. She knew his thoughts well enough that a raised eyebrow was enough to drive her to her knees, a hand motion enough to bend her over. If he addressed her as "Pet," she would get down on all fours and pretend to be a dog, following his commands along with the other dogs. She did not imagine even questioning his commands. Even if she had wished to resist, he had the blood of vampires, and superhuman strength. He need not break a sweat to overpower her. *He has a superhuman sex drive, too. At least four times a day.*

She lived to serve his urges. He liked her mouth and he used it several times a day. She was proud of her skill at oral sex, and a tap on her shoulder was enough to get her started. When she was chained, he felt free to take her however he wished, without preliminaries. In bed, when her hands were free, they were the best of lovers, spending hours smooching, and resting against each other as they fell asleep. *I'm a full service sex slave. I always aim to please.*

She was always naked and available. Even when he was too busy for lovemaking, he never hesitated to invade her with his long thick fingers. But she craved more. She craved his chains, and his hand smacking against her butt. Although tears were streaming from her eyes, she was happy. Her ass was throbbing and she was confined, naked, in a corner. She loved it!

She heard Paul step up behind her. She felt his fingers dig into her shoulders, his grip a steel clamp. He spun her around to face him.

She looked up, and when her eyes met his, she felt a little ashamed, and she dropped her gaze.

"Still crying?" he asked.

She shook her head. "I'm all cried out, my lord."

"It isn't like you to cry because of a spanking. Are you okay?"

"Sir, it was a very hard spanking, sir. It hurt."

"I'm sorry, Donna."

"No, my lord, you aren't sorry. You intended for it to hurt, as I requested. My role is to endure whatever you dish out. I wouldn't have been crying, sir, but it's been a long day and I'm very tired. Please don't feel that you have to ease up on me."

He indicated a gift wrapped box on the table. "I've got something for you," he said. He handed it to her. "Open it."

She shook the box. "It's heavy." She set the box on the table and tore off the wrapping. She had to get a kitchen knife to cut through the heavy tape that kept the container closed. Inside was a sort of gray hoop. She lifted it.

"A collar, sir?"

He smiled. "Look at the front."

She turned it around. The collar was thick, a half inch or more. And more than three inches tall. It was made of polished steel and was a little taller in front. Inlaid gold lettering an inch high spelled out SLAVE. Along the top of the collar were six blue gems, with another six along the bottom beneath the lettering. There was a half-moon extending from the lower front, which was knurled to hold a heavy d-ring. There was d-ring on either side and one on the back.

"You've already signed up to be my slave," Paul said. "Are you ready to wear this collar?"

She beamed a smile. "I am, sir. It's beautiful."

"It's expensive. Those are real sapphires, the jewel that the Mother Goddess loves. That's real gold inlay, too. So you can only wear it on special occasions…weddings, graduations, that sort of thing."

She giggled.

He took it from her and showed how two pins in a raised bump on each side of the collar could be turned and the collar could be split in half. He placed it on her neck and locked the halves together. He checked the fit with his fingers.

"What do you think?" he asked.

"It's heavy," she said.

"I know. I asked them to make it extra thick so you would always feel the weight."

She tried moving her head. "It restricts my head movements. I can't move all the way sideways and I can't look down."

"That's the idea," he said.

"Well," she said, "it works. This puts a crimp on my freedom of movement."

"Will you wear it?"

"If that's what you wish, my lord."

"Do you like it?"

A big smile. "I love it, my lord. It's the best present anybody has ever gotten me."

He smiled indulgently. "Good. You'll wear it all weekend. And, except for when we're in bed, you'll be in chains all weekend. You'll be my little birthday slave, wearing my collar and my bruises so I can see them."

Donna was blissful. Her true lord hadn't deigned to flog her, but he had warmed her butt up pretty good. And now she knew that she would be spending two full days with no freedom at all. *This is the best birthday ever.*

Chapter Thirty-Seven: Billy

Billy Sheffield couldn't stay out of Narvaez County. He'd managed for six weeks in the Daytona area, sleeping on the couches of friends and druggie acquaintances. It was a touch and go kind of life. Billy had started his run with a small stash of money that he'd earned by dealing, and by selling car parts at Garrison's, and by stealing off his victims. He was running low on cash and he didn't have the contacts to deal in Volusia County. He had to return to Narvaez, where he had a few guys he could stay with in Ruffin. He thought that if he stayed away from Pine Hills and the Gulf communities, he'd be cool. They knew him on the west side. In Ruffin, not so much.

It worked. His truck and credit cards were all under the name Jeffrey Wiggins. He even had a driver license in that name. A cop even stopped his truck for speeding and gave him a warning. *No problemo.* Billy's luck was holding. The fact is, he could probably skate indefinitely now that David and Sara were dead. *That's a fricking load off my mind. Jesus!* Except for the fact that that Danielle bitch had IDed him, he'd be gold. Even so, he just had to be careful.

Billy was staying in Sunlite Estates, outside of Ruffin, a community of small houses built for low income people. It was an ethnically mixed community, with white working class people in the majority. Unfortunately, most of the working class folks were now unemployed and clinging to normal life by the skin of their teeth. The place was getting violent, with fights and shootings every few weeks. And families were getting evicted from houses and squatters were taking over.

Billy was staying with a guy named Bill Keller, a cousin. Keller had worked construction but had lost his last gig over a failed drug test. Somehow, Keller had paid off his house, although he couldn't keep the power on consistently. Keller had a skinny, skanky girlfriend who hung all over Billy, but Keller didn't mind. There was one thing wrong with Keller. He knew Billy's real name.

In the back of his mind, Billy was planning to kill Keller and steal his identity. He'd have to waste that skank Cheryl, too. *No loss.* But he resembled Keller. Keller was a little more heavily muscled, but he had the same general facial shape and light hair color. Billy could grow a beard, use Keller's DL, and maybe sell the house and all Keller's shit.

But not yet. Now Billy was getting by with low level dealing. He couldn't do that forever. Even these backwoods cops would eventually find him if he couldn't leave the area, and he couldn't leave without major cash.

So, Billy had contacted his supplier, a man named Dez, and bought enough product to do some business. Now Billy had a shot of, at least, earning a living. He was working a little bar on the east side of the Interstate, as far as he could get from the center of Narvaez and still be in the county. He was answering to the name "Jeff." He was also working a chick, a girl with bleached hair hacked short, a ball cap, a midriff top and jeans. She had a spiked dog collar on her neck and wore way too much makeup. She claimed to be twenty-one, but Billy guessed that she was probably underage.

She was sitting beside him while he was dealing, nestling against him. Billy saw a dude approach. He'd known this guy a while. His name was Lorenzo, Lorenzo Montero. He had dark hair that was close cut on the sides, long on top. He had dark eyes and drooping lids that made him look half asleep. He was wearing a denim jacket over a white tee shirt in ninety degree weather. *Packing,* Billy thought. "You," Billy said, momentarily unable to remember the chick's name. It came to him. "Dee. Take a hike. I'm conducting business here."

"It's okay, Jeff. I won't say anything."

Billy was about to get insistent but Lorenzo pulled up a chair. "Jeff Wiggins," Lorenzo greeted him. "I've got two hundred bucks. You got anything for me?"

"I'm not holding that much," Billy said. "I've got two nickels. I was going to parcel it out in dimes."

"I'll buy it all," Lorenzo said easily.

Billy thought about that. He could probably make more money selling short dimes, but this would get him home sooner. "Okay," he agreed.

He looked around to make sure nobody was looking, then slid the package from his laptop bag. He placed the package…baggies of weed wrapped in brown paper…on top of the table. Lorenzo reached inside his jacket. Billy pulled his .22 and pointed it across the table. "Don't try it," Billy drawled. "A hundred bucks worth of grass. Not worth it."

Lorenzo nodded and flashed an uneasy smile. "Just getting my money," he said. He produced a long leather wallet with a chain on the end. "Here's your Benjamin." He slid a one hundred dollar bill in Billy's direction.

"Your weed," Billy said. He slid the package to Lorenzo.

"Freeze!" he heard a female voice shout. He turned. Dee was standing behind him and holding a semiautomatic pistol with both hands, aimed straight at his head.

"What the fuck!"

Billy raised his hands. Lorenzo took the .22 from his hand.

"You're under arrest, Jeff," Lorenzo said. He pulled a Sheriff's Department badge from his jacket pocket. Billy shook his head as the uniformed deputies started pouring through the door.

☙❧

"So, we've had him for the past three weeks?" Sheriff McCready looked up from her desk at Ty Rodriguez, who was standing across from her next to Henry Klass.

Rodriguez was tall, thin, with weight lifter shoulders and a rather soft face, emphasized by close cut black hair. Donna had once gone out on a date with Rodriguez, only to find out that he was married. She had then engaged in some impromptu marriage counseling and Rodriguez had become, if not a close friend, a dedicated supporter.

"I guess he couldn't stand it anymore," Rodriguez said. "He finally broke down and called Mom to bail him out. We had officers standing by to re-arrest him by the time he got home."

"The gun he had…the .22. I need ballistics on that, ASAP. If he's the one who shot the dog, we have a link to the corpses at the junkyard. And I need the records on the credit cards he was carrying, again, ASAP."

"We're on it," Klass replied crisply.

Donna leaned back in her chair. “Finally, we’re getting somewhere.”

ଔଌ

Adrian Nelson, known as “Baby Face” behind his back, sat in a comfortable chair in the office of Estelle Alvarez, the Assistant State Attorney. Donna’s chair was not so comfortable but she was sitting on the correct side of the table, next to Alvarez.

Donna had heard of Nelson but she had never met him. He was young and had a full head of dark hair. He was a little short for Donna’s taste, no more than five-eight. He was wearing a decent charcoal blazer with fake gold buttons and a bright yellow shirt and red tie. Donna didn’t like him but he was a defense attorney, so she felt that she was probably reacting to a bias. It was, after all, not his fault that Judge McClure had appointed him to represent Billy Sheffield.

“You’ve had my client for almost six months now,” he said. “You’re holding him on a sexual assault that you know is bogus. What I’m asking is that you simply make your sale of marijuana case and let him bond out. You’re disrupting a young man’s life for a charge you can’t prove.”

“I’ve got his DNA,” Alvarez told him. “He was smart enough to use a condom, but he still left DNA.”

Listen to yourself,” Nelson said. “He used a condom. In her own statement the so-called victim admits that she went to his house voluntarily. She had sex with him voluntarily. Where’s the assault?”

“Did you read the part about the hunting knife and the zip ties?” Donna asked.

“My client argues that they were playing a bondage game. Kinky, but it doesn’t rise to the level of sexual assault. And note that there was no sexual intercourse after she was bound.”

“There’s the matter of the kidnapping and the beating,” Alvarez argued.

“In his mind, she went with him voluntarily. He was not present when the other alleged assaults occurred and, frankly, this is where your victim’s story goes off the rails. She claims to have simply shoved the deceased, Sara Sheffield into the wall. But the Medical Examiner describes the injuries as being similar to a fall from a multistory building, or a high speed motorcycle accident. I'll guarantee that you do *not* want me to cross examine your victim."

Alvarez drummed her fingers on the desktop.

Nelson continued: "The people who your victim accused of injuring her are both dead. We have only your victim's word that any of that happened. She herself claims to have killed Sara Sheffield, a story that a jury will find puzzling. And let's not forget that the Sheriff herself killed David Sheffield, the only other witness. A jury will find that particularly strange."

"What are you implying?" Donna asked, suddenly alert.

Nelson smiled. "I can document that your office has had it in for Billy Sheffield. You were looking for him before any of this happened. And I've discovered that the alleged victim in this case is an employee of your husband and a personal friend of yours. There's something going on in the background here, Sheriff. Keep pushing this indictment and it will come out at trial."

Donna glared at him.

"Meanwhile," Nelson went on, "I'm going to file a motion that bond be set. There's no reason for my client to be remanded. I don't think your case will survive a motion to dismiss on the first day of trial."

"Bond the son of a bitch out and I'll arrest him again," Donna said.

Nelson laughed. "On what charge this time?"

"Felony animal abuse."

"What?"

"He shot the dog at the junkyard," Donna explained. "The bullets in the dog match his gun. We know that he did it. We know that David and Sara didn't do it because Billy already had the gun when they were killed."

Nelson gave a scoffing laugh. "Your logic doesn't hold water. But even if it did, that would be at worst a misdemeanor. We'd plead to that. Time served."

"No pleas," Alvarez said. "Push comes to shove, we'll take it to trial."

Nelson shook his head. "Are you serious?"

"Your client is a serial killer," Alvarez replied.

"You cannot prove that." Nelson was suppressing his anger. "You have nothing, zilch, to link my client to those killings."

"I know for a fact that William Sheffield and David Sheffield tortured Rachel Sternburg to death in 2007," Donna said. "I can't use the evidence I've got, but I know it to a moral certainty. If your client can't cut a deal with Estelle, I'll put him in the ground."

Nelson shook his head. "You're threatening a defendant now?"

"I don't make threats, Mister Nelson. I am telling you what is going to happen."

Nelson turned his attention to Alvarez. "Our offer is a guilty plea to drug possession with intent. Three years."

"Try second degree murder," Alvarez said. "If he confesses to every single murder he has committed within the state of Florida, and leads us to the bodies. Twenty-five to life."

"That's ridiculous."

"Let's talk with your client about it," Alvarez answered.

ᴥ

It was another two weeks before everyone's schedule lined up and Donna, Estelle Alvarez, and Adrian Nelson were able to meet with Billy Sheffield. The meeting took place in a conference room in what was now known as the old jail, since Conquest Correctional Services, a division of Conquest Security, Inc. was busily building the new jail not far away. Billy's legs were shackled and his wrists were cuffed, but not attached to the leather belt that was wrapped around the waist of his orange jump suit. Donna smiled to see him safely chained.

Estelle Alvarez outlined the case for a second degree murder plea. Nelson outlined his grounds for requesting that a bond equivalent to that originally posted on the drug charge be set, since the sexual assault indictment was so shaky and the defendant did not present a flight risk. Nelson's motive was to show that the request for bail was likely to be granted.

Billy shook his head. "If I understand this, you're thinking I had something to do with all those bodies. But I don't know anything about it. All you've got me on is dealing. I didn't do anything to that Danielle chick, either. She came on to me. She told me that she was kinky. I'm innocent on that."

"The body in the freezer," Alvarez pressed. "Nose cut off, nipples sliced off. Fingers cut off or broken. Genitals mutilated. Multiple contusions and broken bones from a long, repetitive, brutal beating. And you want us to let you go?"

"Like I said," Billy responded, "I don't know anything about that."

"You picked up the women," Donna said. "Those you didn't kill, you turned over to your psycho brother and your psycho sister in law to torture and murder. That's how you worked – three psychopathic sexual sadists."

Billy turned to face Donna. His voice was calm, almost flippant. "You're talking to me about killing people? You're the fucking bitch who killed my brother."

Donna glared into his eyes. "I'm the fucking bitch who's going to kill *you*, Billy. I am going to put a needle in your arm. I *will* make that happen unless you cut a deal with the state and tell us everything you know."

"Sure you will, bitch. If you could do that, you wouldn't be sitting here talking about a deal. You've got nothing."

Donna smiled. She took a manila folder out of her case. "I've got this." She slid it to Nelson.

"What's this?" Nelson asked as he opened the envelope.

"It's a rendition request from the state of California. It turns out that a few years ago, Billy and his brother and sister in law took a little vacation. Ballistics on Billy's gun match the bullets in the body of Ruth Ormsby, a forty-four year old white female who was murdered during a home invasion. Billy's Jeffrey Wiggins credit card records place Billy in San Bernardino at the time. We know David didn't shoot the woman because he left the scene and got into a fracas somewhere else at the time witnesses heard the shooting. The detectives in San Bernardino are sure they can make a case." Donna turned to face Billy. "So, while you're waiting for trial in California, I will be working night and day to make a case here. Have it your way. Don't talk. I'll attend your execution."

Billy stood up. “Take me back to my cell. And fuck you, Sheriff.”

ଓଃ

Donna, wearing nothing but her leather dog collar and a rope leash lay on the sofa with her head and shoulders resting in Paul McCready’s lap. She stared up at the ceiling, her face blank, as Paul used her leash to tie her wrists together, with eight inches of rope connecting them to her collar.

“No chains tonight, sir?” she asked.

Paul smiled. “You’re giving off a strange vibe, Donna. I think I’ll just tie you up here and handle you all night.”

“Sounds good, sir.”

“So, little concubine, what’s up?”

“I broke a big case today, my lord. I set up Billy Sheffield to face trial in California. They have a lot of evidence. They’ll probably put him away.”

“That’s a great accomplishment. Do you want me to let you loose?”

“No…” Donna started to sit up, but caught herself. “No, my lord. Why would I?”

“I thought you might want to have a drink or two, celebrate.”

She closed her eyes. “Oh, sir, you don’t know how much I love this. When I get out of the car and take off my clothes, I’m like a whole different person. I come in, and you chain me up and it’s like I’m settling in. I don’t have to worry about anything.”

“So you want to keep the deal?”

“Oh my God, yes. Just fix me so I can’t use my arms and take me over. I want you to control me, to *operate* me, relieve me of any volition. When you have me in chains, nothing matters. If I’m uncomfortable or even in pain, it doesn’t matter. It’s just the environment. It doesn’t distress me. I love it when you handle me, make me do things, put me in positions. If I could, I’d link with you telepathically, so that I could do what you want as soon as you think it.”

"You don't feel that way all the time," Paul pointed out. "Sometimes you're pretty grumpy in the morning."

"But if you think back, when we've argued, it was because you were being too easy on me."

Paul laughed. "True, baby. I'm just not mean enough for a hardass like you."

"Oh, Paul, my lord, you're perfect for me. I'm trying to be your perfect slave, that's all."

Paul rubbed her belly, and she practically purred with pleasure.

"May I speak, my lord?"

"Sure, babe. Are you in a talkative mood tonight?"

"I am, sir, if you'll indulge me."

"Go ahead."

"Sir, I'm sorry I gave you so much flak about using *charm.*"

"That's water under the bridge, babe. You've agreed to it now."

"I was wrong, sir. I realize now that it just makes me more yours. If you can make me hot, and if you can make me come with just your mind, I really am your property, your slave. I'm not scared of that anymore. I want to be under your control."

His hand touched between her legs and she shuddered. "Oh, Paul!"

"It's not completely voluntary, you know," Paul said. "When I get excited, it spreads to you. I don't completely control it."

"That's even better," she said.

His finger stroked the outside of her fleshy hood.

"Sometimes I wish I could use my hands on you," she said.

He laughed. "You do that when we're upstairs in bed. Around the house, you do a really fine job with your mouth."

She smiled. "I'm glad you like it, sir. If you like, I'll turn over and do that now."

She shuddered as he touched her most sensitive spot.

"I think not," Paul said. "Let me get you all excited for a while. Besides, you wanted to talk. You can't do that if – you know."

She giggled.

Then her face turned serious. "Paul, can your slave girl ask you for a favor?"

"She can ask."
"My lord, will you give me a hundred thousand dollars?"
His hand stopped moving. "Are you serious?"
"Yes, sir. I'm going to need to charter a plane."

Chapter Thirty-Eight: Progress

Summer was ending and the nights were turning cool. When Donna came home after dark, and stood beside her car and took off her clothes, the gravel was cold on her feet and the wind was almost painful against her bare skin. But she braved it and did not complain. It was another test for her, a challenge to her desire to be a slave.

Donna had always liked Henry Klass, but she hadn't taken him that seriously. His appearance and his tolerance for his termagant wife had led Donna to think of him as weak and unmotivated. But Klass flat out hated men who murdered young women. He still hated Nathan Gibbs, who was still the best bet for Shelley Lowndes, and who was now sitting out his sentence at Union Correctional up in Stark. And Klass hated Billy Sheffield with equal fervor.

While Donna was satisfied with Sheffield's 25 to life sentence in California and had mentally moved on, Klass continued looking for evidence in the Narvaez killings. He wanted to find the missing women and send their killer to hell.

So he had taken to spending weekends at the illegal dump site where they'd found Shelley Lowndes's car. He knew that her body wasn't there, but he'd learned something from the body in the freezer. He was looking for plastic.

He'd turned the cans and bottles and lawn waste over a couple of times before he saw the little triangle sticking out of the dirt that surrounded the site. He took pictures. He called the crime scene techs. And he painstakingly excavated the three feet of dirt that had been piled on top of the folded plastic sheet. He'd given it to the crime scene techs to haul back to their lab at SO headquarters.

It was an irregularly cut sheet of clear Visqueen, roughly ten by ten feet. When it was unrolled, it was found to be covered with dark bloodstains. Leila Williams herself examined the sheet with UV lighting and a magnifier camera. She had the sheet for more than a week before she spotted what she wanted…a barely visible latent print which she carefully imaged and then lifted from the sheet. The latent was in a yellowish stained area which, the FDLE lab would later determine, was diluted blood. This was a great piece of evidence: A fingerprint left in blood. The print matched Billy Sheffield's left middle finger.

Sheriff McCready held a ceremony and gave Captain Klass an award for service above and beyond the call of duty.

ఌ

"I haven't seen you in a while," Donna said. She was sitting across from Danielle Travis at the McCready table at the Fireside. Donna was having a salad and drinking sparkling water. Danielle was having an extremely rare steak. It was lunchtime for Donna, but for Danielle it was breakfast. As an attorney, she couldn't keep vampire hours, but she could work from 2:00 PM to 10:00. As long as her job involved Conquest business in California, she could take advantage of the time difference.

"You've been busy," Danielle replied. "A lot has happened."

"How are you and Whitey getting along?"

"We're still getting along, Donna. He's not afraid of me anymore. Our hours, though…"

Donna shrugged. "He's a ranking officer. We need him on days."

"I know," Danielle said. "It' just something we have to work around."

"Are you still in touch with Michael Dalton?"

"We communicate. Michael's got a new identity, an 'inherited' fortune, and a good job. The Foundation really looks out for him."

"Foundation?"

"I can't talk about that," Danielle said. "I'm just a little jealous. Your husband takes good care of me, but I don't have a mansion in Malibu like Michael."

Donna decided that the less she knew about the financing of the Community, the better.

"We've got some evidence against Sheffield in the Lowndes killing," Donna said. "We might be able to convict him here after all."

"I hope you don't need me to testify. Scrutiny is something I don't need."

Donna patted her hand. "I know. We won't push his assault on you. That's a weak case. We might be able to burn him for murder."

Danielle fell silent.

"What is it?" Donna asked after a few moments.

"It's just that you are so determined to destroy this killer. But I've killed more people than he has. Have you really forgiven me?"

Donna considered the question and answered hesitantly. "Danielle, I haven't *forgiven* you. But there is no justice for what you've done. You killed for food – to live. I can reconcile that, just as I can reconcile killing in war. Or in my case, killing in self-defense. You killed to save your own life. These people, the Sheffields, killed for their own gratification – to satisfy their sadistic lust. It's a different moral issue. You, me, Paul, soldiers in general, were forced to kill to survive. These three destroyed the lives of young women for, basically, sex.

"I'm glad that you and I put two of them in the ground. Now I want the third one out of this world. Dead if possible, but in prison for life at least."

Danielle was silent. She took several bites of her steak without speaking. Donna watched her face and sipped her drink.

"In other news," Danielle finally said, "I've been to the Miasma."

Donna raised an eyebrow.

"I went to your stone island. The Mother Goddess came and spoke with me."

"Really? What did she say?"

"She said that you were her daughter in all the worlds, and that you would help me in any world I found myself. She said that you were my friend in all the worlds."

This surprised Donna. "Really? Did you go to any other world?"

"No, I woke up. But it was a sweet dream. The Mother is so beautiful in her human form. Her body is perfect, and her eyes draw you into forever."

Donna felt a tinge of jealousy.

ꕥ

That evening, a naked Donna shivered as she walked to the house. Because her skin was so cold, the hot shower felt scalding. She dried herself off and hiked downstairs to present herself to her husband, who was standing at the living room bar, sipping a drink . After she had done her pirouette, she fell to her knees, unzipped him, and satisfied his sexual need. When he was spent, he grabbed her by the hair and pulled her to her feet.

"How was your day, slave girl?" he asked.

She smiled. "May I ask a favor, my lord?"

"Sure."

"My lord, could you chain my arms and blindfold me? And put me someplace isolated when you've had your way with me?"

He tilted his head to examine her face. "If that's what you want, little concubine," he replied, his voice gentle.

ଓଃ

Donna finds herself in blackness. She is blindfolded. She cannot move her arms, which are pinned behind her back. She flexes her knee to take some weight off her hips and breasts but her motion is limited by the short chain that connects her ankles. She tries to roll sideways, but there is a tug on her collar. She is lying on the floor, restrained by a short leash.

She doesn't know where she is in the house. It isn't the main living area, because it is slightly chilly, therefore out of the area served by the main heat ducts. She thinks that she is on the hardwood, but without using her fingers she can't even be sure of that. Paul has granted her request and left her chained and alone in darkness.

She smiles. Paul is so good to her, in a way that only she can appreciate.

I have to relax, she thinks. I'm still too much in the real. So she relaxes and accepts that she must tolerate the position that she's in, her weight resting on her breasts and pelvis, her cheek flattened against the unforgiving floor. Incredibly, she finds herself asleep.

She hears a voice.

"What are you doing now, my daughter?"

It is the voice of the Mother. Donna is still in darkness. She can see nothing. She sits up.

She feels a hand under her armpit, pulling her to her feet. "Look," the Goddess says. "Open your eyes, my daughter, and look."

Donna obeys, and she sees her own naked body chained to the floor, the blindfold buckled behind her head, her face resting in a puddle of drool.

"Do you like what you see, my daughter?"

Donna doesn't know how to answer. If this were another woman, say on an Internet porn site, she would find the scene somewhat arousing. Her body is, after all, nearly perfect. Donna is aroused by vulnerability, and this woman on the floor is completely vulnerable. A hand under her waist would bring her rear up and ready for use. But it's my body, Donna thinks. She feels that she should be embarrassed, but she isn't. She sees herself as Paul must see her, a prized possession secured in place until he has need of her.

Finally, Donna answers. "I do like it, Mother. I am a naked slave, bound per my master's requirement, waiting for his hands upon me."

"So you are," the Goddess answers.

Donna realizes that she hasn't yet seen her Mother. She looks around. She is in Paul's office, and her body is chained to the eyebolt under his desk. There is silence. She should be able to hear the television, or some music. It must be late at night. Paul must already be in bed.

"Come, my child," the Goddess says.

Donna finds herself in a familiar place, the great stone floor surrounded by the carved stone balustrade, the gazebo held up by fluted stone columns in the center of the construction. Donna is sitting on a stone bench, which is cold against her ass. The balustrade is behind her. In front of her, beyond the gazebo, is the giant moon hanging round and enormous in the dark blue sky. Far beyond and far below are the sketchy outlines of hills and mountains, dark purple excursions from the dark purple earth, only slightly darker than the sky.

The great white owl appears from nowhere and lands across the table from her. Donna watches the now familiar metamorphosis as the owl becomes the Mother Goddess, or at least her human aspect.

The Goddess is naked, with wavy dark hair to her waist, dark pubic hair against olive skin, dark brown nipples, round and perfect on globular breasts. The Goddess smiles and sits and gazes into Donna's eyes.

"You have sought me out, Donna my daughter."

"I have, Mother. I wanted to ask you about Danielle."

"Ask."

"Danielle said that she has come here and seen you."

"She has, my child."

"How is that possible?"

"My daughter, you and I are one. In the real, I live inside you. If Danielle is your friend in the real, she is my friend in all the worlds."

Donna considers that.

"Danielle has committed many crimes," she says.

"Nevertheless, you have made her your friend."

Donna sighs. "I have. But you have punished her in Koth."

The Goddess laughs and her laugh is the tinkling of tiny bells. "You and I made Koth, my daughter. Her punishment is part of the warp and woof of the world I elaborated from your fantasy. But in Koth you are Ba-el Shanah and, although a slave, you have some power. You can ameliorate her condition, bring her into the Lord's household for example."

Donna nods at this.

A woman appears bearing a huge glazed ceramic pitcher. The woman is solid and muscular, perfectly shaped with generous breasts and long dark hair, cut in long bangs across her forehead. She wears a patterned cloth choker and a loincloth held by a rope around her waist. Wordlessly she pours the purple fluid into the large ceramic mugs that have appeared by magic on the stone table.

The woman turns and strides toward the gazebo. Donna watches the exaggerated motion of her bare butt as she walks away.

"What of Paul?" Donna asks.

"What of him?" the Goddess responds as she takes a sip of nectar.

"He is my true lord," Donna says, "but I fear him."

"Why is that, my child?"

"He has the power of vampire charm and he can arouse me from a distance."

The Goddess smiles. "Is that a problem?"

"He has the power to completely enslave me."

The Goddess answers. "In the worlds, you are Ba-el Shanah, the daughter of the Goddess. In Koth, you are both my priestess-oracle and the slave of the Great Lord. In Koth, the Great Lord has many slaves to tend you and mind you and lead you around in chains. He has squads of soldiers to guard you. He has you absolutely under his control, but do you not have power over him?"

"The real is not Koth, Mother."

"It is not. Since in the real, Paul lacks troops and slaves and a law that gives him control over you, I gave Paul another power, the power of charm – charm and love. It is your nature to be a slave and I have built Paul to be your master. I have given him wealth and strength and the power to manipulate your desire as he chooses. You have spent your life seeking him and wishing to be his toy, his possession. But now you fear him?"

"I do, my Mother. In the worlds I am a demi-goddess. In the real, I am a powerful government official. I have two natures. I fear being drawn into complete slavery."

"Is Paul a cruel master?"

"No, Mother. He is sometimes harsh but never cruel."

"Can you influence Paul to bend to your wishes?"

"I can, my Mother. I'm sometimes frustrated that he isn't as firm as I would like."

The Goddess examines her curiously, leans forward and strokes Donna's face. "Paul loves you, my daughter. You must trust him and submit to him. But I must remind you of something."

"What is that?"

"You and I built Koth to suit you, Donna/Ba-el Shanah. We have built the real to suit you as well."

"You and I didn't build the real," Donna protests. "It is solid. It is a reality built by consensus."

"But we have built your portion of the real, and if it doesn't suit you, you can change it."

The vision fades and Donna is once again in blackness, her limbs immobilized by chains, her neck chained to the floor. She is able to lift herself up and turn her head, shift a little to change where her weight rests against the hardwood. She tries to go back to sleep, but manages only brief snoozes until Paul finally releases her blindfold, and she can see that it is morning.

ଓଃ

It was a warm afternoon, the temperature in the eighties. It was Saturday and Naomi Spears had come up to Narvaez County, ostensibly to work on her house but really because Doug Ackerman was away until Saturday evening. Naomi had arranged for Doug to meet her at her house in Ruffin and they'd spend the night there. Meanwhile, there was always Donna.

Donna was naked most of the time, and she was always ready to put out a blanket beside the pool and lie out in the sun, trying to maintain her honey tan. Naomi liked lying in the sun as well but, being employed at a hospital, didn't have the time to do it as much as she'd like. So, the two women put on sunglasses and took out their favorite books and went out to lie in the afternoon warmth.

Eventually, Donna decided to lie on her back and try to get the tan on her breasts to match her arms and legs. She lay there naked, eyes closed. It was too much of a temptation for Naomi, as Donna had known it would be. "It's starting to get a little chilly," Donna complained.

"I can warm you up," Naomi said. She slid onto Donna so that their breasts rested against each other, and Naomi positioned herself so that they were pubis to pubis. Donna closed her eyes and Naomi's mouth found Donna's lips, beginning a long lingering kiss as Naomi's tongue probed into Donna's mouth, to be met by Donna's own flickering tongue. Donna, her arms free for a change, embraced Naomi and pulled her body tight against her own. Naomi's hand frantically dug between Donna's legs.

Donna loved smooching. She and Paul sometimes would do it for hours. Of course, she also loved being helpless and chained, and being positioned by Paul's irresistibly strong hands as well, so she sometimes didn't get as much smooching as she liked. But with Naomi, there was only smooching. No hair pulling, no being forced to her knees or bent over the couch. So she loved smooching with Naomi. Naomi knew how to make her hot.

Donna opened her eyes when she heard the screen door slam. *Ohmigod! It's Paul.* She felt Naomi sit up. She heard Paul's amiable voice. "Hi, Naomi. I didn't realize you girls were out here. Sorry to interrupt. I'll be inside."

Donna started to sit up, but Naomi's pressure on her shoulders forced her down again. Naomi became frantic and Donna kept up. They ended with Naomi's legs in the air and Donna using her mouth to bring Naomi to a noisy climax.

The women lay panting, Donna's head on Naomi's belly, until they were recovered enough to go inside.

Paul was sitting on a barstool, sipping a drink when the two naked women entered the living room. "I didn't mean to embarrass you," he said.

"Maybe Donna's embarrassed. I'm not," Naomi responded.

Paul laughed. "Donna's not allowed to be embarrassed."

"No harm then," Naomi said.

Donna walked over to stand beside Paul, who stroked his hand down her back and buttocks. Naomi stepped over and stood beside her. "I'll fix us some drinks," Naomi said. "Margaritas?"

"Remember, Donna is the slave here. She'll fix the drinks. Three margaritas, Donna."

Donna walked around the bar and took out the blender.

Naomi sidled next to Paul and put her arm around his shoulder. Paul idly stroked her back and, Donna noticed, let his hand slide to her butt. Donna smiled. She knew that Naomi must be in a state of bliss, having Paul handle her. Donna wasn't jealous. She had once stripped for Naomi's boyfriend and let him fondle her as Naomi stood by.

"You should have stayed out there and watched," Naomi said. "We would have put on a hot performance for you. Right, Donna?"

"We would have, yes," Donna replied with a giggle.

"It's how it all started, you know. Donna and I would sit out in the sun and fantasize about threesomes, and about putting on performances for you and Doug."

Paul smiled as he took his margarita from Donna's hand. "If you two want to put on a show for Doug and me, I'll watch. Just me and you two doesn't seem safe to me."

Naomi laughed. "Paul McCready, you are such a prude!" She gave his arm a little slap.

They eventually moved to the sofa where Paul sat with a naked woman on each side of him, both of them slightly drunk and playful. He caressed both women and fondled their breasts and thighs, but he made certain that was as far as it went.

When Naomi got up to go to the bathroom, Paul turned to Donna. "Naomi's really wound up today."

"She always has had the hots for you," Donna said. "I bet you could tap her right now if you wanted. I'd be cool with it."

"Enough martyr slave stuff," Paul told her. "You're the only woman I'm tapping in the foreseeable future. But I've got something to tell you. Are you sober?"

Donna giggled. "More or less."

Paul pulled her to him and squeezed her breast. "That hundred thousand dollars you wanted?"

Donna was suddenly serious. "What about it?"

"I moved a hundred thousand into our joint account. You can write checks on it whenever you need to."

Donna looked up, delighted. "Sir, you are so sweet."

When Naomi returned, her face fell when she saw Paul and Donna locked in a long kiss.

ঞ

The final piece of the puzzle came unexpectedly. Billy Sheffield had initially been caught because Ty Rodriguez's department had been running a long series of stings that involved infiltrating the local drug scene and picking off the minor dealers one by one. The operation had continued, although Lorenzo Montero was blown as a nark and was now back in uniform. Dee, aka Angelina Mendez, was still in the field with another cover identify. She'd set up man named Morris Reid, w/m age 26. He had been born in Florida, had a slight Southern accent, and had worked in construction before the bust. Now he drove a delivery truck for twelve dollars an hour, which he supplemented by selling weed and pharmaceuticals, mostly oxy.

Montero had set up the operation and scooped Reid up. He'd brought him to the aquarium in the Sheriff's headquarters. Montero and Al Cadbury were questioning him while Rodriguez watched from behind the glass.

"Come on, man, we're not interested in your sleazy ass," Montero told him. "We want the name of the big guy."

Reid was getting frantic. "I don't know. Dez, that's all I know. I don't know his freakin' real name."

"You'd better give us something. Otherwise…" Cadbury let his voice trail off ominously.

Reid looked around desperately. "I want my lawyer."

Cadbury laughed. "A lawyer won't help you. We're not trying to get you to confess. We've got you dead to rights. You sold more than twenty-five grams of weed to an undercover cop. That's a felony. You're looking at five years in prison. If you want, we can stop talking right now and it won't make any difference. Unless you tell us something we can use, you're doing hard time in the Everglades."

"I don't know Dez's name," Reid screwed up his face in desperation. Then something occurred to him. "I do know something about Billy Sheffield."

Cadbury stood up. "Hold that thought. Let me make a few calls."

ങ്ക

"What could he know about Sheffield?" Donna asked. She was standing behind the glass looking up at Ty Rodriguez.

"Beats me. I thought we'd get this public defender twerp and Estelle Alvarez over here before we went any further."

Cadbury was on the other side of the mirror and had just finished introducing everyone.

"I want immunity," Reid said firmly.

"We'll consider misdemeanor sale," Alvarez said, "if it's something we can use."

"Okay, I think I heard Billy Sheffield tell where some bodies were hidden."

The public defender turned to Alvarez. "Good enough?"

"Sure, if it turns out to be real."

The lawyer nodded.

"Okay, I was sitting in the Long Branch a couple of months ago and I was shooting the shit with Billy and some other guys. One of them said, 'Hey, Billy, what happened to that chick you were with the other night?' and Billy goes, 'Oh, I buried her in the backyard.' We were all laughing and shit, because we didn't, like, believe it."

"The Long Branch? Marilyn Rogie?" Cadbury asked.

"No, man. Marilyn was the chick that left her Ford Focus in the parking lot. This was before all that."

He has no sense of time, Donna thought.

Rodriguez turned to Donna. "Does that tell us anything?'

Donna shrugged. "Not really."

"Where was Billy staying at the time?" Cadbury asked.

"I'm not sure, man, but I think he was staying with his mom."

Rodriguez gave Donna a meaningful look.

"I'm on my way to find a judge now," she said.

Chapter Thirty-Nine: Closure

"I've never had the prosecution fly me on a private jet and put me up in a hotel before," Adrian Nelson said as he waited for the corrections officers to bring his client.

"It wasn't the prosecution," Estelle Alvarez replied. "On our budget we couldn't fund a ride on a hang glider. It was the Sheriff."

"My husband, actually," Donna said. "I told him I needed a charter jet and hotel rooms in California and he gave me the money."

"He must really love justice," Nelson remarked.

Donna gave a half smile. "Well, he loves me."

"You must be great in bed," Nelson bantered.

Donna smiled knowingly. "Oh, I'm very good. In bed or anyplace else he wants to do it."

"Jesus, you two!" Alvarez exploded.

"Thank you," a relieved Henry Klass said.

The officers brought Billy Sheffield into the small meeting room. Billy was puffy and pale, the effect of prolonged incarceration. His orange jump suit was nicely accessorized with a wide leather belt, to which his wrists were chained. He walked bent slightly forward and with a side to side shuffle, as his legs were shackled.

"How's prison treating you, Billy?" Klass asked.

"I don't know. I'm still in the local jail."

Klass smiled cruelly.

"What's this about?" Billy asked.

"We've nailed you to Shelley Lowndes," Donna said. "Captain Klass here found the plastic sheet you wrapped her body in. It had your fingerprint on it. And you ran your mouth one too many times. One of your drug buddies remembered that you'd mentioned burying a girl in your back yard. We dug up your mom's property, Billy. Guess what? We found two sets of remains. One we identified as Rosalinda Nunez, the other as Shelley Lowndes."

Sheffield shrugged. "Big fuckin' deal. I'm already doing twenty-five to life."

"I can convict you of the Lowndes murder," Alvarez said. "It will be a two day trial. If we put you on trial in Florida, I have no doubt that you'll get the death penalty."

Billy sneered."So what's stopping you?"

"The families need closure, Billy," Henry Klass said. "We've got remains that we haven't identified. And there are probably victims we haven't found."

Sheffield gave a harsh laugh. "What? You want to do some kind of deal?"

"Listen to them," Nelson urged. "This is your only shot at avoiding the death penalty."

Sheffield finally sat down. "What are you offering?"

"Twenty-five to life," Alvarez said, "running consecutively, after your California sentence. If, for some reason, California decides to release you, you go straight to Florida to start doing time there."

"That's not much of an incentive."

Alvarez narrowed her gaze. "I can have you sitting on Florida's death row within nine months. You'll be in a six by nine cell for years until finally they drag you out and strap you to that gurney."

"Okay," Billy said, appearing bored, "what am I supposed to do?"

"Plead guilty to killing Lowndes and Nunez. Confess to and provide details of all the killings you committed within the state of Florida, and tell us where you dumped the bodies. You'll get immunity on those. The whole deal, of course, is contingent on complete truth. If it turns out that you've lied to us, the bargain is set aside and we go to trial."

Billy shrugged. He turned to Nelson. "What do you think?"

"You don't lose anything," Nelson told him. "California isn't going to parole a known serial killer anyway. And Florida doesn't get to kill you."

Billy shook his head. "Fine. How do we do this?"

ଓଷଓ

Three days later, at one of those airport bars that is a little too bright, and which has ferns in pots hanging in macrame harnesses,

Henry Klass shook his head and turned to Donna. “Damn! I was sure that Gibbs was good for Torricelli. But Billy did her, too.”

Donna turned and raised her glass. “Here’s to justice,” she said.

“Justice,” Alvarez and Nelson echoed.

“That was damned good work, Henry,” Donna said.

Donna walked through the front door of her house. She was wearing Nikes, slacks, and a blouse and jacket. Paul was sitting in his chair, reading something on his tablet. “Hey, babe, how’d it go?”

“We made a plea deal with Billy Sheffield in exchange for a full confession. We still have remains we haven’t identified, but at least we know where he got them.”

Paul nodded and stared at her.

“What?” she asked.

“You’re wearing clothes today?”

“Today, yes. I’ve really accomplished something, Paul. I’ve led my department, my team, in solving the major case of my tenure so far, and I’m bringing closure to a dozen families. So, I don’t feel like a slave today.”

Paul shrugged. “Okay.”

“I’ve been thinking about the deal, Paul. Can we revisit it?” She walked deeper into the living room and stood in front of him, her hands behind her back.

He looked up at her, his forehead wrinkled. “Okay, babe. Say what you want to say.”

“You know I love the deal, Paul. You know how I love to be dominated and handled.”

“Okay.”

“But, sweetie, I’m getting older. I’ve got a serious job now. And sweetie, I love you so much. Part of that love goes into giving myself over to you completely, but part of it…Paul, as I am now, all the burden is on you. You feed me, walk me, chain me up for the evening. I love being your slave, your sex toy. But I want more than that. I still want to serve you, but I want to cook for you and take care of you. I love you, but I want to show it in different ways. I want to be more like a normal wife."

He raised his eyebrows. "That's a switch."

She dug her fingernails into her hands. "I don't mean all the time, sir. Maybe just a day or two a week. I'll still go naked all the time. I'll still call you 'sir' and 'my lord.' And of course I'll still be fully available to you. But I'd be free…to cook for you and talk to you and…you know, be your wife. It will be like it was before between us." She stopped, uncertain of his reaction. "It will only be a couple of days a week. The rest of the time I'll still be your slave concubine, all chained up and under your strict control."

Paul shrugged. "Okay."

She stared at him. "Okay? That's it?"

"Sure. We can work out which days you're a normal person and which days you're my slave. I don't see a problem."

"Paul…"

"What, you wanted me to argue?"

She stopped. "I…I expected you to."

"No, Donna, the deal is what it is because of what you are. You wanted to feel enslaved. You wanted me to be a harsh unyielding master, like the warlord of Koth. So that's what I've tried to be and, if I do say so myself, I've done a damn good job of reducing you to absolute servility." She smiled and nodded her agreement. "But relationships evolve. We can vary things if that's what you want. I'm all about making you happy. We're the ones who made the deal and we can change it. Let the whole thing be in flux for a while until we find what works."

Donna was overcome with relief. "Oh, sweetie!" She leaned down and kissed him.

"I'll tell you what, little concubine, I've missed you. Let's do something together today. What would you like?"

She considered for a moment. *Freedom! But what do I want, now that I can choose?*

"I'd like to not be rich for a while," she said finally. "Let's take my Jeep and hit the road. Let's catch some seafood in one of the Pinellas tourist traps, and maybe find a rundown motel to spend the night in. We can watch porn channels on TV and smooch all night."

“That sounds like fun, babe. Why don’t you go put on some loose clothes, so I can slip my hand under them while we’re stopped at a light.”

She beamed with happiness. “You’re on, mister. And you’d better have that vampire stamina you’re always bragging about.”

“Don’t worry about that,” he said with a laugh. “But, Sheriff, you’d better hurry up. Time’s a wastin’.”

ଔଔଔ

Donna Parker and friends will be returning in *What My Father Saw* later in 2015. You might like the earlier books in this series: *The Cabin: A Time Travel Adventure, The Food,* and *Blood Spirit: Books 1 and 2.*

For excerpts and previews, along with links to sellers, see my website at

www.dallasdunlap.com

And, if you are inclined to review the book, please do so at amazon.com or barnesandnoble.com.

Reviews are greatly appreciated.

www.ingramcontent.com/pod-product-compliance
Lightning Source LLC
Chambersburg PA
CBHW080821250626
47160CB00008B/2817